THE SONG OF SEARE

C. E. LAUREANO

BENEATH
the
FORSAKEN CITY

a novel

A NAVPRESS RESOURCE PUBLISHED IN ALLIANCE
WITH TYNDALE HOUSE PUBLISHERS, INC.

NAVPRESS ⬙®

NavPress is the publishing ministry of The Navigators, an international Christian organization and leader in personal spiritual development. NavPress is committed to helping people grow spiritually and enjoy lives of meaning and hope through personal and group resources that are biblically rooted, culturally relevant, and highly practical.

For more information, go to www.NavPress.com.

A NavPress resource published in alliance with Tyndale House Publishers, Inc.

NAVPRESS and the NAVPRESS logo are registered trademarks of NavPress, The Navigators, Colorado Springs, CO. Absence of ® in connection with marks of NavPress or other parties does not indicate an absence of registration of those marks.

TYNDALE is a registered trademark of Tyndale House Publishers, Inc.

ISBN 978-1-61291-631-6

Cover photography of people by Kirk DouPonce, DogEared Design.

Cover symbol photograph copyright © zhevi/istockphoto. All rights reserved.

Cover photograph of background copyright © Ben Battersby/istockphoto. All rights reserved.

Published in association with WordWise Media Services, 4083 Avenue L, Suite #225, Lancaster, CA 93536.

Printed in the United States of America

21	20	19	18	17	16	15
7	6	5	4	3	2	1

For Dad,
My most enthusiastic (and unexpected) fan.
I'm writing as fast as I can, I promise!

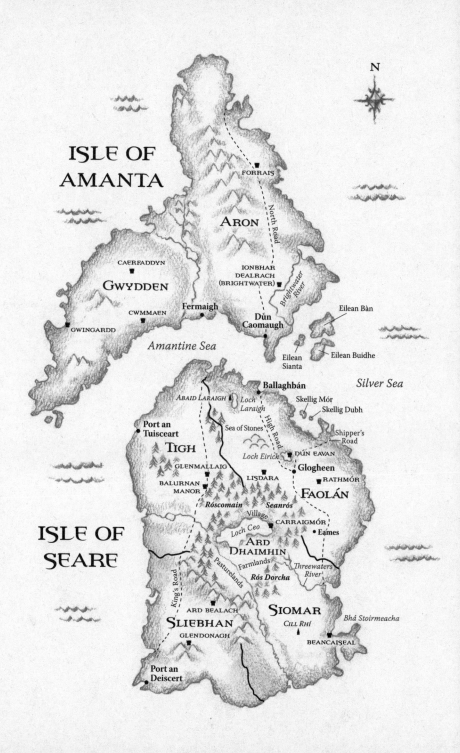

N

ISLE OF
AMANTA

FORRAIS

ARON

North Road

CAERFADDYN

GWYDDEN

IONBHAR
DEALRACH
(BRIGHTWATER)

CWMMAEN

Fermaigh

Brightwater River

GWINGARDD

Dùn
Caomaugh

Eilean Bàn

Amantine Sea

Eilean
Sianta

Eilean Buidhe

Silver Sea

Ballaghbán

ABAID LARAIGH

Loch
Laraigh

Skellig Mór

Skellig Dubh

Port an
Tuisceart

Sea of Stones

High Road

Shipper's
Road

TIGH

Loch Eirich

DÚN EAVAN

GLENMALLAIG

LISDARA

Glogheen

RATHMÓR

BALURNAN
MANOR

FAOLÁN

Róscomain

Seanrós

CARRAIGMÓR

ISLE OF
SEARE

Village

Loch Ceo

Eames

ARD
DHAIMHIN

Pasturelands

Farmlands

Threewaters
River

King's Road

Rós Dorcha

SIOMAR

ARD BEALACH

SLIEBHAN

CILL RHÍ

Bhá Stoirmeacha

GLENDONAGH

BEANCAISEAL

Port an
Deiscert

CHAPTER
ONE

Conor Mac Nir leaned against the railing of the *Resolute* in the dark, watching the choppy seas splash along the cog's wooden hull. Overhead, storm clouds roiled, threatening to unleash their fury on the small ship. Squalls on the Amantine Sea were hardly unusual, but this one had hovered for nearly two days, circling like a bird of prey. No natural storm behaved this way, which left only the other, more unsettling explanation.

The druid is dead. I saw him fall. No one could have survived a wound like that.

Yet, after all they had been through, the memory held little reassurance. He'd seen the extent of the druid's powers before they fled Seare. Diarmuid commanded his warriors with sorcery and compelled the creatures of the mist to do his bidding. Conor's uncle may have begun the bloody war that laid waste to the island, but the druid controlled it. Conor could not deny the possibility that the sorcerer had once more cheated death.

Conor cast a glance back to the passenger cabin beneath the bulkhead, where his new wife, Aine, still slept peacefully. Taking her back to her birthplace would keep her safe for only so long.

Her visions implied that the druid had a far larger plan than the mere conquest of their tiny island. It was only a matter of time before war touched Aron as well.

Unless I stop it.

A sudden gust whipped his blond hair from his braid, and the first drops of rain spattered down on him. He should go inside before the storm worsened, hold his wife, and enjoy their last few days together, but Aine was far too perceptive. She would look into his eyes and know what troubled him. He rested his forehead on the cool, damp railing and let out a sigh.

"I think it's watching us."

He jerked his head up again. Aine stood beside him on the deck, her honey-colored hair blowing loosely around her shoulders. His breath stilled for a moment. Even in the ill-fitting dress she had scavenged in their flight, her eyes shadowed by exhaustion and anxiety, she was breathtaking.

Perhaps all men felt that way about their wives. Or perhaps it was just the knowledge of the even greater obstacles awaiting him that made him want to remember every moment of their short reunion.

"Do you sense something?" he asked, looking back out onto the choppy sea.

Aine ducked beneath his arm and lifted her face to the sky. "It feels wrong. But that could just be my own worry."

Not likely. They both possessed gifts of Balus. While his gift allowed him to transform the language of music into magic, hers gave her, among other things, an awareness of the power that surrounded them, light or dark. Her sense of the storm's wrongness only confirmed his suspicion about the source.

The smattering of raindrops increased to a steady rain, and Conor squinted at the sky, wondering if the storm could possibly know their thoughts.

"Come inside before we both get soaked." Aine laced her fingers through his and tugged him back toward the cabin.

He followed her, ducking beneath the low frame, and shut the door firmly behind them. Dim lamplight illuminated the tiny berth: wood-paneled walls, a narrow bunk, a single stool affixed to the floor. He'd begun to think of the ship's cabin as a haven, isolated from the worries outside. Here they were ordinary newlyweds, beginning their life together, not storing up memories for a separation that might become permanent.

"You're wet." Aine gestured for him to hold up his arms and pulled the damp tunic off over his head. Her hands lingered on his shoulders and then softly slid down his chest.

"You're trying to distract me."

"I'm assessing your injuries," she said sternly, but her lips quivered against a smile. Then she sucked in her breath, and her playful manner slipped. "I don't believe it."

Conor looked down at himself, startled. Two days ago, his body had been mottled with blue and purple bruises left from almost constant travel and fighting. Yesterday they had already faded to the yellow and green that indicated healing.

Today they were gone, as if they had never existed.

Aine lifted her gaze in surprise and then turned him to examine the gash on his arm, the one he'd gotten when fighting their way free of his uncle's fortress. The stitches were still in place, but where the wound had been now lay only a weal of healed skin.

"How is this possible?"

Conor shook his head. It shouldn't be. He'd never shown any particular inclination toward fast healing. Then again, during his time with the Firéin brotherhood, he'd discovered a number of things about himself that shouldn't be possible.

"What do we do now that it's healed around the stitches?" he asked.

"The gut will dissolve on the inside. I can try to cut the bits on the surface, but it will hurt if I have only a dagger."

"It can wait until we make landfall." The idea of cutting tiny stitches with a sharp blade on a pitching ship didn't sound appealing. Conor grinned at her. "Besides, I can think of better ways to use our time."

Aine blushed, but she lifted her face to accept his kiss. He spun her around and pulled her onto his lap on the narrow berth, his arms tightening around her.

She stilled and looked into his eyes. "You're going back, aren't you?"

His heart lurched. Right now, the last thing he wanted to think about was leaving her. He forced his muscles to relax. "If I can find the harp and rebuild the wards, it will cripple their forces. It's my responsibility."

"I know. Whatever happens, just remember I love you."

"And you are my world, Aine. Never forget that."

He kissed her again, and his resolve slipped. It wasn't right. He'd given her up once with the intention of doing his duty to Seare, and where had that led? They'd been betrayed, Conor nearly killed, and Aine kidnapped. They'd barely eluded Diarmuid's grasp, and for all Conor's trouble, he was no closer to finding Meallachán's harp, the object of power he needed to rebuild the wards. If he'd only kept her close, men wouldn't have died needlessly protecting her.

Aine was his wife now. That made her his responsibility, didn't it? What kind of man was he if he abandoned her?

The ship jerked sharply, and Conor thrust out an arm against the bulkhead to keep them in the berth. The movement was followed by a drop in the other direction. Overhead, the tap of raindrops turned into a deafening roar.

"I should see if they need an extra set of hands." Conor eased her onto the bunk beside him and reached for his tunic. He shrugged it on and then leaned over and dropped a light kiss on her lips. "I'll be back."

The situation on deck was worse than Conor had expected. He slipped and slid across the wood as sheets of rain poured down on him. A jagged fork of lightning split the sky, followed by a crash of thunder that nearly vibrated him off his feet. The deck tilted at an odd angle, and he went down on one knee. When the ship righted itself, he struggled to his feet and made his way toward the stern.

Captain Ui Brolacháin braced himself on the starboard side, feet spread, attempting to hold the rudder steady amidst the chaos.

"What can I do?" Conor shouted.

The captain gestured to where crewmen fought the wind's pull on the ungainly square sail. Conor started toward them as a huge wave crashed over the port rail. Water swirled around his calves and nearly swept his feet out from under him, but still he slogged forward.

Foreboding prickled the back of his neck. He glanced over his shoulder, and his blood turned to ice. Aine clung to the cabin's open door, her hair and clothes plastered to her by the driving rain, water rushing around her feet. Her lips moved, but her shout was lost on the wind.

"Stay there!" he yelled as he made his way back to her. "Go back inside!"

Conor was nearly within arm's reach when a huge wave abruptly turned the ship sideways. He hit the deck hard and skidded toward the railing, grabbing a coil of rope to slow his slide. Aine scrabbled for a handhold, but her fingers just scraped over the slick decking. A scream ripped from her as the flow of water carried her over the rail.

The ship shifted back to level. Conor scrambled to the side in time to see Aine surface between the massive swells, surrounded by jetsam and pieces of splintered wood.

She can't swim.

The terrified thought crystallized in his mind, blotting out all else. Without stopping to consider the wisdom of his action, he clambered over the rail and dove cleanly away from the ship.

The impact of the water momentarily stunned him. Instantly, the cold curled through his extremities as the churning waves bore him downward. It took him several moments to figure out which direction was up. He broke the surface with a gasp and threw a panicked glance around him.

There. She was still above water, but the terrified look on her face said she wouldn't last long.

Conor swam against the pull of the water with powerful overhand strokes until she was within arm's reach. But each time he came near enough to grasp her hand, the swell carried him backward again. When her head dipped below the water, it took longer for her to resurface.

Then, finally, the water gathered beneath him, promising to carry him that last inch to her side.

"Grab my hand!" he shouted.

His fingers slid over her wet skin and then held. But before he could pull her to him, a wave crashed over him with the force of a war hammer, breaking his grip. Aine slipped from his grasp, taking with her his hope and his last shred of consciousness, everything but the roiling blackness of the sea.

CHAPTER
TWO

Eoghan sensed the changes in the land surrounding Ard Dhaimhin as soon as he crossed into the old forest. He'd never been able to identify the protective wards that allowed the trackers and sentries to monitor the passage of travelers through the dim, dense woods, but somehow he felt their absence all the same. Since the druid had broken the wards, the Fíréin were as good as blind in their own forest.

He told himself it was that knowledge that sent a shiver of foreboding through him, but that wasn't the whole truth. He had disobeyed Master Liam—or rather, broken the laws of the brotherhood, which was the same thing—and he wasn't entirely sure what awaited him upon his return. Physical punishment? Banishment? Execution?

Eoghan sensed movement in the trees to his right, and his hand moved to the dagger on his belt. Then he relaxed. "Odran."

The tracker emerged from the forest, his footsteps silent. "You came back. Everyone assumed you'd be on your way to Aron by now."

So news had traveled fast. He shouldn't be surprised. With or without the wards, the brotherhood knew everything that went on in the kingdoms. "Master Liam?"

"The Ceannaire would like to see you."

"In bonds?"

Odran shook his head. "He knew you'd return."

Eoghan exhaled, though he'd guessed as much already. The fact that Liam had reared him like his own son would not have kept the Ceannaire from issuing the death order had he truly doubted Eoghan's loyalty. In that case, he'd already be trussed on the forest floor like a boar. Eoghan could beat Odran in a fair fight, but no one could match the tracker in an ambush.

"How did you find me without the wards?"

"The usual way. Master Liam has tripled the border watch. No one escapes notice for long."

"Any incursions yet?"

The tracker shook his head.

"Good. Perhaps the druid's death will cool the Mac Nir's enthusiasm for the High City."

"The druid's not dead. Beagan can still feel a sorcerer at Glenmallaig."

Eoghan paused, taken aback. "Conor saw him fall."

Odran just shrugged.

Eoghan switched topics. "You going my way?"

"No. I just thought you'd want to know what awaited you at the city."

Eoghan nodded his thanks, and the tracker faded back into the foliage with no more sound than the wind. Eoghan continued toward Ard Dhaimhin, his tread light but his mind heavy.

The brotherhood was not yet safe. If the druid was still alive, it was only a matter of time before the Mac Nir attempted to seize the city. If he could convince . . .

Eoghan cut off that line of thinking immediately. Once, perhaps, he'd had some influence with the Conclave, as successor to the brotherhood's leadership.

Now he would be fortunate to survive the day.

✦   ✦   ✦

Full night had fallen by the time Eoghan reached the switchback that led down to the moonlit city. The usually bustling village lay silent, the brothers already retired for the night in the squat clochans and cottages that served as barracks. It was the very reason he'd tarried so long in the forest, as news of his disobedience and desertion had surely spread through the city. Too many brothers knew him to allow for a quiet return.

He traversed the path down the hill, the trill of nightingales preceding him—sentries, sending word that an authorized traveler had arrived. By the time he reached the fortress, the Ceannaire would surely know his prodigal apprentice had returned.

Finally, Eoghan turned onto the lakeshore road, concentrating on the rhythm of his steps to calm his heartbeat. He had done what was required. He had known the consequences of his actions before he left. Whether those consequences involved his death was now out of his hands.

Your death does not serve My plans, came a voice in his head, the words as clear as if they had been spoken aloud. *But you shall still suffer the consequences of your disobedience.*

Eoghan sagged in relief, not just at the reassurance he would not die today but at the return of the voice that had been a constant companion throughout his life. It had been silent for too long, and he'd been afraid to wonder what that might mean.

Aye. I chose to break the law. I will take my punishment.

He could probably avoid that punishment if he just told

Master Liam the truth, but that was impossible. For one thing, he would have to admit he had hidden his unusual gift from the Fíréin his entire life. For another, he wasn't sure the Ceannaire wouldn't think him insane as the parents who'd abandoned him had. Most Balians believed their Creator guided their steps, but there were precious few to whom Comdiu spoke directly.

Eoghan climbed the hundreds of stairs automatically, his footing sure on their slick surface. The traditional tales of Carraigmór, the home of the first and only Seareann High King, spoke of a keep on a cliff. In reality, the dwelling had been carved *from* the cliff, its chambers burrowed deep underground with only the glass windows and narrow terraces on the sheer face hinting at what lay beneath.

When he reached the top and entered the balcony, a glint of surprise crossed the guard's face. "Brother Eoghan. The Ceannaire wishes to see you."

No doubt the guard was one of those who supposed he'd fled with Conor. Eoghan simply nodded and let himself through the heavy, iron-bound door into the fortress.

The great hall was more of a cavern than a room, a dome-shaped space lit with torches and candles and lined with the high-backed chairs used by the Conclave. Beyond them stood the Rune Throne, an ancient tangle of polished roots cradling an etched marble seat. Eoghan turned down a corridor and followed the tunnel to where it ended in a door atop a short flight of steps. He rapped and then entered.

Master Liam sat at a large table, making notations on a sheet of birch-bark paper beside a pile of wax tablets. He didn't look up. "Are they away from Seare?"

Of course Liam already knew. What information his sight didn't provide, his vast network of sentries and informants did.

"Aye, sir. They're safely aboard a ship to Aron. I submit myself to your judgment."

"You could have gone with them."

"I could have." Eoghan's palms prickled with sweat. "But I took an oath, and even if I hadn't, the others who helped me would be punished."

"You know I am within my rights to order your execution."

"Aye, sir."

Liam sighed and rubbed his eyes wearily. "Yet I cannot bring myself to destroy my own apprentice, my successor, for following his conscience. Tell me, why didn't you give me the courtesy of a request?"

"I couldn't be sure you would agree, sir. If I left without permission, I broke only the brotherhood's laws. If I left after you forbade it, I would have disobeyed a direct order."

"Aine is my mother's daughter, and Conor is one of us, even if he chose to leave the brotherhood. I might have looked sympathetically on your task, had you seen fit to ask."

Eoghan studied the wall behind Liam's head. Given the Ceannaire's refusal to become involved in the kingdoms' wars, he'd been so certain Liam would withold aid. "I'm sorry, sir. I did what I thought best."

"I understand that. But you broke both our laws and your oath. I cannot ignore that, even for my own successor. I must sentence you to twenty-five lashes before the brotherhood, to be carried out at dawn tomorrow."

Eoghan jerked his head up. "What?"

"Do you disagree with my punishment? Would you prefer death?"

"No, sir. I accept your judgment."

"Good. You may go." Liam waited until Eoghan reached the door before calling out, "Eoghan, one question. How did you know Conor needed your help when the first report reached Ard Dhaimhin only the day after you left?"

"I wish I were able to give you a reasonable explanation," Eoghan said, avoiding Liam's eyes. Then, despite the fact that he was already in enough trouble, he let himself out before the Ceannaire could ask any more questions.

+ + +

Word spread quickly after the morning horns, and the assembled brotherhood moved en masse to the amphitheater used for devotions. Eoghan didn't need to ask about the procedure for his punishment. In his lifetime at Ard Dhaimhin, he had seen a handful of floggings, and the memories were enough to twist his stomach into knots.

When he arrived, two massive posts had been set into deep holes, ropes hanging from rings set into their tops. Eoghan slowly descended the stairs to where Master Liam and the nine Conclave members awaited him, glad he had skipped the morning meal. Surely even battle could not be as nerve-wracking as the realization he would soon be completely at another's mercy. When he approached, the men stepped back into a line before him, and the hum of voices in the amphitheater hushed.

Master Liam moved forward. "Brother Eoghan, you have admitted to breaking the laws of the Fíréin brotherhood by leaving the city without permission. You have been sentenced to twenty-five lashes with the whip. Do you wish to say anything in your defense?"

"No, sir."

"Very well, then." Master Liam withdrew a handful of straws and leveled them in his fist. "The Conclave will draw to determine who will carry out the sentence."

One by one, the nine members drew straws. When Brother
Daigh, the oldest of the Conclave, drew the shortest one,
Eoghan's heart sank. Daigh was not the strongest of the men,
but he was the sternest. He would not let pity stay his hand.

Liam glanced at the lanky, blond-haired warrior beside him.
"Brother Riordan, restrain Brother Eoghan."

Regret crossed the man's face. After Liam, this brother had
played the biggest role in Eoghan's upbringing. He also happened to be Conor's father, a fact of which few knew and even
fewer spoke.

"Remove your shirt," Riordan said.

Eoghan pulled off the linen tunic and tossed it aside, keeping
his expression blank.

Riordan buckled leather straps around Eoghan's wrists and
then threaded the ropes through the ring on each.

"I tried to speak with Master Liam," he murmured.

"I knew what I was doing. Your son is safe. And by now,
I would think you have a daughter as well."

Relief and pleasure mingled with pain in the older man's face.
He placed a green willow rod between Eoghan's teeth. "Comdiu
protect you."

The ropes pulled through the rings, stretching Eoghan's arms
out in a vee above his head, rendering him powerless, vulnerable. A frisson of fear scurried through him as Brother Daigh
approached with a five-tailed cord whip in hand. At least it
wasn't leather like those they used on brothers who purposely
harmed one another. This whip was meant to inflict pain, not
to maim.

Eoghan steeled himself for the first lash, but even so, it stole
his breath. Fiery pain seared across his back and rippled through
his nerve endings. He clenched the willow rod between his teeth.

It was worse than he had imagined. But he would be silent.

He would not show weakness. He braced himself for the second lash while the moments ticked by, each one an agony of anticipation. Only when the sting had faded to a manageable level did the whip crack again and pain seared him once more.

It took Daigh nearly twenty minutes to deliver the requisite twenty-five strokes, pausing between each to let the pain abate before he started again. Eoghan's determination to remain silent disintegrated somewhere around number six, when he could no longer stifle his cries. By the end, his body was slicked with sweat or blood, and he sagged in his restraints until his arms felt as though they would be pulled from their sockets.

At last, two brothers lowered the ropes. Eoghan lay facedown on the ground, his muscles cramped and his throat raw, while calloused hands unbuckled the straps around his wrists.

"On behalf of my son," Riordan's voice whispered, "thank you."

Eoghan managed to lift his head. "It is my privilege to serve Comdiu." Then he collapsed on the hard ground.

CHAPTER
THREE

Thirst, powerful and insistent, broke through the haze of
Conor's unconsciousness, followed by an ache that seemed to
come from everywhere at once. A distant roar sent his head
into a furious hammering that squelched all thoughts of movement. He lay still and gritted his teeth against the pain until
it passed.

Slowly, he opened his eyes to the source of the roaring, which
was actually just the lap of low tide. He was sprawled on a sandy
beach, sand in every last crevice: eyes, nose, mouth. It hurt to
move or even blink, and it took every last bit of strength to push
himself to a sitting position.

A level swath of shoreline stretched in either direction, long
grasses marking dunes along the gentle slope. Not Seare. Amanta
perhaps. But how had he gotten here?

Memories flooded back. The storm that stalked them from
Seare, biding its time like a living thing. The massive waves.
Aine struggling in the churning sea.

His heart nearly burst from his chest with its sudden pounding. He scrambled to his feet and scanned the beach. He'd

almost had her. Their fingers had touched just before something had knocked him unconscious.

But Aine couldn't swim. The chances she had survived . . .

"Aine!" The shout cracked his salt-parched throat. "Aine, can you hear me?"

He stumbled up the beach, straining his eyes in the filtered light that shone through the clouds overhead.

She was dead. She couldn't have survived that storm, not when she couldn't swim.

No. Conor shut his eyes to clear those dark thoughts. He hadn't been able to swim when he was unconscious. If he had washed up on the beach, perhaps she had as well.

He trudged along the shoreline, hope battling logic in his foggy brain. The southern coast of Amanta was sparsely settled. He might walk for miles without seeing another living soul. But even as he called Aine's name, he knew it was futile. If she had survived, she could be anywhere. The chances against both of them surviving and then washing up together on the shore were astronomical.

She's dead, Conor.

I thought that before.

That was a dream; this is real.

But she can't be dead.

That's only your own wishful thinking.

Movement in the grasses caught his eye, so fleeting that he thought it was just his imagination tormenting him. But, no, there it was again. Hope swelled. Could she have wandered inland and, now that she heard him calling, come back to find him? He took a step toward the grassy dune.

Then the heads of three men crested the rise, followed by bulky, muscular bodies. Bleached hair fell around the shoulders of their brightly dyed cloaks, beneath which were knee-length tunics and close-fitting trousers. Their movements as much as their weapons marked them as warriors, but he knew immediately that they weren't Gwynn or Aronan. In Amanta, that left only one other possibility.

A sharp, humorless laugh slipped from him. He had escaped certain death in Seare, only to be captured by the Sofarende who plagued Gwydden's southern coast.

Conor's amusement was fleeting. A fighting man caught on foreign shores was too dangerous to keep as a captive and useless as a hostage. That left only one probable alternative.

If he were going to die, he would die on his own terms, not at the hands of some barbarian executioner. He reached over his shoulder for his sword and remembered he had left it hanging in the *Resolute*'s cabin.

He still had his dagger, though, secured on his belt. He would never get close enough to use it if he gave them any reason to see him as a threat. Deception was his only chance.

He waited for their approach, his hands open by his side, and put on a terrified expression. If he could just draw them in and convince them he wouldn't fight, he might have a chance. When they were within speaking distance, Conor threw up his hands. "Please! I surrender! Don't hurt me!"

The one in the middle said something, and the others laughed. He caught the word *coward* in Norin. Then the leader said clearly to him, "Turn around."

Conor didn't move. No need to show he understood their language. The man motioned impatiently to him, and Conor turned, his hands still by his ears.

One of the other men strode toward him with a length of rope, and Conor realized he was to be bound. The man in the middle, who seemed to be the leader, warned them that Conor might be an Aronan spy. A second man approached from the other side.

In a split second, Conor's course of action flashed before him. He freed his dagger and plunged it into the side of the man next to him, a killing blow to the heart. Before the others could react, he swiveled and sliced across the second man's thigh. The warrior fell to the ground with a howl of pain. His hand clamped the wound to no avail—he would bleed out in minutes. That left only the third man. Blood pulsed through Conor's veins, fueling his exhausted body with a surge of energy. He yanked the sword free of the dead man's sheath. But even as Conor lifted the weapon to block the last man's sword, he knew he was too slow.

That single moment, that last breath, stretched into an eternity as he waited for the strike of the blade, that instant of pain followed by blackness. Faces, names, regrets all flashed through his mind.

Riordan. Eoghan. Liam. Aine. If he died, he failed them all.

Forgive me, Comdiu.

He sensed the breeze as the sword cleaved the air toward his neck, flinched before the bite of steel that would end it all. It never came. His eyes snapped open and looked straight into a pair of watery blue ones that appeared as shocked as he felt.

"Blessed Askr," the warrior cried, looking down at the sword in his straining hands.

The moment stretched as they both stared at the Sofarende's blade, fixed in place as if the air had turned to mortar. Before Conor could regain his wits enough to strike, the warrior knocked the sword from his numb fingers. A booted foot crashed first into his chest and then into his head. Conor struggled to hang on to consciousness while blood poured into his eyes, but the light was like the slipping of the tide, receding by inches until only dark remained.

+ + +

"You should have killed him."

"We can't kill him. Haldor will want to question him."

"He killed two of our own. Do you want to tell Haldor why we let him live after that?"

The sharp argument just at the edge of Conor's hearing was the first indication that he wasn't dead, though at the moment, he very much wished to be. If he had thought he felt bad waking up on the shore, it was nothing compared with the pain he felt now. He lay still, waiting for the pain and nausea to pass, and then pried his eyes open. Blurry images shifted and overlapped, angling over each other like the facets of a prism.

"Enough. He's awake. Get him up."

It took Conor a few moments to recognize the addition of a third voice, even longer to comprehend they were speaking Norin. If he still understood another language, he couldn't be too badly injured, could he?

Hands pulled him up from where he lay on the hard ground and sat him on something even harder, a bench perhaps. He could smell burning pitch, the close odor of sweat, and the metallic tang of his own blood. No air currents. He must be indoors. He wrenched his eyes open again and made out the blurry shapes of men around him. Just that small action taxed him so much that his eyes drooped closed again and his head lolled forward on his chest.

A fist yanked his head up by the hair, and a hand slapped him hard across the face. The low throb in Conor's skull escalated to the pounding of skin drums.

"Ask him his name," the commanding speaker said.

An accented voice asked in the common tongue, "What's your name?"

Conor opened his swollen eyes long enough to take in the new speaker's rough-spun tunic and clean-shaven head. A slave. Through his split, swollen lips, he rasped, "Conor."

"Your clan name?"

Conor considered, his thoughts coming slowly through the pain. "I have none."

"He's lying," the Sofarende murmured in his own language. "He's no commoner. Prompt him."

A fist collided with Conor's cheekbone, bringing another explosion of pain. Something told him he shouldn't identify himself as a Mac Nir. He gasped out his answer. "No clan name. Fíréin."

Silence settled over the room. Quietly, the slave said, "The Brotherhood of the Faithful. Warrior priests. Like your Wolfskins, just better educated."

"Who sent him?" the Sofarende asked.

Fading in and out of consciousness, Conor mumbled an answer before the question could be translated. "No one sent me. Shipwrecked."

The slave interpreted his answer, and snorts of derision rang out around him.

Conor sensed someone bend down, his face right in front of his. The Sofarende's tone was low and dangerous. "You speak our language?"

"Aye," Conor whispered.

"Who sent you? Olaf? Ingvarr?"

He gurgled a laugh, pain and despair making him reckless. "If you think I'm a spy, reports of your intelligence are greatly overrated."

The blow did not come in the form of a fist to his face this time but rather some sort of object to his ribs. A cry sprang from his lips, and he panted through the waves of agony. He reached for the trick he'd learned long ago to distance his mind from his body until the pain slackened its grip. When he had himself mostly under control, he forced open his heavy eyelids.

The warrior leaned close to him. "You stopped my blade. How did you do that?"

Conor's pulse sped, setting off another round of throbbing in his head. He licked his cracked lips. The answer to this question would determine whether he lived or died. What *had* happened? One moment, he'd realized he'd never be able to stop the arc of the sword in time. The next, he was staring into the eyes of his enemy, who looked at him as if he were a spirit—or a god.

"I don't know," he said finally. "Perhaps the favor of Comdiu was upon me."

Silence fell over the gathering, only the quiet rustle of clothing betraying movement. The air around him grew thick with consideration.

"Kill him," the warrior said finally. "In the square."

They fell on him, tearing clothes from his body. When they'd stripped him naked, they wrenched him to his feet. He stumbled forward, determined to stay upright on his wobbly legs. Should he fall with his hands bound behind his back, he would be kissing the dirt.

Another round of inappropriate laughter welled up. They were taking him to be executed, and he was worried about stumbling.

The warriors propelled him from what he now recognized as a timber hut into glaring day. He squeezed his eyes shut against the sunlight, focusing instead on the breeze that cooled his battered face. His bare feet thudded on wood planking, but his head throbbed too fiercely to come up with a reasonable explanation.

He wrenched his eyes open when the first piece of rotten

produce hit him. It exploded in a wet, putrid mess on his chest before sliding down his skin. He closed his nose against the smell and turned to the child he assumed had thrown it. Whatever his gaze may have held, the boy stepped behind his mother. Conor only got the impression of apron, skirt, and a steely glare. The boy might fear him, but the woman did not.

And indeed, why would anyone fear him in this state? He was naked, bound, covered in dirt and blood, and barely able to walk under his own power.

They think you have magic.

He tried to hold on to the thought. It was important somehow. But it slipped away in the spinning of his brain. Norin words flowed around him, no longer making any sense, just lulling him into the peaceful arms of the dark.

And then he was being forced to his knees. A moment of clarity came back at the touch of a blade to his neck.

I don't want to die.

He focused on those words to keep the darkness at bay. If he died, there would be no one to help Aine. If he died, Seare would suffer beneath the druid's rule without anyone to deliver them.

They think you have magic.

He raised his head and forced defiance into his tone. "What makes you think you can kill me now? You failed before. Do you want to fail again before your people?"

"We shall see, shan't we?" The blade lifted from his neck as his executioner prepared for the killing blow. Conor tensed, fear flooding the space his feigned courage had left behind.

"What's the meaning of this?"

Conor jerked at the new voice, heavy with command.

"He's a spy. He should be executed as such."

A hand grasped Conor's hair and yanked his head back. "Where are you from, boy?"

Conor found himself staring into a pair of sea-green eyes. Was it his imagination, or did they seem curious? He forced enough moisture into his mouth to answer. "Seare."

"And what interest does Seare have in us?"

"I cannot speak for Seare, but I have no interest in you other than convincing you not to kill me."

The man's brow furrowed, but before Conor could determine what that might mean, another voice cut in. "He killed Rún and Bjarne. He possesses magic."

The commander's expression darkened. He released Conor abruptly and stepped back. Conor tried to focus, but he could make out only bulk and pale hair. "Restrain him in the goat shed. If he survives his injuries, I'll question him myself."

Once more, hands lifted him to his feet, but he could barely coordinate the movement of his legs through his rush of relief. He would not die—at least not today.

His captor shoved him into a shed smelling of hay, animal, and manure. He sprawled on the hard earth.

"You won't survive your injuries," the man muttered.

Only then did Conor notice the three men who trailed the first.

Fear vanished into agony as blows rained down on his entire body, delivered by foot and fist and spear haft. He curled into a ball, trying to evade the punishment even as he wished for a killing strike. He had wanted a clean death, a warrior's death, not to be bludgeoned on the ground like vermin. And then, at last, the final blow came, bringing with it the blessed relief of oblivion.

CHAPTER FOUR

The Aronan galley Beacon pulled in its oars as the first breath of wind filled its sails. Its crew had been on duty for almost six months, patrolling the Aronan coast not only for Sofarende invaders but also for Seareann attacks. With the defeat of Faolán a recent memory, King Bress of Aron would not assume that the new monarch's avarice would end with his conquest of Seare.

Cass Mac Onaghan, captain of the *Beacon*, had seen enough wars to know how quickly they could boil over into neighboring nations, so he, like the others, kept his eyes peeled on the horizon. Still, he didn't expect trouble today, and his mind was more fixed on the uncomfortable flare of gout that troubled his feet. He was already fifty in a land where most men would not achieve another decade, and the longer he spent at sea, the more his dream of comfortable retirement looked unlikely.

A shout went up on the opposite side of the ship, and Cass hurried larboard. His first mate, Miach, pointed at a speck on the water in the distance. Cass squinted.

"Probably a seal," he said. "Too small to be of note."

But as the *Beacon* drew nearer, Cass could see a splash

of white in the dark ocean, floating atop the water. Not a seal but a woman, snagged on a piece of wood that might once have been a barrel or a crate.

"Lower the dinghy," he ordered. "She's probably a victim of the storms."

Miach called for three men, and within minutes, the dinghy cut through the water toward the victim. Cass watched as the men retrieved the corpse and hauled the waterlogged woman into the boat. They rowed back quickly—too quickly—and when the boat neared, Miach shouted, "She's alive!"

Cass snapped his fingers at the cabin boy. "Prepare my quarters. Plenty of blankets."

Crewmen lowered a sling to haul up the woman, and then more men helped lay her gently on the deck. The way they immediately stepped back to give her room prompted Cass to take a closer look. She was young, her skin pale and translucent, her lips tinged blue from exposure. With her hair splayed out in a wet tangle on the deck and her tattered dress clinging to her body, Cass could nearly believe she was a selkie in her human form.

But that was ridiculous. A human woman she was and, by the barely perceptible rise and fall of her chest, alive by only the thinnest of threads.

"Take her to my cabin." Cass looked at Miach, who wore the same stunned expression. "It looks like we're back into port after all."

Miach dragged his eyes away from the girl and then called for the oars again. As the galley crawled toward shore, Cass followed the man who carried her back to his cabin. He was not given to flights of fancy, but even he had the feeling there was more to this than a mere shipwrecked survivor.

+ + +

Aine was cold—bone-deep, shivering, nauseatingly cold. The water relinquished its grip, bringing with it the weight of gravity as she was lifted from the buoyant swells of the sea. But her eyes would not open and allow her to see what had plucked her from the waves.

Then something warm and dry wrapped around her, and someone rubbed her hands and feet. They stung as feeling returned to them. She wanted to cry out, but her mind and voice were still buried beneath half-consciousness. She had no choice but to endure the torment, shuddering as warmth returned to her chilled body. Then the sensations finally subsided and she slept.

Aine's next conscious sensation was the gentle sway of a ship, comforting like the rocking of a cradle. Had she just dreamed it all? Were the storm and her near-drowning and the piercing cold merely figments of her imagination?

She pried her eyes open and found herself staring at a wood-paneled ceiling. A wool blanket scratched her chin. She was in a bunk somewhere, but it was not the cabin on the *Resolute*.

"How are you feeling?" A man's voice, soft but colored with a distinct Lowland accent.

She turned her head and tried to focus on the speaker's face. Red hair, close-cropped beard, kind brown eyes. She remembered the question and whispered, "Thirsty."

He filled a cup from a pitcher and pressed the rim to her lips. She drank until he took it back. "Not so quick. You'll make yourself ill."

"Where am I? Who are you? How did I get here?"

She tried to sit up, but he placed a hand on her shoulder and pushed her back against the pillow. "My name is Cass Mac

Onaghan. You're aboard my ship, the *Beacon*. We pulled you out of the water a few hours ago."

"Who's your lord?"

"Lord Riagain of Ionbhar Dealrach. He's the chief of—"

"Clan Comain, I know." The words came automatically. The captain's expression changed.

"You know him?"

Aine didn't know whether to laugh or cry. The coincidence was almost too much to bear. "He's my cousin."

"But that would make you—"

"Aine Nic Tamhais."

Cass paled. "You're supposed to be in Faolán. We'd assumed you were dead!"

"Nearly. My companion and I escaped. Did you . . . did you find anyone else among the wreckage?"

"No, my lady. Just you. And there was no wreckage."

Perhaps the *Resolute* had survived after all. Perhaps they had pulled Conor back on board. He might still be alive. Hope bloomed in her chest, but Cass's next words filled her with dread again.

"There are dozens of ships missing, my lady. We can inquire when we reach Dún Caomaugh."

"Dún Caomaugh? We were sailing for Fermaigh!"

"I find that hard to believe, my lady. Fermaigh is far north-west of where we found you. Isn't it likely you are mistaken?"

Aine fixed him with a cool stare. "We were sailing for Fermaigh. Perhaps we got blown off course."

"Aye, of course, my lady. I meant no offense."

Aine sighed. Alienating the man would not help. He might call her *my lady*, but he was still a Lowlander. "No offense taken, Captain, I assure you. What do we do now?"

"We put in at Dún Caomaugh and send word to Brightwater and Forrais."

Unease crept into her gut at the mention of the two fortresses. Instinct, perhaps. Or was it Comdiu's leading?

"Perhaps we should hold off on that. I'd rather no one know I'm alive until I arrive at Forrais." She held Cass's eyes for a long moment. "Can I trust you to assist me?"

"Of course, my lady."

"Thank you. Do you suppose you could find me some clean clothes and a basin of water?"

Cass nodded and averted his eyes. Perhaps he was just now realizing that her clothes were in rags and hanging off of her. He stood, gave her an awkward little bow, and hurried out of the cabin.

Aine buried her face in her hands. She could barely sort through her battered emotions for words of prayer. *Thank you for saving me, Lord. Once again I live when I should have died.* There was no other way to explain her survival. But what about Conor? Could he still be alive? Perhaps the crew of the *Resolute* had been able to retrieve him, even if she had been washed away.

Cass returned with a basin of water and a folded set of clean clothing, probably borrowed from a cabin boy. His fingers brushed hers as he handed them over. He jerked his hand away. "There's a comb in the drawer, my lady. When you're ready, I'll have some food brought to you."

"Thank you, Captain," she said. "Your kindness is appreciated."

As soon as he left, Aine stripped off her salt-stiffened dress and shift. The man's shirt, tunic, and trousers were worn but clean, and they fit her reasonably well. She found the comb where Cass had indicated and then fashioned her stiff, tangled hair into a queue. With any luck, she could pretend to be a boy once they reached Dún Caomaugh.

A knock at the cabin door startled her. A cabin boy poked his head through the door and nudged it open with his shoulder, holding a tray of food. He set it down on the small table.

"Thank you," she said.

The boy met her eyes for a moment before dropping his attention back to the decking. "You're welcome, my lady." He paused uncomfortably for a moment and then turned on his heel and fled the room.

Aine forced herself to take a seat in front of the tray. The meal was just fish soup and bread, hearty and warming, but her stomach was suddenly too tight to eat. She bowed her head as tears rolled down her cheeks.

My husband, my heart . . . where are you? Are you even alive?

This couldn't be happening. She and Conor had been separated for three years, reunited, separated again, finally married, and now after two days as husband and wife, she didn't know if he lived or died. Her chest felt as though it were in a vice, but she still managed to choke out a sob.

Is this a test, Lord? How could You let this happen to us again? Is he even alive? Please, please, let him be alive.

Somewhere inside her, she knew that Comdiu never caused bad things to happen, nor did He allow anything to happen that she couldn't handle with His help. Still, that knowledge did nothing to ease the ache. What more did she have to lose? Both her parents were dead. Ruarc, her faithful guard, had been killed protecting her, most likely Lorcan with him. Her siblings—Calhoun, Gainor, and Niamh—had undoubtedly been slaughtered after Lisdara's fall. And now Conor had been taken from her by an unnatural storm.

She pushed away from the table, lay down on the narrow bunk, and sobbed.

✦ ✦ ✦

That night, Cass supped with Miach in the first mate's small cabin. They had anchored just off the coast of Dún Caomaugh, within sight of the harbor lights, close enough that they should have docked and allowed the men to take their shore leave for the evening. But that would have meant finding an inn for his special passenger, and he wasn't quite ready to relinquish her, nor answer questions about how she had come to be aboard his ship.

She could have no idea of the difficult position her arrival put him in. She was much too young to remember the conflict between Alsandair Mac Tamhais and his Lowlander cousin. It had already been fanned into a blood feud by the time Mac Tamhais rejected a suitable Lowland bride in favor of the Seareann queen, Lady Ailís. Ostensibly he had meant to build alliances across the Amantine, but most thought Mac Tamhais just refused to dilute Highland stock with Lowlander blood. And so the feud had festered for nearly thirty years.

The whole situation was not without irony. The only thing a Highlander hated more than the Lowland clans was magic, something Seare had in abundance. There had even been some rumors about Lady Ailís, considering her eldest son had been sent to Ard Dhaimhin in the old tradition.

All of which led Cass to his unfortunate lie. He had no choice but to notify Lord Riagain of Lady Aine's presence, and the chieftain would want her sent on to Brightwater. Lord Alsandair's daughter was too valuable a hostage to be given up so easily.

Cass tapped his foot anxiously under the table. It was only then he realized the pain that had plagued him all season was gone. Frowning, he stuck his booted foot out beside him.

"What are you doing?" Miach asked.

Cass yanked his boot off. The swelling in his ankle was completely gone. He probed the flesh experimentally, but the expected twinge never came.

Impossible. Just this afternoon he was cursing his gout and limping around deck. And now . . .

He thought back through the day's events. A slow smile spread across his face. The girl. When she had touched him, a jolt of energy had flashed through him, so quickly he'd written it off as imagination. Oh, this just kept getting better.

"What are you looking so pleased about?"

Cass's grin widened. "Miach, my friend, the gods have smiled on us today." Perhaps that comfortable retirement was not as far out of reach as he'd thought.

CHAPTER
FIVE

Aine sat up in the berth and rubbed her swollen eyes. It must
be morning, though she couldn't tell from the windowless
cabin's unchanging light. It took several moments to register
the change in the ship's motion from the rocking of waves
at anchor to the forward momentum of the oars. They were
going ashore.

Her stomach backflipped at the idea. Would she hear that
the *Resolute* had been among the storm's casualties? Or would
there be no word at all? Dún Caomaugh was far from Fermaigh.
Wreckage would be washing up on the Aronan coast for weeks,
and if Conor had perished at sea, she might never learn what
had happened to him.

Aine splashed water from the basin onto her face and neck.
She couldn't lose hope until she knew something for certain.

A sharp rap on the door made her dry her face quickly and
straighten her borrowed clothing. The captain poked in his
head, his eyes averted. "Lady Aine. May I enter?"

"Of course, Captain. It's your cabin."

"We've docked," he said, and Aine realized that the motion

had indeed stopped. He held out a cloak. "We will be going ashore soon. You should put this on."

An unexpected spike of fear skewered her as she took the garment. She clutched it to her chest as if it could offer her some protection against the unknown.

Minutes later, Aine disembarked from the *Beacon*, accompanied by the captain and several crewmen. She surveyed the teeming dock quarter from the safety of the cloak's voluminous hood. Thickly muscled men secured the vessels to the docks with heavy ropes; fishermen unloaded their catches; merchants transported chests and casks to and from their ships in oxcarts. Farther in, hawkers' carts displayed their wares, from fish and produce to leather goods and cloth.

At last, they stopped before a tiny inn, little more than a large thatched-roof cottage at the quiet end of a market street. Tantalizing scents wafted from a nearby bakery, and the soft whicker of horses came from a stable down the way. They were comforting details, familiar.

Aine followed Mac Onaghan into the structure, where a balding man, about five-and-thirty, greeted them. "Cass, the room's ready as you asked. Come with me."

"The room is for my young friend," Cass told the innkeeper as they passed through the common room to the back corridor. "See that she isn't disturbed. She's had a difficult few days and could use the quiet."

The innkeeper glanced back at Aine. "She'll take her meals in her room, then?"

"Aye, thank you. And could Ingrid find her some clothing? I think she's your daughter's size."

"Sure thing, Cass. Will you be back later to check on her, or should I—?"

"I'll be back at sundown."

Cass ushered her into the room and then quickly shut the door behind them. Aine dropped back her hood, taking her first easy breath since setting foot on shore. "You seem to be on good terms with the innkeeper."

"Alan is my nephew. You'll be safe here alone, and nobody will disturb you. His wife, Ingrid, will see to your needs while I'm gone. I'll check on you before I go back to the ship for the night. Will you be all right?"

"Aye, I'll be fine. Will you ask after the *Resolute* while you're here?"

"I will. Don't get your hopes up, though. If you were bound for Fermaigh, no one here would have any reason to hear of it." Cass opened the door and gave her a sympathetic smile. "Rest. I'll be back later."

Only after the captain left and she latched the door behind him did she realize she was still wearing his cloak. Quickly, she unlocked the door again and poked her head into the empty corridor. Muted voices coaxed her toward the common room.

"I need this message to go to Lord Riagain with all haste," a man said in a low tone.

Aine's heart rose into her throat when she recognized the captain's voice. Surely it wasn't what it sounded like. He'd promised.

"Are you sure about this, uncle?" Alan asked. "You know very well—"

"It isn't as if we have a choice, and you know it. Just look after the girl until his men arrive. Make sure she doesn't go anywhere. And don't use the regular courier. Go to the Piper's Gate. Their messengers ask fewer questions."

"I don't like it, Cass. But I don't want to anger Lord Riagain any more than you do."

Blood pounded in Aine's ears. She backed slowly away from

the doorway until she bumped into something solid behind her. A hand clapped over her mouth before she could scream.

"Not a sound, or we're both in trouble," a heavily accented female voice said in her ear.

Aine froze and then nodded. When the hand went away, she turned to find a tall blonde woman standing behind her.

"Back to your room," the woman whispered. "Quickly."

She dragged Aine down the corridor and then shoved her inside her room, shutting the door behind them. "You must leave now."

Aine stared at her. "Who are you?"

"Ingrid. Alan's wife. As soon as they send that message, Lord Riagain's men will come for you. And if they take you to Brightwater, you will not leave."

For the second time in a handful of minutes, Aine felt as though the wind had been knocked out of her. "How long do I have?"

"If you're smart, you'll get as far as you can before Cass knows you're gone. Get dressed. I'll put together some food." Ingrid shoved a neatly folded stack of clothing at her and disappeared out the door.

Aine took the clothing numbly, her hands trembling too hard to undress. She squeezed them together and took deep breaths while she willed calm into her nerves.

"Pull yourself together, Aine. You can do this. You've faced down much worse than a little walking by yourself."

She rode that conviction long enough to strip off the boy's clothing and pull on the items Ingrid had brought her: a long-sleeved linen shift and a dusky pink sleeveless gown. They fit as if they had been made for her, though the style was clearly meant for a younger girl. She clasped the captain's cloak around her neck. No one would be looking for her until later, and with the garment to conceal her, she should be able to safely travel the main road without anyone guessing her identity.

That thought made her insides quiver, so she spent the next several minutes concentrating on the breath moving in and out of her lungs. By the time Ingrid returned with a canvas pack and a water skin, Aine had almost convinced herself she was calm.

"There's enough food for two days if you're careful," Ingrid said. "You'll have to refill the skin as you go. I couldn't spare any coin; Alan would notice. If you can travel with other women and children, do. Otherwise you're safest alone." She helped Aine put on the pack before draping the cloak over her again.

"Why are you doing this?" Aine asked.

Ingrid didn't meet her eyes. "I've spent more time in captivity than I care to remember. I won't condemn you to that fate. If you strike out due east from the inn, you'll hit the road north." She gave Aine a long, regretful look, as if she knew the immensity of the undertaking. "I'm sorry I can't do more."

Aine nodded and then impulsively threw her arms around Ingrid. "Thank you. I hope I haven't caused you any trouble."

"Oh, I can cause enough trouble for myself without your help. Don't waste your worry on me. Be safe and go with Comdiu."

Somehow, Aine found herself on the street. *Due east.* She got her bearings and struck out down the road at a steady pace. She felt as if she must have a sign announcing her intentions tacked to her back, but no one gave her a second look.

Once she reached the North Road, stark fear propelled her forward and she had soon cleared the boundaries of Dún Caomaugh. The city was small after all. Too bad. It wouldn't take them long to determine she wasn't hiding in town. Riagain's men would send riders down all the main roads, and unless she left them in favor of open country, they would soon catch up to her.

Please, Lord. I know you provided this escape for me. How else

*can I explain Ingrid's help? I have to trust that You won't allow me
to be captured. I don't know how You will do it, but I trust that
You will.*

Her energy wore away quickly, reminding her that less than a
day ago, she had been fished out of the ocean, unconscious. She
didn't even know how long she had been there, since she kept
forgetting to ask what day it was. The road stretched endlessly
before her, but still she continued steadily, her head bowed and
her eyes down. From time to time, horses and carts passed in
each direction, but no one seemed to notice her.

By the time the sun set, Aine's legs and feet ached, blisters
burning inside her ruined boots. She had no idea how many
miles she had covered, but it couldn't be more than seven or
eight. Forrais still lay hundreds of miles away. It was a depress-
ing thought.

Once the sun dipped completely below the horizon, Aine
gave up the pretense that she was capable of continuing. She
chose a small stand of ash trees several paces from the road to
make her camp, aware of how helpless and unprepared she
was. She had no tinder box or flint, so there would be no fire
to warm her tonight. She didn't even have a blanket beyond
the oversized cloak, nor a knife with which to defend herself.

She had never been so completely dependent on Comdiu's
mercy for her survival.

Perhaps that's the point.

The thought stunned her. Could Comdiu have allowed her
isolation as a lesson in trust? She had embarked on her tasks in
Faolán with the faith He would keep her from harm through her
loyal guards. But her trust had still been a step removed. It was
all too easy to give credit to human hands.

Aine hugged her arms around herself. The temperature was
falling steadily, warning of a cold night to come. She forced

herself to eat a few bites of bread and cheese and drank from the water skin she had refilled earlier in the day. It took far too little time, and the long, lonely night stretched ahead of her.

She'd never really been alone. The fearless woman who had surveyed wards on the battlefield and led men into Fíréin territory seemed far away now. It had been borrowed courage, born from her reliance on those men's capability. How little had she valued them when they were alive?

She hugged her arms to herself, staggered by the unexpected, crushing weight of loss. It took her a full minute to catch her breath and even longer for her swimming vision to clear. *Dear Lord*, she began, but she couldn't put the prayer into words. The grief was too raw, too close. She curled up at the base of the tree, her head pillowed on her arm, the cloak wrapped around her. Tears pricked her eyes. The ache in her heart only intensified when she tried not to think of Conor. Had Comdiu allowed them to be separated to make her realize how much she depended on her earthly support?

The night stretched on endlessly. The normal sounds of the dark countryside—animals scrabbling for food, the chirp of crickets, the muffled flap of an owl's wings—took on an ominous cast, awakening her after short snatches of sleep. Toward dawn, she rolled over and murmured something to Conor before she remembered only cold ground lay beside her. That brought on another wave of tears that didn't subside until the sun crested the horizon.

CHAPTER
SIX

When consciousness returned to Conor, it brought with it blinding pain, layer upon layer. He ground his teeth, his mind too consumed by agony to remember where he was or how he had gotten there. It felt as though he were dying slowly, the life dragged from him with every breath, every heartbeat.

"Stay still," came a quiet, oddly accented voice in his ear. "Drink this."

Something cool and smooth—an earthenware cup—pressed against his lips, and cold water trickled into his mouth. He swallowed automatically. The liquid seared a path down his parched throat.

Despite his sticky, swollen eyes, Conor could see shafts of light cutting into the darkness all around him. Where was he?

Immediately, the answer came to him. The beach. The brief questioning. A Sofarende camp.

Aine.

Her image sprang up before his eyes, bringing with it a crushing blow of grief. Surely she was dead. She could not have survived the angry sea. She had been on the verge of going under when he had struggled through the waves toward her.

Oh, my love. Not you. I can't . . . His thoughts dissolved into a meaningless jumble, an ache far worse than his physical pain. Aine was dead, and he would not leave this camp alive. The fact he was still here seemed like a cruel joke.

The cup pressed against his lips again, but Conor turned his head away. He was injured and ill from exposure. If he didn't eat or drink, he would just slip away in his sleep. It would be better this way. There was nothing left for him if she was gone.

But Conor underestimated his body's determination and the persistence of his unknown caretaker. When he awoke later, trembling with fever, he gulped down the water gratefully. Something cool and damp lay across his forehead, chasing away some of the fever, and his shaking gradually subsided.

Just let me die, he begged, but again and again he drank the water that was offered to him before lapsing into unconsciousness.

Then one day, Conor became aware of the soft drip-drip of water somewhere above him. He opened his eyes, surprised they obeyed his bidding. He focused on the small space of gray that indicated a gap in the thatched roof and followed the drip to where it fell on his bare chest.

He didn't feel it land.

Panic surged through his veins as he commanded his body to move, but it remained heavy and unresponsive. He cast about with his eyes, the only part of him that seemed to obey his bidding. He was in a goat pen, lying naked on a bed of hay. Had they simply cast him here to die?

Then a blurry face surfaced in his vision. He blinked until it resolved into a clear image: angular and fine-boned, light eyes, dark hair. A scruffy beard covered the bottom half of the man's face.

"Calm yourself." Conor recognized the man's peculiar accent as belonging to the slave who had translated his words when he was captured. The man pressed a cup to Conor's lips, and cool liquid slid over his tongue.

"Why can't I move?" Conor whispered, hating the tremor in his voice.

"Don't worry. It's just the all-heal. You were thrashing so much while you were unconscious, I thought you might puncture your lung. Your ribs are broken, I think."

The man spoke with knowledge and authority, but Conor still stared. "Who are you?"

"My name is Talfryn. I'm a prisoner here, like you."

Talfryn. The man was Gwynn. That explained the accent. Conor closed his eyes. "You should have let me die."

"I couldn't. Haldor's orders."

"Why?"

"I don't know. You should be dead already. It wasn't as if they didn't try."

Conor turned his head away, determined not to take any more food or water. What was the point of living when he would only languish in a Sofarende prison? What was the point of enduring any more suffering when the only person who mattered to him was gone?

To his chagrin, sleep eluded him, even though he couldn't move from his position on the floor. Guards retrieved Talfryn at midday, leaving Conor alone in the shed with nothing to do but stare. His Fíréin training had not deserted him: his heart said he wanted to die, but his mind still surveyed his surroundings, considering avenues of escape.

The structure itself was not a problem. From the breeze and the movement of animals in and out, he guessed that one entire side was open. But the scuff of feet and occasional low voices outside told him he was being guarded. It hardly mattered when the all-heal kept him immobilized on the filthy ground.

Then one morning, he reached up to scratch his neck and froze. He flexed his hand and then wiggled his toes, triumph rushing through him. Apparently Talfryn had backed off the herbs. Conor pushed himself upright on his elbows and then just as quickly collapsed back onto the hay.

Sweat broke out on his forehead. Who would have known broken ribs could hurt so much? Gingerly he palpated his body, looking for other injuries. Bruises covered him from head to toe, and the cuts in his scalp still felt swollen and raw, but the ribs seemed to be the worst of his injuries.

He waited until his breathing steadied and then gathered all his energy to push himself into a sitting position against the wall. Another bolt of pain ripped through him. This time he welcomed it. Didn't he deserve this, for his failure? He'd had one task: to protect Aine and take her to safety in Aron, and he hadn't even managed to do that right. All the lives taken, all the bloodshed, for naught.

Conor leaned his head back against the wall. How had he come to this? He'd wanted to be a musician, not a warrior. Even Aine had once told him there was enough fighting in this world without him contributing to it. Yet everything he had done was for her.

Without her, there had been no point to any of it.

Was that what this was all about? Was Comdiu punishing him? He'd been so sure he was meant to rescue Aine, but accompanying her to Forrais—marrying her—had been pure selfishness. Perhaps now he was paying for his disobedience with his life, and hers as well. If that was the case, why should he resist? He should just break for the entrance and die cleanly by one of the guards' swords.

A too-deep breath banished that fantasy. He almost laughed, but the pain reduced it to a grimace. No. He lacked the strength even to die properly. That would have to wait, unless the Sofarende leader did it for him. Instead, Conor watched the goats come and go, counting them, naming them in his head, looking for patterns in their behavior as a way to pass the time and distract himself from his aching body.

The thud of footsteps came shortly after sundown. He turned his head, expecting Talfryn. Instead, a guard entered, scanning the dim space until his eyes lit on Conor.

"You. Eat." He tossed him a heel of bread, but Conor couldn't move quickly enough to catch it. It thudded to the ground several feet away. He didn't consider what had been on the floor before he snatched it up. His stomach tossed as the first bite of bread hit it, but he still forced the food down, piece by tiny piece until he was sure his body would retain it. The stale crumbs stuck in his throat, and his eyes settled on a trough filled with murky water.

He inched across the dirt pen until he could kneel beside the trough. A slimy film lay over the top of the water, but he dipped his hands in anyway and lifted them to his mouth. The taste nearly gagged him, but at least his mouth no longer felt as if it were stuffed with dust. Then he crept back to his bed of hay and stretched out to relieve the pressure of his swollen midsection on his lungs.

Only then did he recognize the truth: for all his brave thoughts about dying a clean, honorable death, of accepting Comdiu's punishment for his sins, he wanted to live. As long as there was the slimmest chance Aine could still be alive, he owed it to her to endure.

Which meant he had to convince this Haldor to keep him alive, no matter the cost.

✦ ✦ ✦

Conor awoke the next morning to a nudge in the ribs that felt more like a kick. His breath hissed from between his teeth as his eyes snapped open. The light from the doorway outlined a man's form beside him.

"Get up." The guard pitched Conor his confiscated trousers. "Put these on. Haldor wants to see you."

Conor struggled to his feet, sucking in a sharp breath at the stab in his side, and swayed for a moment. It took him seconds more to pick up the trousers and what felt like a year to put them on. The warrior took out a length of rope, slipped the loop over Conor's head, and nudged him toward the doorway.

Conor squinted in the bright light, sensing more than seeing a second guard join them. The point of a weapon prodded him forward. Amusement surfaced through his pain. He was so weak from injuries and lack of food that he could barely put one foot in front of another, and they somehow thought he was dangerous enough to require two guards?

"Where are we going?" he asked in Norin. They didn't answer.

As Conor's eyes adjusted to the light, he took in the details of his surroundings he had neglected earlier. It was not a warrior camp but a village, the main boulevard lined with timber and crowded with long, rectangular cottages. Metal clanged— a blacksmith. The putrid smells of salt, sulfur, and animal skin drifted to him—a tannery. A woman gave him a curious look as she passed with a large basket in her arms, but she moved on without comment.

These were not raiders come to strip the land bare and return back home. These were settlers with women and children. In time, these foreigners would come to regard Gwydden as home, and then they would be impossible to beat from the land. Men fought far more fiercely to defend their homes than for plunder.

At last they came to a larger longhouse down another wood-planked road. The guards pushed him through the door. The man holding his leash dragged a bench into the center of the room next to a stone hearth, and the other man shoved him down onto it. He bound Conor's arms behind his back, looping the rope around the chair legs, and then did the same with his ankles.

"Don't move," one of the men said. "Haldor has given us permission to kill you if you try to escape."

Conor studied the man. He was lying. The leader wanted him alive.

That certainly worked in his favor. He just needed to discover what the commander wanted from him. He looked around the rectangular cottage, hoping for some sort of insight into the warrior they called Haldor, but the room gave him very little. A raised wooden platform ran around the outside edges of the structure, several wooden benches and chests spaced along it. A thick straw mattress covered in woolens and furs indicated a bed, and a meager collection of cookware sat by the square wooden hearth. Haldor had no woman or children with him here. That was telling. Either he didn't plan on staying permanently or their settlement was too tenuous to bring his family from Norin.

The door opened once more, and Conor turned his head toward it. A man stood in the doorway, his broad shoulders nearly touching the sides of the frame, his head brushing the lintel above. Blond hair, naturally pale rather than bleached yellow like that of the other warriors, barely reached his shoulders, brushing a blue wool cloak fastened with an intricately wrought silver pin. The pommel of a sword peeked from beneath the cloak.

The man jerked his head to the warriors in dismissal and watched Conor until the door shut behind them.

"You heal fast," he said in Norin. "A few days ago, you would not have been able to make the journey here."

Conor said nothing. Unlike the other Sofarende he had come across, this man was completely unafraid of him. The commander retrieved a bench from the platform and set it near Conor. His massive frame made it look as if it were sized for a child. He leaned forward, his forearms braced on his knees.

"My name is Haldor the Brave. To distinguish me from my father, Haldor the Fierce."

Still Conor said nothing. He met the man's gaze, determined to show neither fear nor curiosity.

"I could attempt to coax information from you, but you have already shown you can endure pain. So I find myself in a quandary. You are plainly a warrior. Warriors are of no use to me. I give you a tool, you try to kill your guards. Yet you intrigue me."

Conor noted the carefully chosen wording, the soft intonation. Haldor was no barbarian. He was an educated man, a thinking man. He would not fall prey to fear and superstition like his warriors.

"Have you nothing to say?"

Conor stared at him blankly.

"Very well. Just listen then. I understand you were asking about a woman."

Conor couldn't keep the flicker of alarm from his expression. He couldn't recall having mentioned Aine, but who knew what he had uttered while in the throes of fever?

"Ah, I see I have gotten your attention. In answer to the question you will not ask me, I do not have her. But I could find out if another settlement does."

Conor moistened his cracked lips, contemplating his answer. "In return for what?"

"I want to learn of your people. Your language, your religion, your magic."

"I know nothing of magic."

"I do not believe you. But let us assume I do. My Gwynn slave tells me the Fíréin are something of legend. I take a particular interest in legend."

He only wants to know what kind of threat he might face should he invade Seare. To come out and deny him would only earn Conor a quick death. He tried to turn the conversation another way.

"Why the interest in magic? Your men seem to fear it. Is that why you want to know? To instill the respect that your men lack?"

Haldor merely cocked his head. "What makes you say that?"

"They disobeyed your orders by trying to kill me."

The Sofarende leader let out a booming laugh. "Do not think because you understand our language that you understand our ways. I was not telling them to unhand you. You killed two of my best men. I needed to know if your life was worth two of theirs."

"Is it?"

The amusement left Haldor's expression, and his eyes turned hard. "We will see." He stood and called to the guards, "Eluf, Ove!" The door opened immediately, and the guards stepped inside. "Take him back now. We're finished."

The guards untied the rope from the bench and jerked Conor to his feet, but they kept his hands bound behind his back. He complied, his face impassive.

"I will give you until this time tomorrow to consider my offer. If you still refuse, you will be executed."

Conor struggled not to show the thrill of fear the words sent through him. If the choice was between betraying his homeland or his own death, he knew which one he should choose. But it was not only his life at stake here. Eluf shoved him toward the door. Before he could step through it, Haldor called after him, "Not all Sofarende are as enlightened as I am, Conor. Before you make your decision, you might ask Eluf what the others would do with a female captive."

Conor jerked his eyes to his guard, who grinned suggestively. Haldor nodded, his point made. "Tomorrow. I hope for the sake of your woman you make the right decision."

The walk back to Conor's prison went more easily, perhaps because his mind was fixed on Haldor's ultimatum and not the trembling in his legs. He barely noticed the shoves Eluf aimed at his back to unbalance him as he calculated the likelihood of Aine's survival. If she were alive and in Sofarende custody, he would do anything to spare her. After all, it wasn't as if there were much left of Seare to save. Would it be so bad if Fergus had to focus his attention on a Sofarende invasion?

He didn't immediately notice that Eluf was not taking him back to the goat pen but instead toward the opposite side of the village. Conor slowed. "Where are you taking me?"

Eluf responded with a shove. Conor resisted for a brief moment before he gave in to his guard's prodding.

Eluf stopped before a smaller hut, its roof thatched but its walls poorly insulated. The guard yanked open the door and shoved Conor inside. He stumbled and caught himself on his hands and knees. Thin straw pallets covered in stained linen lined the hard ground, and a bucket stood in the corner. From the smell, he assumed it to be a makeshift chamber pot. He suddenly wished for the goat pen.

"You will stay here until you are called again. If you try to escape, you die. Haldor's orders."

Before Conor could respond, Eluf stepped out and shut the

door. Conor found a spot away from the bucket and lowered his aching body to the ground, the squalor around him a stark reminder that should he live, he would be a slave.

Warriors are of no use to me. I give you a tool, you try to kill your guards.

Haldor was no fool.

Right now, though, Conor could barely walk, let alone fight, which meant that Haldor's offer was the only way out.

That evening, a guard came in with another scrap of bread and a bowl of thin soup. Conor ate slowly, his stomach still uneasy after days of mostly liquid. There had to be other men quartered here, but they must eat someplace else. Someone had ordered the guard to make the extra effort of bringing him food.

Why? Was Haldor that sure Conor would accept his offer? Why waste food on a prisoner who would be executed?

He finished the meal and inched himself back against the wall, where he sat, breathing carefully lest he disturb his injuries, until the door opened again. A line of men filed in, each one just this side of malnourished and cloaked in the aura of defeat that only those who had given up hope could possess. All except one.

Conor studied him for a long moment. Talfryn. The man kept his head down and his movements controlled, but he still possessed a quality that unmistakably screamed *warrior*. How was it that they let him move so freely among them?

The Gwynn sat against the wall a few feet from Conor and shot him a sidelong glance. "So Haldor decided not to kill you after all?"

"Not until tomorrow at least. It depends."

"On what?"

Conor studied him for a long moment. "On you."

"How's that?"

"Haldor says he never keeps fighting men alive. So how's it that you're still here?"

"Me?" Talfryn's eyes widened in surprise, and a man beside them guffawed. "What gave you that idea?"

Conor frowned. Talfryn's build, his mannerisms—Conor knew instinctively that this man was comfortable with a sword. "I'm rarely wrong about these things. I pegged you for a warrior. Likely a good one."

Talfryn's expression changed. "Interesting."

"I don't . . ."

The other man shook his head. "I'll explain later. You said it all depends on me. What did you mean by that?"

Even though Conor was clearly missing part of the story, his instincts told him he could trust Talfryn, especially after the man had nursed him back to some semblance of health. "He gave me a choice. If I teach him about Seare, he will inquire after my wife in the other settlements. If I don't, he'll execute me."

"Haldor's an intelligent man," Talfryn said. "He knows you wouldn't betray your country to save your own life, but for someone you love . . ."

"You told him."

"It was necessary. What are you going to do?"

"What did you do? You must have made some sort of deal to keep yourself alive."

"I didn't." Talfryn moved closer and lowered his voice. "You are the only one who has been able to perceive me as a warrior. Everyone else believes I'm a eunuch. A house slave."

Conor's eyebrows flew up. Talfryn could alter others' perceptions of him? That was a gift he'd never heard of. "Then you're Balian."

"You don't seem surprised by my ability."

"I've seen things a lot more unbelievable than this." It explained plenty, though—why he'd recognized the Gwynn's voice but not his face. "You were the one translating the day I was captured."

"I'm the only one who speaks both Norin and the common tongue."

"And how did you learn Norin? As a slave?"

"I could ask you the same thing." Talfryn threw him a smile. "But those are stories for another day. After you've made your decision."

Talfryn was right. Conor stretched out on a filthy pallet and stared at the dimly illuminated thatching while he pondered his options. Aine was probably dead. Acknowledging the thought seemed to suck the air from the room. The honorable thing to do would be to refuse Haldor's offer and accept his execution. But what if there were even the slightest chance Aine could be alive and in Sofarende control?

The surge of hope surprised him. He and Aine had a connection before. Did he have some sort of awareness that she lived? Or was it just wishful thinking?

What would You have me do, Lord? Do I betray my homeland? Is it even a betrayal? What harm could come from teaching Haldor to speak Seareann?

Then, *Is Aine alive? I want to believe that You saved her once more. I don't want to fail this test.*

He waited for a sign, some deep certainty about his path. It didn't come. In fact, when the guard came for him the next morning, he still had no idea what answer he would give.

Once more, the guards lashed his wrists and ankles to the bench and waited nearby. As the minutes passed and Haldor still did not arrive, Conor's pulse accelerated. He imagined himself remaining tight-lipped, accepting a pronouncement of death rather than betraying his homeland's secrets. But it was not his own execution that sprang to mind.

Haldor chose that moment to appear, and Conor couldn't help but think the delay had been calculated to make him nervous. He stiffened on the bench, preparing himself, but the big warrior simply regarded him expectantly. "What have you decided?"

Inspiration struck. "I will accept your offer. On one condition."

"What makes you think I'm interested in your condition?"

"Because you want what I can offer more than you want to execute me."

"What is it, then?"

"Send word to the other settlements about my wife immediately, and if they have her, ensure her release. I don't want her spending any more time imprisoned than necessary."

"You think more of my influence than you should. I have no control over what the other settlements do."

Conor studied Haldor. The brooch that held his cloak on one shoulder was silver, studded with precious gems. The hilt of his sword was elaborately carved ivory. Taken with his educated speech, Haldor must have been an important man back in Klasjvic. Besides, his men had thought Conor was a spy. That meant Haldor had enemies, and men only had enemies when they had influence.

"No. You're someone important. I would stake my life on it."

"Easy to say when your life is already in my hands. How do I know you will still tell me what I want to know once she's safe?"

"How do I know you will ensure her release?" Conor countered. "Are we men of our word? If not, you might as well kill me now."

Haldor considered and then gave him a single nod. He looked to the guard. "Unbind him."

The guard reluctantly unknotted the ropes. Conor flexed his

hands but otherwise didn't move. Gaining Haldor's trust was the key to getting what he wanted.

"Leave us," Haldor said to the guard. The man obeyed wordlessly.

"Tell me, Conor with no clan name, why did you make this decision?"

Conor remembered the last thing he had said to his wife. *You are my world, Aine. Never forget that.*

"Because I value my wife's safety above my own," he said finally. "Besides, Seare is under the control of a despicable man. I wouldn't mind him being occupied with you instead of my countrymen for a while."

Haldor laughed. "I like you, Conor. You keep your end of the bargain, and I'll keep mine. I'll send my messengers today. Come tomorrow morning after breakfast."

Talfryn looked unsurprised to see Conor that night in the prison hut. "You made your decision, then."

"You don't approve?"

"I think anything that saves your life and buys you time is a sound decision. I just hope you have a plan. When Haldor gets what he wants, he'll have no more reason to keep you around."

Conor nodded solemnly. He had bargained for Haldor's help in finding Aine. His own life hadn't much entered into the decision.

CHAPTER
SEVEN

Shortly after dawn the next morning, two guards appeared at the door of their prison and roused them with a shout. Conor groaned and pushed himself into a sitting position, shaking off the grogginess of another restless, nightmare-filled night. The other men automatically lined up at the door, expressionless.

Talfryn nudged Conor. "Up, quickly. You don't get in line, you don't eat."

With difficulty, Conor made his stiff limbs obey and fell into line behind the Gwynn warrior. He moved toward the dim light of the door, but one of the guards stopped him with the haft of a spear.

"Hands," he said in Norin.

Conor obeyed and held out his wrists to be bound. The guard also knotted a rope around his ankles, leaving just enough slack for him to walk in small, shuffling steps. He would have been flattered if the whole idea were not so ludicrous. Were he really capable of escape, a length of rope would hardly be a deterrent.

He hurried forward to catch up with the others, helped along by the occasional jab of a spear point between his shoulder blades.

Talfryn shot him a wry smile over his shoulder. "The most dangerous prisoner."

"Until I have need of breathing deeply."

"Quiet!" The guard thwacked the back of Conor's thigh with the spear, hard enough to make him stumble.

Conversation effectively cut off, Conor instead looked to his surroundings. The village was larger than he had first thought. The curve of the stone and earth walls seemed to suggest a large circle, and timber-planked walkways formed the main thorough-fares, intersected at right angles by other, smaller walkways.

The line halted at a little square formed by several small build-ings, in the middle of which hung a heavy iron cauldron over a cook fire. An old woman in a linen shift and wool overdress ladled porridge into wooden bowls, strings of beads swinging from the two brooches at her bosom as she worked. Substitute a man for the woman, and it wasn't so far from what he'd been accustomed to in Ard Dhaimhin.

The line moved slowly forward. Conor held his hands out wordlessly for a bowl, but the woman paused before placing it into his hands. Her lips twisted into a sneer, and she spat into his bowl. "Balian filth."

Conor cringed, but he took the food anyway, not knowing when the opportunity to eat would come again. The other men crouched in a circle nearby, eating with their hands. He squatted beside Talfryn and scooped out the spittle floating on top of the thick oat mush.

"She gave you something extra today, did she?" Talfryn said with a wicked grin.

"She called me Balian filth."

"Ah, don't take it personally. Yesterday, she spat in Geralt's and called him the son of a cross-eyed mule. She's completely mad."

"I feel so much better." Conor tried not to think of what had been in his porridge. It was still probably cleaner than his fingers, though, which seemed to be the only utensils he'd be getting.

Across from them, Dyllan, the biggest of the prisoners—though, given their emaciated states, that wasn't saying much—took the bowl from an adolescent boy. The young slave protested, only to get cuffed in the ear for his trouble. Conor shot a look at the grinning guard and then stood up.

Talfryn clamped a hand on Conor's shoulder, eyes never leaving his own bowl. "Don't interfere."

"But—"

"It is not your fight. They already fear your reputation as Fíréin. Don't give them another reason to look your way."

Conor lowered himself back down, though fury at the injustice burned inside him. Someone had to stop it. But not him. Not today. Aine's life depended on his staying alive and being of use to Haldor, at least long enough to find her and order her release.

Another warrior approached and spoke quietly to Conor's guard, who booted Conor in the hip. "Get up. Haldor wants you now."

"Good luck," Talfryn mumbled.

Conor struggled to his feet, only to be pushed forward by the new guard. It was the warrior who had tried and failed to kill him, twice. As they walked, Conor tried to note landmarks, get his bearings, but the village's symmetrical nature defied his efforts. They neared a barn, and the guard unceremoniously pushed him into the nearest trough.

When Conor surfaced, spluttering, the guard grinned. "You smell like goat dung. Wash."

The water was hardly cleaner than his body, but it was better than nothing. Conor dunked his head under again and scrubbed the filth from his hair and face and then did the best he could to wash his trousers while they were still on his body. When the guard yanked him from the trough, he was hard-pressed to say if it were an improvement.

The warrior tossed him a rough-spun tunic, barely cleaner than the trousers.

"Put it on."

Conor held up his bound hands. "How do you suggest I do that?"

"You wait. Now let's go."

Conor tucked the shirt beneath his arm and wrung the mucky water from his trousers as he walked, shivering in the brisk morning breeze. The warrior had done an admirable job of making him uncomfortable. By the time they reached Haldor's house, Conor's teeth were chattering.

Just as he had the previous day, the guard pointed Conor to the bench, but he did not secure him to it this time, nor did he make a move to untie the bonds. He merely stood nearby with his hand on his sword, glaring at Conor as if daring him to make a move. Conor clamped down his chattering teeth and gripped his hands together in his lap.

The door to the cottage opened abruptly and Haldor strode in. He removed his sword belt and set it aside, not looking at Conor or the guard.

"Untie him and then leave us."

"Sir?"

"You heard me."

Grudgingly, the Norin warrior untied Conor's bonds, muscles tensed as if he expected some sort of attack. Then he strode from the room.

"I can barely move," Conor said. "What does he fear?"

"Magic." Haldor fixed a searching gaze on him. "But if you

had the ability to strike him down with a word, I imagine you would have done it already."

"Would I? Perhaps I want information about Aine more than I wish you and your men dead."

Haldor stared and then broke into a smile. "Very well. Let us begin. After you dress."

Conor nodded and shrugged on the tunic but stayed seated. "We need something to write with."

"Aye." Haldor rummaged in a chest and produced two wax tablets and a stylus, though he never turned his back on Conor. "Does it surprise you to know I read and write?"

"Not at all. We'll start here." Conor took the stylus and carefully wrote out the Seareann alphabet, sounding the letters out as he went. Haldor repeated them, not at all self-conscious.

The Sofarende warrior proved to be an apt student, and he absorbed everything Conor taught him, even if the Seareann language sounded rough and strange on his tongue. When they were done for the day, Conor asked, "Why are you so interested in my language?"

"I thought you of all people would understand. Knowing the enemy's language is useful, is it not?"

"Aye, it is. Why do you trust me?"

"I don't. You are my enemy, and you will kill me if you get the chance." Haldor stood and took the stylus and tablet from him. "But unless your brotherhood teaches you to do something magical with wax and wood, I will count myself safe enough. For now."

Conor nodded. Haldor seemed like an honorable man, but the Sofarende leader was still an enemy, no matter how respectfully he acted. Conor recalled Talfryn's words. When Haldor got what he wanted, Conor's presence among them would no longer be worth the risk.

He needed a plan. Fast.

CHAPTER
EIGHT

Aine's food lasted two days.

She continued to fill the water skin from the stream that meandered alongside the road, but she ate the last morsel of cheese at midday rest. What was she to do now? She'd barely walked twenty miles from Dún Caomaugh. Her legs, back, and feet ached with every step, and her stomach grumbled in annoyance.

If she could just make it to a crossroads inn, she could dispatch a message to Forrais. Surely Lady Macha would send a carriage for her if she knew she were alive.

And how do you plan on paying the messenger? Here in the Lowlands, no one would take her word that payment would be forthcoming when the message was delivered. Besides, she couldn't openly identify herself. Aine chewed her lip thoughtfully. She had no skills that could earn her coin and a bed while she waited, at least none she wanted to reveal in her superstitious homeland. And if she had a way to earn some coin, she'd be better off hiring a ride to Forrais. No, at least for now, she would have to keep walking.

Aine trudged on with her head tilted down inside her hood. The twinge of hunger turned into a gnawing ache as the day went on. When she could walk no more, she withdrew from the row into another copse of trees.

Lord, what do I do now? Hysteria tinged the words in her mind. Two days. Only two days and she'd begun to panic. How much longer would she survive on her own?

She didn't dare sit until she'd refilled her water skin. She wouldn't be able to get back up if she rested now. She tramped through the brush toward the stream, sliding the strap from her shoulder.

A smile crept onto her face for the first time in days. Watercress spread along the edge of the stream and several feet up the bank like a lacy green carpet. It hardly qualified as a proper supper, but just the idea of tasting something besides the faintly musty water from the skin cheered her.

Thank you, Lord. I'll trust You'll bring something more substantial later.

She gathered fistfuls of the ruffled, thin-stemmed plant and returned to the spot she'd chosen for her bed. Her smile widened.

A patch of flat beige mushrooms clustered between the roots of a tree. A close inspection assured her they were an edible variety. As far as filling her stomach was concerned, the unexpected bounty was almost as good as meat.

That night, her meager forage felt like a feast. She couldn't live forever on greens and mushrooms, but it was enough to take the edge off her hunger. She wrapped herself in her cloak and lay down beneath the shelter of the trees.

Protect me, Lord.

Before she could put words to a more proper prayer, she was asleep.

✦ ✦ ✦

Aine jerked awake, blinking in the sudden brightness. Blue-gray morning light lit her tree-sheltered abode. The cold air nipped her skin when she ventured a limb from beneath her cloak. She yanked her arm back under the wool with a gasp.

Unease nagged at the edge of her consciousness, a sure sign that something had woken her. It certainly wasn't because she was rested. Behind the urgent pounding of her heart lay exhaustion that would take more than an evening to erase.

Even though she was alone, she moved deeper into the trees to perform her morning tasks and then headed back to the stream to bathe her hands and face in the frigid water. She rose, still dripping, and turned back the way she'd come.

And stifled a scream at the man barring her way.

Tall and muscular, covered by a wolfskin mantle, he just smiled at her. No sooner did a startled gasp escape her lips than a hand clamped over her mouth from behind.

"No screaming," the first man said, his hand touching the hilt of his sword. "It'll be easier for you if you go gentle."

Aine sucked air in through her nose. Her heart ricocheted in her chest. *Think! Don't panic.* Build and scars indicated a warrior, as did his weaponry: long sword, dagger, small knife, bow. The man holding her felt strong too, but it didn't take much muscle to overpower a woman her size. He smelled of sweat, damp wool, and leather, but not the stench that would indicate an unfamiliarity with regular bathing.

Lord Riagain's men had caught up with her.

Aine closed her eyes and let her body go limp as if she'd succumbed to a swoon. As soon as her captor's grip loosened, she kicked back at his leg and broke free.

She made it only a few steps toward the road before

something heavy bore her to the ground, scraping her palms and forearms on the rocky earth and shredding the sleeves of her underdress. Despite the pain, she struggled forward on her hands and knees, but the man flipped her over and pinned her to the ground. His hands cut off the circulation in her wrists while his knees dug into her legs.

She desperately searched for some sign of humanity in his bearded face, something to which she could appeal. How could his blue eyes look both cold and angry at the same time?

"Dunchaid, let her up," the other man said, but he sounded more amused than annoyed.

"Riagain wants her for her magic, not her body. No reason we shouldn't have some fun with her. Look. I think she likes me."

Aine's stomach roiled. *Please, not that! Anything but that!* As if he heard her plea, he released her hands, but her surge of relief was short-lived when he fumbled with the hem of her skirt.

A scream tore from her lips, and she struck out, her nails just grazing his cheek. His expression turned savage then, lips curling into a sneer, and he hit her openhanded across the face. Her vision blanked from the pain.

He's going to violate me and then take me to Brightwater, where Comdiu only knows what Lord Riagain will do with me. The thought broke through her haze of pain and panic.

Comdiu, help me!

His movements stilled. Aine opened her eyes and saw first the blade at her attacker's throat and then the blurry figure of a man holding the sword.

"Up, slowly, if you value your life."

The coldness in the voice made her shiver before she recognized the Highland accent.

Apparently Dunchaid recognized it too. He laughed, but he

eased his weight off her. His hand inched toward the knife
sheathed in the baldric across his chest.

"Blade!" she screamed.

Dunchaid ripped the knife free, but before he could do more
than clear the sheath, her rescuer's blade opened the man's throat
in a shower of blood. Dunchaid's expression froze. Then he
toppled to the ground at her feet.

Aine scrambled back on her hands and heels, the torn skin
burning at the friction. "You killed him."

"Aye. A cleaner death than he deserved."

Aine looked up at her rescuer in disbelief. Tall and middle-
aged, he wore a short fur cape over leather and plate. His dark,
unbound hair tangled in the brass-studded sword baldric across
one shoulder. He might have been handsome if not for the scar
that tugged one side of his mouth into a permanent half sneer.

Aine met his eyes and shivered at their coldness. "Who
are you?"

He ignored her question and offered his hand. After a
moment of hesitation, she took it and he hauled her to her feet.
He looked her over as he might examine a horse, dispassionately.
"Have you been injured? Did I interrupt him before or after?"

Blood rushed to her face in both humiliation and relief.
"No. He hadn't yet." She touched her throbbing cheekbone and
looked over her scraped hands and arms. "Just scratches."

The man gave a tense nod and swiveled on his heel. Only
then did Aine notice that her rescuer was not alone. A blond
man, young and muscular, held Dunchaid's companion at
swordpoint on his knees.

The dark-haired warrior smiled as he approached, his booted
feet scuffing the ground in a way that seemed somehow calculated. A feral smile creased his face, or perhaps his cold green
eyes just made it seem that way. Aine's chill returned.

"Lord Gabhran, you're a difficult man to track. I didn't expect to find you doing your own dirty work."

Surprise and confusion rippled across the captive's face. For a moment, Aine almost felt sorry for him.

"Oh, you don't remember me? Let me remind you, then. My name is Taran Mac Maolain. You killed my daughter, Caer, after you offered her your protection as a nobleman. You ordered her tortured without mercy, as I shall now do with you."

Understanding dawned on Lord Gabhran's face. Taran lifted his sword, still wet with Dunchaid's blood, and placed the tip against Gabhran's chest. He drew it slowly downward, slicing fabric, and if Gabhran's gasp were an indication, flesh beneath it.

Aine looked among the three men in bewilderment. What had she wandered into? It sounded as if Taran had been tracking this Lord Gabhran. Had it been mere coincidence he'd caught up with him in time to save her?

No. She didn't believe in coincidence.

Taran turned to the blond man. "You captured him. Do you dispute my claim on his life?"

"Do with him as you wish." The words were laced with an unfamiliar accent. "*After* we question him."

"No. I haven't the time or the tools to question this man as he deserves."

Taran withdrew his sword, and Gabhran let out a slight breath, his mouth tipping up in a cocky smile.

"Don't be so relieved, Lord Gabhran. If I questioned you, I'd be tempted to cut out your lying tongue before putting a blade through your heart, which is a mercy you don't deserve." Taran sheathed his sword. Then, as if an afterthought, he drove a booted heel into Gabhran's ribs. The prisoner grunted and doubled over in the other warrior's grasp.

"That's all he'll get from me. We'll save him for Lady Macha."

Gabhran blanched, and Aine's pulse sped again. There were definitely nuances to this situation she didn't grasp.

Taran finally turned to her, his expression lightening the barest degree. "Come, Lady Aine. We've much ground to cover tonight, even with a prisoner. Lord Riagain surely sent more than just two men to retrieve you, and contrary to what you might believe, I've neither the time nor the inclination to shed any more blood today."

"How do you know my name?"

The warrior shook his head. "You wouldn't believe it if I told you."

"Try me."

He stopped and sighed. "Comdiu sent me. For whatever reason, you must not be allowed to die."

CHAPTER
NINE

Aine stumbled after the warrior. "What do you mean, Comdiu
sent you?"

"Just what I said." Taran nudged his captive forward with his
elbow, holding the rope that fastened Gabhran's hands behind
his back.

"Do you work for my aunt?"

Ahead of them, the Lakelander snorted and the older warrior
chuckled. "Not quite. But she'll pay handsomely for this captive."

"So you're mercenaries." Aine stopped and stared at the two
of them. She'd never have taken them for sellswords, not from
their educated speech and fine clothing, though she'd hardly
had enough contact with any other kind to know the difference.

Taran kept walking, though his tone dripped with sarcasm.
"Mercenaries who just saved your life, *my lady*. I'd think you'd
show more gratitude."

"Taran," the other warrior said quietly. "She's just a girl."

"No, he's right. I am grateful. I just don't understand. Why
are you here? No one even knows I'm in Aron."

Taran jerked his head toward their captive. "Someone knows

you're in Aron. And that someone is prepared to pay twenty silver pennies to have you, relatively intact."

Aine trembled again at the reminder of what Taran had saved her from. No, Lord Riagain cared nothing for her, only her gifts. That had been the reason she'd waited so long to tell Calhoun. In the end, her visions hadn't been much help to anyone, anyway.

In fact, her visions had sent Conor to his death. Her husband had just proved to be harder to kill than anyone had expected.

The pain, sharper for being unexpected, pierced her midsection, and she caught her breath. Not now. She couldn't address her grief and still function in the present. "Do you intend to take me to Lord Riagain?"

"Weren't you listening, girl? Gabhran here slaughtered my daughter. On whose orders do you think he did that?"

"Oh, it was Riagain's orders," Gabhran put in. "But the pleasure was mine."

Taran spun and laid a well-aimed punch across the captive's mouth. "I'm not daft enough to let you goad me into killing you quickly. But don't think I won't break every bone in your body, strap you to your horse, and let Macha have whatever's left of you."

Gabhran spat blood, his face pale, though it might have just been the pain of the strike. Surely the huge man had broken some teeth and rattled his brain a bit. Taran yanked the prisoner forward again, a twitch of his head indicating that Aine should follow.

She tried to figure out the situation through her fear-addled thoughts. So they weren't working for Lady Macha, and they weren't after her for the bounty. That meant they had reasons of their own for rescuing her, reasons they had not yet disclosed.

Unless Taran's statement that Comdiu sent him was not mere hyperbole.

They broke from the trees onto the road, where another dark-haired man, this one short and slender, stood with five horses. He wore a sleeveless leather jacket and an elaborately stamped leather baldric, which held his short sword and a pair of daggers. Another member of their group?

"Ah, you found her," the man said in another unfamiliar accent, this one both soft and guttural. "And in one piece, I see."

Taran gave a terse nod. "Any sign of others?"

"Alone. Didn't want to share the reward, most likely."

The blond sent a look in Gabhran's direction. "This one couldn't care less about money. He enjoys being Riagain's lackey."

It was all too much. The scene swam around her. Taran kicked Gabhran's feet out from beneath him and then guided her to a fallen log. "Sit, Lady Aine. You look as if you're about to collapse."

"What happens to me now? When Gabhran doesn't bring me back, will Lord Riagain send more men?"

"Don't worry. It will take time for Riagain to realize that his lapdog isn't returning. It remains to be seen how long Lord Gabhran continues to enjoy the light of day."

In that moment, Aine couldn't blame Gabhran for blanching. The viciousness in the mercenary's voice was bad enough, and it sounded as if what Lady Macha would do to him was far worse.

What kind of place had she come home to?

+ + +

The death of Riagain's man conveniently left an extra horse, a gelding nearly as fine as those she'd ridden in her brother's stables at Lisdara. "You can ride?" Taran asked.

Aine nodded and moved to the massive horse's side. When the smaller mercenary appeared at her elbow, she took a halting step back.

"Forgive me. I did not mean to startle you." He gave Aine a sweeping, courtly bow. "Taran has forgotten his manners again. I am Pepin, at your service."

"Easy, Pepin," Taran said. "She's under my protection. If you touch her, I'll have to kill you."

"I would not dream of it." Pepin pretended to be offended as he took Aine's hand and kissed the back of it. "Taran is bad-tempered, but you could ask for no better protector."

Taran smiled faintly. With his head, he indicated the light-haired man who guarded their prisoner with a placid expression. "That over there is Sigurd."

Norin. She should have guessed. Sigurd gave Aine a sober bow and then returned his eyes to Gabhran.

Because Pepin was the most likely source of information, Aine turned her smile on him. "How did the three of you come to work together?"

"That, my lady, is a story that requires a roaring fire and a cup of good wine. Suffice it to say that our northern friend, Sigurd, got himself into a bit of difficulty in Cira, and yours truly came to his aid."

"That's not how I remember it," Sigurd said. "Thanks to your aid, we barely escaped the city with our lives."

"A misunderstanding. How was I supposed to know that *two* people wanted Lord Gaius dead?"

Sigurd stared back, clearly unconvinced.

Pepin waved a hand in dismissal and then winked at Aine. "An oversight. They keep me around because I'm a crack aim with a throwing knife and, shall we say, good in less accessible spaces?"

Aine looked between the two men, unsure whether she should be amused or alarmed. Considering she depended on this group for safe transport, she wasn't about to insult them. "What about you, Sigurd? Are you Sofarende? How does a Northman come to Aron?"

"I get seasick." As Sigurd turned away, the edge of his mouth twitched up in a smile.

"Enough talking." Taran hoisted the prisoner up by his tied hands and hauled him over to the horse.

Gabhran held up his hands. "This would be easier if you'd unbind me."

"Not interested in making things easier. Find your way atop the horse or you'll be running behind it."

Gabhran heaved a sigh, obviously having decided that mild irritation would play better than outright fear, and managed to haul himself onto the horse's back. Taran looped a slipknotted rope around his neck. Should he attempt to flee, he would be yanked off his horse and strangled at the end of the noose.

The prisoner noticed Aine's eyes on him and met her gaze with a smug grin. She turned away. Why couldn't Taran have just killed him back in the forest?

The bloodthirsty thought surprised her, but no more than the brutality of her first few days back in Aron. Somehow she had thought that once she set foot on home soil she would be safe. How had she ever felt safe here?

"My lady, allow me." Pepin knelt at the side of the horse and offered his knee as a step. Aine grabbed a handful of the horse's mane and hauled herself atop its back and then tugged her skirt down over her legs. The others mounted and the group moved as one, surrounding Aine and the prisoner. Taran took the lead and urged the party into a brisk walk.

After several moments, Aine asked, "What did you mean when you said Comdiu sent you?"

"Do you always ask this many questions?"

"No, not usually."

"Comdiu did not send a bolt of lightning or write the command on the wall, if that's what you mean." A hint of a smile colored Taran's voice. "I've been after Lord Gabhran for years. When I heard about the bounty, I knew he would be first in line to go after you, so we picked up his trail. When I saw you there, I knew Comdiu meant me to intervene. Somehow you're important."

"You're a Balian, then."

"Comdiu may have abandoned me when I needed Him, but I did not abandon Him. Where He directs, I obey."

Aine frowned. There was no hint of humor or irony in the mercenary's voice. He truly believed Comdiu had failed him, yet he still obeyed—this man who had turned his back on his lord, if he had indeed ever served one. How did one respond to a statement like that?

With gratitude, she decided at last. She cleared her throat. "Then thank you. I will gladly accept your help returning to the safety of my aunt's house."

Taran remained quiet for so long, she began to wonder if she'd offended him. Then he cast one more unreadable look over his shoulder. "That's where you're wrong, my lady. There is no safety in your aunt's house."

CHAPTER
TEN

"How bad is it?"

Aine jerked upright at Taran's voice behind her, feeling as if she'd been caught doing something wrong. She rolled down her shredded sleeves to conceal the scrapes she'd been washing in the stream and straightened her dress before turning.

"Not bad. Just needed cleaning to avoid infection." She kept her tone light, but the memory of those terror-filled moments pinned to the forest floor made her shudder. She wrapped her arms around herself and trudged up the bank toward camp.

Taran came alongside her. "Are you all right?"

How was she supposed to answer that question? Aine had not allowed herself to dwell on the day's events, but they still hovered in the back of her mind. In fact, all the terrible things that had happened—Conor's ambush, her kidnapping, their bloody escape from Glenmallaig, and then her near-drowning in the Amantine Sea—hung like a dark cloud over her subconscious. But that wasn't the answer Taran sought. He wanted to know if she could hold herself together until they arrived at Forrais, nothing more.

"I'm fine." Aine gave the mercenary a wan smile. "Can I help with camp?"

Taran shrugged and fell into step beside her as they walked back to the men.

Nearby, Sigurd stood watch over Lord Gabhran, where he'd been tied to a tree. Pepin was putting dried meat, vegetables, and fresh herbs into a wooden bowl of water. Aine watched, baffled, until he nudged several small rocks from the fire and used his leather vest to drop the stones into the bowl. Steam hissed from the water, which began to boil before her eyes.

Taran immediately took up a hand ax and began to chop kindling. Apparently their discussion, cursory as it had been, was over.

There was no room for another person in this well-rehearsed dance, so Aine found herself a seat on a rock out of the way of camp preparations. Unfortunately that brought her closer to their prisoner than she wished to be.

"Girl," Lord Gabhran called to her.

She stiffened, but she ignored him.

"You might as well tell me. Why does Lord Riagain want you so badly?"

Aine turned her head away and fixed her eyes on the crackling fire, determined not to answer him.

"Are you a witch? Is that why my lord wants you? You know, your aunt takes a dim view of witchcraft. You might have been better off at Brightwater." Gabhran paused, and his tone was softer when he next spoke. "I'm sorry, you know. It was bad of me not to stop him sooner."

Aine jumped to her feet and spun to face him. "Sooner? Don't fool yourself, *Lord* Gabhran. You are no more noble than the horse you ride. You would have let him have his way with me, and then perhaps you would have been convinced to have a turn."

Gabhran's gaze raked her from head to toe, and a smile parted his lips. "You may be right on that. You are a beautiful woman, Aine Nic Tamhais. Especially when you're angry."

"No." Her voice shook with the effort of holding herself in check. Sigurd stood by, his eyes flicking between them, but he didn't look inclined to intervene. "I'm not angry. I'm furious."

Her eyes homed in on the dagger at Sigurd's waist. Before either of the men could react, she yanked the mercenary's blade from the sheath and fell upon the prisoner. She jerked his head back by a handful of hair and pressed the point of the dagger to the soft spot beneath his jaw.

Gabhran stiffened, not daring to move a muscle, his eyes wide with shock.

"How does it feel, Lord Gabhran, being completely at another's mercy?" She put more pressure on the blade, and a spot of blood appeared at the point. "Knowing that any moment, I could kill you or maim you and there's nothing you can do about it? That's what fear tastes like."

"Aine." Taran's hand touched Aine's shoulder.

"Someone stop her!" Gabhran appealed first to Taran, then to Sigurd. "The woman is mad!"

Sigurd crossed his arms across his chest and stared at Gabhran, his expression never changing.

"Stop me? Like you stopped your man back there?"

"Aine, that's enough."

Taran's quiet voice broke through her anger. She withdrew the blade from Gabhran's throat and turned away, her heart pounding so hard it crushed the air from her chest. Fury still surged through her veins. For a moment, she'd considered killing him, and Taran wouldn't have stopped her. She blew out her breath and found that her whole body was shaking.

Taran cleared his throat behind her. "My lady?"

Aine didn't turn. When she spoke, her voice was clogged with unshed tears. "I'm sorry."

"Don't be. It's rather less than he deserves. Lord Gabhran incites bloodlust in every woman he comes across, I'd think." His tone was joking, but Aine heard the steel beneath it. He had just as much reason—more, really—to want the man dead as Aine did.

"You are allowed to be angry," he continued. "But the man who threatened you is dead, and Lord Gabhran will wish he was once he reaches your aunt's dungeons."

"I wanted to kill him," Aine whispered. "I could have. I never thought I was capable of such a thing. What is it about this place that makes one have such savage thoughts?"

"Aron is a hard place, my lady. You were just too young and sheltered to see it before. The strong and the savage prey on the weak and the helpless. It's not right, but that's the way it is."

Aine faced Taran, and for the first time, she glimpsed the pain behind his hard veneer. He was no longer the hired sword but rather a father still mourning the loss of a child. Was that what he had meant when he'd said Comdiu had abandoned him? Was that why he was helping her? As penance, or perhaps as a chance to save someone else's daughter?

If it had been Ruarc or Conor or one of her brothers, she might have taken comfort in his arms. But Taran was a stranger, and they were still days from Forrais. She straightened her spine and swiped a dirty sleeve across her eyes. If she were to survive, she had to be strong.

"By the gods, you *are* a witch!"

Aine and Taran spun toward the prisoner, who was staring at Aine with a mixture of revulsion and wonder. "My ribs! He broke them, and now they're healed. I feel not even a twinge of pain."

Taran strode to Gabhran's side and jerked his head back as Aine had done and then ripped open the front of his shirt. Even at this distance, Aine could see that the blood remained, but the wound the mercenary had inflicted was already closed.

Taran looked wide-eyed at Aine and then scrubbed his hands wearily over his face.

"Now we are going to have to kill him."

+ + +

"I told you before, I don't know how I did it." Aine sighed in frustration and wrapped her cloak tighter around her shoulders as if it could deflect the hard stares from three pairs of eyes.

Four pairs, if she counted the prisoner's. Gabhran watched Aine as if he weren't quite sure whether she was his salvation or his damnation. She could be either, depending on what was decided in the next several minutes.

"Tell us what you do know," Taran said.

The calculating glint in his eye unsettled Aine, but she nodded anyway. "My gift was healing, but not directly. When I touched someone, I could feel their sickness, but I relied on my training as a healer to cure them. I had no idea it had changed into something more."

"So it's possible you touched someone and accidentally healed them, like you did with that sorry bag of flesh and bone." Taran jerked his head in Gabhran's direction. "The innkeeper, his wife . . ."

"The ship's captain." It made sense. Cass Mac Onaghan had wanted her safe and secluded. He must have known Riagain would reward him for turning her in.

Aine should have guessed, though. Hadn't she been marveling at how quickly Conor had healed, how his wounds had miraculously disappeared in mere days? But Conor had his own magic. She had seen him do things that should have been impossible. How was she to know it was due to her and not his own innate abilities?

"We can't take him to Forrais," Pepin said to Taran. "He'll trade the information to Macha the minute we turn him over."

"Probably. I can't say I haven't dreamed of ending his sorry life myself, but I haven't the time to do a proper job of it."

Sigurd shrugged. "There are ways of making sure he dies slowly without having to wait around to watch."

Taran loosened the dagger at his waist and weighed it in his palm for a moment, his jaw clenched. Finally, he nodded. "Pepin, stay with her. Sigurd and I will take him into the trees. The lady shouldn't have to see this."

The Lakelander rose to follow Taran while Aine stared, openmouthed. They were discussing a man's life as if they were discussing their supper. And now, in half a minute, they'd decided to kill a landed Aronan lord to keep Aine's secret. Slowly and painfully, if she understood aright.

"Wait! Stop!"

Taran turned. "It's the only way."

"Why? Macha is my aunt. Surely she won't let Riagain have me."

"Riagain? No. But you know how Aronans feel about magic."

"I know it's frowned upon—"

"Under your father, perhaps. Under Macha's leadership, it carries a sentence of death. King Bress is content to let the clans make up their own minds about such things."

Aine swallowed the sudden lump in her throat. "She wouldn't kill me."

But even as she said it, she doubted her conviction. Macha had barely tolerated her. Given a legitimate way to rid herself of Aine, would clan ties really stop her? No wonder Taran had said there was no safety in her aunt's house.

But even that didn't justify this action. "I can't let you kill a man in cold blood for my sake."

Taran deflated. When he spoke, his voice held a new weariness. "You don't understand what this man did to my daughter. She was only thirteen years old. She was under Lord Riagain's protection, meant to marry Lord Gabhran to bring peace between the clans. Instead of marrying her, he slaughtered her."

Gabhran let out a harsh laugh. "Lady Macha was foolish to think she could buy peace with a minor nobleman's daughter after the affront Lord Alsandair gave the clan. She sent Lady Caer to die. It should be Macha with whom you've a blood feud, not me."

Aine looked between the two men, finally understanding what she should have put together long before. "*Lord* Taran? You're supposed to be dead! Killed on campaign!"

"Lord Taran *is* dead." The mercenary glanced at her. "He died when your aunt's ambition murdered my daughter. Lady Macha will sacrifice anything or anyone to get what she wants."

Aine pressed a hand to her abdomen, struggling to breathe. She'd wandered into something far wider and more dangerous than she'd understood. Taran Mac Maolain had been one of the clan's loyal lords. His disappearance had put the lands that lay between Clan Tamhais's and Lord Riagain's in Macha's hands. What if it hadn't been an accident? What if Macha really had sent Taran's daughter to die, figuring he'd be killed in a quest for revenge? Could she have intentionally put a girl's life in the hands of an unprincipled—no, downright evil—man such as Gabhran?

"He deserves whatever you would do to him," Aine said. Gabhran stared at her in shock, as if he'd thought she would save him. "But I do not believe Comdiu sent you to do this."

Taran exhaled heavily. "Then what do you suggest, Lady Aine? You understand now what could happen to you if he's allowed to tell of your abilities."

"Let him go," Pepin said. "He'll report back to Lord Riagain, but by the time he reaches Brightwater, Aine will be at Forrais."

"Some comfort that is," Aine muttered.

A smile passed Sigurd's lips, but he focused on Taran. "You know full well how it feels to have another's blood on your conscience. Do you wish that for her?"

"No. I don't. But you cannot begin to know how much this pains me." He moved toward the captive, his knuckles white on the hilt of his dagger. Aine held her breath, sure the blade would find a home in Gabhran's chest. But Taran only sliced through the rope that bound the Lowlander to the tree.

"Go."

Gabhran pushed to his feet, unsteady. He held out his wrists.

"Find your own way out of your bonds. If you are still in my sight in twenty seconds, I will kill you."

Gabhran nodded solemnly. He looked at Aine, who minutes before he had taunted, who had wanted him dead as well. Then he dropped his gaze, apparently struck by whatever he saw in her face.

Taran's hand tightened on his dagger, shaking from the effort of restraining himself. "Now you only have ten."

"Thank you," Aine whispered. "I know that was not easy."

"You have no idea what you've done. People like Riagain and Gabhran and Macha—there is no honor in them. Be prepared, my lady, because your position affords you only so much protection. In fact, your status puts you in more danger."

"I don't understand. What position? What status?"

Taran shot her an incredulous stare. "As your father's heir. Macha may have inherited clan leadership, but you inherited his wealth."

When Aine showed no comprehension, Taran took her by the shoulders. "Aine, you are one of the wealthiest women in Aron."

CHAPTER
ELEVEN

Eoghan's back was on fire, and two days had done nothing to lessen the pain. After the flogging, he'd been taken to the healers' cottage, where they slathered on foul-smelling salve to stave off infection and promote healing, and he'd been granted the rest of the day to recover. The next day, however, he was back to his regular duties and banned from weapons training until further notice.

Now he knelt in Carraigmór's great hall with a horsehair brush and a bucket of soapy water, scrubbing the accumulated grime from the stone floor. He hadn't bothered with a shirt this morning. There was no point hiding his shame, not that he felt particularly shamed by it, and the rough linen only dragged against his lacerated skin. As it was, his movements stretched and pulled his healing flesh, and he could barely resist scratching the wounds open again.

"Daigh showed great restraint."

Eoghan sat back on his heels and twisted toward Brother Riordan. "If this is restraint, I'd hate to see him lose control."

Riordan grinned. "He barely drew blood. There are few men with greater control of a whip. Have you ever stopped to wonder why Brother Daigh draws the short straw so often?"

Eoghan hadn't, but it was true. Daigh did carry out most discipline of this type. Liam, with his sight, could conceivably have stacked the odds in Daigh's favor.

Riordan's smile faded, and he crouched beside Eoghan, his voice low. "The other day, you told me, 'It's my privilege to serve Comdiu.' What did you mean by that?"

Eoghan felt the blood drain from his face. He hadn't realized he'd said it aloud. "I was delirious with pain."

"No, you weren't. You were completely lucid."

Eoghan shrugged and went back to scrubbing. The scratch of bristles against stone filled the space left by his silence.

"Liam seems to believe you have the gift of sight like him, but I sense no magic in you at all. Yet you knew Conor needed your help before the first reports came from the forest. How do you explain that?"

"That depends. Are you asking? Or is Master Liam?"

"You saved my son's life. I want to understand how."

Eoghan sighed. Riordan had always been perceptive, even more so than Liam. He'd believe nothing but the full truth. "Comdiu told me."

"You mean, you felt—"

"No, I mean a voice in my mind clearly said, 'Go to Conor and aid in his escape from Glenmallaig. Go now.'"

Even though he must have expected an answer of this sort, Riordan looked stunned. "Comdiu speaks to you directly. How long has this happened?"

"All my life. Don't you wonder why my parents abandoned me in the forest? They must have thought I was insane. In any case, I tarried too long, debating whether to ask Master Liam's permission. Conor already had things well in hand by the time I arrived. I just helped secure their passage out of Seare." Eoghan didn't tell how he had found Conor nearly unconscious in the forest, a sword in his hand and covered in blood, not all of it his own. Nor did he mention the haunted look in the young man's eyes when he spoke of how that blood had gotten there.

"I don't understand why you wouldn't have told anyone. Surely, if Master Liam knew—"

"It changes nothing. It was my choice to break the law, and now I pay the consequences. You will not tell the Ceannaire?"

He phrased it as a question, but it was not a request.

"I will not tell him," Riordan said, straightening. "But there will come a time when you will wish you had not kept the secret. I promise you that."

CHAPTER
TWELVE

Conor dreamed of fighting, of screams of pain and death. Over and over, he fought his way to Aine, only to have her remain just out of his reach. A river of blood swirled around his knees, pulling him down. Then it rose in a wave over him, washing him toward her. Their fingers were so close—he almost had her, but he couldn't breathe . . .

Conor started awake to find a dark shape huddled over him, a hand clamped over his mouth. Instinctively he jammed his knee into his assailant's midsection. The man let out a soft groan, but didn't loosen his grip.

"Cease, Conor, it's Talfryn!"

Conor stilled his struggling as his eyes adjusted to the darkness and he made out the Gwynn's familiar face.

"Are you awake now?"

Conor nodded mutely.

"Good. I'm going to release you." Talfryn rocked back on his heels, pressing a hand to his stomach. "You were making enough noise to call the guards down on us. Trust me, you don't want to do that."

Conor pushed himself up on the straw mat, blinking away the last shreds of sleep. The dream had seemed so real, so terrifying, but it had just been his pent-up fears, his buried guilt, getting the best of him.

"I'm sorry. I was dreaming."

"About your wife?"

"Aine could be out there anywhere. After everything we went through to escape, I've lost her again. I couldn't keep her safe."

"That isn't your responsibility, Conor."

"I'm her husband. I killed for her. I would have died for her. Do you understand that?" He squeezed his head in his hands as if he could physically push back the memories. He had told Eoghan he didn't regret any of the things he had done to rescue her from Glenmallaig, but they still plagued him. He could picture the face of every man he'd killed, even if he didn't know their names. Men who had just been following orders, who had been serving their king and ensuring their families' survival. Men exactly like him.

Talfryn stayed quiet for a long moment. "You are a warrior. But you grieve the lives you take."

Conor simply nodded. He had done what was necessary, but he could not bring himself to rejoice over the bloodshed.

"One day you will be faced with the choice to fight or die. If your wife is out there somewhere, do you not owe it to her to escape? To look for her?"

"Haldor is sending word—"

"The Sofarende are not the only ones who would like to have a Highlander woman in their grasp. Even if they do, do you think Haldor will keep his bargain? These men are not like us, Conor. Their concept of honor does not extend to their enemies."

Despite the logic behind Talfryn's words, Conor knew the Sofarende captain was an honorable man. Haldor would keep his bargain because his word meant something to him. But even if it didn't, would it matter? Conor meant what he said about his oath being to Comdiu and not to man. If it came down to it, could he bring himself to break his oath and fight?

"Think about it." Talfryn slid away onto his own mat. "There will come a moment, a single opportunity, and if you are not ready for it, it will pass you by."

Conor lay back down and stared at the dark ceiling. Was Talfryn planning something? Or was he just warning him against having too much trust in his bargain with Haldor? Conor didn't need a reminder that his position was precarious, that he might someday be forced to fight or die. For now, he had no choice but to act in good faith and trust Haldor to do the same.

Still, Talfryn's words planted a kernel of doubt. As they walked to breakfast in the morning, he watched the movements of the guards, looking for times when the warriors were lax, opportunities to seize a weapon. He found few. The Norin warriors might not have been particularly disciplined, but they were well-trained and experienced. They kept their weapons under their control and stored tools or other objects that could be used against them far out of reach of the prisoners. When they did allow the prisoners to use shovels and picks, it was under the scrutiny of several fierce and heavily armed warriors.

Just as well. When Conor was not with Haldor—who gave him nothing more dangerous than a wooden stylus—he was kept under guard in the prison cottage. Occasionally he would be brought out to carry water or lug grain sacks. Either the bucket or the grain could be used to throw his guard off balance long enough to seize a weapon, but he wouldn't make it far on his own in daylight. Too much space to cover, too many warriors to face. Even using his ability to fade, he'd never make it more than a few feet toward the outer wall.

Besides, now that Haldor knew of Aine's existence, her safety depended on Conor's cooperation.

So he cooperated, ignoring the searching looks that said Haldor expected him to break their agreement at any moment. Instead, Conor patiently taught his pupil to write Norin words with the common alphabet until he deemed him ready to begin learning vocabulary.

"We'll start with verbs," Conor said, pulling a new tablet toward him. "Simple actions."

Haldor stared at him as if trying to peer into his thoughts.

Conor repeated the Seareann words with their Norin counterparts and waited expectantly.

Abruptly, Haldor stood and strode across the room to his chest, where he retrieved a scrap of parchment. He returned to Conor and handed it to him.

"Can you read it?"

Conor's heart leapt as he unfolded it. Angular Norin lettering stretched from right to left across the page. He read silently, translating in his head.

"This settlement doesn't have her?"

"No. But that is the nearest settlement. It will be days until a message returns from the others."

Conor nodded, not sure whether he was more relieved or disappointed. Perhaps Aine had escaped the hands of the Norin raiders after all. Or perhaps she had not drifted this far south.

Or perhaps she is dead.

"Thank you." Conor rerolled the message and handed it back to Haldor. "Shall we continue? 'I go. He goes. She goes.'"

Surprise crossed Haldor's face. He sat beside Conor, ignoring the tablet. "Tell me about this woman of yours."

Conor jerked his head up. What could he say about Aine? He hardly wanted to rave about her beauty, lest it inspire

Haldor to seek her himself. Nor could he say anything about her unusual gifts.

Finally, he said, "I loved her from the first moment I saw her and every single minute we were apart. She is better and braver than I could ever hope to be."

Something glimmered in the depths of the Norin warrior's pale eyes. Was that pain he saw?

Before Conor could be sure, Haldor turned away. "Leave now. We will continue tomorrow."

Conor obeyed, confused, and went to the door, where Ulaf stood waiting for him. He put his hands out to submit to the bonds, but he couldn't keep his eyes from drifting to the hilt of Ulaf's sword, within reach just beneath the man's left arm. He raised his gaze and smiled.

The Sofarende warrior yanked the ropes around his wrists, so tight his fingers instantly went numb. *Foolish.* He should be trying to lull them into complacency, not reminding them of the Fíréin's reputation to soothe his own ego. That little bit of folly could end up getting him killed.

Conor flexed his hands in a futile effort to get blood moving back into his fingers while Ulaf nudged him forward. He walked meekly back toward the prisoners' hut.

"You think they will let your woman go?" Ulaf sneered. "Haldor may send the letters, but they do not have to listen."

Conor's steps faltered, but he kept moving forward.

"I think you would not be so concerned if she were not beautiful. Do you know what happens to a beautiful slave?"

Ulaf proceeded to detail his vilest imaginings while Conor struggled to keep his fury in check. The warrior was just trying to goad him into making a move, giving him an excuse to beat or kill him.

"And then when she's used and broken, they will kill her slowly and feed her to the dogs."

Conor spun so quickly that Ulaf jumped back and had his sword half free of its sheath before he realized he wasn't under attack.

"I am here because of her. If you convince me she is dead, do you think that makes me less dangerous or more?"

Ulaf blinked. Conor turned slowly and began walking again, not caring whether the Sofarende followed.

That night, in line for a bowl of watery soup, Talfryn nudged him with his elbow. "You look troubled. What happened?"

"Nothing happened."

"Your moment is coming. Be ready."

Hope surged inside Conor and was just as quickly squelched by reality. If he ran, Aine was as good as dead.

If she wasn't already.

CHAPTER
THIRTEEN

After all she had been through, Aine had thought she knew the depths to which humans could sink: their propensity to be fooled by lies, how easily they could be seduced by darkness. Even on the battlefield, her life had been easily divided into black and white, right and wrong, friend and foe. Now, riding north to the fortification of a family member who would be far happier if Aine had turned up dead, protected by mercenaries who fought and killed for money rather than honor, she wondered if she hadn't gotten it all wrong.

Seare had once seemed hopelessly backward, rough. Aron, despite its clan organization only loosely governed by a king, had always seemed very civilized and modern. Even its dislike of magic, while inconvenient, meant that few people fell prey to the superstitions of the less-enlightened world. But when the mere existence of Aine's gifts put her life in danger, she had to wonder if her homeland weren't the one clinging to its outdated superstitions.

"What are my options?" Aine asked Taran on her second day with the mercenaries.

"I was wondering when you might ask that." He reined his horse beside her, his eyes still scanning his surroundings. "I'm not sure you have any, besides returning to Forrais. Should you fall into another clan's hands, they will use you against your clan as bait, bargain, or punishment. As long as Macha does not learn about your gift, you have the strength of clan law and your extensive holdings to protect you in Forrais."

"What do you know of those holdings? And why didn't they revert to Lady Macha when she took clan leadership?"

"Those that belonged to the clan did. But your father was a wealthy man in his own right. You would have to speak to Macha's exchequer to learn the full extent of his estates."

"You're well informed for the lord of a midland clan. Maolain has shifted allegiances a dozen times in the last two hundred years, hasn't it?"

Taran chuckled. "Your father was one of the few men I truly respected in the north, Lady Aine. I might have even liked him, as much as you can like a man such as him."

"What do you mean?"

Taran shifted his position on the horse's back, the upward cast of his eyes telling her he was considering his words. "He was hard. Unyielding. Expected things to be done his way without question. Yet he was also fair and honorable, and he put his tenants' well-being before his own. Not many lords would be roused in the middle of the night to help fight a barn fire or arrange subsistence for a family who had lost the head of their household. The people on his land both feared and respected him. I daresay some might have even loved him."

It was no less than she'd ever expected from Alsandair Mac Tamhais, but it was the first time she had heard it from the mouth of someone with nothing to gain. "And Lady Macha?"

"She is your father's sister, but I fear she lacks his more

altruistic qualities. Lady Aine, you must be prepared that she will not take your reclaiming your birthright well. She has benefited from the rents and taxes on your lands. That means thousands of tenanted acres of farm and pastureland, not to mention the livestock and the hives."

"What would you do?"

"What I would do and what you *should* do are two entirely different things. Your best hope is to rely on clan law. Give Macha a chance to do the proper thing. She will not want to risk losing the support of the clansmen by taking your rightful inheritance. But she might take some convincing."

"And exactly whose sort of convincing would that be?" Aine asked with an arch of her eyebrow.

Pepin laughed behind them. "My dear, as much as I would love to serve you, our sort of convincing would cause more problems than it would solve."

Aine smiled. She'd come to like these men, especially Pepin with his lilting accent and flirtatious charm. His endearment aside, he seemed to look on Aine with the distant affection of an uncle or older cousin. She couldn't help thinking they were good men, despite their chosen profession.

"We should be reaching Forrais tomorrow," Taran continued. "Prepare yourself. You may not be welcomed as warmly as your position demands. Concentrate on making allies among the household. Spread word of your return as quickly as possible. The more who know of your existence, the safer you are. You do have status as your father's daughter, and as Macha's heir."

"Macha's heir? What do you mean? I have two uncles still."

Now it was Taran's turn to look surprised. "You didn't know? They died of the summer fever last year. Did no one send word to Seare?"

"They may have, but I've been on the battlefield for the past two years. The message must not have been passed along to me. Or perhaps we were so consumed with war that no one thought to convey the information." What exactly did this mean for her? By the law of Aronan succession, she was next in line for clan leadership after Macha. Which left . . .

"Macha's sons," she murmured. "Should I die, all my property will pass to Macha's family for dozens of years. Longer if they have children."

"You see the danger," Taran said softly.

The last piece of the puzzle clicked into place. It had been about control of the clan and its wealth all along. Had her father not married Lady Ailís and had an heir, the succession would have passed to Macha and then directly to her sons, if only she managed to outlive her younger brothers. No wonder Macha had despised Aine and her mother. She must have had this planned since Alsandair's first wife died childless.

Had Aine known any of this before, she might have had a chance to plan a strategy. She had no experience in the level of politics and scheming into which she was about to be thrown.

They reached the outskirts of Forrais's village by noon the next day. After Seare's decidedly rural bent, the activity of this small town took Aine aback. Smoke from the foundries and blacksmith shops stung her eyes, melding in her nostrils with the mellower scent of hay and livestock.

Further in, where the freestanding structures became more closely packed around the central lane, the scent of fresh-baked bread and roasting meat joined in. She wrinkled her nose against the faint undercurrent of sewage and rotting vegetables. More people meant more smell, and here in the crowded quarter beneath the great hill that housed the fortress, nearly half of the folk under Macha's responsibility lived and worked together.

The main road took them to the base of that hill, where the group reined in abruptly.

"This is where we leave you, my lady," Taran said.

Aine nodded, resisting the urge to ask them to stay. They had done enough for her already, far more than she had dared hope. "I thank you for your help, all of you. You did not need to bring me all this way, at no benefit to yourselves."

To her surprise, Taran looked moved. "May Comdiu bless you, my lady."

Her heart squeezed at his serious tone. She bowed her head in respect and then turned to Pepin.

The Merovian reined his horse near and bent over her hand. "Bless you, Lady Aine."

"Thank you, Pepin."

To her surprise, Sigurd dismounted and moved to her side. He engulfed her hand in his two large ones. "If things were different, my lady, it would be an honor to serve you."

"The honor would be mine, I think."

She couldn't help feeling that something more should be said, but there was nothing else to express. She gave a nod and cued her horse up the winding road that led to the fortress.

She didn't expect the sense of loss nor the surge of panic she felt at once again being alone. So much for her independence. She'd needed rescuing so badly that Comdiu had sent her mercenaries—men she'd normally think to be protected from, not by.

Guilt crashed over her. She had been so focused on herself and her situation that she'd never acknowledged the miracle Comdiu had wrought on her behalf. She was worth twenty silver pennies to them, and instead they had delivered her safely to her aunt's household.

Tears pricked her eyes. *Thank you, Comdiu. Once more, You are gracious where I am undeserving.*

And yet, even her gratitude couldn't push back the surge of pain at the thought of those who should be with her now: Ruarc, Lorcan, Conor.

Automatically she wrapped her fingers around the ivory charm, blinking back tears. She and Conor were supposed to be making this trip together, and now she didn't know if he was even alive. Once, he had heard her through the magic of the charm. If she concentrated hard enough, would he again?

I'm alive, love. Are you out there somewhere? I can't believe Comdiu would save me and not you.

As she approached the gates, she dropped the charm beneath her bodice again and forced her trembling hands to be still. She had to be strong. Macha possessed the feral brutality of a she-wolf: any sign of weakness and she would lunge for the throat. Aine's only hope was to present herself as strong, hard, demanding— someone of whom Macha couldn't take advantage.

A pair of heavily armed guards looked her over suspiciously at the fortress gates. One stepped forward and took hold of her horse's bridle. "State your business."

Aine tried for an imperious tone. "Inform Lady Macha that her niece, Lady Aine Nic Tamhais, has returned to Forrais."

The guard threw his head back and laughed. "And I'm the chieftain herself. Be gone with you, girl. We've no need for your cruel jests."

So he needed convincing. Aine swept back the hood of her cloak and stared the guard straight in the eye, her chin lifted. It took every bit of her courage to make her voice strong and haughty. "I am who I say. I would like an audience with my aunt—now. Send a boy to fetch her and see me to the hall."

"I don't know who you are, miss, but Lady Aine was killed in Seare. Your swindle is ill-timed. Go peacefully before we're forced to remove you."

So Taran had been right. Macha had wasted no time declaring her dead, and it would take more than the word of a disheveled little girl to change the guard's mind. She sighed and slid from her horse.

The guard laid a hand on the hilt of his sword. It would have been laughable had the threat not been so real.

"I am Lady Aine. Call the Mac Tamhais herself and find out."

The man's stony expression faded slightly. He glanced at his fellow guard.

"Lady Macha will confirm my identity. Please. Would you rather be the man that returned a lost daughter to the clan or the man who turned her away at the gate?"

Perhaps it was her accent or her manner of speech, too refined for a commoner, or perhaps he could just see the weariness that threatened to engulf her with each passing second. Either way, the resistance slid from his expression. "My apologies, my lady. Welcome back."

"Thank you, sir. Your name?"

"Cé, my lady. Bain will take you to the keep."

"Very well, Cé. Thank you."

Aine took the gelding's reins and fell in beside her escort. Bain's pinched frown said he wouldn't be as easily persuaded by her explanation as Cé. She needed to convince a few of the fortress's guards of her identity if word were to spread quickly among the clansmen.

"I've been gone for nearly four years," she said. "Is Diocail still in charge of the guard here?"

"Aye, he is."

"And Guaire is still the steward?"

A bit of the defensiveness melted from Bain's posture. "Aye. But Síle is no longer the head cook. She retired last year."

"There was never a cook named Síle here. Our head cook was

Sim. And he certainly wasn't old enough to retire. I did have a nursemaid named Síle for a few years, however."

The guard stopped abruptly. "You are she."

"Aye, I am she." Aine smiled up at him. "I don't blame you for your doubt, Bain. You only wish to protect your chief. I respect your loyalty."

Bain looked embarrassed. He took the reins from her and handed them to a boy who appeared at their side. Then he led her up the stairs to the front doors of the keep. The two men on guard immediately opened the doors for her.

Just before she stepped through, Bain gripped her arm. "We served your father faithfully, my lady. Be wary."

He gave her a sharp nod, spoke a quiet word to a servant, and left her to face the hall alone.

CHAPTER
FOURTEEN

Aine shivered, pressing her hands together as she entered the hall. It was always cold at Forrais, and not just because the vast expanse of stone reflected the Highland chill. With its high, peaked roof and tapestry-lined walls, the keep rivaled the continental cathedrals in its grandeur, but it still fell far short of the warmth and welcome of her half brother's hall in Faolán.

A pang of longing struck her. How strange to realize that in a few short years, Seare had become her home.

"They said you were dead."

Aine turned at the hard voice behind her and found herself looking into an even harder set of dark eyes.

Aine might have changed in her absence, but Lady Macha had not, no more than the standing stones of their pagan ancestors weathered in a few short years. At first glance, she looked like any other noblewoman in Aron. A braid bound salt-and-pepper hair away from her face, and her silver-embroidered dress draped a body as hard as an oak, erect and unyielding. Her hands, however, gave her away—muscular, calloused, scarred from sword work. A woman, aye, but there could be no mistaking her for anything but a warrior.

Dislike washed over Aine. "As you can see, I am very much alive."

"And I suppose now that you're back, you'll be wishing for lodging."

Aine's nervousness dissolved in a sudden flush of anger. Macha may be chief, the leader of this clan, and a warrior in her own right, but Aine was no mere girl. She had healed on the battlefield, led men, counseled kings, and escaped a druid's grasp. She would not let this battle-ax of a woman intimidate her.

She straightened her spine and looked Macha directly in the eye. "I'll be looking for my rightful place as a daughter of this clan."

Macha held the gaze, something dark and unsettling behind her eyes. Then a tiny shift in the set of her shoulders conceded the argument. "Very well. A servant will show you to your old chamber. Do your best to make yourself presentable for supper. I expect you to give a full explanation before the court this evening."

Aine dipped her head. "Thank you, Aunt."

Another sharp nod and Macha turned on her heel, striding out of the room as though she had a broomstick down the back of her bodice. The fight seeped from Aine with the fading of her aunt's footsteps. Macha had tolerated Aine as a child because her father was chief, and then after his death because Ailís demanded it. Now only the rights and responsibilities of blood kept her from refusing Aine a place at court.

"My lady?" A girl, no more than thirteen or fourteen, appeared at Aine's elbow, trembling. "I'm to show you to your chamber."

Aine dismissed Macha's rudeness in the face of the maid's cringing posture. "What's your name, dear?"

"Lia, my lady."

"Very well, Lia. I've been gone long enough that I might lose my way in the corridors."

"Aye, my lady. It's this way."

Aine followed Lia down one of the tapestry-lined corridors, even though she could never forget this place. She swallowed a lump of grief when they passed her mother's old quarters, the ones Ailís had been assigned when Father died and Macha took over as chief: deep in the east wing, as far away from the chief's apartments as possible. Aine had been too young to understand the slight, but she did now.

It was a reminder that however familiar Forrais might be, it was no longer home.

"Here we are, my lady." The maid pushed open the door to a cavernous, high-ceilinged room.

Aine's chamber seemed to have been untouched since she left. Heavy curtains covered tall, leaded-glass windows, and cloths draped the sparse furnishings, protecting them from the film that lay thick over every other surface. Stale rushes in the mattress gave off a musty, abandoned smell instead of the usual sweet scent of hay and sunshine. Her fantasy of collapsing into a plump, freshly made bed dissipated like the cloud of dust around her feet.

"I'm sorry, my lady. We had no notice you were coming."

"Then speak with Master Guaire right away." Aine quickly smiled at the girl to soften the sharp edge of her words. Lia wasn't responsible for her aunt's cold welcome.

"Aye, my lady." Lia curtsied and scurried out the door.

Aine rubbed her pounding temples with her fingertips. She was tired, achy, and hungry, three things about which she could do nothing at present. But perhaps she could fill her time while she waited.

Lady Ailís's chamber was unlocked. Aine took a thick candle from the corridor and stepped into the pitch-black room. It was smaller and darker than she remembered, without the tall windows that lit her own space. It was not what she would have expected of a chamber belonging to a former clan chief's wife.

My mother gave me the chamber meant for her. How did I never realize that?

Aine wandered around the space, opening chests and wardrobes, but they were all empty. Where were her mother's things? Surely they hadn't been discarded. The idea that Macha might possess Ailís's jewels, furs, and weapons made her stomach twist. They were Aine's by right. She would demand them—

Aine stopped the thoughts in their tracks. To demand Ailís's possessions would only make her look like a petulant little girl. She turned and strode into the corridor, her boot heels echoing in the empty hallway. When she burst into her chamber, two male servants were already sweeping, dusting, and scrubbing.

"Do you know where Master Guaire . . ."

A gray-haired man turned to her. A smile split his face, the first genuine expression of pleasure she'd seen since arriving at Forrais. "Lady Aine. It truly is you."

Despite the utter impropriety of it, the steward enfolded her in his arms. Aine allowed herself the briefest moment to revel in the welcome before she stepped back. "Master Guaire, where are my mother's possessions?"

The steward hesitated, the pleasure in his lined face dimming.

She placed a hand on his sleeve in silent appeal. "Please. I've arrived home with nothing. And now I find I haven't even the comfort of those familiar objects."

"They are yours," he said finally. "I know clan law as well as our chief. I'll have Ailís's chests retrieved from storage and brought here when your chamber is once more fit for use."

Aine caught the implied dismissal and gave a small bow of acknowledgment. She turned and made as dignified an exit as she could manage with her victory surging through her veins.

She was not the same naive girl she had been when she left. She would not allow them to treat her as such.

"My lady?"

Aine stopped with her hand on the latch. "Aye, Master Guaire?"

A smile touched his lips, but there was a spark in his eyes that made her think he knew her thoughts.

"Welcome back."

CHAPTER
FIFTEEN

A knock roused Aine from a sound sleep. She pushed herself
up onto one elbow on the freshly stuffed mattress, blinking
grit from her bleary eyes. In the dark room, lit by only a single
candle, she couldn't tell if it were day or night.

"Lady Aine?" a muffled voice called from behind the door,
followed by a more insistent knock.

Aine cleared her throat. "Enter."

The door swung inward, revealing Lia's nervous face. She
may have been timid, but she was efficient. Not only had Aine's
room been thoroughly cleaned under Master Guaire's direction,
but Lia had also had a tray of food waiting when Aine returned.

"Lady Ailís's trunks have arrived."

Aine swung her legs off the bed and fixed her dress. "Send
them in."

Two men, the same ones who had cleaned her room, half-
carried and half-dragged the first chest inside and then darted
back out for another.

"There are more, but Master Guaire thought you would want
to start with these."

Aine smiled her thanks to Lia and positioned herself in front of the door. "What are your names?"

Surprise flashed over the face of the younger servant, pink creeping up his neck. "I'm Tamlane, my lady. This is Fingal."

"You were the ones who cleaned my chamber?" At Tamlane's nod, she flashed another smile. "Then thank you both for being so quick and thorough."

"Aye, my lady," Fingal said. They gave her quick bows and hurried out the door.

"You've made two new admirers, my lady." Lia flushed. "Forgive me. I spoke out of turn."

What kind of place had Lisdara become when mere common courtesy elicited this kind of response? "If you would call for a bath, I'd like to look through these and then prepare for supper."

"Of course, my lady." A hasty curtsy and Lia was out the door as quickly as the two men.

As soon as the door closed, Aine lifted the lid of the first chest. A wool blanket lay tucked around the top. She removed it and drew in a breath.

Her mother's gowns. Lady Ailís had never dressed as opulently as some of the other ladies at court—she was Seareann, after all—but her elegance and beauty had inspired songs. Even those lords who had scoffed at Lord Alsandair's choice to wed the foreign queen had been won over by her grace.

Aine would do well to remind Macha's court of that resemblance.

She sorted through day gowns and riding habits until she touched a swath of midnight-blue watered silk. She withdrew a beautifully simple gown, followed by its underdress of light-blue linen and smiled. If she were to face Macha's court, she should do it in her husband's colors.

After a moment's hesitation, Aine removed her stained dress

and slid the silk over her head. The laces tied up the back, but she could tell the bodice would fit. The hem, however, puddled on the floor around her.

A knock preceded Lia into the room. "Oh, my lady, that's . . . it's lovely."

Aine smiled. "Do you know how to baste a hem, Lia?"

"Of course, my lady. Let me find a needle and thread."

Boys came and went with steaming water while Lia retrieved sewing supplies. The girl knelt before Aine and began pinning up the bottom of the dress with steel pins. Aine let her work in silence before she asked, "How many people know I've returned?"

"Why, everyone, my lady. It's difficult to keep such news a secret."

"How long ago did Lady Macha have me declared dead?"

Lia yelped as she jabbed herself with a pin. She thrust her bleeding finger into her mouth. "I really shouldn't speak of such things."

Aine gentled her tone. Macha had thought she was doing Aine a disservice by assigning a lower servant as a lady's maid, but she'd only given her an avenue to the girl's loyalty. "Lia, what were you doing before I arrived?"

Lia dropped her gaze. "I was a chambermaid. I cleaned the hearths and laid the fires."

"Would you like to continue serving me?"

"Of course, my lady!" Lia's eyes widened. "Unless, of course, you wish someone older, more experienced."

"No, Lia, I would like you to continue. But you must be honest. I promise that anything you say to me will be held in confidence."

Lia paused as if considering, and then she nodded. "As soon as word came of Lisdara's fall, she put about that you were dead."

"But it's barely been a fortnight!"

"Indeed, my lady. But I couldn't tell you why."

"That's all right. What else have you heard? Surely there's been talk."

The first light of mischief touched Lia's eyes. "Granddad says word has already spread among the guardsmen. There are many who claim to remember you."

Aine grinned. "Perfect. Who is your grandfather?"

"Master Guaire, of course. But that doesn't mean I receive any special treatment." Lia put aside the sewing basket and pushed to her feet. "There. I've got the length right. Shall I sew while you bathe?"

"Please."

Moments later, Aine was up to her elbows in warm water. Nothing had ever felt so luxurious. She'd never really been able to get the stiff salt feel from her hair, even after washing in the stream on the way to Forrais. She scrubbed it clean with a cake of herbal soap, focusing on the mundane details of her toilette to avoid thinking of what was to come.

"There. It's not perfect, my lady, but it's near enough that no one will notice." Lia held up the newly shortened dress to check her work and then laid it carefully on the bed. She helped Aine from the tub and wrapped her in a length of clean linen before leading her to a chair by the brazier.

"You've done this before," Aine said.

"My mother served Lady Macha for a time. She made sure I understood the duties of a maid so I might better my station."

Aine nodded. How strange to think of an entire family serving one clan their whole lives, from grandfather to granddaughter. True, life as a servant at Forrais was far easier than life as a crofter or baker or almost any sort of craftsman. But to have so few options . . .

How is that any different than your life? What options do you have? What real freedom do you possess to follow your own path?

But it *was* different, because Aine had the means to do what she wished. She simply lacked the courage.

"My lady?"

Aine glanced up and realized the girl was waiting with a comb in her hand. "I'm sorry, Lia. Go ahead."

The girl combed the damp length of Aine's hair and then arranged it in a swirl of braids atop her head, woven with an embroidered blue ribbon. It was style befitting a married woman, not a maiden. Was that Lia's idea? Exactly how much did the inhabitants of Forrais know about what came before?

When Lia handed her the brass mirror, Aine nodded in satisfaction. She looked nothing like the travel-stained slip of a girl who had wandered in that morning. She was a chieftain's heir, a queen's daughter.

A warrior's wife.

Inspiration struck. "Lia, would you send for your grandfather? I need one more thing."

✦ ✦ ✦

Aine stood before the doorway leading into the great hall, fingering the new addition to her wardrobe.

"That was good thinking," a man's voice said at her shoulder.

Aine spun, her heart pounding, her hand flying to her throat. The speaker smiled and stepped back, then swept into a low bow.

"Forgive me, Lady Aine. I did not mean to startle you. I am Uallas, lord of Eilean Buidhe. Welcome home."

Under another circumstance, Aine might have found Lord Uallas handsome. Well built, with red hair and a trim beard, he somehow managed to avoid the ruddy, boyish look so many men of his coloring seemed never to lose. His green eyes twinkled, a sign of perpetual good humor. Aye, she would think him attractive if not for the impulse to compare every man she met to Conor.

"Thank you, my lord," she managed at last. "Welcome to Forrais. You are far from home."

"Not as far as you."

His eyes drifted to her waist, where her other hand still rested. "Your mother's, I take it?"

Aine released the bejeweled, silver-chased dagger. The weapon had been a wedding gift from her father to her mother, a tradition that dated back to the days when men would marry their sweethearts on the eve of battle. They would leave weapons behind to keep their wives safe and to mark them as a protected member of their clan. Gradually, the gifts became more and more ornate, until the daggers were as much a symbol of status as they were of the marriage bargain.

As a warrior's wife, it was Aine's right to wear one, even if her husband had not given it. And it would remind the entire assemblage of her heritage. Macha wouldn't be as eager to push her to the margins with such a reminder.

And somehow, Uallas knew it.

His eyes found hers again. "Perhaps it is improper, considering I'm a stranger here, but may I escort you to your table?" He held out his hand, his gaze unwavering.

Aine automatically put her hand in his, and a pang struck her to her core. It was too familiar: his words, the situation. Conor had done the same thing his second night in Lisdara, despite the fact he too had been a stranger in her brother's hall. The fingers of loss tightened around her lungs, squeezing the breath from her chest. The edges of her vision grew murky.

"Lady Aine?"

She sucked in a breath, and her view expanded once more. "Thank you, Lord Uallas. You are very kind." Aine straightened herself to her full, unimpressive height and strode into the hall, wishing with every step that it were Conor walking beside her.

To her relief, the space was barely even half-full. Only a handful of nobles remained at court, the rest of them overseeing harvest and late planting on their lands. Platters of food already sat at the long tables, and the tap of knives and spoons against wooden trenchers punctuated the drone of voices. She hadn't realized until this moment how much she missed the ever-present music at Lisdara.

Lady Macha sat at one such long table, undistinguished from the rest except by its position at the front of the hall. A handsome gray-haired man sat beside her: her husband, Aenghus. The youngest child in a family of nine, he'd given up his distant claim to his own clan's leadership to handfast with Macha. Their two sons, older than Aine, sat at the table adjacent to their parents'. She felt their eyes, as hard and dark as their mother's, on her as she entered.

Macha's eyebrows rose when she saw her on Lord Uallas's arm. She gestured for Aine to join her in the empty seat to her left. Lord Uallas bowed to both Aine and the chieftain and then found his own seat at the next table.

"Impressive. You've been here a day and already you've caught Lord Uallas's attention. You do not waste time."

"We met in the corridor. He offered to escort me."

The little smile that curled on Macha's lips said she clearly didn't believe her. She gestured to the platter before them. "Eat. Seareanns may like to take emaciated waifs to wife, but Aronans need strong stock to breed sons."

Aine's shoulders slumped until she saw Uallas's questioning look from across the room. Somehow, it gave her a boost of confidence. She straightened in her chair and helped herself to a joint of meat from the platter and then several small potatoes.

"I appreciate your concern, Aunt. But I've no need of suitors, considering I already have a husband."

Lady Macha choked on her food, coughing into her hand before she swallowed the offending piece down with a long pull of wine from her goblet. "I must be mistaken. I thought you said you have a husband."

Aine hid her own smile in her cup. It had to be a sin to enjoy her aunt's discomfiture so much, but the chieftain had done nothing but try to keep her off balance since she'd arrived that morning. It was much too pleasurable to turn the tables.

"Aye. I married Conor Mac Nir when I left Seare."

"Then where is he?"

"I don't know. We were separated in the storm. I expect he's making his way here at this very moment. I do hope you will offer him a less suspicious welcome than you gave me. He is the sole reason I'm alive."

She took Macha's slack-jawed expression as permission to elaborate and told her the story of how she'd been betrayed by one of King Calhoun's lords, captured by the Red Druid at the fortress in Tigh, and then rescued by Conor. When she got to her attack on the road, she paused.

"You should know that Lord Riagain fully intended to take me back to Brightwater as a hostage. Had it not been for the help of some passing travelers, I would be in the hands of your enemy now." Macha probably wouldn't care if Aine were captured by Riagain, but she would take offense at the sheer audacity of the assault on her clan.

"It sounds as if you composed yourself in a manner befitting your Tamhais blood," Aenghus said. Not for the first time, Aine wondered why such a kind-seeming man had married her aunt. "Or do you claim Nir as your clan now?"

Even Conor didn't claim Nir as his clan, but they didn't need to know that. "We handfasted, Uncle, as you and Lady Macha did. It seemed wisest given the circumstances."

"You couldn't have possibly had a legal handfasting in a few days and on the open sea, no less," Macha said. "I'm tempted to believe this is all a fabrication. Will we learn in a few months that you're carrying a bastard child?"

Aine recoiled at the venom in her aunt's words. "I hope that I'm fortunate enough to be carrying my *husband's* child now. And considering we were married by a former Fíréin brother and the captain of our ship, I'd say that makes it at least as legitimate as your own. My lady."

"Except my husband is here to attest that the marriage actually happened." Malice glimmered in Macha's eyes, and her lips lifted in a satisfied smile. "But there's no need to publicize that matter. Especially since the man you claimed to have married died almost four years ago."

Aine swayed in her seat, her heart lodging somewhere in her throat as she realized how neatly she'd been set up. Macha knew all about her life in Seare, about Conor's supposed disappearance. But she couldn't possibly know that reports of his death had been intended to divert from the fact that he was training with Fíréin brotherhood. Without any proof, everyone would believe whatever Macha said about her, particularly if she turned up pregnant.

Aine's hand drifted to her flat stomach and then dropped into her lap before Macha could note the gesture. She and Conor had had only two days together, little enough time to conceive a child. It would be easier if she had not: much of the speculation would fall away in several months. But if Conor were truly lost to her, could she be blamed for wanting some piece of him?

Macha went back to her food, apparently satisfied she'd put her upstart niece in her place. Aine ground her back teeth together. She couldn't let Macha see how much she'd been rattled, how badly she'd been beaten. Her only hope of survival at Forrais was to find some way to force her aunt's respect. Otherwise, she'd be marginalized, pushed to the side, ignored if not outright scorned.

Aine stayed at the table only as long as necessary to avoid looking as though she were storming out of the hall. Curious gazes followed her from the room, none more intent than that belonging to Lord Uallas.

She waited until she cleared the attention of the hall before she let her dignified walk break into a run. Hot tears stung the back of her eyes. It was all a lie, not just to Macha but to herself. Conor was probably dead. To think otherwise would only bring greater heartbreak.

She managed to throw herself through the doorway of her chamber and bolt the latch behind her before the first tear spilled over. Her fingers fumbled for the ivory charm beneath her dress and she pressed it between her hands.

"Please," she whispered. "Just give me a sign, some indication you're still alive. You can't be gone. You just can't be."

But however much she willed the warmth to flare in the charm, it remained as still and cold as ever.

CHAPTER
SIXTEEN

Riordan had never been able to sense the wards, but even he felt the difference as he moved through the forest. The wrongness beyond Ard Dhaimhin's borders was palpable, like a snowstorm in the middle of summer. Never before had the margin between the High City and the kingdoms been so clear, and it made his task that much less appealing.

As he broke free of the tree line, he couldn't hold back a shiver. Dark clouds roiled on the horizon, an ominous sign. Legend held that in the rule of a good and noble king, the sun would shine and the crops would thrive, while in the rule of an evil king, darkness would cover the land. He'd never believed it, thinking it one of Seare's pagan superstitions, but now he wondered if there weren't some truth to the stories.

Just as he now questioned the brotherhood's policy of separation. There had been good reasons for it once, but was tradition an adequate justification now that they saw the darkness their inaction had wrought? The brotherhood was descended from the loyal palace guard who had protected Queen Shanna from the wrath of her sons after they murdered her husband, and their only purpose for five hundred years had been to hold the High City for the return of the king. But what good was holding the throne and the fortress if the people the High King was meant to serve were suffering under the rule of an evil man?

His uneasiness built, but he shook off the feeling as he shouldered his staff and trudged into the open meadow. It had to be the sidhe. The spirits had done enough damage while they were bound. It seemed that they were bound no more.

You should not have come here. Your place is at Ard Dhaimhin, not here in the world. Go back to your comfortable prison.

The pang of foreboding nearly doubled him over. He paused, breathing deeply. "You cannot harm me," he said quietly. "I walk in the light of Balus."

The oppression eased somewhat, and he moved forward, taking his heading from the position of what little sun peeked through the clouds. He'd meant to make for Clogheen, a market village that stood at the intersection of the road from the port of Ballaghbán and the shippers' road that led from Siomar toward Lisdara. Its constant influx of travelers offered both anonymity and the promise of fresh news. But now he wondered if he'd chosen wrong. Walking in that direction was like trudging through molasses. His feet were moving, but it took an extraordinary effort to continue. Was it just an overall malaise brought on by the sidhe, or was he being specifically targeted?

"Be gone in the name of Comdiu and his son, Balus," Riordan commanded, and the presence fled. He drew in another deep breath. Whatever he would learn in Clogheen, the sidhe did not want him to know.

It was bad enough that they had been released. Even worse that they now seemed to have purpose. Riordan struck out southeast, traveling overland so he wouldn't meet up with the road until he came to Clogheen. A fine mist wet his skin, growing increasingly thicker and more persistent the closer he came to the town. Of course. The sidhe fed off human passions and delighted in creating mischief. A market town with its cross sections of travelers, some of whom had never heard of Balus, was the perfect place in which to gorge themselves.

No sooner did Riordan reach the boundaries of the town than the oppressive stench of misery and fear fell over him. He shuddered, sending up a silent prayer for protection. The town was small by any standards other than Seareann, a scattering of huts and thatched-roof cottages. Pony- and ox- and handcarts displayed all sorts of wares. He squinted through the mist and brushed moisture from his skin as he walked slowly down the main street, the usual market sounds dampened by the fog.

A shout caught his attention, followed by a clatter as a produce cart tipped over and late-summer vegetables spilled onto the road. Riordan jumped out of the way just as two men crashed into the street, grappling in the dirt and shouting vile names Riordan hadn't heard in years. The one on the bottom— the customer, Riordan thought—seemed to be getting in his fair share of licks, punching and kneeing the man on top, who groaned as each strike met flesh. Then, without warning, the merchant pulled a knife from his belt and plunged it into the other man's chest.

The murderer stood and wiped his blade on his own tunic, then met Riordan's eyes. Riordan shuddered again. There was something empty and hopeless, vacant, about those eyes. The sidhe had found another victim. Beneath his cloak, Riordan curled his hand around the hilt of his own dagger, but the man just turned and walked back to his toppled cart, leaving the body alone in the street.

Not for long, though. A pack of urchins scrambled into the road, rifling through the dead man's possessions. His shoes went first, followed by his cloak. One girl howled in fury when his coin pouch turned out to be empty—probably the reason for the fight in the first place.

Riordan turned away, sickened. The children always turned feral first. They were too susceptible to the lies of the Adversary's minions, too desperate to survive at any cost. Most of them would die on this street before they ever reached adulthood, and there was nothing Riordan could do about it.

Comdiu, help me. Protect me from this evil. Do not let me fall prey to this darkness.

The grip on his heart eased again, and he drew a long breath before continuing on down the street. There was an alehouse here somewhere, no doubt the most dangerous spot in the entire town, but ale tended to loosen lips and free tales. And tales were what he was after.

He found it at last, housed in one of the town's few timbered buildings and topped with a real slate-shingled roof. Naturally it would be the most prosperous business in town. Riordan pushed through the door, trying to make himself inconspicuous, but the combination of his height, his weapons, and the old-fashioned cut of his clothing made that impossible. A dozen pairs of eyes fixed on him.

He ignored the scrutiny and found an empty table in the corner, a feat much more difficult than it should have been, given the morning hour. A hollow-eyed, weary-looking lass barely older than his son approached immediately. "What can I get you, traveler?"

"Mead. Brown bread and butter if you have it."

"No one's got butter the last few weeks. Not a cow within a hundred miles of here whose milk's not soured. We've got the last of the honey, though."

"That's fine, thank you." Riordan nodded and gave her a

slight smile. She faltered as if the expression were unfamiliar and then turned and headed back to the kitchen.

Soured milk? That was another faerie story from Seare's past that Riordan had dismissed as mere fancy. Perhaps the stories of Daimhin bringing the light to Seare were not just metaphor. He'd always wondered how the mercenary king had managed to gain the fealty of the clans so quickly and bloodlessly. If this were the way things had been before Daimhin had come with his magic, maybe it wasn't so hard to understand after all.

The girl came back a few minutes later with a wooden mug of mead and several thick slices of brown bread spread with honey. Riordan pushed a coin across the table to her and curled his fingers around her wrist when she reached for it. "What's your name?"

She jerked her hand away, fire flashing in her eyes. She still managed to snag the coin off the table, though. "Take your interest elsewhere. I only serve food, you understand me?"

"I didn't mean to frighten you. I'm not looking for a woman. Can you sit for a minute?"

"Why should I?"

"Because you're the only person in Clogheen with a spark of life behind her eyes. I want to know what's happened here."

"Everyone knows what happened here. You a foreigner?"

"Something like that." Ard Dhaimhin felt farther away by the minute. "If you'll spare the time, I'll make it worth your while." Riordan reached into his pouch for another coin and placed it on the table with a click. Avarice lit her eyes while she considered.

Finally she pocketed the coin and slid into the seat across from him. Her posture remained wary. "Old Enda's in his cups. He won't notice a minute or two. What do you want to know?"

"Your name, for starters."

She relaxed a degree, and a fleeting smile passed her lips. "Bryn."

"A ladylike name. Do you know the story of Queen Bryn of Faolán?"

"Who are you?" The suspicion crept back into her expression. "Never mind. I don't want to know. You paid for a copper of my time and it's slipping away. Ask your questions."

"What happened here?"

She snorted a laugh. "You are from a far-off land. The Mac Cuillinn fell. The family was slaughtered. The 'High King' sits at Lisdara while the unholy mist destroys us from the inside."

"You're a Balian, then," Riordan said softly.

She looked away, confirmation enough. "Balians are killed in the worst ways imaginable. No one is a Balian anymore."

"I am."

"Then I should not be talking to you." She stood, but Riordan reached for her hand again.

"Please. Stay. Do you know about the Fíréin?"

Recognition lit her face and she slid back into the chair. "You're one of them? You're from Ard Dhaimhin?"

"Aye."

"They say that's the only place free of Lord Keondric's reach. But everyone says you'll be killed if you venture into the forest. Is it true?"

"Unless you have a good reason to be there, it's true. But wait a moment. You said Keondric. What happened to Fergus and his druid?"

His admission seemed to ease her doubts about him. "No one has ever seen the druid, only whispers. But he must still be alive because there are stories about men losing their will and bowing to the new king. Strong men. Men who had vowed to fight 'til their last breath."

Riordan nodded slowly. "And Fergus?"

"Dead. Killed by Keondric himself, they say."

"How is that possible?"

"I wouldn't know. But his head is mounted upon Lisdara's gate as a warning. All Fergus's men have sworn loyalty to Mac Eirhinin, and more join him every day. Even those who come back, come back . . . changed. Is it true that Ard Dhaimhin is beyond the druid's reach?"

Riordan blinked at the change in subject, but he owed her honesty in return for her risk. "I don't know about that, Bryn. But you're probably right that it's the safest place in Seare."

She rose and pushed the copper back across the table. "Keep your coin. I want to show you something. Will you meet me out back when you're finished?"

Riordan nodded. He drank his mead and ate his bread, troubled by Bryn's revelations. There was only one possible explanation, and it was not comforting. He rose from his chair, checked his weapons out of habit, and made his way out the front door. From there he circled around to the back of the alehouse, where Bryn waited for him.

"Just a moment." She ducked through the back door and returned with a boy. He couldn't have been more than eight years old, rail thin with a mop of dark hair, a canvas sack slung across his back. "Please. You must take him with you to Ard Dhaimhin."

Riordan's heart sank. "I cannot. I have more stops in my travels. It would not be safe."

"You call this town safe?"

"What of his father?"

Bryn stared him in the eye. "Lost to us. He became one of *them*. And if my Treabhar does not leave here, he'll do the same. They are conscripting them younger and younger, my lord."

Riordan wavered. Bryn grabbed Riordan's hand and pressed it to her heart. "I know you probably can't understand this, but I would do anything to keep my son safe. Even if it means giving him up."

Riordan turned to the boy, who stared at him with such a mixture of fear and hope, it hurt to look at him.

"I understand better than you know."

CHAPTER
SEVENTEEN

It didn't take long for Conor to lose track of the days he spent in the settlement. Each day was the same, stretches of mind-numbing boredom interspersed with hours of intense concentration while he taught Haldor the common language of Seare and Amanta and answered his questions. The warrior had not asked about the magic that had ostensibly saved Conor's life. Perhaps he sensed he would not yet receive an honest answer. Or perhaps he was waiting for it to occur to Conor that he would die here.

"When faced with their own mortality, there are two kinds of men," Talfryn said one night. "Those who decide that honor means nothing, and those to whom honor comes to mean everything. He's waiting to discover which one you are."

Half the nights Conor woke from terrifying nightmares, either experiencing his worst imaginings about Aine or reliving the bloody fighting that had preceded their escape from Seare. The other nights, he slept not at all, his churning thoughts covering the same ground in much greater detail. He could not escape his worry. He knew he should pray, lay his worries before his Maker, but his troubled heart would not make the words.

Some days, he was sure Aine was dead. In those dark moments, he again considered the fastest way to get himself killed. Yet he still visited Haldor, his words and actions measured, calculated. Not all of the settlements had replied. As long as he fulfilled his bargain, it was as if he kept Aine alive.

Foolish thoughts. But in those moments of hope, when his spirits lifted, he imagined he heard her.

I'm alive, love, he heard once. *Are you out there somewhere?*

And another time: *You can't be gone. You just can't be.*

But it was always too quiet, too distant, to know if the voice were real or if it were just his own wishful thinking.

Comdiu, keep her safe, wherever she is. Let her be alive.

Haldor made rapid progress in his studies, and even though it seemed tantamount to a betrayal, Conor felt a spark of pride in his student. They did not speak of personal matters in the leader's longhouse. Haldor remained focused while they worked, and his sharp mind picked up the language far quicker than Conor had expected. In less than a month, the Sofarende warrior had acquired a solid-enough grasp of syntax and vocabulary to move on to more difficult passages.

The only passages Conor knew by heart were Scripture. He wrote out the first ones that came to mind while he waited for Haldor to arrive one morning. He'd wanted to know more about their culture. Balianism was—or at least had been—a large part of that.

Conor had neatly etched several verses onto the tablets when Haldor entered and put aside his sword on the bench.

"What is this?"

"You're ready to move on to something more difficult. Take your time reading it. We will work through the unfamiliar words."

Slowly, Haldor read, "'For Comdiu did not wish eternal

punishment for man, the creation whom He loved. So He sent His son, Balus, Lord of heaven, clothed in flesh to die for men. That through His blood mankind might be saved.'" He stumbled over a few of the words they hadn't studied yet. "What does this mean, Lord of heaven who died for men? You follow the dying god? Like our Lelle?"

Conor wracked his brain for some recollection of the Norin myths he had learned from his tutor. "I don't know your Lelle, I'm afraid."

"He died of a poisoned arrow shot by his brother. Our people believe he will come back to a new world someday."

"I see," Conor said. "No, our Lord Balus is different. He knew He would die, but He came to earth anyway. The people didn't believe He could be the one prophesied in the old writings, and they tortured Him on the wheel."

"This god must not be very strong if he could not fight mere men."

"He could have saved Himself with a word. He could have called His Companions to come down and slay all those who persecuted Him. But He did not, because only by His death could all mankind live."

Haldor shook his head, clearly unimpressed. "You are a warrior. You should not follow a weak god who would let himself be slain."

"So you would not allow yourself to be killed?"

Haldor looked offended. "Of course not."

"What if it meant saving every person in this village? Every person in Norin? Every person in the world?"

"Most of the world is my enemy," Haldor said, but consideration flickered behind his eyes.

"That is the difference between us and Lord Balus. We are His enemies, yet He died for us anyway."

Haldor stood with a snort of derision. "I would not die for my enemy."

Conor said nothing. His purpose was not to try to convert Haldor to his beliefs. If anything, he had just given the Sofarende the wrong impression of Balians: that they were weak, that they would not fight. Fine. Let him believe that Seare would be easy to conquer. He moved on to a verse about the creation of the world and focused on Haldor's pronunciation rather than the words' meaning.

Still, Conor could not shake the feeling that he had somehow failed. It felt uncomfortably like the nudging of Comdiu.

What would You have me do, Lord? I cannot force him to adopt my beliefs. I am merely a prisoner. I am here only because I love Aine more than my freedom.

But the pressure didn't relent. It only grew stronger.

"What's wrong?" Talfryn asked him one night while they waited in line for their food.

Conor shook his head. He couldn't explain it even if he were inclined to try.

Talfryn dropped the subject, instead looking him over surreptitiously. "You're healing."

Conor nodded. It still hurt to fully expand his lungs, but the bruises were fading and his dizziness was gone. Now the ache in his muscles was due to inactivity rather than injury. Had he been back at Ard Dhaimhin, he would be longing to join sword drills or even one of the work details in the far fields. He flexed his hands, wondering how much strength he'd lost in the past few weeks.

Talfryn followed the movement. "Be careful. While you're still injured, you're invisible."

Invisible was just another word for useless. Conor had been invisible for most of his life.

Movement on the other side of the circle caught his eye. Once more, as happened several times a week, Dyllan took the boy's bowl from him. And once more the guard turned a blind eye.

"Don't," Talfryn said.

Conor ignored him. He addressed the guard in Norin. "Are you going to do something?"

The guard only smirked at him.

"Don't," Talfryn repeated.

Conor set down his bowl and walked slowly to Dyllan. The guard didn't stop him. Apparently the prospect of entertainment trumped enforcing his orders.

"He needs to eat, same as you," Conor said quietly.

Dyllan laughed. "What are you going to do about it?"

Conor stared, unflinching.

Dyllan arched his eyebrows and set the bowl down. The boy snatched it up and backed away while the attention was off him. That was something at least.

Conor topped the man's height by several inches, but he was still injured and bound. The Gwynn smiled right before he lunged. Conor ducked out of the way before the punch could connect. Instead, he hooked his heel around the other man's foot, tangling the rope around it, and yanked. As they fell together, Conor looped the rope binding his hands around Dyllan's neck and pulled back. The man thrashed and clawed at the rope, not experienced enough to strike at Conor's injured ribs, instead letting panic consume him. Conor waited for that moment of slackening that would indicate unconsciousness. It was a fine line from there, a short step to death.

Before that could happen, the Sofarende guard sprang for them and aimed a kick at Conor's side. Conor groaned, but before the guard could drag him away, he put his mouth near Dyllan's ear and said, "Leave the boy alone."

Conor braced himself for the guard's punishment, but the blows never came. He didn't resist, simply let himself be dragged back to the prison hut. Why didn't the guard beat him? Why didn't he make an example of him?

Then Conor understood. Prisoner or not, he was under Haldor's protection. How much could he get away with without inciting the guards' retaliation if they were so obedient to their commander?

"That was unwise," Talfryn growled when the rest of the prisoners returned. He lowered himself onto the mat. "Now they'll be watching your every move."

"Maybe I'm tired of seeing Dyllan get away with it." But it was more than that. He'd once had a purpose. If he had the power to help but did nothing, what did it matter if he lived or died?

"This will not go unaddressed, you realize."

Conor followed Talfryn's gaze. Dyllan stared at him with unveiled hatred. He'd made an enemy today, but hopefully he'd also made a point. If he'd diverted the bully's attention from the boy, it would be worth the renewed ache in his ribs.

That night, the prickle of danger startled Conor awake fractions of a second before a foot collided with his side.

Conor raised his hands and knees to protect himself, trying to roll to his feet, but the blows that rained down on him gave him no opportunity. A weight fell on his chest, followed by a fist to his face. The room spun, and he tasted blood.

"Where's your courage now, boy?" Dyllan leaned close, enveloping him in foul breath. "Do you see? Not one of these prisoners you think you can help will come to your aid."

Conor blinked through the throb of pain in his face, the stab to his reinjured midsection. Even now, he knew he could get free, gain the upper position. Dyllan would be at his mercy. Yet the quiet nudge inside restrained him.

"What do you say? Was it worth making an enemy of me, knowing you can never sleep without wondering if I'll kill you?"

He locked on the Gwynn prisoner's face, any number of defiant retorts flashing through his mind. When he opened his mouth, the words that came out surprised even him. "Leave the boy alone."

Dyllan's brows knit together, and then his weight lifted from Conor. He gave him one last halfhearted kick and returned to his pallet.

Conor let out a long shuddering breath and took stock of his injuries. Nothing felt broken, though his lip was already swelling and his ribs complained when he took a deep breath. Why hadn't he fought back? Why had he frozen when he could have gotten the better of the man?

"You all right?" Talfryn's whispered question came from his right.

Conor rolled to his side and stifled a groan. "No thanks to you."

"You know why I couldn't intervene."

"Aye. I do." He winced as he tried to find a comfortable position and closed his eyes. The Gwynn had been right about one thing: he could not expect help from any quarter.

No one spoke of Conor's injuries the next morning, though from the tightness in his face, he knew they must be ugly. When he caught sight of his reflection in a trough, he almost didn't recognize himself: cheek and lip double their normal size, blue ringing one eye from a blow he didn't remember. Not even the Sofarende's punishment had taken such a toll on his face.

Even Haldor's eyes widened when he met Conor that afternoon. Without pausing to lay aside his weapon, the commander pulled up a bench in front of him.

"If that is what you look like when you win a fight, I would not want to see you when you lose."

"This was my punishment for winning the fight."

"And yet the Gwynn works today without a mark on him."

Conor just stared back. Haldor looked away while he considered his next words. It may have been the first time Conor had ever seen the warrior uncomfortable. "Why did you not fight back? You cannot tell me you do not have the skill, even injured."

"It would have served no purpose but to make more of an enemy of him." What else could he say? That Comdiu had reached down and convinced him not to fight?

"Ulaf tells me that even though he insults your woman every day, you do not try to fight him. Why?"

Conor raised his head, surprised. "Because I gave you my word. I will stay here and teach you, and you will send word after Aine."

"I am already your enemy. And still you are determined to keep your word?"

Conor nodded and said nothing.

Haldor stood and paced before him. "I do not understand you. You are a warrior. You fight your fellow prisoner but not your enemy. My men insult your honor, your woman, force you to act as a slave, and you allow them. Is it because you follow this dying god?"

This was not just an idle question. Conor sent up a prayer for guidance. He could be facing his end. Or he could have an ally.

"In a sense," he said finally. "We consider oaths to be solemn before Comdiu. If we break an oath, we break our word to Comdiu, not just man."

"What if I say I plan to kill you?"

"Will you keep your word to have Aine released, even if I am dead?"

Haldor shook his head in wonder. "You sacrifice yourself for a woman. We value women in my land, it is true. What Ulaf says about your wife is just words, unless she is sold as a concubine. But a woman is not worth a warrior."

Conor studied Haldor. Something in his tone carried an underlying sadness. "Are you married? Do you have children?"

Haldor's breath hissed out from between his teeth. "My wife is dead. We had no children."

"I love my wife, whether she is deemed worthy or not. Because I love her, I count her life as more important than mine. Even if that means I die. Do you understand?"

Haldor stared at him, so intently that Conor had to resist the urge to reach for a weapon, even though he clearly had access to no such thing. Finally the warrior reached into his tunic and pulled out two parchments.

"Here. The last settlements. They do not have her."

Conor's heart squeezed in his chest as he took the scrolls and skimmed them. No one had seen any Aronan woman resembling Aine in the last several weeks or months. He let out a sigh of relief even as a cold tendril of fear wormed its way into his heart. He handed the scrolls back to Haldor and indicated the tablets that held their lesson. "Shall we continue?"

Haldor fingered the intricately carved ivory hilt of his sword. "You will continue your teaching?"

"You have kept your word, and I will keep mine. It is my oath before Comdiu."

Haldor settled beside him, but this time he did not remove his sword. They worked through Conor's chosen Scriptures without another word on the matter.

In the days that followed, however, Haldor's weapon was never far from hand.

CHAPTER
EIGHTEEN

Aine refused to leave her room for two days, remaining wrapped in her embroidered bedcovers and eating only when the cook sent a tray with Lia. She couldn't face Macha and her lords, the speculation, the whispers. Lia had put about that Aine was recovering from her ordeal and didn't feel up to dining in the hall. It wasn't far from the truth.

On the third day, a knock sounded at her door. Aine rolled over and buried her head in her feather pillow. Lia would enter without knocking, which only left people with whom she had no interest in speaking.

But the pounding continued. Aine threw the blankets aside and padded to the door. She finger-combed her tangled hair and straightened her chemise before she cracked it open.

Master Guaire stood there, a tray in his hand. "May I enter?"

Aine swallowed and dipped her head. The steward nudged the door closed behind him and then set the tray on a low table by her bed. "Do you mind if I sit with you while you eat?"

"Why?"

Guaire smiled. "I've served Clan Tamhais since I was a child.

I was manservant to Lord Ruaidh, your father's father. Then Alsandair. And your mother. Of all the ladies of Forrais, your mother was my favorite."

"Why?" The question escaped for a second time, this time from curiosity.

"You cannot help but notice that Aron is a hard place. And hard places breed harder people. But your mother—she had a light about her. An unusual grace."

"Is this where you tell me I remind you of her?"

Guaire chuckled. "No, though it's true. I have a question for you. Do you think your mother was happy here?"

Aine had never thought about it. Lady Ailís had always been placid, loving, dutiful. She'd acted as the wife of a chieftain should, always for the good of the clan and the people who depended on them. But now Aine was ashamed to realize she had never asked.

"I don't know," she said finally.

"Neither do I."

Aine jerked her head up.

"When she came, she was like you. She cried for days over leaving her children back in Seare. I think she wondered if she'd made the right decision."

That was another thing Aine had never questioned. Why had a Seareann queen married a foreign clan chief in the first place? She looked to Guaire, the question hovering on her lips.

"Things were different twenty years ago," the steward said. "Faolán had just spent years warring against Sliebhan with great losses on both sides. I don't recall what began the conflict, if I ever knew. Both the king and his tanist were killed in battle, and Calhoun was barely eight and ten when he was elected king. Siomar saw that as a weakness they could exploit. So did one of Faolán's lords. He began to sway others in his favor. Gainor was even younger than Calhoun, though he already had shown a mind for strategy. If Calhoun and Gainor could be shown as unfit to rule and removed by the council, power would pass from the clan."

"Mac Eirhinin. Keondric's father." It made sense now. Then Aine realized what Guaire was really saying. "My mother bought Calhoun's throne."

"Your father was in a situation similar to your brother's. He had no heir, and he was under pressure to make peace with Lord Riagain. He refused. Instead he linked Clan Tamhais to Faolán's royal line—a match no one could refuse—and sent enough clansmen south to secure Calhoun's throne."

"Why have I never heard this?"

Guaire smiled sadly. "Because no one could ever know. It simply looked as if Calhoun had hired mercenaries and Ailís had left out of grief over her husband. People suspected, of course, but there was no proof."

It explained so much that Aine had never thought to question. "Why are you telling me?"

The steward put a fatherly hand on her shoulder. "Your mother made sacrifices. In some ways, she never stopped grieving. But she didn't let it change who she was or prevent her from doing all in her power to help those around her."

"You're telling me to stop hiding in my room feeling sorry for myself."

"I'm telling you that your mother found contentment in having a purpose." Guaire rose and gave her a deep bow. "It does my heart good to have you back at Forrais, my lady."

Aine stared at the wall long after the steward left. Guaire was right: she had no way of knowing if Conor were dead or alive. If he had risked all—sacrificed all—to bring her back home, didn't she owe it to him to make something of her life here?

"My lady?" Lia poked her head into the room. "Granddad—Master Guaire—said you were ready to dress."

So he'd been that confident in his success, had he? A reluctant smile creased Aine's face. "I suppose I am. We'll need to summon a dressmaker soon. I've only the pink and the blue."

"And the green." Lia dipped her head. "I hope I didn't overstep, my lady, but I hemmed another of Lady Ailís's gowns. I thought you might need a plain day dress."

"Thank you, Lia." Was the girl really only fourteen years old? But of course, she was Guaire's granddaughter, and the steward was looking out for her. "May I see it?"

Lia smiled, less shyly this time, and disappeared out the door. She returned with a sage green wool gown draped over her arm. "Shall we, my lady?"

The maid helped her into the matching underdress, then the overdress, and laced up the sides. Aine fingered the fabric, noting Lia's other modifications.

"The sleeves were old-fashioned. I hope you don't mind that I changed them."

"Not at all." Aine took the brass hand mirror and studied her reflection. Master Guaire wouldn't let her mope in her chamber all day. That meant she needed to make her presence known at Forrais. "After you do my hair, I'd like to meet the staff. Will you make the introductions?"

Lia bowed her head and curtsied in acknowledgement, but not before Aine saw the gleam of satisfaction in her eyes.

By the time Aine made the rounds of the fortress, her head ached with the effort of holding all the names and faces in her memory. Not that the servants would expect it of her, but she'd never wanted to be the sort of noblewoman who snapped her fingers and called every female servant *girl*.

"What about Diocail and the guard?" Aine asked when they'd finished their rounds of the keep.

Lia's eyebrows lifted, but she steered Aine into the rear courtyard. Aine paused to lift her face to the dim gleam of sun through the clouds. Somehow the familiar smells calmed her—earth and hay, smoke, food, animals. No matter the location, the scents and sounds of a noble keep were the same. If she used enough imagination, she could see herself striding toward her own little workshop, spending her mornings grinding powders and mixing tisanes.

Well, why not?

Her breath caught in her throat. Why couldn't she? She might be trying to hide her healing abilities, but she knew as much herb lore as any of Aron's physicians, thanks to Mistress Bearrach's tutelage. If she were careful, she could heal with herbs without anyone becoming the wiser. How could Lady Macha object to that when she'd permitted as much before Aine left?

"My lady?"

Aine opened her eyes. "Shall we find Master Diocail, then?"

CHAPTER NINETEEN

Whereas the front of the palace at Forrais faced a cliff, the back courtyard stretched out upon the flat top of the mountain, encompassing a scattering of buildings and a grassy field within its high stone walls. It was the grassy area they sought now, where a handful of men trained with swords and staffs. A long line of archery targets stood against the weathered outer wall.

Aine and Lia paused at the edge, watching as a dozen guardsmen drew and fired with precision. Clan Tamhais had always been known for their archers, and Aine could see why. Before they'd seen more than a few volleys, a man strode in their direction.

Aine's stomach fluttered. She'd always been slightly uneasy around the master of the guard. Perhaps it was because he'd been an unyielding, unsmiling tutor throughout her cursory training. Or perhaps it was that particular edge of steel in him that all men bred to warfare seemed to possess. He strode toward her and then pulled up short in a precise bow.

"Lady Aine, welcome back to Forrais."

Aine studied him as he straightened. The only nod to the passage of time was a bit more gray in his dark hair, the slight deepening of lines in his face. She had no more idea of his age now than she'd ever had as a child.

"Thank you, Master Diocail." She couldn't utter the expected words that it was good to be back. She would prefer to be almost anywhere but here.

"Are you here to train, my lady? I remember that you were once quite accomplished with a bow."

"I fear you've embellished my skill beyond reality, sir."

He did not smile. "I do not embellish, my lady. It might do you good to have a bow in your hands once more."

He was serious. Aine tipped her head. "Perhaps you're right. Another day, though. Today I just wished to greet those who are responsible for the workings of Forrais."

"I am at your service." Diocail gave another bow, deeper this time. When he straightened, the corners of his mouth tilted up. "Tomorrow, then?"

"Tomorrow."

The captain nodded sharply. "Excuse me, my lady. I must get back to my men." Then he strode back toward the archery range, calling instructions as he went.

Lia stared at the man, her lips parted as if interrupted mid-sentence. "He smiled at you."

"That was a smile?"

"The closest Master Diocail gets." Lia turned a searching gaze on her. "You really don't see it."

"See what?"

The maid shook her head. "Perhaps I'm imagining things. Come, my lady. It's nearly time for dinner."

Aine watched the captain for several moments before following Lia. What had she missed in that exchange? And why did it seem as if everyone knew far more about her than she herself did?

She still took her dinner in her room alone, not yet ready to face the scrutiny of Macha's lords and ladies. Yet as she sat down to her meal, the thoughts that had surfaced earlier in the day came back with troubling persistence. Guaire wanted her to find a sense of purpose to take her mind off Conor. What else did she know how to do besides heal?

When the maid came to remove her tray, Aine tasked her with finding writing materials. Lia quickly returned with two wax tablets and a stylus, and Aine settled at the desk to make a list of things she would need to get started. She then found Master Guaire in the kitchen and handed the tablet to him without a word.

His eyebrows lifted. "So it's back to healing, I see?"

"What have I forgotten?"

"You'll need a work room, certainly."

"I thought I might use my mother's chamber." Aine held her breath. Servant or not, Guaire had final authority of the keep.

"I think Lady Ailís's chamber would do nicely," he said finally. "You'll be needing a workbench and shelving, I imagine?"

"Will that be a problem?"

"Not for me. It may take me a week or two to lay hands on these materials, but it will be done. You'll need to speak with Master Diocail about an escort to gather herbs on your own."

She did indeed need to see Diocail, though she had no idea if he would provide her an escort. They were, after all, his men. Though she was a member of the household and well within her rights to request such a thing, Aine also knew that demanding her rights as daughter of the clan would cause more trouble with Macha than she wanted. Covert action was her best option, at least while she was setting up her work space. Once she began seeing patients, it would be impossible to hide her activities and the extra attention they brought.

It remained to be seen what Macha would do about it.

✦ ✦ ✦

Aine barely knew Master Diocail, but something told her that if she were going to request a favor from him, she'd need to give him something in return.

The next morning, she rose, dressed in the green wool, and strapped on the leather bracers Lia had procured for her. Her stomach erupted into butterflies, despite the fact she needn't make a great showing, merely a passable one—enough of an effort to elicit more than a handful of words from the taciturn captain.

She went straight to the armory. Diocail wasn't present, but one of the watch captains was. She gave him a friendly smile. "Might I trouble you for some help, sir?"

He straightened from the blade he was honing and swept a hasty bow her direction. "My lady? I'm at your service. How can I assist you?"

"I need a bow. Naturally, a long bow isn't going to be suitable."

"That's no problem. We've lightweight bows for the boys to use until they're strong enough for a war bow. Begging your pardon, my lady."

"Not necessary. Might you find me one and a quiver as well?"

He gave a quick nod and disappeared into one of the back rooms, then returned a moment later with an unstrung short bow and a cloth quiver. She took them with a smile, which made the young captain flush, then asked, "I don't suppose you know where Master Diocail is?"

"I'll fetch him, my lady. You can go to the range if you like."

That had been easy. Almost too easy. She'd have thought, given Macha's attitude toward her, the members of the keep would be more reticent, but they'd been positively eager to help. Was the chieftain disliked by others that much? Was helping Aine a small rebellion on their part?

The archery range was deserted this morning, though the sounds of wood and metal drifted from some other point in the courtyard. Sword training today, then. Just as well, assuming the watch captain followed through on his promise of fetching Master Diocail. She found a spot at the center of the firing line and braced one end of the bow at her feet while she bent the yew and attached the other end of the string.

Aine planted several arrows into the ground in front of her, then settled into a comfortable stance and nocked one. She sighted down the arrow's shaft and let it fly.

It bounced off the target and fell into the grass.

"You're drawing with your arm, not your back," a male voice said behind her. "Try again."

Aine glanced over her shoulder to where Diocail stood a dozen paces away, arms crossed over his chest. He gave her a nod, an invitation to continue. She turned back to the target and concentrated on drawing the bow properly.

This time the arrow traveled straight, striking the target within the painted red ring.

She shot a satisfied glance Diocail's way. The slightest hint of a smile touched his lips. "You always did have a talent with a bow. Your father's daughter indeed."

Aine returned the smile and went back to her practice, each time improving her accuracy, even though her arms and back immediately began to ache from the exertion. Too bad Conor wasn't here to see her. When she'd told him she was a fair archer, he'd barely been able to keep from laughing. Then again, he hadn't yet grown into manhood or his fighting skills. She'd comforted him by telling him that not everyone was cut out to be a warrior, yet that was exactly what he had made of himself.

Had he not been quite so determined to prove her wrong, she wouldn't be alive today.

But he might be.

"My lady?" Diocail's quiet voice caught her attention.

Aine realized that tears were rolling down her face. She swiped them away impatiently.

"That's enough for today, my lady."

"No." Aine sniffed and dried her face with her sleeve. "It's better that I stay busy."

The captain cast a look over his shoulder, and his expression changed. "It looks like you have a visitor."

Aine followed Diocail's gaze. Lord Uallas stood a respectful distance off, a bow and quiver over his shoulder and a curious smile on his face.

"What does he want?" Aine muttered.

"Probably wants to compliment you on your . . . skills." Diocail's sour tone made him sound like a father faced with his daughter's unwanted suitor.

"Well, he can wait until I'm done." Aine marched toward the targets and yanked her arrows out of the straw target. Lord Uallas must have somehow taken this as an invitation, because he ambled to where she had been standing. She struggled not to stomp back toward him. The last thing she wanted to do was banter with a young lord who wanted something she could not give.

But she was still a lady, so she put on a noncommittal smile and gave him a nod. "Lord Uallas."

"Lady Aine." He bowed deeply and found her gaze with his own when he rose. "I'm glad to see you've recovered."

"Recovered?"

"Lady Macha said that you were indisposed. But I'm guessing that was just an excuse. Forgive me for bringing up subjects best left alone."

"It's fine, Lord Uallas." She gave him the best smile she could manage and planted the arrows back in the earth, save one. That she fitted to the bow and aimed.

The arrow bounced off the target onto the grass below. She sighed. The island lord's presence wasn't exactly helping her concentration.

"May I?" He gestured to the target.

She glanced back at Diocail, who simply scowled. Aine sighed and braced herself for some sort of "lesson," but Uallas merely took one of the arrows, nocked it, and fired at the target. It struck low and to the left. Rather than make excuses, he took another and tried again.

So he wasn't going to force conversation. Aine let out her held breath and retrieved another arrow. Without the tension, she hit her mark, dead center.

"Impressive," Uallas murmured.

"Thank you."

After a few more minutes of shooting in silence, they exhausted the arrows, and Uallas went to retrieve them. When he returned, he stuck them into the ground. His eyes once more sought Aine's face.

"You don't like Forrais much."

"I grew up here." Aine's heart throbbed in her throat. Had Macha sent him to get some information out of her? Or to convince her to leave?

"I don't much care for it either." Uallas plucked an arrow from the ground.

"Then why are you here?"

"Obligation. It is tradition that the lord of Eilean Buidhe bring tribute to his clan lord every five years."

"And this is the fifth year."

"Actually, it's the sixth." He turned away and raised the bow again. "My wife died last year. Even Lady Macha would not go against the traditions of mourning."

Despite herself, a pang of sympathy struck Aine. "I'm sorry. That must have been difficult."

"It was. We had been married only three years."

"Children?"

"One. A son." He gave a bare smile. "At least she lived to see him draw his first breath. But not long after."

"I'm sorry." Aine had attended enough births to know that even with a skilled midwife or physician, things sometimes went wrong. One never knew when a loved one would be snatched away. Aine's vision went blurry before she realized the tears were back.

Uallas lowered his weapon. "I hope your husband is alive, Lady Aine. I will pray to Comdiu for it."

He bowed, just as deep but more sober. Without another word, he took his quiver and walked back across the yard toward the keep.

"What did he want?" Diocail stepped up beside her, the edge still present in his voice.

Aine followed the red-haired lord with her eyes. "I don't know." She turned to the captain. "But I'm glad you're still here. There's a favor I wish to ask of you."

CHAPTER
TWENTY

After days of confinement to Carraigmór, Eoghan wondered if perhaps his flogging had only been an excuse for his real punishment. It wasn't that he minded scrubbing floors and fetching water and beating the dust from tapestries. He had been raised taking his turn in service at Carraigmór. It was being banned from the practice yard that rankled, not being allowed to take anything more dangerous than a mop in hand.

Eoghan lifted four buckets on a wooden yoke. Today's task was changing the soiled water in the guest chambers' tubs and replacing it with fresh. Normally this would have been an easy task, but the war had sent an influx of young boys and men into the forest. Two more had arrived this morning, their eyes filled with knowledge far too heavy for such a tender age. Personally, he couldn't blame them for seeking refuge at Ard Dhaimhin. If these young men would be called upon to fight, wasn't it better to send them to the Fíréin, where they would be properly trained and cared for and raised in the ways of Comdiu?

Eoghan might have hinted to Conor that he wished for a different sort of life, but the brotherhood was all he knew—the grueling training, the strict obedience. That obedience was being tested with each new task Master Liam and the Conclave found for him at the fortress. To a man who'd had a sword in hand since childhood, the restrictions on his practice felt like having a limb amputated.

Eoghan rolled his shoulders experimentally, feeling the tug of healing skin on his back as his muscles flexed. At least the enforced "rest" combined with the healer's effective poultices had reduced the weals to faint marks, even if he would bear them for the rest of his life. That hardly bothered him. It was an honor to be punished for doing Comdiu's will, and the scars were a reminder of how much trouble he could get himself into when he didn't act in faith.

So you're willing to endure a lashing for My will, but you're not willing to endure some scrubbing?

Eoghan could swear he felt a hint of amusement in Comdiu's words.

He nudged open the chamber door with his foot and headed down the corridor to the garderobe sewer. "It's not the scrubbing that I mind; it's the time away from my training."

Comdiu didn't need to say anything for him to know He was less than impressed by the excuse.

And that was another reason Eoghan did not tell anyone of his gift. More often than not, Comdiu spoke to him like a doting father to a beloved child, with no small measure of amusement. To some, portraying their great and powerful God in such a way would be blasphemy. This was the Creator of the heavens and earth, the judge of the wicked and defender of the righteous. Why would He bother Himself with the activities of one insignificant man scrubbing tubs and stone floors in the far corner of the known world? And why would He bother to speak directly to such a man?

It sounded, even to Eoghan, like madness.

"Then what do You wish me to do, if it's not to wield a sword?" Talking aloud made him feel less insane, though it probably looked the opposite.

Obey.

Very well. He would obey, even if Comdiu didn't give any more direction on *whom* he was meant to obey.

He was heading back to the other empty chamber to perform the same service when Brother Daigh approached in his usual measured stride. The elder brother's expression did not reflect that he had recently delivered an extreme punishment to the Ceannaire's successor.

"You're wanted in the hall, Brother Eoghan. The Conclave has been called."

Eoghan's stomach did an acrobatic twist. He had never been included in a meeting of the Conclave. Either it was a sign his punishment was going to be lifted, or it was a sign of changing things to come. He left the buckets and yoke in the chamber— no doubt he'd have to go straight back to this task—and followed the stern brother through the winding corridors into the great hall.

Rather than the semicircular arrangement of chairs used when a brother or apprentice requested an audience, today they were placed down both sides of a long table in the center of the hall. An extra chair had been pulled up on the end.

"Brother Riordan! You're back!" The words escaped before he could restrain them.

Riordan didn't smile. The layer of dust upon his cloak said he had not even spared the time to bathe and change before he convened a meeting of Ard Dhaimhin's leadership. What could be so urgent?

The other Conclave members filed in and took their seats.

Eoghan folded his hands atop the table so he wouldn't fidget. He was a grown man, but this gathering of elders still made him feel like a young boy waiting for chastisement. At last, Liam appeared from the direction of his private chamber and took a seat on the far end, facing the Rune Throne.

"Brother Riordan has brought us some disturbing news," Liam said. "You all must hear it. We have decisions to make."

Riordan cleared his throat and launched into an account of what he had seen in Faolán. Eoghan just stared. Fergus dead, the druid gone, and Mac Eirhinin claiming the throne? He would have been less surprised to find that the sorcerer had sprouted wings.

When he finished, no one spoke. Finally Eoghan asked the question that filled the room like a silent specter. "Where is the druid?"

Riordan looked at him. "He's there. I can feel him."

"In hiding?"

"In a sense."

"He's taken another body," Liam said.

All attention shifted to the Ceannaire, and Liam sighed. "Thus far, I have not shared all I know. This druid is neither young nor a stranger. You know that part of the reason the wards were estab-lished was to limit the activities of the sorcerers, particularly the ones known as the Red Druids. Ceannaires relied upon the wards for centuries. But what the brotherhood did not anticipate was the potential for corruption from within."

Eoghan's heart beat harder. This information was something no one, outside of the Ceannaire himself, had likely ever known.

"One of my predecessors was a man by the name of Niall. At least, that's the name recorded in the rolls of the brotherhood, though we have no way of knowing whether that was the name to which he was born. He was extraordinarily gifted. He could sense magic in others and instantly identify the type. He could fade in front of someone looking directly at him. But he was not satisfied with the power Comdiu gave him, nor with the small realm he led at Ard Dhaimhin. He called on the darker arts of our forefathers, communed with the sidhe, and gained unimaginable power. When his Conclave suspected he was dabbling in forbidden magic, they attempted to remove him. Instead, through dark magic, he killed his old body and took a new one, that of a young apprentice. Through the years, he has cheated death, changing bodies at will when the old one no longer serves him."

"And you believe Keondric is simply Diarmuid or Niall or whatever you wish to call him, in a new body," Eoghan said.

Liam glanced at Riordan. "I do. There is no other explanation of how Keondric commands Fergus's and Diarmuid's loyal men."

"That explains why Conor thought they had killed the druid but Beagan still sensed a sorcerer at Glenmallaig." Eoghan should have known it. Keondric was the man who had kidnapped Aine and taken her to Glenmallaig as bait for Conor. If he'd already been under the druid's control, it would have been that much easier to take his body.

"What happened to the real Keondric, then?"

"Gone, most likely," Liam said. "Two souls cannot reside in one body. The druid, through magic, would have forced his soul to flee and then taken over the space it left behind."

"I would not have thought it possible," Gradaigh said quietly. One of the younger members of the Conclave, he'd only recently become a dominant voice on the council. "This is the work of faerie stories, not reality."

"Where do you think faerie stories come from?" Liam asked. "The world is an ancient place, and there is evil beyond these walls that you cannot even imagine. What Niall—or Keondric—controls is only the smallest fraction of the dark power the Adversary has at his disposal."

A chill raced over Eoghan's skin. "How does this affect us?"

"He wants to eliminate all who might stand against him," Riordan said. "First the Balians in the kingdoms. Next will be Ard Dhaimhin. We must prepare to defend Carraigmór."

Dal let out a scornful laugh, drawing attention to where he sat at the end of the table. He was another Conclave member emboldened by the changes in Ard Dhaimhin, and if Eoghan were completely honest, he didn't care for him. "No army can defeat the brotherhood. Even with sorcery, those men are no match for the Fíréin. He will never take the Rune Throne."

"He does not come to rule," Liam said. "And it is not the throne that he desires."

A sick, sinking feeling crept into Eoghan's middle. Somewhere deep down, he knew what Liam would say before he said it.

"He wants to wipe every last trace of Comdiu's gifts from the earth."

CHAPTER
TWENTY-ONE

"You're moving better."

Talfryn lowered himself to the ground beside Conor, where he ate his morning porridge. This time the extras were a few mushy bits of stone fruit, probably too overripe to be eaten by the settlement. Conor didn't care. It was food—extra energy—and at least it gave flavor to the otherwise tasteless gruel.

Conor ran his fingers over his healing ribs. His short altercation with Dyllan had reminded him how far he had to go before he was fully healed, but at least it no longer hurt to breathe or walk.

"A few more weeks," he said as he shoved the last of his breakfast into his mouth with his fingers.

"You may not have a few weeks. I don't like the way the guards look at you. They know the last messages asking after your wife have come back, and now they know you're well enough to fight. They're waiting for you to make your move."

"Then they will continue waiting. My work is not done here yet."

Talfryn looked at their guard to see if their conversation had been noticed. "You owe them nothing. You owe Haldor nothing. Are you prepared to die here as a matter of honor?"

Talfryn was right, but Conor couldn't bring himself to betray Haldor's trust. He had asked a few more questions about Conor's beliefs—not anything significant—but it was obvious the Sofarende leader was trying to reconcile Conor's actions with his own expectations. He seemed to think, like Talfryn, that Conor was going to make his move any minute.

And if you're smart, you will. Aine could still be out there somewhere. If she's alive, she could be alone. Or she could be waiting for you in Aron. Are you going to languish in a Sofarende prison until Haldor tires of you?

Yet something in his spirit told him to stay.

"You must make a decision, Conor. Time is growing short."

"Time for what?"

Talfryn just shook his head. "Be ready. Soon."

Conor rose and took his bowl to the trough, where he rinsed it under close supervision and placed it in the bucket beside it, his mind spinning. Did Talfryn plan on making his escape and taking Conor with him? What could he possibly be planning? His chances alone were no better than Conor's. Even if they overcame their guards, they'd be captured before they could ever breach the wall. The defenses the Sofarende had built against the Gwynn just as effectively kept the prisoners in.

Except Conor knew from his sleepless nights that there was a point when the guard changed and only one man stood watch over their hut. The walls were wicker and clay. It would be easy enough to break out, kill the single guard, and take his weapon before fading into the compound's shadows. They would have perhaps ten minutes before the body was discovered—ten minutes to find a way out through the heavily guarded gate.

Conor shook his head, drawing a suspicious glance from the

guard. It would never work. He was hardly at his best. He had no weapons. If he were caught, he would certainly be killed. What would Haldor make of an escape attempt after all the talk about honor and oaths before Comdiu?

Did you really mean it? Or were you just buying time?

The bonds seemed to chafe more than usual as a different guard walked him to Haldor's longhouse and let him inside. Conor prepared the tablets distractedly, etching several verses without thinking about what he was writing.

Hear me, O Lord, defender of the meek.
I am beset by my enemies.
Raise Your sword in my defense,
And protect Your sons who are defenseless.

Conor stared at the verse he had just written. It was barely familiar, as if he had read it long ago but forgotten it until this minute. Why had he chosen those lines? Was he trying to justify his own conflicted thoughts? Or was this a direct message from Comdiu?

"It is hard, doing nothing, is it not?"

Haldor startled him from his thoughts. Conor set the tablet aside and tried to make his expression blank. "Pardon me?"

"You are accustomed to being useful, not hobbled like a horse in a pasture." Haldor jerked his head toward Conor's bonds. He hadn't even noticed that the guard had forgotten to take them off, he'd become so accustomed to them. He shuddered at the significance.

"Men are not allowed to be idle at Ard Dhaimhin, no matter their role in the brotherhood. Our elders scrub floors and carry water, the same as the novices. Since Comdiu sees men as equals, so does the brotherhood."

"These thoughts of yours are very strange. You say all men are equals, yet you have kings."

Conor thought back to what Riordan had said to him when he first came to Ard Dhaimhin. "Leadership is a privilege and a responsibility, not a right. Those who are trusted with much are expected to do much."

"As I said, strange." But Haldor smiled. "I do not wish to practice your language today. Tell me about your brotherhood."

So now they came down to it. "What do you wish to know?"

"You are warriors, aye?"

Conor nodded his head once.

"But you do not make war."

"Not unless the war comes to us."

"Who would be foolish enough to bring war against men who do nothing but learn to fight and use magic?"

"Men who fight with darker magic."

Haldor's eyes burned suddenly bright. "Tell me about this magic."

Conor considered. The northerner could be trying to learn about the one thing the Fíréin feared, but Haldor's tension, his intense interest, told Conor it was much more personal. But where to begin?

At the beginning, he supposed. "Balians believe in one God above all, who created both men and the beings we call the Companions. At the beginning of time, one of the Companions named Arkiel rebelled against Comdiu. He lost and was cast out of heaven with those who stood with him. Arkiel and the fallen, those our people call the sidhe, are allowed to influence the earth. Yet when Balus came to die for mankind, He gave the gifts of magic to help counteract the sidhe's influence. To bind their power. Many of our brothers possess these gifts."

Haldor nodded thoughtfully, and Conor could see him fitting together all the pieces Conor had given him in the last several weeks. "It is the sidhe that your brotherhood fights against."

"In a sense. There are druids, like priests, who serve the Adversary and commune with the sidhe. Even if we don't understand the full extent of their powers, what might they do if the gifts of Balus did not hold them back?"

Haldor just stared through him, unseeing.

A possibility surfaced in Conor's mind. "Haldor, why did your people leave your homeland?"

The Sofarende leader turned to him, and Conor knew. These incidents were not just limited to Seare. Perhaps the situation was different, but there was none of the surprise or disbelief he had expected to see in Haldor's face. He had seen such things himself.

"You may go now, Conor."

On the way back to his prison, Conor realized it was the first time Haldor had ever used his given name.

That night, Conor tossed and turned on his mat, the glare of the moon through the gaps in the hut's mortared walls interrupting his sleep. As if he could have slept anyway. Haldor understood the oppression of which Conor spoke; he was sure of it. Was that why he was meant to be here? To show Haldor the weapon— belief in the one true God—that could combat the evil that had overrun his northern home as it now swept over Seare?

Shouts rang out in the compound outside the hut. Conor jerked straight up on his mat. Talfryn crouched beside him, his teeth gleaming in the dim light. "Are you ready?"

The sounds of horses, men's shouts, and clashes of steel grew louder, shuddering through Conor with sickening familiarity. The village was under attack. Talfryn crept to the door, but rather than try to open it, he threw his shoulder against a cracked section of the wall again and again. The plaster crumbled, the wicker frame splintering under the impact. Finally, with one last thrust, a section of the wall collapsed completely, spilling torchlight and moonlight inside.

At once, the prisoners rushed for the hole, stumbling over each other in their haste. Talfryn and Conor pressed back out of the way, waiting. A cry pierced the air as one of the prisoners was taken by the guard, followed by a Norin curse as the other men fell upon him. Talfryn tapped Conor's arm and gestured toward the now-quieter exterior of the hut.

Men on powerful stallions rampaged through the village with swords and spears, killing all in their path. Across the planked thoroughfare, Conor glimpsed Haldor in his elaborately decorated helmet, ivory-hilted sword in hand. He cut down one of the horses and fell upon its rider before turning to face another warrior.

"Go!" Talfryn shouted. "What are you waiting for?"

Conor's feet remained rooted in place.

"Your freedom awaits you! Run!"

Stay.

Conor's blood thrummed in his ears, dulling the sound of battle. This could be his one and only chance for escape. After this attack, vigilance would be doubled. He would never get another opportunity.

Stay.

In front of him, a Norin warrior fought a man on foot, their swords clashing for a second. Conor realized in shock that it was Ulaf. The other man, whom Conor assumed to be Gwynn, fought with a smaller, lighter sword than the Sofarende's heavy broad weapon, and he wielded it with a facility that most Fíréin would envy. One quick feint, which Ulaf was slow to parry, and the sword slid into the northerner's middle.

Ulaf collapsed. Conor rushed to the warrior's side and pressed his hands to the gushing wound.

"Go," Conor gritted out to Talfryn. His insides twisted at the thought of what he was giving up. "Escape while you can."

"Conor, don't be stupid! He's the enemy. You can't save him."

Conor looked at the blood seeping through his fingers and knew the words to be true. But something, that quiet hand on his spirit, would not let him stand up and walk away.

"It's Comdiu's will that I stay. Now go, quickly, before your chance is lost too."

Talfryn looked stricken, but he turned and ran, taking up a sword from a fallen Gwynn warrior as he went.

Ulaf choked on a breath, blood bubbling from his lips and splattering his bleached beard. Conor cast around desperately until his eyes fell on a woman, brandishing a club as fearlessly as the men.

"You! Here! Your apron!"

The woman gawked at Conor, and he realized he had shouted in his own language. He repeated the command in Norin, and after a hesitation, she came to his side, pulling her apron from the front of her dress.

"Press here," he told her, bunching up the linen to staunch the wound. Almost immediately, it turned crimson. "More pressure."

"He's already dead."

He looked at the warrior's face. Ulaf's eyes stared sightlessly to the sky. Conor sat back in the dirt, unable to understand the sudden flood of despair. This man was his enemy. He had spewed the vilest imaginings, detailed terrible acts, yet Conor was struck by a pang of grief at the knowledge that Ulaf's spirit was gone.

He sent the Lord of heaven as sacrifice, so that none need be lost.

Conor bowed his head beneath the weight of sudden understanding. He had said it himself only hours ago: Comdiu saw men as equals. Not as enemies fighting over land and resources, but as sinners who were lost. To Him, Ulaf was no different than Conor except that Conor had accepted the sacrifice made for him.

"You're still here."

Conor looked up. Haldor stood over him, holding a dripping

battle-ax, his face, hands, and clothing spattered with blood. He looked like a Norin god, bent on vengeance.

"I made an oath before Comdiu to you. I will not go back on it."

Haldor stared at him while the fighting dwindled around them. He looked at Ulaf and then the blood on Conor's hands and arms. He shook his head. "I do not know you, stranger. Leave this place."

He said it in the common tongue.

Conor watched him walk away, almost too shocked to react. The woman looked between him and Haldor, just as surprised. Conor reached down and eased Ulaf's broadsword from his limp fingers, cast one last look at Haldor's departing back, and melted effortlessly into the darkness.

✦ ✦ ✦

Conor escaped the settlement without difficulty, staying close to the walls and concealing himself in the shadows. The front gate lay open, splintered, evidence of the battering ram used to break in. This was no hasty raid, but it wasn't a full-scale assault either. Only a few of the Gwynn horsemen remained, fighting their way out, not in. Surely that meant they had accomplished their goal. Had they come to rescue Talfryn? Who was he to justify an attack on the Sofarende settlement?

Conor kept his eyes peeled for any signs of him, but the man had disappeared as quickly and quietly as Conor. Did the Gwynn have powers of concealment beyond changing his appearance, ones that Conor's perception couldn't penetrate?

The man—and the horsemen who had created the diversion—were surely his greatest chance for safety. The full moon illuminated the churned earth, scarred from the horse's hooves. He followed the tracks northeast around the village and up a nearby rise, still concentrating on remaining unseen. He propped the flat of the heavy Norin blade against his shoulder. His arms, shoulders, and back ached as they had his first days at Ard Dhaimhin, and as his breathing became increasingly labored, pain stabbed through his ribs. He gave a mental prayer of thanks when he reached the top and slumped forward to catch his breath.

Warning prickled the back of his neck. He barely managed to raise the sword in time to block the oncoming strike.

"Halt! I'm a friend!" Conor circled to meet a second blow from the cloaked figure.

"Enough."

A voice, laden with authority, cut through the fight, and his attacker disengaged. Conor glanced up to where several dozen horsemen waited. A man cloaked in a fur mantle moved toward him. Talfryn.

Conor didn't lower his sword until the other warrior sheathed his weapon. Talfryn nodded to the man, who gave a deep bow before backing away. "My lord."

Talfryn's entire demeanor had changed. No longer was he the cringing, unassuming man pretending to be a house slave. He stood now with an air of command, armed with a sword that even in the dim light, Conor could see was inlaid with gold and precious gems.

"You escaped after all," Talfryn said. "What changed your mind?"

"My lord," one of the warriors called. "Forgive me, but we must be away to Cwmmaen before the Norin decide to give pursuit."

Cwmmaen? Conor sifted the half-forgotten details of Gwynn genealogy in his mind. King Llewellyn had three sons, the second of which was—

"Prince Talfryn?"

A smile stretched Talfryn's face. "Indeed, I am. I'm impressed,

Seareann. Where does a common warrior learn the details of foreign succession? Unless you are not as common as you pretend. Didn't King Galbraith have a son named Conor who was killed tragically young?"

Conor grinned. "Aye, he did. But you shouldn't believe every report you hear."

"Then, Conor with no clan name, let us be away. You ride?"

Conor followed Talfryn to where two riderless mounts waited. A man offered him the reins. "This was planned? I don't understand."

"I will explain. But not now."

Conor looked down at the leather saddle with its hanging loops. Apparently Gwynn did not ride bareback like Seareanns. He thrust his foot into the loop and swung his leg over the gelding's back. Convenient. This was a custom he wouldn't mind bringing back to Seare.

He settled the reins in one hand and rested the sword against his shoulder once more.

"Can you use that thing?"

Conor glanced at Talfryn. "Aye. Though I'm better with a short sword."

"Good. Because as soon as my wife learns you're the reason for my captivity, she'll likely try to separate your head from your shoulders."

"I'm the reason for your captivity? You were there before I was!"

"Comdiu sent me to wait for you." Talfryn grinned at Conor. "I suppose it could be worse. Hyledd will forgive me since the mission was successful. If I came back without you, I would never hear the end of it."

CHAPTER
TWENTY-TWO

The men remained vigilant as they rode north from the Sofarende encampment, but best they could tell, they had not been pursued. Perhaps Haldor had decided it wasn't worth risking his men to recover a pair of slaves.

After a few minutes, their escort split into several detachments and took off in different directions, leaving only a handful of warriors behind to accompany them. Conor took that to mean they were nearing Cwmmaen, but the sky had begun to lighten to a steely gray before they descended into a low valley.

Talfryn gestured for Conor to ride up beside him. "I take it you do not wish anyone to know your real identity?"

"It doesn't serve me to be known as a Mac Nir," he said. "Not considering all that has been done in Seare."

"You don't wish any mention of the Fíréin either?"

Conor shook his head. Men typically took that bit of information as a threat or a challenge. The last thing he needed was the scrutiny of the warriors in the prince's household. As it was, anyone who knew Talfryn's true reason for being in the enemy camp would have a reason to dislike him.

They descended into the valley and then back up the next

rise, where a sprawling fortress came into view. Its inner walls, earth and stone, protected a structure more elegant than most palaces he'd seen in Seare. Circular walls rose to meet a peaked timber roof, the carved eaves displaying elaborately entwined mythological creatures. Several outbuildings, their slanted tops barely visible over the high walls, flanked the main keep. Two of their party rode ahead, and the great gates cranked open on their approach.

Conor hung back with the other men while Talfryn rode up front. A host of servants appeared before them to take the horses' reins. He dismounted, suddenly conscious of his appearance. Even without a mirror, he knew his hair was matted, his skin and clothing filthy. It was a small comfort that the prince looked and smelled no better than he.

The massive carved wooden doors opened, and a beautiful woman in an embroidered dress came out. Intricate braids bound her blonde hair atop her head, and gold and jewels covered her throat and hands. She strode straight for Talfryn, gripping handfuls of her skirt before her, and then drew back her hand and slapped him soundly across the cheek.

Conor held his breath, muscles tensed while he waited for Talfryn's response. But the prince just rubbed his cheek ruefully. "Could you be less predictable, darling?" Then he yanked her to him and kissed her. The men around them laughed.

"Ugh. You reek." She struggled away from him, though the press of her lips suggested she was not as irritated as she pretended. She turned to a tall, thin man beside her. "My lord husband will bathe in the barracks. Our guest as well."

Her gaze had slid so quickly over Conor that he'd thought she hadn't noticed his presence. Talfryn nudged him with his elbow as she spun on her heel and went back inside. "This is to be my punishment, I see. Is your wife so demanding?"

"I wouldn't know." The ache crept into Conor's chest again. "We were separated only a few days after we were married."

Talfryn sobered. "I'm sorry—"

"Think nothing of it, my lord."

"Oh, not you as well." Talfryn shook his head and clapped a hand on Conor's shoulder. "No 'my lord this' or 'my lord that.' Men who have been in captivity together have no use for such formality."

"If you say so, my l—Talfryn."

The steward stepped between them. "My lord, your bath awaits you."

Talfryn chuckled and shrugged, then gestured for Conor to follow him.

The barracks were as well appointed as Conor's rooms at Glenmallaig. Talfryn and Conor were shown to separate bathing rooms with stone tubs set into the ground and drains in the bottom. Conor gaped openly at the hot water flooding from piping into the bath.

"Ciraen design, sir. This fortress was left behind when the armies withdrew almost a century ago. We benefit from their ingenuity. Hot springs, you see."

Conor nodded, though he really didn't see. The bathhouse at Ard Dhaimhin made use of the hot springs beneath, but those were just natural pools around which a structure had been erected. This was a marvel of engineering, water routed through piping that could be turned on and off at will.

"Do you need assistance, sir?"

"No, thank you. I can manage on my own."

"Very well, sir. I'll be back with clean clothes."

Conor nodded. Once he was alone, he stripped off his stinking, filthy garments. Thank Comdiu the Gwynn were as fanatical as Seareanns about bathing. His tutor had told him that on the continent, bathing was thought to cause the plague and other diseases. He shuddered at the thought of what a hall full of continental courtiers must smell like. At least the smell in the slaves' quarters had been an honest stink, not layered with perfume and incense.

When Conor had scrubbed every inch of his body with strong lye soap and the bath water had turned an alarming shade of gray, he climbed out and wrapped the clean cloth around his waist. The steward had placed a comb, a single-edged blade meant for shaving, and a hand mirror on a tray atop a low table. Conor attempted to draw the comb through the ends of his matted hair for only a moment before he set it down in exasperation and eyed the razor.

What did it matter? His long hair was just another bit of vanity—the symbol of a warrior from a homeland that had fallen and a brotherhood he had abandoned. He hesitated for a moment before he raised the razor to the nape of his neck and sawed through his braid.

When the steward returned minutes later, he looked twice at Conor before nodding approvingly. He handed a folded stack of clothing to him. "Your meal awaits you in the hall, sir. Prince Talfryn has ordered—requested—that you dine with him and his family."

Conor fingered the garments, finely woven silk and linen heavy with embroidery. They looked to be straight from the prince's own wardrobe. Why was a Gwynn prince, a stranger, taking such an interest in him? He had said Comdiu sent him. Surely he just meant he saw a greater purpose in his captivity. He couldn't mean it literally.

Then again, stranger things had happened. And Talfryn had the resources and the contacts to make inquiries about Aine.

Even the fiercely independent Highland clans wouldn't ignore a missive from a prince of Gwydden.

Conor brightened at the thought and dressed quickly, his stomach rumbling. It had been weeks—no, months—since he'd had the benefit of a proper meal. He combed his newly shorn hair away from his face in an attempt to make himself presentable, straightened his silk tunic, and stepped outside to find the prince waiting for him.

"Ready to face the wolves?" Talfryn asked with a cheery smile.

"Wolves? Are your lords at court?"

The prince chuckled. "No. I meant my wife and daughter. Prepare yourself, Seareann. You are bound to be plied with questions."

With that cryptic comment, Talfryn settled his fur mantle around his shoulders and headed into the courtyard. His men called welcomes to him, and he paused to clasp arms or exchange a few words with each. Conor followed, watching and waiting. Appraising glances slid over him, the men no doubt wondering what was so important about him that their lord would have risked his life for him. Perhaps they resented the fact that his existence put their prince in danger.

Conor met their eyes squarely and nodded in greeting, not holding their gazes long enough to be taken as a challenge. Instead, he stayed several steps behind Talfryn, his hands clasped behind his back.

The prince entered by a small door that led into a narrow corridor and then emptied into a hall larger than Carraigmór's and Lisdara's put together. More of the carving adorned the upper reaches of the hall and the massive ceiling beams, and elaborate tapestries decorated the stone walls.

For all its magnificence, Conor expected the space to be packed with courtiers, yet it lay open and empty, two long tables set in the middle of the room like islands in a sea of stone. Several men in plain garments sat at the far table. Warriors, clearly, but not only that, if they had a place in the hall.

Lady Hyledd met them halfway to the main table, holding her hand out to Talfryn. "Husband. Much better."

Talfryn held back a smile. "Hyledd, may I introduce our guest, Conor?"

"Conor . . ."

He gave her a deep bow. "Just Conor, my lady. I am grateful for your hospitality."

Hyledd gave Conor a practiced smile and inclined her head politely. "You are most welcome, sir. Please, join us for an early meal, and then you and my husband can rest." The look Hyledd shot Talfryn said he shouldn't expect any rest until she told him exactly what she thought about his absence.

Hyledd stepped aside then and gestured to the beautiful young woman behind her. "Conor, may I also introduce our daughter, Briallu."

Conor blinked at the girl standing before him. Where had she come from? She was fair-haired and slender like her mother, with eyes the most peculiar shade of green-gold. She glided forward and gave him a curtsy. "Welcome, Conor. It's my honor to meet you."

She held out her hand, and he bowed over it. A bolt of energy shot up his arm, making his breath seize in his throat. It was not so different from his reaction the first time he had seen Aine, but this sensation was not altogether pleasant.

He dropped her hand and took a step back while he tried to find his voice. "And you, my lady."

Talfryn smiled at them. "Food. After a month of Norin cooking, I'm anxious for some Gwynn delicacies."

"Your own fault," Hyledd muttered as she walked with her daughter to the table.

Conor followed Talfryn and took the seat beside him. Within moments, servants placed trenchers of hot porridge—far superior to the thin gruel they had been served at the Sofarende camp—along with roasted partridge, blood sausages, and pots of steaming tea. He tried to make himself eat slowly, knowing his body would not likely tolerate the food, but he couldn't prevent himself from shoveling in the porridge like a starving man. His stomach cramped immediately, and he set the spoon aside with a wince. Instead, he surveyed the rest of the table, only to have his gaze collide with the piercing green eyes of Lady Briallu. She didn't bother to veil her interest.

Conor looked away. He would have to make it clear he was married. Talfryn knew as much, though it was hardly his host's fault that Conor had been taken off guard by the presence of his beautiful daughter. He'd just never felt any sort of connection with a woman other than Aine.

Until now.

That thought drove him to his feet, garnering surprised looks from his Companions. "Forgive me. Apparently my exhaustion is greater than my hunger. Might someone direct me to my quarters?"

Talfryn raised his hand, and a male servant stepped forward. "Follow me, sir. Your quarters are on the other side of the fortress."

Conor bowed slightly to the table. "Thank you again for your hospitality. It is greatly appreciated." He caught Talfryn's eye, and the man nodded. There would be time to talk after they rested.

The corridors that led away from the hall, unlike the one that delivered them to it, were plain, unadorned stone without any sign of the scrollwork carving that decorated the rest of the fortress. Conor barely managed to duck through a low doorway without cracking his forehead.

"This is the old Ciraen section," the servant explained.

"You're not leading me to the dungeons, are you?"

The servant looked back at him with a thin smile. "If you think our prince would risk his life for you just to throw you in the dungeons, I question his decision to retrieve you in the first place."

Conor took the reprimand evenly. So everyone knew the prince's business, and no matter how polite or well-trained the servants might be, they would look at Conor as the man who had put their prince at risk. Briallu, however, didn't seem to have any such prejudice. That was odd, wasn't it? Unless she had so little regard for her father that she didn't care about the threat to his life.

But that didn't make sense either. Clearly Talfryn doted on her. If he recalled, the prince had several grown sons. Briallu was probably the only girl child, favored, protected, and spoiled— the type who had never experienced any hardship and so could not imagine that tragedy could strike her personally.

Aye, it was easier to write her off as a petulant, spoiled noble-woman, even though his instincts told him she was nothing of the sort. Those same instincts just gave him little else by which to judge her.

"Sir, your chamber." The servant opened a door on the left and stepped aside for Conor.

The chamber was comfortably appointed, much like his chamber back at Lisdara—not overly lavish, but with every requirement a guest could need. Conor took a single glance around the space, yanked off his boots, and fell asleep facedown on the bed.

CHAPTER
TWENTY-THREE

Conor awoke to yellow light sifting through the small, high window. A few hours past midday, perhaps. He pushed himself off the bed and made a face at the wrinkled mess he'd made of his borrowed silk tunic. He should have at least had the grace to take it off before he collapsed.

Not that sleep had righted anything. His body ached from the luxury of a soft bed after nearly a month sleeping on hard ground, his mouth felt dry, and his stomach seemed shriveled to the size of a walnut. No wonder he'd had such difficulty with the heavy Norin sword. His muscles shook from bearing his own weight, let alone a dozen pounds of iron.

Someone—probably the same disdainful servant—had come in and placed a ewer and a basin on the small table next to the bed, along with a clean, folded cloth. Conor splashed water on his face and rinsed his mouth, then combed his hair back from his face. The abrupt end of the motion took him by surprise. He had forgotten he had hacked it off rather than suffer through the process of dematting his braid.

He grinned ruefully at his own vanity. Aine would make fun

of him. Or would she be disappointed? He had clear memories of her burying her hands in his hair on their wedding night. . . .

He sighed. He couldn't think of those things now. Though it did bring to mind what he was supposed to broach with Talfryn: would the prince be willing to use his resources to find Aine?

When he reached the hall, however, it was empty. A servant passing by in one of the corridors paused. "Sir? May I bring you something?"

"No, thank you." Conor detoured down the corridor that led to the side door and stepped into the glaring afternoon sunlight.

The clack of wood on wood and the good-natured shouts of men drew him to the far corner of the large courtyard, where at least a dozen warriors gathered around the prince. Talfryn faced four of his men, stripped to the waist with sword in hand.

"Ah, you can do better than that!" he taunted. "Afraid to bruise your prince?"

His opponents grinned and redoubled their efforts—with practice swords, Conor saw—but the prince held them off at every turn. He'd been right in his earlier assessment of Talfryn's ability: the man was every bit as skilled as his warriors. Watching the match made Conor itch for the feel of a weapon in his own hand.

"You feel naked."

He jerked his head around. Briallu smiled at him, a hint of mischief glinting in her eyes. "Without a sword, I mean."

Conor cleared his throat. "How do you know I'm a fighter?"

She threw her head back and laughed, a lilting sound that wormed its way into his chest. "Surely you jest. I have brothers. I was raised among men. Fair hand with a sword and bow I am myself. And you ask me how I recognize a warrior." She winked at him and gestured with her head for him to follow. Against his better judgment, he obeyed.

"Where are we going? Won't your father be upset about you being alone with a stranger?"

"You hardly qualify as a stranger. But even if you did, I have my father wrapped around my finger. He won't object. Not when he knows what I'm up to."

An odd sense of foreboding slid over Conor, and his steps slowed. Briallu glanced back at him, her expression reproving. "Come, now. Afraid I'm going to lure you away and steal your virtue? What kind of woman do you think I am?"

Conor's flush began at the tips of his ears and spread across his face. "Forgive me, my lady. I am a married man. I attempt to avoid any appearance of impropriety."

"Well, you are a proper one, aren't you? Fear not, Lord Conor—aye, you are as clearly noble as you are a warrior—I will not give your wife any cause for complaint today. But you will regret it if you do not follow me."

Terrible idea, Conor told himself. But he followed.

She led him to a small stone structure beyond the barracks and pushed open the iron-bound door. "Come. See."

Conor stepped inside the dark space, his eyes adjusting to the dimness. He propped the door open with his foot to let in more light. "The armory."

"Aye, the armory. I suspect my father would understand you're in need of a sword. After all, it's unseemly for a nobleman to be without a weapon, is it not?"

Conor met her eyes, for the first time feeling more kinship than wariness. "It is. And since you seem to know your way around, I'll let you point out the obvious choices."

She smiled and sized him up with uncomfortable thoroughness. "Short sword and dagger, aye?"

"Aye. Good guess."

"I mean no offense, Conor, but it's hardly a guess." She went to a rack that held at least a dozen plain swords, all with well-made steel blades, brass pommels and leather-wrapped wooden grips. Soldiers' swords, almost Ciraean in design. "One of these, I'd think."

Conor took one after another from the rack, testing the feel in his hand, the distribution of weight. He'd been trained to fight with whatever he was given or whatever he could pick up on the battlefield, but the first two felt wrong. The third reminded him of the weapons to which he had been accustomed at Ard Dhaimhin. It was the most worn of the bunch, its handle and crossguard scarred, but it was balanced and the blade was true. "This one."

She nodded toward another wall where an array of fleece-lined sheaths with their leather harnesses and baldrics hung side by side. He chose the first that fit the blade and tested the draw to make sure the sword would not stick or slide out.

"Now for the dagger." Briallu moved to a large bench upon which was displayed an array of short blades. Conor reached out, but she raised a hand.

"A man chooses his own sword, but a woman must choose the dagger." She gave him a smile once again tinged with amusement. "It is usually the wife's responsibility, but since you are inconveniently without yours, I will have to do."

"I'm not familiar with that custom."

"Does it not make sense? If a man loses his sword and must use his dagger, he no longer battles for honor or glory. He fights to return home to his loved ones. His wife's heart goes with him and gives him strength."

It was the kind of superstition Conor had been taught to cast aside by his Balian instructors. But he remembered his relief when he had woken up after the ambush in Siomar and found they had forgotten to take his dagger. Aye, he had been fighting for his loved one then.

Briallu moved to the table, closed her eyes, and hovered a hand over the weapons.

Conor couldn't help himself. "This is your selection method?"

"Shhh." She didn't open her eyes. "I am never wrong. Don't distract me."

After a few moments of wordless "searching," she closed her hand around one and lifted it in triumph. "This one is meant for you." She turned to him and presented it, hilt first.

It had absolutely nothing to commend it above a dozen other similar daggers, but the moment he grasped it, the hilt warmed in his palm. His eyes widened.

"I told you. I'm never wrong."

About what? Surely, he'd just imagined the sensation, based on the power of her suggestion.

She retrieved the leather baldric he'd chosen, slid on the sheathed sword, and gestured to him. "Let's fit this."

He obeyed, far too taken aback by the radiating dagger to do anything else. He dipped his head so she could slip the harness over his shoulder and beneath his left arm. Then she reached around him to buckle the belt at his waist, her hands brisk, businesslike. Even so, he found himself holding his breath at her nearness.

"In Gwydden, only long swords are worn on the back. Short swords go at the hip." Her hands went to the buckle at his chest to take up the slack in the strap.

"I feel like one of your horses with all this tack."

She chuckled. "You will become used to it with time, I'm sure."

With time. He sobered. It had been a month since he had lost Aine, and he was no closer to finding her than before. He shifted the unfamiliar baldric on his shoulder and gave Briallu a sober nod. "Thank you."

Her smile faded, a hint of hurt surfacing in her expression. "You're welcome."

Outside, Talfryn was standing by, watching the other men practice. He glanced up when he saw them approach, his eyes lighting on Conor's weaponry. "I see my daughter already got to you."

She winked at Conor. "It's shameful that a warrior should be without his weapons, Father. Someone needs to see to the important details around here."

"I know you do. Just don't tell your mother I said that." Talfryn chuckled and bestowed a doting smile on Briallu, leaving Conor to again wonder about the informality of this family.

"My lord"—Conor grimaced at Talfryn's reproving look, but he continued—"might I speak with you in private when you have a moment?"

"We do have things to discuss, don't we? Come." Talfryn headed toward the side door near the barracks. Conor followed him down one corridor and into another one, where he pushed open a chamber door. A library, it seemed from the books, or perhaps the prince just enjoyed having his study filled with reading material. He gestured for Conor to take a seat at the long table and sat down across from him.

"You have questions about how I came to be in the Norin camp."

"Aye. You said Comdiu told you to find me."

Talfryn leaned forward in his chair. "I don't expect you to believe this. I almost don't believe it myself. I am a follower of Lord Balus, Conor, but I always thought that visions were reserved for prophets or priests. Men more devout than me.

"But I had a dream that very clearly showed me I was to ride up to the Norin encampment west of Cwmmaen and get myself captured. I was not to resist, but simply wait for a foreign warrior. And then we were to escape on the first full moon after his arrival."

Conor studied the prince, fascinated. "And you just accepted that as a vision?"

"Of course not! I dismissed it as a dream. But the next night, I had the same dream. And the next. And the night after that. Never varying, always the same down to the smallest detail. Except the last time, I saw the arrival of a message from my brother, Prince Neryn. When I awoke the next morning to a messenger from Gwingardd, I knew I was being told to obey. What do you make of that?"

"I am grateful you obeyed," Conor said with a grin.

"I am sure you are. But now it is my turn." Talfryn folded his hands on the table, his brown eyes glinting. "I have been wondering this whole time: why you?"

Conor shook his head. "I don't know."

"Well." Talfryn flopped back in his chair. "Here I thought you would give me some elaborate explanation of your calling, your charge for Comdiu."

Conor flushed. In his capture and his fear for his wife, he had nearly forgotten the task he was supposed to accomplish. "I may be the only person left alive who can retake Seare from my uncle and his sorcerer."

"And you forgot to mention that?"

"I don't know if it can be done. I don't know if I am the one to do it. I certainly don't know why Comdiu tasked you of all people with this job. But I'm afraid I must ask for your help one more time."

"You want me to inquire after your wife."

"Please. I cannot return to Seare without finding her. My hope is that she's safe in Aron by now, but she could have fallen into the hands of one of the Lowland clans."

"I will make inquiries," Talfryn said. "We have no quarrel with the Aronans in the north, so I would expect a quick answer from them. But the southern clans have been feuding with Gwydden over borders for almost as long as they've been quarreling with the Highlanders. Do not expect much from that quarter."

Conor let out his breath. It was not the news for which he had hoped, but he could ask for no more. "Thank you, Talfryn. You have been asked to do more on my behalf than most men would bear. Please know that I am truly grateful."

Talfryn nodded and rose. "You will find paper and ink in the drawers on the far wall. Write your missives, and I will have them sent under my personal seal. We shall find your wife one way or another."

CHAPTER
TWENTY-FOUR

Eoghan rapped on the heavy wood door, his heart in his throat. Ever since Riordan's startling revelation the week before, he hadn't been able to shake the sense of foreboding, the vague awareness of a coming storm. Worse yet, Comdiu had been mostly silent, responding to his worried questions with one word: *obey*. Now Liam had called Eoghan to his office, and he couldn't help feeling that the storm had arrived.

Liam called his permission to enter, and Eoghan pushed the door open. The Ceannaire sat in his chair, a wax tablet in front of him, staring at it as if it contained some desperately interesting puzzle, when in reality it was probably just the tallies of their grain storage. "You wanted to see me, sir?"

Liam looked up and pushed the tablet aside. "Come, I want to show you something."

Eoghan frowned, but he followed Liam back out the door and down the stairs, making a turn into a short corridor that ended in solid rock.

"It's time you learn some of the Ceannaire's secrets." Liam spoke a single word—or maybe it was a handful of words—and a hidden door disengaged from its jamb, springing a fraction of an inch outward. Eoghan blinked. How could that be? He would have sworn it was simply a hallway. He tried to keep the password in his mind, but every time he thought he grasped it, it slipped away, like water flowing through his fingers.

As if he knew Eoghan's thoughts, Liam smiled. "The password is passed down from one Ceannaire to the next, and no one who does not have the right to speak it can recall it."

"How is that possible?"

"There is magic here at Carraigmór, magic that is more powerful than anything we can currently perform. Perhaps no one but Daimhin himself ever knew it. We simply don't know. The password was passed to me when I accepted leadership from my master."

Gooseflesh pricked Eoghan's arms as he stepped through the door into a cramped tunnel. There were no torches, yet a dim glow illuminated the staircase. When the door whispered shut behind them, he had the sensation of being sealed into a tomb. Could someone get trapped in here if they didn't know the password to get out? That wasn't an encouraging thought.

Liam led him down the long, narrow stairway, only the sound of their shoes scuffing stone to break the silence. The walls of the corridor pressed so close he had to force himself to breathe normally. He'd never been afraid of enclosed spaces, but something about this tunnel set his heart rattling in his chest like an animal caught in a trap.

They finally came to the end of the corridor, a dead end, and Eoghan waited for Liam to open another magically hidden door. Instead, he just turned sharply into an angled passage that was little more than a split in the rock. Eoghan inhaled deeply and followed him into a chamber.

More soft, unidentifiable light illuminated the cavern, which was several arm spans wide and twice as deep. Wooden compartments lined the walls, each space holding a book, scroll, or folio. The smell of old paper and animal skin added to the musty, crypt-like atmosphere.

"This chamber is Carraigmór's greatest secret and its greatest treasure," Liam said reverently. "It's called the Hall of Prophecies, but it's much more than that. This room not only contains all the prophecies that have been gathered over the last five hundred years, it also preserves the history and the rolls of the brotherhood. Where we came from, where we are going. All that you will someday need to know. All that you must swear to protect, with your life if necessary."

Something in Liam's voice made Eoghan think the Ceannaire was not telling all, but he didn't push. This was too much to take in at once. Instead, he asked, "What would happen if Keondric managed to access this chamber?"

"Disaster. You understand why I show this to you now."

"Because I may have to protect it," Eoghan said. "If the druid was once the Ceannaire, he knows it's here."

"And he knows what's inside. Even I don't know all that's here. It would take a man more than a lifetime to read it all. Comdiu has guided me to what I needed to lead justly and to do His work."

Eoghan walked slowly around the room, peering at the various writings on the shelves but afraid to touch. There were scrolls in every known language, some so old they looked as though they would crumble if they were handled. Parchments ancient enough to have the hair of the animal still attached to the back. Scraped birch bark that looked like it might disintegrate at a breath. Most of the characters he didn't even recognize. Conor might, but Eoghan didn't have his friend's extensive education.

For the first time, the enormity of his undertaking hit him. Liam was to have been a king. His education, even up to his tenth birthday, was more comprehensive than most people received their entire lives—far more extensive than any of the brothers' studies at Ard Dhaimhin. How on earth was Eoghan to be trusted with the knowledge in this room when he couldn't even read half of it?

"I've debated whether to show this to you, but it's time. It's *past* time."

Eoghan turned and saw Liam holding a folded square of uneven vellum. "What's that?"

Liam pulled up two stools from the corner of the room and settled himself on one. "What do you remember of your parents?"

"Nothing," Eoghan said. "My first memories are of Ard Dhaimhin."

"I don't believe that. Close your eyes and think hard. What do you remember?"

Eoghan sank onto the stool across from Master Liam and shut his eyes. This was a ridiculous exercise. He had come here at three years old, abandoned by his parents in the forest. He didn't remember anything but the scent of lavender, attached to a woman: dark-haired, laughing sometimes, but more often worried.

"You remember," Liam said quietly. "You remember your parents."

"My mother. But I can't see her face." Eoghan opened his eyes. "Why bring this up now? What purpose does it serve?"

Liam toyed with the parchment, worrying the rough edge with his thumb. "I have not been completely honest with you, Eoghan. I have debated for years when to discuss the matter, if at all. And I'm afraid we are long past the time when you deserved to hear it. Do you know why you came to Ard Dhaimhin?"

Because my parents thought I was insane. Out loud he said, "They didn't want me. Or maybe they just couldn't care for me."

"No. They were afraid for you, Eoghan. And because you told them that you must come here."

Eoghan stared at his master. Impossible. He had been only three years old.

"They did not just abandon you within our borders. Quite the opposite, in fact. Your mother took you into the forest and waited for a tracker to find you. She said you were destined for the brotherhood and she was following Comdiu's will by giving you up."

Eoghan shook his head. "How could you possibly know that's true?"

"Because I was the tracker."

Eoghan opened his mouth, but nothing would come out. When the words finally did come, they weren't what he intended. "What was her name?"

"Fionnuala. I don't know your father's clan, but she claimed to be a Fearghail."

Eoghan recognized the clan name from history lessons, though he couldn't recall exactly why. "She was Sliebhanaigh. I'm Sliebhanaigh."

"Indeed. Nobility of some sort. I suspect she was afraid to name your father's clan for that reason. They were also Balians."

Understanding dawned. "At a time when the Balian faith was punishable by death."

"Aye. Despite their best efforts to conceal their beliefs, they always feared they would be punished and you would be taken from them." Liam hesitated. "Then there were your particular gifts."

"Gifts?"

"From your first words, you would have conversations with yourself. At first they thought you were mad. Then they realized that some of what you said came true. One day, you told them very clearly, 'Men will be coming for me. I must go to the forsaken city.' It was that wording, so unusual for a child, that convinced them you had access to something the rest of us are denied. Interaction with the Companions, perhaps Comdiu Himself.

"It didn't take them long to figure out what the 'forsaken city' meant. I told Lady Fionnuala I would look after you and give you a good life at Ard Dhaimhin. I have done my best to keep that vow."

Words wouldn't come. All these years believing he had been abandoned, unwanted, when really he had been left for his own safety, at his own request. "Why didn't you tell me?"

Liam bowed his head and studied his clasped hands. "I don't know. Selfishness, perhaps. I never had a family of my own, and you were as close to a son as I would ever get. Perhaps I thought if you knew your family was still out there, you would want to look for them."

Eoghan would have, in his younger years. Now it was a wound so old and calloused that to reopen it would cause everyone unnecessary pain. "You should have told me."

Liam raised his head, pain flashing through his expression. "I know. Eoghan, I have made many mistakes in this life. Taking you as my apprentice and my successor was not one of them. I have fumbled along, trying to follow my imperfect understanding of Comdiu's will. Sometimes I have done good. Sometimes I have not. But you, Eoghan—I have always known that you would be a different person, a different leader. Maybe it's the product of your particular gifts, or maybe you are just a better man than I. Don't repeat my mistakes. Seek the counsel of Comdiu. Follow His instruction."

Eoghan sat silent for a moment. "Conor told me the same thing once."

"Conor was another of my mistakes. I didn't understand until it was too late . . . Ah, but that doesn't matter now. I'm sorry I didn't tell you. You had the right to know you were not abandoned because of a lack of love but because your family loved you too much to do otherwise."

It was too much to take in at once. Eoghan's gaze fell on the piece of vellum in Liam's hand. "What's that?"

"A letter to you from your mother." He held it out.

Slowly, Eoghan unfolded it. Elegant script traveled across it in neat rows.

My dearest son,
I am sorry we had to give you up. We tried to hide you and
your gifts, but you insisted you would be caught. You seem to
believe I will come with you to Ard Dhaimhin. I am sorry
that I cannot. Know that your father and I love you very
much. We will always love you. We wish you the life that
you deserve.

Your mother,
Fionnuala

Eoghan flipped it over. That was it? She was sorry? No more explanation than what Liam had already given? Aye, it was good to know they had loved him, that they regretted having to leave him with strangers. But there was nothing more about them, not even his father's name. Had it not been for Liam's memory, he would not even know his mother's clan.

Eoghan handed the vellum back to his master, his heart heavy. He had longed for this moment his entire life, and now that it was here, it made no difference. He had still been raised among men in a life he did not choose for himself. He had still been a pawn in others' games. He hadn't the opportunity to know his family, to court a girl, to be married and have his own children someday, all because they had trusted a word of a three-year-old over their desire to protect him themselves.

And how is that any different than the boys coming to Ard Dhaimhin to escape Keondric's army? You said you didn't blame them. You said you would have done the same thing.

That was different.

Because it's you. Because you want to believe you were wronged. Because you do not want to acknowledge that perhaps it was My plans that Liam carried out and not his own.

Eoghan rose, convicted by the sharp words in his mind. "I need some time to think."

Liam returned the stools to their place in the corner. "Come to my study when you're ready to continue. There is more we have to discuss, and our time is growing short."

Eoghan nodded, barely hearing the words. He pushed through the door and strode down the hall.

So perhaps it hadn't been Liam's decision at all. That just left a single, uncomfortable realization.

Comdiu was the one he should have been angry with all along.

CHAPTER
TWENTY-FIVE

Liam noted Riordan's presence before his friend joined him on one of Carraigmór's granite balconies. It was his usual choice when he needed to think over a difficult matter, and he and Riordan had had many conversations here over the years. Usually, though, the Ceannaire gave the advice to Riordan, not the other way around.

"I told him."

Riordan stepped to the railing beside Liam. "How did he take it?"

"He's angry. Disappointed. Expected something more dramatic, perhaps." Liam rubbed his eyes. "I suspect he'd like to go off somewhere to sulk, but he has too much self-respect to be seen doing so."

"I imagine he does. He's an impressive young man. You have done well by him."

"Have I?" Liam wasn't so sure. All these years of treading the road he thought Comdiu had set before him, secure in his justifications for his actions, were crashing down around him. "I lied to him. Or, rather, I allowed him to believe a lie, which is much the same thing."

Riordan was quiet for a moment. "I did the same with Conor."

"Aye, on my direction. It seems I've made many such questionable decisions."

"What is this really about? I've never known you to be so melancholy."

Liam pushed away from the rail and turned his back to the Fíréin city. "The druid is amassing an army. You know this; you saw and heard firsthand how he is conscripting men and boys."

"We will be under siege."

"Aye. And many will die, on both sides. Niall knows that even his trained men cannot stand up to the skill of the Fíréin. He just seeks to throw bodies in our way, the younger the better. If we kill them, the sorcery in their blood is a threat to us. If we take pity on them and let them live, they will find a way to strike at us from the inside. And while we are distracted, he can seek his true objective." Liam crossed his arms over his chest. "The city will fall, and all we have built, all we have protected, will be gone."

"And the victory?"

Liam had to give Riordan credit. To most men, news that their brothers would die and their city would fall would automatically mean defeat. "Comdiu has not shown me that. So much still depends on Eoghan. And Conor."

"What does Conor have to do with this?"

"More than you know. More than I can tell you. His time in Seare is not finished. But I will soon become unnecessary."

Once, Riordan would have tried to reassure him, but they both knew the time for that was past. No matter the outcome, the brotherhood's part in Seare's history was coming to an end.

CHAPTER
TWENTY-SIX

"My lady, everything has been prepared for you."

Aine looked up from her spot at the workbench and gave Guaire a grateful nod. "Thank you, sir. If you'll let the men know I'll be out shortly, I'd appreciate it."

Guaire gave her a little bow. "As you wish, my lady."

Aine watched the steward leave her work room, a smile on her face. Her suspicion that the steward's enthusiasm came from a desire to thwart Lady Macha had continued to grow as Lady Ailís's chamber was emptied of its furnishings and new items more suited to Aine's purpose arrived.

She turned a small circle, her smile widening. Gone were the bed and the wardrobe, in their place a long wooden table along one wall and a tall bank of shelves. The wood bore the bright tan-yellow color of newly split timber, a sign they had been made especially for her, not repurposed from elsewhere in the keep. Bottles and jars lined a few of the shelves, though most were still empty. Buckets of lard, tallow, and beeswax—bases for ointments and salves—waited beneath the bench, and a grated brazier stood in the far corner. The only things she lacked were the herbs that would become her healing remedies.

Aine slid a heavy-bladed knife, equally suited for defense or harvesting, onto her leather belt and then shoved thin fabric sacks and waxed parchments into a satchel. If she remembered the Aronan countryside as well as she thought she did, she would come back with enough herbs to keep herself busy for weeks.

After pulling on a pair of fine leather riding gloves, she slung the satchel over her shoulder and made her way down the corridor to the back door. Her spirits lifted at the prospect of escaping Forrais for a day. Since coming to Aron, a gloom had settled over her spirit like the gray autumn clouds that spread over the Highlands. Ensconced in the keep, it was too easy to shed bitter tears over Conor and feel sorry for herself. A ride—preferably a long one—would do her good.

Diocail himself stood in the courtyard with three men, while a stable boy held a trio of nearly identical chestnut horses and a smaller gray mare. The captain of the guard swept a low bow when she approached.

"Lady Aine, Master Guaire told me you were in need of an escort today."

She blinked. "One man, sir. I hardly expected you to spare three from the watch."

"Volunteers, my lady." That rare smile tilted the corners of his lips. "May I introduce Oisean, Lachaidh, and Roidh?"

Aine nodded to each in turn, noting all were armed with swords and bows and wearing light leather armor. "You look ready for battle. I'd only planned on a day's ride to gather herbs."

"Even so, it pays to be prepared." The glance Lachaidh flicked toward Diocail made her think it was on the captain's orders. "Never fear, the three of us can look after you reasonably well."

"Four."

Aine turned to find Lord Uallas leading a hulking gray gelding from the stable. He offered her a friendly smile and a little bow. When he straightened, the horse nudged him in the shoulder and threw him off balance.

"Easy, Ailpein," he muttered. "First the lady needs to agree."

Aine cast a look at Diocail, who shrugged. "I never turn down an extra sword."

She shifted her attention back to Uallas. Thus far she had only seen him in court attire: silks and embroidered linens, unarmed but for the dagger at his belt. Perhaps she'd even thought him a little soft. In his plain tunic, trews, and leather vest with a long sword on his back, he looked anything but soft. In fact, he reminded her a bit of her brother Calhoun.

Or Conor.

Pain spiked through her and left the niggling trace of guilt in its wake. But that was silly. Surely she had nothing to feel guilty about.

"My lady?" Uallas's careful question made her realize she'd been staring at him. Heat rushed to her cheeks.

"Forgive me, my lord. I was just thinking how much you remind me of my brother."

A self-deprecating smile tilted his lips. "I'm not sure that was the comparison I'd hoped for."

Aine swallowed, and her cheeks burned hotter. "In any case, Lord Uallas, we'd welcome the company."

"Ailpein thanks you, as do I." He grinned at her, and she found herself returning the smile.

The guardsmen took their mounts, and the stable boy led the mare to her side. "This is Banrion, my lady. She's gentle. You should have no fear of her."

Aine hid her smile and gave the boy a somber nod. "Thank

you. I'm sure we will do just fine." Assuming she could coax a canter out of this four-footed dove.

Uallas was at her side in an instant. "Allow me, my lady."

For a second, she held her breath, thinking he meant to lift her atop her mount, but he only knelt and laced his fingers together. She grasped the horse's mane and accepted the leg up and then settled herself atop the horse's blanketed back.

Uallas hovered near the mare's head. "Take care, my lady. I wouldn't want you to swoon the minute she starts into a brisk walk."

The lord's eyes twinkled and Aine repressed her laugh. He returned to his own mount and vaulted atop it with the ease of a natural horseman. She flushed when she realized her attention was verging on admiring and jerked her eyes away. She had done nothing worthy of guilt. So why did merely noting another man's existence feel like a betrayal?

She loved Conor, and she would continue to love him until the day she died. They were meant to be together. How else could she explain the connection she'd felt to him the first time they saw each other in Lisdara's hall, that feeling of destiny? She had been so sure when they left Seare and sealed their union officially aboard the *Resolute* that it would be forever.

What if she'd been wrong?

What if she would spend the rest of her life alone, loving the memory of a man she had been allowed to know for far too short a time?

Lachaidh took the lead from the courtyard through the front gates. Except for a flicker of surprise from Cé, who was again on duty, no one seemed to mark their passing. The guardsmen closed ranks around her, Uallas in the rear, as they made their way down the switchback toward the village below. Once there, they turned northeast and Lachaidh held his horse back to speak with her.

"Where to, my lady?"

"There's a meadow a few minutes north of here that has some plants I need. Let's start there and we'll proceed to the river."

"As you wish."

Aine smiled her thanks. Once they cleared the village, she lifted her face to the sky and inhaled the scent of earth and vegetation. Despite the gray clouds overhead, the fresh air was a balm to her wounded heart. Guaire was right. Having a purpose didn't lessen the pain she felt over Conor, but it gave her the means to live through it. She sifted through her mental list of locations and herbs. If she didn't tarry too long, she would be able to gather all the items on her list and still return in time for supper in the hall. The fact that Macha had not yet commented on her activities said that she either didn't know or didn't care. Whichever it was, Aine preferred to keep it that way.

After about twenty minutes, the rocky hills emptied into a wide, shallow meadow filled with grasses and late-summer flowers. She called a halt and dismounted, then rummaged through the satchel for one of her fabric sacks and her small hand-spade.

Roidh and Lachaidh remained on horseback, but Oisean dismounted and nocked an arrow to his bowstring in readiness.

"Are you expecting an attack?" Aine asked.

Oisean shrugged. "Diocail's orders."

"You cannot blame them, my lady," Uallas murmured at her shoulder. "To lose Lord Alsandair's heir because of carelessness . . ."

"Is that what I am?" Aine took a few long strides into the meadow. Uallas followed.

"Among other things." He matched her pace, checking his sword over his shoulder with a movement that seemed more reflex than conscious action. For some reason, it made her edgy.

She knelt beside a bushy tormentil plant, its trailing stems heavy with yellow flowers, and drew out her spade. Carefully, she dug beneath the plant to remove it from the earth, root and all, and tucked it into the sack.

"Right here?"

She twisted to see Uallas mimicking her motion, his knife poised above the earth like a spade. "You're picking flowers for me?"

"Why? Is gathering herbs not a manly pursuit?"

Aine shrugged. "Most men would think not."

"I'm not most men. Besides, I don't plan to braid them together and wear them as a crown." Uallas grinned at her, but rather than easing her discomfort, it only twisted the knot in her chest tighter. He should not be so likable. She thrust the sack at him before tramping off to another patch of flowers several feet away.

They worked in silence for several minutes. Aine gathered the plants in her overskirt until Uallas held out the sack for her. She emptied her bounty and raised her eyes to his face.

"You miss him."

She didn't need to ask what he meant. She took a step back. "I do."

"As do I. My wife, I mean." He cleared his throat. "I don't mean to make you uncomfortable, Lady Aine."

"You don't."

"I won't insult you by saying I'm just trying to be your friend." That quiet smile surfaced again, and this time Aine thought she caught some sadness behind it. "I don't even presume to know you. But I do know what you must be feeling. I know what it's like to lose someone you love."

Love. Not *loved*. She shot a surprised look at him, noted the tension in his jaw. So his marriage had been a love match too, and he was as far from being over his wife as Aine was from being over Conor. Somehow that made her feel better.

And made her ill at the same time. If she acknowledged that bit of commonality with him, it would be like saying she had given up on her husband. That she was abandoning him.

She touched the wheel charm at her neckline, rubbing her fingers over the smooth ivory. At last she managed to force out, "My husband is still alive, Lord Uallas. I must continue to believe that."

"For your sake, I truly hope you're right."

She gave him a jerky nod and turned back to her work, praying as she harvested. *Please, Comdiu. Bring Conor back to me. And whatever this is with Uallas, let it cease.* She couldn't bear the way he looked at her. She couldn't bear that some part of her enjoyed the attention.

She took the sack from Uallas and stuffed her last handful of flowers into it without looking at him. They trudged back to where the other guards waited, and once more he helped her onto her horse.

"There's a marshy spot near Black Creek that will have meadowsweet and oxterful," she said to Lachaidh. "Do you know it?"

"I do, my lady. There's a pond nearby. My brother and I used to fish there as children."

"You grew up near here?"

"Less than a league away, my lady." The guard dipped his head, seeming almost shy. It was an incongruous expression on such a seasoned face. "Had I known, I would have brought a line."

"And Diocail would have summarily dismissed you." Uallas's tone was light, but his expression was serious. Lachaidh gave a quick nod of acknowledgment and adjusted his reins.

Aine looked between the two of them in confusion. Uallas just gave another smile and mounted up. But when they turned east toward Black Creek, the lord guided his horse alongside hers, so close that their legs nearly brushed.

"You may cease now, my lady," he murmured. "Their allegiance is assured."

"Cease what?"

An impish smile crossed Uallas's face. "Your witchcraft."

"Witchcraft!" The exclamation drew startled looks from the guards. "I don't know what you mean! I'm merely a healer. Gathering herbs—"

"You know very well of what I speak. I cannot blame you, given your lady aunt's dislike of you, but much more and these poor men will be useless for anything but being your lapdogs. And that is counterproductive to your aims, I think."

Aine stiffened atop her mare and threw him a stern look. "I have no idea what you're talking about, Lord Uallas. Speak plainly if you must, but quit your accusations."

"You really don't know, do you?" His gaze took her in much too thoroughly for her comfort. "No. You don't. If you did, it would not work nearly so well."

Aine's heart pounded. She was missing something very important here, but Lord Uallas seemed determined to speak in riddles. "What—?"

"Not here. When we stop, I will explain." He nudged his horse into a trot and rode forward to converse with Lachaidh.

Aine's mind whirled as she tried to figure out Uallas's meaning. He thought she was somehow trying to manipulate the guards to switch their allegiance from Macha to her? Why would she do that? How? She hadn't even asked for these particular guards. She'd expected only one companion when she'd asked Guaire for an escort.

Before she could ponder it further, Lachaidh raised his hand and pointed at the patch of trees clustered along a small, rushing creek. "My lady, we've arrived."

CHAPTER
TWENTY-SEVEN

They reined in their horses near the edge of the forest, and Aine dismounted quickly, desperate for a distraction. She took her entire satchel this time, unsure how many herbs she would gather, but before she could make it more than a few steps, Uallas took the pack from her hand. "Allow me."

Aine nodded and kept walking, aware that he kept pace a half step behind. The guards dismounted with their bows and spread out, keeping a close eye on their surroundings. Their vigilance scraped her nerves raw. Did the men think they might come under attack? Had Aron become so dangerous they feared ambush a mere two or three leagues from Forrais, within sight of the keep's towers?

As soon as they reached the edge of the forest, Aine spun to face Uallas. "Explain."

Uallas lowered himself onto a fallen log, but she remained standing, her arms crossed over her chest. A slight smile twitched at his lips. "Men are drawn to you, my lady."

This was what he wanted to talk about? She waved a hand. "Aye, I know. Alsandair's heir, extensive wealth. No doubt if it were not for the little problem of me being married, Lady Macha would already be flooded with suits for my hand."

"Don't think she isn't already." That hint of humor surfaced again. "You would certainly be an attractive wife for what you brought to the marriage. But that's not what I mean. Men seem to lose themselves around you"—he held up a hand before she could protest—"and not in the way you imagine.

"Look at them out there." He nodded back toward the guards. "They met you this morning, yet they're behaving as though they've devoted their entire lives to your service."

"That's their job," Aine said slowly, but she couldn't deny that their behavior was odd.

"How did you make your way alone to Forrais?"

"I had help. Three mercenaries rescued me and brought me home."

"For what gain?"

"No gain." Hadn't she herself thought that was strange, that the mercenaries had taken her all the way to Forrais? Aye, Taran had said Comdiu had sent him, but he'd been willing to kill a landed lord to protect her secret. Even more telling, he'd given up his plans of revenge for her.

"You're beginning to see now," Uallas said. "Whenever you were in need, someone stepped forward to assist you. To protect you."

Her heart rose into her throat. When she'd mapped the wards on the Siomaigh front, the men had looked upon her as a sister to be protected, despite their commander's fears. Then there had been Lorcan's unflagging devotion from the day she'd taken him into her service. Keondric's sacrifice. Hadn't even Lia noticed how Diocail reacted to her that first day in the practice yard? She sank to the log beside Uallas, her hand grasping at her chest as if it could release the band around it.

"Aine, breathe." Uallas gripped her shoulder and shook her. It snapped her out of her panic and made her suck in a deep breath.

"It's true. I never saw." She raised her eyes to his. "Then you know that what you're feeling is just a product of whatever *this* is."

"There are worse things." He reached out and brushed a strand of hair from her shoulder, then leaned forward the barest degree, as if testing.

Aine jumped up before he could do any more. "No. You mustn't. I don't understand what I'm doing, but I do not mean to give you the impression I would welcome your attentions."

Uallas glanced up at her, repressed laughter playing at the corners of his eyes and mouth. "You don't have that effect on me, my lady. Not since I became aware of it."

That was even worse. He'd almost kissed her because he wanted to, because he wanted to see if she would allow it. "What do I do?"

His amusement faded. "You must be careful. You must learn to control it. Barring that, you must learn to use it wisely. Your aunt already fears you. If she learned you can command men with your very presence—"

"But they only feel compelled to protect me!"

"It would simply take a few words to convince the men that Lady Macha was endangering your life."

He was right. And should Macha think Aine was swaying men to her cause, her life *would* be in danger. The clan chief would not hesitate to strike quickly and directly. Aine pressed her hands to her face. Why was this happening to her? Why had Comdiu given her this gift? Despite the problems it could cause, it was undoubtedly a gift.

Uallas's eyes widened. She twisted and followed his gaze just as something whizzed by her and embedded in the tree trunk behind them. An arrow.

"Get down!" Uallas leapt to his feet and pushed her to the ground, drawing his sword in the same swift movement. Aine hit the dirt hard, knocking the wind from her lungs. Before she could comprehend what was happening, an arrow sprouted from Uallas's chest. He sank slowly to his knees.

"Ambush!" Aine screamed. "Help us!" She pulled Uallas to the ground and threw herself over him, making them as small a target as she could while another arrow sailed over her head. Shouts and footfalls neared, joined by the rapid thrum of bowstrings. Uallas shuddered and gasped beneath her.

"Hold on," she whispered. "Don't you dare die on me now. Not when it's my fault."

Uallas gave a gurgling laugh. "I told you your power doesn't work on me." He coughed, and blood splattered from his lips.

Outside the narrow tunnel of her vision, she heard approaching footfalls. She grabbed for Uallas's fallen sword.

"My lady, it's us. You're safe."

Oisean. Relief flooded her as Lachaidh and Roidh stepped up behind him. "Did you get them?"

"No, my lady." Oisean's expression darkened. "But they're gone now."

Uallas coughed, drawing her attention back to the man on the ground beside her. Unlike the others, he wasn't wearing a breastplate. The arrow protruded from his ribs several inches below his heart, likely puncturing his lungs. A blessing, that, or she wouldn't have time to do anything.

"Help me," she said. "We need to get the arrow out."

Lachaidh knelt beside her and surveyed the location. "He'll bleed to death, my lady. If he doesn't suffocate first."

"Trust me, Lachaidh. I can save him. But you must do what I say. Break the fletching and push it out through the back."

Lachaidh didn't look convinced, but he nodded and gestured to Roidh. "Roll him onto his side." He looked at Uallas. "This is going to hurt."

"Compared to the pleasant sensation right now?" Uallas forced a smile, but by the glassy look in his eyes, Aine could tell he was fading fast. When Roidh rolled him to his side, a pool of blood stained the earth.

"Are you sure about this?" Lachaidh asked.

"He's going to die anyway. Do it, and quickly."

Lachaidh grimaced, but he snapped off the arrow, eliciting a deep groan from Uallas. When he gripped the shaft and forced it out through the back, Uallas screamed.

"Almost over," she whispered, gripping the lord's hand. "You must endure a bit longer."

"It's out." Lachaidh held up the bloody arrow. "If you're going to do something, do it now. He's got a minute, maybe two."

And in a minute or two, my fate at Forrais will be sealed.

Aine gestured for Roidh to lay Uallas back down. Then she stripped off her gloves and laid her hands on his chest, focusing on the wounds. *Close. Heal. Please, Comdiu, don't let him die. Let this work.*

But as seconds ticked by, Uallas's body slackened and his eyes drifted closed. Tears pricked her eyes. She had been too late. "It didn't work. I was so sure . . ."

Then a shuddering breath racked Uallas. His eyes snapped open. "What happened?"

Relief took the strength from her legs, and she thunked to the ground beside him. "You almost died, you foolish man." With trembling fingers, she unbuttoned his jacket and pushed up his shirt. The flesh beneath showed only a faint pink scar.

"Blessed Comdiu," Oisean murmured. "What did you do?"

She didn't look away from Uallas's stunned gaze. "I have more than one gift, my lord."

Uallas's hand gripped hers. "Thank you."

She disentangled her hand and looked at each of the men in turn. She hadn't wanted to use either of her gifts, and now she had been forced to exercise both. So be it. "I don't need to tell you what this means for me. If anyone finds out what happened here, my life will be in danger. You cannot tell anyone."

The men slowly nodded their agreement, though they didn't seem pleased about it.

"Your life is already in danger." Uallas pushed himself to a sitting position and held up the broken end of the arrow, fletched with a familiar feather pattern. Her heart sank in recognition even before he said the words.

"Our ambushers were from Forrais."

CHAPTER
TWENTY-EIGHT

Eoghan trudged toward the meeting place, preparing himself. He hadn't spoken with Liam since the revelation in the Hall of Prophecies, and the Ceannaire had been content to leave him to wrestle with his thoughts in peace.

As had Comdiu. Perhaps the Almighty didn't appreciate that his lowly servant was angry with Him.

Eoghan wasn't angry, though. Not really. It wouldn't do any good if he were. He'd chosen a life at Ard Dhaimhin when he committed himself to the leadership of the brotherhood. He'd taken one possible avenue Comdiu had offered him—to train Conor as his apprentice—knowing full well it meant that his friend would leave the High City in his place.

Apparently Liam had decided Eoghan had sulked long enough, because he'd summoned him to the practice yard where the elder brothers and the Conclave sometimes trained in private. But when Eoghan reached the clearing, he found only Liam, working through his sword drills alone, one impressive form after another.

Conor had been extraordinarily talented, truly. How else could he have gone from a weakling to one of the brotherhood's most skilled warriors in only three years? Even so, watching Liam now, Eoghan knew Conor shouldn't have been able to beat the Ceannaire. Comdiu had surely orchestrated Conor's release from the brotherhood, just as it seemed Comdiu had determined Eoghan would never leave.

Liam turned and broke off his form.

"You summoned me?" Eoghan asked.

Sweating but still breathing easily, Liam nodded and crossed to where several weapons lay on a flat rock. He selected a blunt sword and tossed it to his apprentice.

Eoghan automatically caught it by the grip, the movement pulling at his healing flesh.

"Still in pain?"

"Not much. Well enough to train. Well enough to fight."

"Good. I'm giving you a céad."

Eoghan paused in the middle of an experimental stroke with the sword. "Sir?"

"Only to train. Not to lead. When the battle comes to Carraigmór, I'll expect you to be safely behind walls."

Eoghan lowered the weapon. "I'm no coward, Master Liam. I can fight."

Liam put up his own sword and moved closer. "I know. It is not for your sake that I ask this; it's for the safety of the brotherhood. You remember what I said when I showed you the chamber?"

"Keondric must not be allowed to access it. You think he will try to force you to let him in."

"He will try. He will fail. And then he will not hesitate to torture the name of my successor from the other men. Your identity will not remain secret for long."

"What happens if I'm killed? I haven't chosen a successor yet."

"I don't know," Liam said. "It's never been a question. Perhaps anyone could gain access. Or no one. Either scenario would be just as disastrous as allowing Keondric in. When the fighting starts, I will lock you inside the chamber. It is the only way to be sure you and the Hall remain safe."

Eoghan exhaled a long, heavy breath. "It feels wrong. You taught me never to run from a fight."

"I also taught you to be strategic and think of the larger purpose behind your actions. By protecting yourself, protecting our secrets, you ensure the safety of Seare. Will you do what I ask?"

Obey.

Eoghan closed his eyes for a brief moment. Of course now Comdiu chose to speak to him. He opened his eyes and raised his sword. "I will obey."

"Good. Now let's see how much your loafing has slowed you down."

Eoghan fought a laugh. "You should not test me."

"And you should have less confidence in your youth."

Eoghan's smile broke out at the first ring of metal and then faded again when he thought of the one question he should have asked: "How long do we have until they arrive?"

"I don't know," Liam said, sobering. "I just know they're coming."

✦ ✦ ✦

Eoghan moved toward the practice yard where he was to meet his new céad, adjusting the buckle of the sword baldric he had checked out from the armory. Before, the céads had been arranged by age and ability for younger boys, by skill set and function for full brothers. Since Riordan had returned with news of Keondric's mounting army, however, the Conclave had begun reassigning men into fighting units under battle captains. What that meant for Eoghan's céad, considering he had been forbidden to fight, he didn't know. He had just been instructed to evaluate his céad's readiness and bring up weak skills as quickly as possible.

As he entered the training yard where his hundred men gathered, Eoghan faltered. They were boys, not men. The oldest couldn't have seen more than fourteen years, the youngest perhaps ten or eleven. Faces turned toward him, expectant, waiting for orders. These boys, too young to be sent out on patrol or trusted with guard duty at the fortress, would now be called upon to fight, perhaps die. Even worse, they might be required to kill boys even younger than themselves. Was this what the brotherhood had been reduced to? Sending boys to do a man's job?

No, this was not Liam's choice. It was Niall's or Keondric's or whatever he chose to call himself at the moment. The druid would not hesitate to kill the young ones.

Hence Eoghan's charge to ensure their readiness for battle.

Pushing down his creeping sense of sickness, he faced them and made his expression stern. "I am Brother Eoghan, your new céad leader. You will show me what you've learned. Positions."

Instantly the boys spaced themselves with military precision, practice swords in hand.

"First form," he barked, and they simultaneously took the first position.

His eyebrows arched upward in surprise. They were young, not particularly strong, but they were well-trained, even by Fírein standards. He was obviously not taking over an existing céad as he thought but rather one that had been newly formed of the most talented novices and young apprentices.

Eoghan took them through their sword drills at a fast clip, pushing them, looking for weaknesses. By the time he broke them into pairs, his pessimism had faded some. Young they might be, but they possessed a gravity, a maturity, that made him think they had spent most of their lives at Ard Dhaimhin.

He wove through the group as they sparred with their wooden swords, making minor corrections. He stopped beside a pair to watch the smaller of the two. At first glance, Eoghan had dismissed the redheaded boy as the youngest and weakest of the group. Now he saw he handled the sword with the ease of a much older student.

They disengaged and stepped back when Eoghan approached.

Eoghan directed his attention to the younger one. "What is your name, boy?"

"Breann, my lord . . . I mean, sir."

"My lord? You were raised in the kingdoms."

"Aye, my l—sir. Faolán."

"How long have you been here?"

"Two months and a bit, sir."

"What's your clan name?"

"I have renounced my clan ties, sir. I am sworn to the brotherhood now."

Eoghan studied Breann for a moment. Educated, certainly, and with a good grasp of the politics of such a place, even if Ard Dhaimhin differed from the kingdoms. He was clearly a bright boy.

"Very well, Breann. It's clear you have been trained. Care to have a go with me?"

A cautious smile spread over his face. "Aye, sir."

"Your guard."

Breann moved into a respectable guard position while Eoghan drew his sword. The boy's eyes darted to the weapon's sharpened edge and then returned to his eyes. Good. He wouldn't freeze when faced with the real thing. Of course he also trusted that Eoghan, his instructor, wouldn't harm him.

Eoghan started slowly, and the boy met each strike confidently, countering with ease. Eoghan continued to trade strikes and parries, gradually increasing the pressure until the boy was working harder and harder to keep up. Then, in one swift movement, he disarmed the boy and set the flat of his sword against his neck.

"Well done, Breann."

"I lost, sir. I would be dead now."

Eoghan withdrew his blade and looked at the students who had gathered around them to watch. "This is no longer play, boys. There will come a time when you will be facing a man with a real sword who wants nothing more than to kill you."

Their expressions sobered and a few shifted uncomfortably. "You are young. You do not yet have a man's strength. That means you must use what you have: energy, speed, intelligence. You must be smarter than your opponent."

"How do we do that?" one of the younger boys asked.

Eoghan smiled and looked from face to face. He had them now. "I will teach you."

CHAPTER
TWENTY-NINE

They might have been young, but Eoghan's boys attacked their training with enthusiasm. Perhaps it was because he had trained Conor, who was already something of a legend among the younger brothers, a symbol of what hard work could accomplish. Or maybe it was because Eoghan treated them like men. Whatever the reason, they obeyed him unquestioningly, no matter how hard he pushed them.

The same sort of urgency he'd felt with Conor crept into the teaching of his céad, just magnified a hundredfold. He sought every edge he could give them over the enemy, bringing in some of the older brothers to give them a taste of a real fight. He dispensed with the open battlefield tactics as soon as he was sure they were reasonably proficient, teaching them instead how to use their smaller size and speed to their advantage. He taught strikes to disable their opponents: tendons, major arteries. He attempted to teach them ways to minimize exposure to their enemies' infected blood, but how did one fight with swords without getting bloodied?

That brought him to the discussion he dreaded, even though

it was essential. Talk had been rippling through the city ever
since Liam had announced that the Fíréin must ready themselves
for battle.

Eoghan gathered his céad together in the stone amphitheater.
A hundred pairs of earnest eyes stared back at him, but it was
Breann's, too old and wise for his age, that made him look away.

"You've no doubt heard the rumors about what we face. Lord
Keondric has turned his eye toward Ard Dhaimhin, and he commands more than eight thousand men."

"One Fíréin warrior is worth five of the kingdom's," one of the
older boys called, his newly deepening voice laced with bravado.

Eoghan smiled. "That is certainly true. Yet they have a more
dangerous weapon at their disposal. Keondric controls his men
by sorcery, a dark magic that lives in the blood."

"So their blood is a threat to us?" Breann asked quietly. "How
do we avoid it?"

"The best you can." Eoghan hesitated. "You must understand: no matter how well we fight, we may still lose men to the
sorcery. Some may be strong enough to resist it; some may not."

Breann looked at him. "And if we aren't?"

He knew. The boy was prompting Eoghan along, trying to
make it easier. How had an eleven-year-old gotten so wise?

"If you are infected, and you will know if you are"—Eoghan
hoped so, at least—"the honorable thing to do is turn your blade
on yourself before you can betray your brothers or infect those
around you."

Not a whisper moved through the group. Some looked at
him aghast. Others had tears in their eyes, though they held
them back for fear of looking weak. He didn't blame them. It
was one thing to die in battle. It was another to be defeated
by a foe against which you couldn't defend, to die by your
own sword.

"And if they won't do what needs to be done?" The older boy asked, the bravado gone. "What then?"

"If they act as an enemy, they must be treated as an enemy."

Eoghan delivered the words quietly, but they still jolted through the gathering like a shout. The boys looked at one another, wondering if they would be called upon to kill someone with whom they had lived and trained for years.

"Archers," Breann said.

All heads snapped around, and Breann looked startled. "Doesn't it stand to reason we'd be best using our archers, keep them at a distance? We've some good bowmen in this céad."

Eoghan nodded. The same idea had been discussed by the Conclave. The sentries and trackers would eliminate as many as they could when the druid's army breached the borders, relying on their fading ability and stealth. Archers would attempt to decimate their numbers before they broke free of the trees into the city itself. Perhaps an obvious plan, but he was impressed by the young boy's strategic ability. He certainly hadn't been that aware at Breann's age.

"You will be assigned to guard the storehouses. If he's smart, Lord Keondric will target the things we require to live separately and independently." Eoghan was sharing far more than he should, but if he was asking them to lay down their lives in service to the brotherhood, they deserved to understand why. "Our crops, our granaries, our animals. The flax we grow for our clothing. These things keep us from dependence on the outside world. It is more important than ever that we maintain our livelihood."

"We will not let the enemy destroy them, sir," one of the boys called from the back. "Will we?"

A chorus of agreement went up. Even though his heart was heavy, Eoghan smiled. "Good lads. Now take the session off to rest and I will see you at archery. I expect a good showing from you lot."

The boys exchanged smiles as they dispersed, far more enthusiastic about the discipline than usual. It was a solid plan, but considering the numbers they would face, it would almost certainly come down to close combat.

That night at supper, Riordan slid onto the bench across from Eoghan and folded his arms on top of the table. "What do you think of your céad?"

Eoghan looked toward his boys, scattered among the tables near the cookhouse, and his stomach clenched once more.

"I think we have a fair bit of work ahead of us. Is this what it's like to be a parent? This queasy feeling of responsibility?"

Riordan chuckled. "In a sense. They've got potential, you think?"

"Aye. Some talented swordsmen in the group. I wish I could be assured they'll live to reach that potential."

"If anyone can see them through, it's you. What you did with Conor—"

"Has far more to do with Conor than me. Comdiu had plans for him." Eoghan glanced up at Riordan. "What are the chances any of us will live through this? That there will be an Ard Dhaimhin left if we do?"

Riordan placed a hand on his shoulder and then disappeared back into the crowd. Eoghan looked back at his boys. The brother's silence said enough.

CHAPTER
THIRTY

A knock rattled Aine's workshop door a split second before it opened.

"Lady Aine, we must talk."

She didn't pause in her work, though the voice caused a ripple of disquiet through her body. "Lord Uallas, you should not be here alone. *We* should not be here alone."

"In this case, my lady, I disagree."

Aine sighed and set the pestle into the mortar before she turned. Lord Uallas stood by the door, dressed once more in his court attire, his bearing erect, even regal. Nothing to hint that he had taken an arrow meant for her only two weeks before.

"How is the wound, my lord? Any more pain?"

He took a step toward her. "As if it never happened. Which, for our purposes, I supposed it never did. Though it was difficult to convince my manservant of five years he'd simply missed two scars."

Aine grimaced. "Does he suspect anything?"

"He suspects that perhaps I've been dueling without his knowledge. But does he suspect what actually happened? No."

She sank back against her workbench. "Thank you, my lord. These matters are not easy to keep secret."

"No. They're not. That's why I'm concerned for your safety. By your own insistence, we cannot investigate the ambush without admitting what happened afterward. But there is at least one person at Forrais who wants you dead, and that person saw me fall with an arrow to the chest. Yet, here I am, walking about with no indication of injury. If you think that doesn't raise questions . . ."

She had known it would. She'd thought of little else in the two weeks since the incident. "What do you propose we do about that, my lord?"

"You must leave Forrais."

"I've just received Macha's permission to begin seeing patients. You don't think it would be suspicious if I suddenly felt the urge to leave Forrais?"

"Not if you were to marry me."

Aine lifted a hand to her forehead, feeling dizzy. "I am a married woman already, my lord."

"Not by the laws of Aron. I took the liberty of consulting your aunt's lawyers. Handfasted marriages are legal only when performed by a member of the clergy and witnessed by another of equal status."

"And in Seare, members of the Fíréin brotherhood are granted the rights of clergy, which makes my marriage perfectly legal."

"In Seare only." Uallas bowed his head. "Forgive me, my lady. I do not mean to argue that your marriage was not valid before Comdiu. I do not ask you to forget your husband. But surely you can understand that your aunt wishes to see you married, and there is no legal impediment to doing so."

Aine struggled for breath and pressed her hands against her

suddenly flushed face. "Why are you doing this? Why are you so determined to marry me?"

Lord Uallas closed the space between them and took her hand. "Aine, I fear for you. I want to protect you. I also have a young son who needs me, who needs a mother. And if what Lady Macha says is true, if you are indeed carrying a child, that child will need a father. Would you have him branded a bastard?"

Aine flinched at the moniker and looked away. Had she not feared that very thing? Not for her sake, but for the child's?

Uallas seemed to take that as affirmation. He brought her hand to his chest, spreading her fingers over his heart. It beat steadily, if a little too fast. Her own heart sped to match it as his warmth crept into her palm. "I will not speak words of love, but I believe that will come in time, my lady. I offer you safety. Security. A home. If you carry a child now, I will gladly give him a name and an inheritance."

Everything he said made sense. It was perfectly respectable, perfectly obvious. Then why couldn't she breathe? Why did the light seem just a little too bright? On the edge of panic, her question came out too harshly. "And what do you expect in return, my lord?"

"That you treat my son as your own. That, Comdiu willing, we have more children. And that you use your gift on behalf of the people of Eilean Buidhe."

Her eyes found his immediately. "My lord?"

"Unlike Lady Macha, I do not see that as a fault. Life is hard on the islands, harder than the Highlands at times. It eases my mind to know that perhaps we will not have to bury our own children before their time. Do you not want that same thing?"

"Of course I do."

Uallas lifted her hand where it still rested on his chest and brought it to his lips. "I truly believe we will grow to love each other. But in the meantime, a marriage based on respect and mutual need is not a sin. Consider my offer, Aine. Will you at least do that?"

Her thoughts were spinning too fast to make sense of his question. Mutely, she nodded again. He let her fingers slip from his and gave her a deep bow. "I'll let you get back to work, then. But consider quickly, my lady. I must leave in a fortnight or I won't make it back before the autumn snows begin."

Uallas let himself out of the work room. As soon as the door closed, Aine sank onto her stool.

What was she going to do? Everything Uallas said sounded right. She was not foolish enough to believe she would be safe at Forrais for much longer, nor that she could escape marrying indefinitely. The lord of Eilean Buidhe would make a fine husband. He was handsome, kind, protective. He made her smile. He did not seem upset at the idea she might be carrying another man's child. And he saw her healing ability not as witchcraft but as a gift to the people of his clan. What more could a woman ask for in a match?

Would you abandon your love for Conor that quickly? What if he's coming to you? It would take months to make his way north on foot. Would you have him arrive to find out that you'd married another man in his absence? Could you survive knowing he still lived and you couldn't be together? Could he survive?

Aine's fingers went to the charm at her neck. She lifted the ivory to her lips, willing it to warm as it once had when she thought of him. She remembered how she had promised to keep it for him until he returned.

No. She could do nothing if there were the faintest possibility he still lived. She would wait.

Now it was just a question of who would reach her first: Conor or the person who wanted her dead.

CHAPTER
THIRTY-ONE

At Cwmmaen, Conor slowly regained his strength, doing little besides eating and sleeping. Talfryn seemed not to be suffering any ill effects from his captivity; most mornings when Conor arrived in the hall, the prince was already gone. Instead, Briallu kept him company at the table, entertaining him with stories that she deemed particularly Gwynn. Despite the fact she never did anything that could be construed as improper, there was something about her manner that made him uncomfortable, something that signaled she looked on him as far more than just her father's guest.

"You haven't yet left the fortress," she said one morning. "You must be in need of fresh air. Come ride with me."

Conor smiled gently. "Thank you, Briallu. You know that I cannot."

She cocked her head. "Perhaps customs are different in Seare. It's improper for a woman to be escorted alone by an unmarried man, but a married man is considered a suitable chaperone."

"Customs *are* different in Seare. Even married men are not considered immune from temptation."

"So I'm a temptation?" Briallu gave him a flirtatious smile. "I'm flattered, my lord."

Conor shook his head. If she flirted as shamelessly with the other men in the fortress, she was asking for trouble. The way she smiled at him made him think she was offering more than just a pleasant morning ride.

Her smile faded. "Surely your wife had a guardsman. Were you concerned he had designs on her?"

That idea was ridiculous. Aine had inherited Ruarc's service from her mother, and he had looked on her like a father, not a potential suitor. Ruarc had loved her, though, enough to die defending her.

"You see I'm right," Briallu said. "My father will not allow me to leave the fortress without an escort, but his warriors are either so afraid I'll be hurt under their watch that they won't let me ride faster than a crawl or they're trying to better their position by wooing me. The fact you're already married is a relief. You see, Conor, unlike most women of my position, I have no interest in being married myself. What sort of man do you think would give me free rein in the armory once I was his wife?" The mischievous glint returned to her expression.

His better judgment warred with his desire for a change of scenery. "If you promise not to get yourself killed under *my* watch. And if we're back in plenty of time for supper. I don't want to anger your father or all those warriors who think they might win your hand."

She popped up from the bench with a brilliant smile. "I promise. Go have the stable hands ready our mounts, and I'll change into something more suitable."

This may not have been my best decision.

Conor drained the bitter remainder of his tea, stopped by

his chamber to retrieve his weapons, and headed to the stables, where the prince's collection of fine horseflesh was displayed.

"Lady Briallu wishes a ride," he told the stable boy.

The boy grinned at him. "I hope you are a good rider, sir."

"I am." Inwardly, though, he again wondered if he hadn't made a mistake. Perhaps there was a reason Talfryn's warriors insisted she ride at a sedate, ladylike pace.

Briallu arrived moments later, dressed in a wool and silk gown. Unlike her other dresses, which tended to show off most of her neck and shoulders, this one was modest and covered every last inch of skin. Or so he thought until she mounted. It was not a gown after all but a skirt split front and back, worn over a pair of leggings that showed off every contour of her shapely legs.

She arranged the pieces so it appeared to be a dress again and fixed a challenging look on him. "Lord Conor, I do believe you're staring. That is hardly proper for a married man."

Conor jerked his eyes away and mounted his horse without a word. Now he knew he had made a mistake.

Despite his earlier concerns, Briallu kept her mount to a sedate walk through the gates and out into the surrounding country-side. The Gwynn landscape was not unlike his native Seare: forest interspersed with meadow. The promise of fall lingered in the breeze, and a layer of dew sparkled on the grasses in the morning sun. Conor forced himself to relax and filled his lungs full of the sweet smells of nature.

"I knew you needed to escape the fortress," Briallu said. "I get restless within stone walls. How can anyone stay inside when there is all this beauty to be revealed?"

"Your father wishes you to be safe. You can't fault him. In a family of sons, naturally he would dote on his only daughter."

"And yet he raised me as a man," she shot back. "I trained

with the boys in the yard until I came of marriageable age and it was deemed unseemly. If you ask me, it is far more seemly and necessary for a woman of marriageable age to be able to defend her honor with a blade."

"Indeed." Conor couldn't keep his mind from drifting to Aine again. She was by no means weak, but even on the battle-field she had been protected.

"You worry about her. Your wife, I mean."

He nodded.

"You know, we women are stronger than you think. Resource-ful. We find a way to survive. As long as we are women, we have weapons."

"That doesn't reassure me. I don't want her to just survive. I want her to survive unharmed."

"And what if she's been forced to do things in order to sur-vive? What then?"

Conor swallowed hard. He didn't want to think about what she suggested. He would not. Aine would never sacrifice her principles to live.

As if Briallu knew his thoughts, she said, "The will to live is surprisingly strong, Conor. It's something you must think about. If you can't reconcile her instinct for survival with her desire to be yours and yours alone, then you don't deserve her."

A sick feeling crept into Conor's center. "Perhaps this was a mistake. I should take you back."

Briallu reined in abruptly. Her chin dropped to her chest, and her eyes closed. "I'm sorry. I didn't mean to upset you. It's just . . . you haven't been there to protect her. There is a reason why my father will not let me leave without an escort, you know. It's not simply a matter of propriety. You want to find her alive, but you may not find her the same woman you left."

Please, Comdiu, spare her that at least. Let her be alive, and unharmed. I couldn't bear . . .

Bear what? For her to be hurt? Or to know she had been hurt in such a way?

"Forgive me," Briallu said. "I say what I think. I am told it's my greatest fault. I just wanted you to be prepared. If you find her, she will need you more than ever."

"When I find her," he corrected.

"Aye, of course. When you find her. Now look ahead. Do you see those trees up there?"

"What about them?"

"I bet I can get there before you can!" With that, she dug her heels into her horse, and her mount charged ahead several lengths before Conor figured out he had been tricked and gave chase. He leaned forward and urged more speed from his mount, but Briallu was a good rider and managed to beat him to the trees. When he pulled up beside her, she was out of breath and laughing.

"You cheat!" he said.

"It's not my fault if you don't have my reflexes. Some warrior."

"So now you insult me?"

Briallu grinned and dismounted, drawing attention once more to her legs beneath the split skirt. He looked away. "Call it a friendly challenge. Now tie the horses and follow me."

"Aye, my lady." A wry note crept into Conor's voice. It was not just her father she was used to wrapping around her finger.

He tied the horses' reins to a low-hanging branch and followed her into the cluster of trees. The stony stream bank slowed his progress, but Briallu scrambled over the rocks without a care for the shifting foundation beneath. At last she stopped at a spot where a fallen log had created a pool, just barely fed by the trickle of water from the main stream. Its glassy surface reflected them side by side, lit by the dappled sunlight that seeped through the trees overhead.

"This is my favorite spot," Briallu said. "There's been something I've been wanting to try, but I didn't have a good reason to attempt it. Do you believe in magic, Conor?"

He nodded. He had seen too much, experienced too much, *done* too much himself not to. But something told him they were not talking about the same sort of magic.

Briallu settled herself onto a mossy rock at the edge of the pool and dipped her finger in. Concentric circles spread across the surface. "What is your wife's name?"

"Aine."

"Aine. Good. Now you must be quiet." Briallu closed her eyes and put her hands in her lap.

"What are you—"

"Shhh, don't disturb me."

Conor shut his mouth. Seconds passed, then minutes, as Briallu sat silently at the edge of the pool. Then, abruptly, the reflection shimmered as if disturbed by wind, even though the day was still. The ripples moved to the outer edges of the pool, revealing a still image once more.

Except it wasn't a reflection of their faces and sun-dappled trees.

The pond showed a late-summer landscape, patchy heather clinging to rocky hills beneath a deep gray sky. It was an unfamiliar scene that was neither Seare nor Gwydden.

Foreboding shuddered through Conor. "No!" He picked up a rock and heaved it into the center of the pond. The image vanished in a splash.

Briallu scrambled upright. "Why did you do that?"

"You . . . you can't . . ." Words failed him, and he strode from the trees.

She had been scrying. It was magic, all right, but the dark kind, forbidden. Men were led astray by such magic, driven to despair or false hope. There was a reason the Balians preached against it.

Conor stood by his horse, his head pressed against the mare's withers while his heart returned to normal. A light hand pressed against his back. He flinched.

"Forgive me," Briallu said. "I only meant to do you a kindness."

She looked appropriately contrite, her expression pleading. He relaxed. What had she really done? Aye, she was dabbling in forbidden magic, but perhaps she had fallen into it innocently. After all, she had been trying to show him Aine.

"Is she alive?" Conor asked, not daring more than a whisper.

"I don't know. You saw the same thing I did. If I tried again—"

"No!" He grabbed both her hands. "Briallu, you must not do that again. Not for me, not for anybody. It is forbidden to Balians in Seare for a reason. It may seem innocent now, but it will lead you places you do not wish to go. I know this as surely as I know anything."

Briallu looked down at their joined hands, then up into his face. A spark flared between them, that same flash of wildfire he had felt on their first meeting. He dropped her hands and turned away. "We should be going back now."

He expected her to walk away, but instead she put her hand on his arm. "Conor, I would not have tried that if I wanted you for myself. I know your heart belongs to another."

He couldn't look at her. He gave a terse nod and waited for her to remove her hand, then levered himself atop his mount.

They didn't speak on the way back, and he glanced her way only to ensure she was following. His gut twisted, guilt seeping into him, even though he hadn't done anything worth feeling guilty about. He had not asked for her attention. He was not pursuing it.

Yet you rode out with her, knowing full well the way she looks at you, knowing what you feel when you look at her.

He loved his wife. And he was a fool. Those two facts were not in question. He needed to find Aine and go back to Seare before his common sense deserted him completely.

CHAPTER THIRTY-TWO

The sound of horns jolted Eoghan from a deep sleep. For a moment, he lay still, trying to reconcile the sound of the city's wake-up call with the darkness still visible through the hole in the clochan's roof. Then he realized it was not the sounding horn at all but rather the carnyx, which was used to signal only one thing.

War.

Eoghan swung his legs from the shelf bed and lit the torch. The fire whooshed to life, scattering its orange light over the boys, most of whom were blinking sleepily, confused by the early rousing.

"Up and in your clothes, lads." Eoghan kept his voice steady, though his heart was knocking against his ribs. "Quickly now."

"It's time, then?" Breann asked. He'd come to be the unofficial spokesman for the céad.

"It's time." Eoghan went to the chest that held his personal belongings. His sword went on his back, dagger and hand stones at his belt, another knife in the sheath strapped to his calf. The boys would receive their swords and knives at the armory. The older céads had been assigned weapons long ago, but his group had been deemed too young.

The irony grated on him. Too young to be trusted with unsecured weapons, but old enough to die with them in hand.

He shook off the black thought as the boys finished dressing and formed a line in the large open area of the clochan. "Bhris, take the lead."

One of the older boys stepped to the front and led the line up the steps that emptied out of the beehive-shaped dwelling. Eoghan brought up the rear, the unaccustomed tang of fear on his tongue. Not for himself—after all, he would be safe at Carraigmór behind a magically sealed door—but for these boys he'd come to care about.

As they joined the other céads moving in a steady flow toward the armory, Iomhar fell in beside Eoghan. He was one of Ard Dhaimhin's younger brothers and one of its best swordsmen. "I've been ordered to take command of your céad. Master Liam summons you to the fortress."

Eoghan nodded as if it were a surprise. Liam had insisted that no one but they know his location during the battle, but the idea still chafed. What had he trained for if he ran and hid at the first sign of danger? He had enough confidence to believe he would come out of battle alive.

He does not fear your death but your corruption.

That thought, clearly from Comdiu, made him stumble. When the céad halted in formation near the armory, he moved to their front.

"The Ceannaire has called me to the fortress. I will return when I can. Iomhar is to command you in my absence. Show him how you have made me proud. Look to one another's safety. And do not give up."

Most of the boys looked confused, but they immediately focused on the young swordsman. All except Breann, who just looked at Eoghan with those wise, knowing eyes. Eoghan still felt the boy's gaze as he strode away. Orders or not, he was letting them down, betraying their trust.

Eoghan found his way to the steps of Carraigmór, passing groups of boys heading to the armory, falling behind other groups already armed and making their way to their posts. He frowned. Where were the men? Shouldn't he be seeing someone over the age of fifteen?

And why was the air already heavy with the scent of wood smoke? Had the cookhouse fires been lit early in honor of their abrupt awakening?

He shook his head. It was surreal seeing the peaceful city mobilize under the starlit sky, illuminated only by the orange flare of torches. At least he could see the glow of the rising sun on the far horizon, a sign that dawn was only a few minutes away.

He took the steps up to Carraigmór as rapidly as he dared, slowing in places where the water seeped from the mountain. At the top, the brother on duty waved him in. "Master Liam is on his balcony."

Eoghan nodded. Watching the dispersion of his men, no doubt. He wove through Carraigmór's stone corridors, upward to Liam's study, then out onto one of the narrow granite terraces. The Ceannaire stood at the railing, motionless.

"You called for me?"

Liam didn't turn. "I did. Come."

Eoghan moved to his master's side, smoke assailing his nostrils. He followed Liam's gaze to the east. That was not the glow of sunrise he had seen. It was fire.

"They're burning our cover!" Eoghan's heart lodged in his throat. "The sentries—"

"Recalled last night."

"You knew?"

"I suspected. It's what I would do. Much of our strength is

our ability to strike unexpectedly. If the druid burns the forest, we lose our advantage."

Eoghan stared at the far edge of Seanrós, the billowing smoke lending a hazy orange glow to the horizon. The destruction of those ancient trees made him ill. Even if Ard Dhaimhin remained standing, the barrier that had allowed them to remain separate would be gone.

"What now?" Despair tinged Eoghan's voice. "Wait until they burn the forest to ashes and face them in the city?"

"They think they've hemmed us in, but they have given themselves nowhere to go."

So that was why the city had seemed so empty. Liam must have sent them behind enemy lines to take Niall's forces by surprise.

"You've seen it?"

"I've seen what I need to know to save as many lives as I can. There will be fighting, men lost, no matter what. But we can make the price so dear that Niall will never be able to hold the city."

Kill so many of them that there's not enough left to hold it, he means.

Eoghan had seen blood shed, had let it himself. But by the end of this battle, the city would drown in it.

✦ ✦ ✦

Eoghan paced a triangle from the balcony to the corridor to Liam's study as the sky lightened to a smoky orange dawn. The Ceannaire sat at his desk fully armed, sifting through a stack of tablets.

The city was under siege, and he was worried about reports?

Liam glanced at him. "Calm yourself, Eoghan. What is to be will be. Worrying will not change the outcome."

"That's easy for you to say. You've seen what's to come."

"You think that's easier, do you?" Liam leaned back in his chair. "Believe me, I'd rather not know what I do now."

Eoghan stopped his pacing, struck again by the uneasy feeling that the Ceannaire had seen his own demise. "Might Comdiu be showing you what's to come so you can change it?"

"It doesn't work that way. Not for me." Liam nodded his head toward the chair. "Sit. We still have matters to discuss."

Eoghan lowered himself to the chair.

"Regardless of what happens here in the coming days, Niall will not be defeated, not completely. That I have seen. Conor told you of the harp?"

Slowly, Eoghan nodded. "Aye."

"It still exists. It must." Liam's gaze took on a faraway look, as if he were seeing something beyond this room. "Someone must rebuild the wards. That is what you are to be spared for."

"But I can't rebuild the wards. I haven't the gift."

"But Conor does. And Meallachán. And likely others about whom we don't know."

"So, I'm supposed to find this harp—somewhere in Seare, which is in enemy hands—and then find someone who can use it?"

Liam gave him a spare smile. "Aye."

Eoghan wiped his hands across his face. That easy. *Comdiu, I need Your wisdom. I haven't a clue where to begin.*

Liam stood abruptly and jerked his head toward the window. "It's time now."

Eoghan rushed to the window. The flames were gone, replaced by billowing white smoke as if the entire forest had been doused by an ocean of water. From between the spindly, charred-black remains of massive trees, lines of men emerged.

Ard Dhaimhin was under attack.

CHAPTER
THIRTY-THREE

"Hold steady, men."

Riordan crouched in cover on the rocky hillside, the same rock into which the fortress had been carved. The fire raged more fiercely than any natural fire, consuming acres of trees as if driven by some unseen wind. And then, as abruptly as it began, it stopped.

The sorcery prickled his skin.

Now, as the first group emerged from the tree line, he could feel the magic rolling from them like steam from the surface of hot springs. One mind, a thousand evil tentacles to do its bidding. Cut one off and a hundred more sprang up in its place.

"Ready," Riordan called, and hundreds of bowstrings drew taut, their arrows nocked. A few more steps and their attackers would be in range.

"Loose!"

The archers let the arrows fly, a dark cloud that moved across the sky and then fell upon attackers in eerie silence. The men kept coming, trampling the dead and injured.

"Next volley. Loose!"

The second volley had the same effect as the first: no shields raised, no return fire.

They kept coming.

A sick sense of inevitability crept into Riordan's gut as the archers prepared for the third volley. As they released their arrows once more, the hush suddenly broke with a shout and the clash of metal.

Riordan cast his glance to the east side of the village, where the enemy swarmed from the trees, swords drawn. The Fíréin céads moved methodically to meet them, and across the lake, the first of their men fell.

+ + +

"Quickly now." Liam ushered Eoghan down the corridor to the Hall of Prophecies, their footsteps sharp in the stillness. He spoke the words of entry, which lodged no better in Eoghan's mind than before, and the door swung open.

Eoghan stepped into the passageway and turned to face the Ceannaire. "Master Liam, there must be another way. I can't sit idly by—"

"This is how it must be, for the good of Ard Dhaimhin, for the good of Seare." Liam reached out and clasped Eoghan's forearm, then pulled him close into a tight embrace. "Go with Comdiu, my son. You have made me proud."

Then he shut the door.

Eoghan stared at the back of the door for several moments, his heart beating in his ears.

Protect him, Comdiu. I beg You. Watch over our brothers. Bring them through safely.

Comdiu did not reply.

Eoghan sighed and began the slow descent to the chamber beneath the fortress.

The soft light intensified for a moment when he entered the Hall of Prophecies. He paced the edges of the chamber, looking over the scrolls, folios, and parchments without seeing them. He had no idea how long he walked the perimeter of the room, praying a wordless litany and pushing down the fear that threatened to choke him.

Then, as if directed by a hand outside him, he paused before one particular cubbyhole. Hand shaking, he removed the scroll from its spot and unrolled it.

The Kinslayer shall rise, the Adversary looming treacherous over the bleeding land. Day shall be night, and the mist, unbound, shall wreak evil upon the sons of men.

In that hour alone, the son of Daimhin shall come; wielding the sword and the song, he shall stand against the Kinslayer, binding the power of the sidhe and, for a time, bringing peace.

Eoghan sank back against the wall of shelving, stunned.

The sword and the song.

Did that mean their battle against the druid would be won by both steel and magic? Led by one who possessed skills with both? Would the one who defeated this foe in such a way again rule over Seare?

Eoghan lowered the parchment to his lap, suddenly weak. He should have seen it all along. How blind had he been?

Conor was to be their salvation after all, the one to end the age of the brotherhood and usher in a new era of peace for Seare.

His apprentice. His best friend. The High King.

Who was now far out of their reach.

✦ ✦ ✦

Liam strode away from the Hall of Prophecies, his confident steps at odds with his inner turmoil. Eoghan was angry. Humiliated. Worried.

But at least he'd be safe.

In the main hall, Liam passed the brothers whose sole purpose was to defend the fortress against breach. Not that breaching it would be an easy task. There was only one way in, from a narrow balcony through a narrower doorway at the top of three hundred four stairs flanked by a sheer drop-off to the lake below. No, he was not concerned with Carraigmór being taken by force.

Liam stepped out the front door onto that same balcony. It was guarded by a handful of brothers, while more archers perched on the heights. The sounds of fighting drifted to him, and he moved to the arrow slit in the enclosure's wall to peer down at the battle. Enemy warriors swarmed the city, falling to the Fíréin as soon as they raised weapons. Already he could see the bodies of the combatants, far more invaders than Fíréin, but they kept coming. Plumes of smoke billowed from fires: the thatched roofs of cottages, fields the brotherhood had not been able to defend against flaming arrows.

And in the midst of it all walked Niall in his new body, untouched as if enclosed in a bubble, a sword on his back rather than in his hand. The sorcerer's magic drew Liam's attention like a signal fire. Niall looked his way. He knew Liam was there. And he was coming for him.

Liam pushed himself through the barrier of warriors and started for the steps.

"Sir!" one of the brothers said. "You must stay in the fortress, where it's safe!"

Liam fixed the brother with a steely stare, and the man lowered his eyes. The brother meant well. It was his duty to keep him safe, something he couldn't do if the Ceannaire exposed himself. But it was not safety Liam was after.

Despite himself, his heart thudded in his chest. It had been years since Liam had felt true fear. It sparked along every nerve, hummed in his blood. He traversed the slippery staircase, slowing on the final steps. Niall crossed the last bit of open space and waited for him, his arms clasped behind his back.

"We finally meet." Niall looked him over as if they were not enemies but lords meeting at court. "Your reputation has made me anxious to see you face to face."

"And you, Niall. We may not have met, but you left your mark on the brotherhood. Before you betrayed us to follow the Adversary, that is."

Niall cocked his head, a slight smile lifting his lips. The new host was handsome, young, obviously accustomed to fighting. The sorcerer's mannerisms, on the other hand, didn't suit the image. They were old, calculating. The combination struck Liam as unnatural.

"Dispensing with the pleasantries already? And here I thought we could have a civil discussion, one leader to another."

Liam looked around at the still-raging battle, its sounds muted as if heard from a distance. So he was inside Niall's protective bubble. No help would be coming for him. Not that Liam sought help. He knew how this would end. He had seen how it must.

"There is nothing to discuss," he said finally. "You come as an invader, killing my men, destroying our livelihood. There will be no peace between us."

"I would say your men are doing most of the killing." As if to punctuate the druid's words, a boy, no more than fifteen or sixteen, fell at their feet, his eyes gazing sightlessly to the sky, red spreading across his chest. Untrained and barely armed, he hadn't stood a chance against the Fírein brother who felled him.

"This can all end if you say the word. I don't want the city. I don't want the throne. I only want the sword."

The sword? He could only be referring to Daimhin's sword,

the oath-binding sword. What did he want with such a relic? Regardless, Liam would never give in to his demands. "You shall never have the sword."

"I feared you would say that." Niall lifted a hand, and the cottage nearest them went up in a column of blue flame. "I will take apart your city, bit by bit, until I get what I want. You want to protect your men, your way of life? There is only one way." He looked farther afield, and the timbered roof of the bathhouse roared with fire. "This costs me nothing, Liam. I will destroy your city around you. How do you think you will support these men without your fields? Your animals? Your lake?"

Liam followed Niall's gaze. Steam poured in a shimmering cloud from the water, bubbles breaking the surface like a giant cauldron. Within seconds, dead fish began bobbing to the top.

"Why do you want the sword?" Liam asked, buying time while he thought.

Niall shook his head. "No. I won't make your decision that easy. Give me what I want or your way of life is gone. The age of the brotherhood is over."

The age of the brotherhood is already over. Liam reached over his shoulder and drew his sword from the sheath on his back. "Let us see if you remember your training, Niall."

The sorcerer chuckled but made no move to draw his own weapon. "I confess, I've wanted to try this body against you. After a century of living within old men and fools, it's pleasant to be young again. Fit. Keondric was quite the warrior, up until the time that I killed him. Then he was just another fool."

If Niall would not fight, that would make Liam's job that much easier. Lightning fast, he struck at the sorcerer. His sword caught in midair, an inch from Niall's neck.

The sorcerer lifted an eyebrow. "Most unworthy of you, Liam, to strike an unarmed man."

Liam pulled back the sword and thrust it toward Niall's body, jolting to a stop as if he'd tried to pierce a stone wall.

"You see now how you can never win." Niall crossed his arms over his chest. "Did you never wonder why I left the brotherhood? Why I sought the power of the one you call the Adversary?"

"Because you were weak," Liam growled. "Corruptible."

"I was weak. But not in the way you mean. Gracious Comdiu, in all his wisdom, chose to give us his most useless gifts. Prophecy? Music? Sight?" Niall laughed, a tinge of bitterness in the sound. "Suited for weak-minded men who want to stay safely locked away behind strong walls. No way to defend themselves against the spirits who wished to claim the island for themselves. Ah, but you haven't read Daimhin's accounts of those days, have you? There's a reason I destroyed them. Back then, the sidhe roamed freely. Terrorized indiscriminately. Turned men to their vicious appetites."

"And now you have freed them."

"Aye. I have freed them. But they are under *my* command. That is where the real power lies. Not in your passive, weak Balian magic. Not in the pathetic little parlor tricks you like to call gifts. I control the elements, the spirits, all that we see before us."

"No," Liam said. "Your magic controls you. And when the Adversary no longer has use for you, he will devour you."

"I am not going to convince you to join me, I see. I had hoped . . ." Niall shook his head. "Never mind. Your incessant whining would become tiresome. This is your last chance, Liam, Ceannaire of the Fíréin brotherhood. Give me the sword."

The command in the words wrapped itself around Liam's will, and the smallest part of himself stretched to answer: *Aye, I will give you the sword.* He forced it down and sheathed his blade.

Niall smiled. "Aye. That's right. Do not resist me. Give me the sword, and the rest of your men shall live. The brotherhood can be what it once was, and you can be ruler of your own little kingdom."

The seductive power of the druid's words wormed into Liam's heart, urging him to give in. He could not beat him. He could do only one thing to save his men.

Liam eased his dagger from his waist.

"Where have you hidden it? The Hall of Prophecies?" He peered into Liam's eyes and must have seen the truth there. "Good. I would have done the same thing. It's the only truly secure place in the entire fortress. Even I have not mastered the magic that made it, though I have long tried."

"What do you want it for?" Liam stared into Niall's eyes as if mesmerized.

"Do not concern yourself with that. I have said that Ard Dhaimhin will remain safe, and so it shall." His eyes flicked to the dagger, and the satisfaction slipped from his expression. "You have already seen you cannot touch me. And I can feel the desire in you. For what I offer. For power. For the strength to rule."

"Aye," Liam said quietly. "Even I feel the pull of your magic. But this is not meant for you."

In one swift movement, Liam turned the weapon on himself and plunged the blade between his ribs into his heart. Pain like he'd never known burst through him, radiating through his limbs, stealing his breath, his strength. He sank on suddenly numb legs to the ground.

"No!" Niall howled. "You stupid, small-minded man!"

Liam couldn't breathe. He couldn't move. The life ebbed from him along with the blood that soaked the front of his tunic and ran to the ground. The world slipped sideways, growing increasingly dim but for one sharp pinprick of light in his vision.

Forgive me, my Lord. I am coming to You.

The light winked out.

✦ ✦ ✦

They just kept coming. Riordan pulled his sword free in time to turn and meet another. A single crossways slash and his opponent was on the ground. He pushed down his revulsion and sorrow as he moved past the body, just another piled at the tree line, and met the next onslaught.

The next opponent wielded his spear with rudimentary skill. Riordan raised his eyes long enough to see his enemy's face. It was not a man but a boy, not even mature enough to shave the few scraggly whiskers on his jaw. Riordan parried the spear thrust easily.

"Don't do this," he said. "This is not your fight. Turn and go home to your mother, to your farm."

He might as well have been talking to stone. Nothing in the boy's face indicated understanding, the glassy-eyed expression telling Riordan he was in the grip of sorcery. He made another awkward thrust with the spear.

Riordan delivered a sharp strike with the flat of his blade to the boy's hand and used his other to yank the weapon away from him. "Go home. I don't want to kill you."

He began to turn away, when the boy uttered a cry and rushed forward, throwing himself at him with the fury of a wounded animal. Riordan sidestepped, drew back his fist, and landed a solid punch to the boy's jaw. The opponent, if he could call him that, went down, unconscious before he hit the ground.

Riordan stared at his hand, for a second mesmerized by the smear of blood across his knuckles. His own?

The chill of sorcery rippled across his skin, searching, seeking. No. He couldn't become infected. He dropped the spear and sprinted toward the lake, only a few dozen strides away, cutting down opponents in his way. His arm was numb to the elbow, his lungs frozen with panic. He fell to his knees and plunged his hands into the frigid water.

Except it wasn't cold. Riordan jerked his arms free with a howl. Had the sorcery taken him already? Was it toying with his senses, making him think cold was hot? He scrambled back from the edge and rose to his feet, staring at the flushed red skin on his arms, already beginning to blister as if he'd thrust them into a cauldron of boiling water.

The pain came a moment later, delayed: fire licking his skin, glazing his vision, making him want to crumple into a heap at the water's edge. He'd been beaten, stabbed, had bones broken, but nothing compared to this searing agony. Only then did he see the bubbles that roiled the water, the fish bobbing lifelessly on the surface.

No wonder it felt as if he'd washed in a cauldron. The lake *was* a cauldron.

In his pain-fogged state, Riordan only then realized the seeking presence of the sorcery was gone. He heaved a sigh of relief that turned into a groan. He couldn't fight like this. He could barely curl his blistering hand into a fist, let alone grip a sword with any semblance of strength. Still, he forced himself to pick it up and return it to the sheath on his back. What did he do now? Stay and die with his men because he couldn't defend himself, or return to Carraigmór like a coward?

He cast his eyes to the fortress steps as if the answer were written there. Then he froze. He could barely see the man through the smoke that billowed from fires in the village, but he could feel the dark magic emanating from him. The druid.

"Archers! The stairs!"

Two of the archers still concealed in the rocks rose to their feet and turned in the direction he pointed, confusion written plain on their faces. "Where?"

"There!" It was no use. They couldn't see him. Riordan's gift must have rendered him immune to whatever magic the druid was using for concealment.

He rushed to the archers' side and took the bow from one, barely biting back a scream at the pressure of the wood against his blistered hand. He swayed as he nocked an arrow and drew back the string. *Hold it together a moment more. You must not miss.* He took aim, not daring to even breathe, and loosed the arrow. It flew straight and true, seeming to hang in the air when it struck its target. The druid grabbed at the shaft that protruded from his shoulder and stumbled back against the wall.

The archers looked between Riordan and the druid, wide-eyed, apparently now able to see what they earlier had not.

"Brother Riordan?" one asked in concern, taking the bow from his hand.

The wood ripped a layer of burned skin from his palm. Riordan screamed in agony, and the world shattered around him.

CHAPTER
THIRTY-FOUR

At some point during his confinement, Eoghan slept, slumped against the wall between a stool and a wooden rack that held scrolls in languages he couldn't even identify. He awoke what could have been minutes or hours later to the faint sound of voices in the corridor above his hiding place.

His hiding place. Even the words in his mind made him burn with shame. Men were fighting, dying outside, and he was cowering in the corner of a hidden room like a child.

". . . him to his study!" A muffled voice rose above the rest. It must have been a shout to penetrate through the countless spans of rock. Eoghan rose. Was it Master Liam? Was he wounded?

Eoghan paced the room while he debated. He had been given strict orders to stay here until the battle was over or Liam retrieved him. But there was no way of knowing in this nearly soundproof fortress of rock if the fighting had stopped, and if Liam was unconscious, he couldn't very well come and get him.

Decision made, Eoghan donned his weapons and took the staircase upward, where he pushed lightly on the door. It eased open, allowing him a moment to listen for sounds in the hallway. Nothing. He slipped out and pushed the door closed behind him. It sealed back into the wall with a soft whoosh.

Then he saw the smear of blood in the hallway, leading toward the Ceannaire's study.

His heart in his throat, he broke into a run, taking the steps two at a time before bursting into the room. Brothers' hands went to weapons before they recognized him, their startled expressions quickly turning to sorrow.

He shoved past them to where Liam lay on the hard floor with his eyes closed and his hands folded on his chest. His clothes were soaked in blood, but it wasn't pooling beneath him. That was good, wasn't it? If he were mortally wounded, it would be gushing out. "What are you doing? Find a pallet! Someone help him! Quick!"

"Eoghan, I'm sorry. He's gone." A brother—Eoghan didn't even recognize him through his panic—put a hand on his shoulder.

Eoghan shook it off. "That's impossible. He can't be dead. I would know. I'm his successor." He fell to the ground beside Liam, felt for a pulse, watched for the rise and fall of his chest. Only then did he realize that his master's skin was cool. Too cool. He jerked his hands away.

"No. No. It can't be."

Someone gripped his elbow and raised him to his feet. "I'm sorry, sir. I know you were close. I know he was like a father to you."

Eoghan focused his suddenly blurry eyes on the speaker. Daigh. "'Sir'? Why are you calling me 'sir'? He's not dead. He can't be." *I would have known. He said I would know when leadership passed to me.*

"He's dead, sir, by his own hand," Daigh said quietly. "He gave himself up rather than allow the druid access to Carraigmór and its secrets."

A wave of sickness crashed over Eoghan, more shock than grief. Liam had known this would happen. He had known what he would have to do all along. That's why he had been so sure confining Eoghan would protect the Hall.

The password.

Eoghan pushed his way from the study, following the trail of blood down the hallway, and then turned into the corridor with the invisible door. He waited for the password to surface.

Nothing came to mind.

What were the words Liam had spoken this morning? No matter how hard he searched his memory, they still remained nothing more than the drift of smoke, not substantial enough to grasp. What did that mean? Perhaps Liam wasn't really dead. Perhaps he could be healed.

Or maybe Eoghan wasn't meant to be the Ceannaire after all.

But if he wasn't, who was?

He stumbled back to the Ceannaire's study, unable to form a coherent thought amidst his crush of emotion. Only now did he recognize the men there as members of the Conclave: Gradaigh, Dal, Manog, Daigh.

"Sir, I know this is a shock, but we need orders." Daigh positioned himself in Eoghan's vision, drawing his attention away from Liam's lifeless body in the corner.

"I am not the Ceannaire. I cannot be."

"You are his chosen successor, sworn on the sword before the Conclave. We witnessed it. You are the Ceannaire, and we need our orders."

Eoghan pressed his fingers to his eyes and forced himself to think. There would be time enough to sort this out. Right now, the Conclave believed he was the Ceannaire, and they would accept orders from only him.

"Tell me of the battle."

"Over," Gradaigh said. "Brother Riordan alone could see through the druid's magic, and he wounded him. Niall could no longer maintain his shield, so the army retreated."

"And you let them go? With the druid wounded?"

"We'd already sustained enough casualties," Dal said. "The city is glutted with bodies. We'll have enough trouble safely disposing of them without adding to the count."

"How many?" Eoghan asked. "How many casualties?"

"Most recent estimate, two hundred fell in battle. Thousands exposed, perhaps four hundred infected. Most of them did as commanded and ended their own lives if they could not resist. The others . . ." He swallowed and wouldn't finish the sentence.

The others had been killed by loyal Fíréin, men with whom they had sworn brotherhood. The toll on Ard Dhaimhin was far higher than the six hundred men they had lost today.

Eoghan choked down his sorrow. "How many of theirs? How many to dispose of?"

"Thousands, sir."

Eoghan jerked his head up and made his way over to the window. Piles of bodies clogged the walkways, the forest's edge, the village. Mostly the enemy's, but some of theirs, too.

"Make bonfires," he said. "Organize parties to retrieve the bodies and burn them as quickly as possible. Assign overseers to each group. If anyone is exposed to the blood, make them wash immediately and quarantine them under guard while we have time to see if they're taken by the sorcery."

A sigh of relief filled the room as Eoghan gave the men direction. These were strong, smart men, but they were conditioned to obey. Without a leader . . .

"And our fallen?" Dal asked.

"We have no way of knowing for certain who is infected and who is not. Burn them immediately like the others. I'm sorry."

Eoghan continued to survey the wreckage of the city, mentally listing their less immediate, but equally crucial, tasks. Smoke still billowed from fires in the villages and croplands beyond, and wisps of steam drifted from the surface of the lake. "What happened at Loch Ceo?"

Gradaigh answered. "The druid boiled it as a demonstration of his power."

Dread crept into Eoghan's body, spreading cold through his limbs. Matters were even more critical than he'd thought. He turned away from the window, gathering strength. Password or no password, he was the closest thing to a leader the brotherhood had, and he knew what had to be done.

"Organize bucket brigades to put out the fires that are still burning. Assign men to take inventory of our losses. Animals that were killed must be butchered and taken to the smokehouse immediately. Salvage what fish you can from the lake. Without our crops and our animals, it will be a long winter indeed. I will be down as soon as I can."

The men dispersed, all but Daigh, who lingered behind. "You have my sympathy for your loss, sir."

"Thank you." Then Eoghan realized who had been missing from the room. "Brother Riordan? Did he . . . ?"

"Badly burned, but he lives. I'll send him to you. He's in the infirmary."

"No, I'll find him later." He gave Daigh a bare smile and waited until the door closed before he turned back to Liam's lifeless, peaceful body. He sank to the floor beside him.

"You sacrificed all for the brotherhood. We will honor you. You will not be forgotten."

Eoghan reached out to touch Liam, but he jerked his hand back before he could feel his master's cold skin. They would have to organize a proper remembrance for him before the brotherhood. As his designated successor, it was Eoghan's responsibility to lead the men in their mourning.

Except he wasn't truly the Ceannaire. Something had gone wrong. The authority that was supposed to transfer with magic—the knowledge, the passwords—it had not happened.

And now the secrets of Ard Dhaimhin were locked away from them.

+ + +

Eoghan oversaw the activities in Ard Dhaimhin with numb efficiency. The enemy bodies were burned with as much care as they could manage, overseen by senior brothers who made sure no one became infected. Mass funeral pyres were built for their men in one of the burned wheat fields, the fall harvest now reduced to charred ash. Patrols were set along the burnt forest edge as well as the rest of the borders.

The men of the brotherhood were strong and disciplined, but Eoghan could see the strain that came from saying farewell to their brethren. Almost as bad was burning the enemy corpses, some of whom were boys not yet old enough to be out from behind their mothers' skirts. This was not a victory they celebrated.

Eoghan oversaw Liam's pyre himself, stacking kindling beneath the frame of felled saplings, arranging the wood and straw so it would burn fast and hot. He had debated dressing him in new clothing, but in the end, Eoghan could not justify destroying supplies they would need to sustain them through the coming lean seasons. Instead, he ordered Liam covered in a length of worn linen to conceal his mortal wound and laid upon the pyre.

As Ceannaire, it fell to Eoghan to say the blessing over the bodies of their fallen comrades, but he hadn't the words. Instead, Riordan stepped to the forefront, his burned hands and arms wrapped in clean linen bandages, and recited some relevant passages from Scripture.

Eoghan barely heard them, his eyes fixed on the body of the man who had practically raised him as his own son. He took the torch forward and lit the wood beneath Liam's body. It exploded in a rush of flame. He passed the torch to the next brother, until all the pyres containing the dead were alight.

He stared numbly into the flames, hypnotized by the twisting fingers of yellow and orange and blue that consumed the mortal housing of spirits now residing with Comdiu. He sent up an anguished prayer for their city, more a cry of the heart than coherent words.

"It's time now." Riordan nudged Eoghan. He looked up and realized the pyres had burned to ash. The stiffness in his limbs said he had stood motionless for hours, though he didn't remember it. Now other brothers would collect the ashes and scatter them in the forest, as was their custom. Cook fires burned elsewhere, mingling the smell of baking bread with Ard Dhaimhin's charred remains.

"Convene the Conclave," Eoghan said in a low voice. "There are matters we must discuss."

Riordan gave him a nod that was just short of a bow and hurried away. Despite the excruciating pain he must be feeling, he never hesitated to do his duty. Eoghan was the Ceannaire now, and Riordan would do his bidding.

Until he learned the truth.

Up at Carraigmór, Eoghan waited at the hall's massive table, staring blankly at the wood grain, while the other Conclave members finished their duties and traversed the steps to the fortress. This numbness he felt must be shock. Disbelief over the outcome of the battle, grief over burying men he had known his whole life, the knowledge that until he spoke the truth to the Conclave he was a pretender.

The men entered the hall in groups and took their seats solemnly around the table. When the last man arrived, Eoghan stood and poured himself a drink from the jug at the center of the table.

"Mead?" Gradaigh asked.

"It seemed appropriate to raise a cup to our fallen." He didn't say that he also needed it for his nerves, to steel himself for what he was about to tell them. The men served themselves from the jug, and then Eoghan lifted his cup.

"To Master Liam: a courageous leader, a loyal friend, a true servant of Comdiu."

"To Liam," they echoed, and they all drank.

Eoghan sank into his seat. "Brothers, there is a matter we all must discuss. You know I swore an oath to take the leadership of the Fíréin brotherhood after Master Liam's passing. It was why he insisted that I sit out the battle, to preserve the line of succession and secure the secrets of the brotherhood that only the Ceannaire may access."

Heads nodded.

"I am sorry to say his plan failed."

Silence fell around the table, and Eoghan shifted under the weight of eight pairs of eyes.

Riordan drank deeply before he spoke, an edge to his voice that could have come either from pain or from Eoghan's announcement. "Tell us how."

How was he supposed to explain when only the Ceannaire was to know of the existence of the Hall of Prophecies? "There are hidden places in Carraigmór that can be accessed only by one possessing a password, embedded by an old magic. That password is supposed to transfer to the Ceannaire's successor at his death. It did not."

"Password or not, you are still the rightful leader of this

brotherhood," Daigh said. "We witnessed your oath. We understand Liam's intentions. You will take your oath before the Conclave and assume your office. Perhaps once that's completed, you will have the knowledge you need to access those secret places."

"I do not think so," Eoghan said. "And in any case, that is impossible."

All eyes focused on him, sharper this time.

"The oath-binding sword is locked inside that place of which I speak."

Dal slammed his fist on the table. "This is nonsense! How is this possible? It is not as if this is the first time power has had to pass to the Ceannaire's apprentice!"

No one wanted to answer that, least of all Eoghan. It may not have been his fault, but he felt responsible all the same.

"Master Liam said this was the end of the brotherhood. Perhaps that's what this means."

Eoghan jerked his head toward Riordan, who looked even paler now beneath the sweat beading on his face. Eoghan refilled Riordan's cup, which the older man drained in one swallow. It returned some color to his skin, but he still shuddered when he put down the cup.

"Had Eoghan been meant to take the oath of leadership upon the sword, we would have the sword," Riordan said softly. "So we must assume that our traditions are broken. The only question is what to do now."

"This is preposterous," Fechin snapped, rising to his feet. "I will not throw away five hundred years of tradition because of some mistake!"

Eoghan gestured for Fechin to sit, and the man sat. So he still did have some power here. The thought almost made him laugh. The senior brother might take his cues from Dal, but he wasn't willing to go against Eoghan while he was still acknowledged as Liam's successor. "I do not believe this is a mistake. The time of the High King is at hand. Perhaps there can be no Ceannaire because the king must command the brotherhood, not as guardians but as soldiers."

"And who is the High King, then? You?" Manog spoke more quietly than Fechin or Dal, but it took only a handful of words for Eoghan to discern that he would side with the other two men if it came to a vote. "You wish to rule? Over a land in the hands of a sorcerer, that is terrorized by the ancient spirits?"

Eoghan shook his head. "I do not wish to rule. And I do not believe I'm meant to rule. Master Liam clearly told me what I must do. With our forest gone, we're more exposed than ever. The only thing that can keep us safe from another attack is to rebuild the wards. And in order to do that, I must find the object of power that built them."

"And someone with the ability to use it," Riordan said.

"Aye. That was the task given to me by Liam. Which means I will be leaving Ard Dhaimhin soon. The men who remain will need someone to command them." He met Riordan's eyes. "I think it should be you."

Riordan said nothing. He only stared at his bandaged hands.

"What say the Conclave? Brother Riordan once ruled as king of Tigh, before he forsook his clan for the brotherhood. He is well-respected among the men, he was privy to Liam's plans for the Fíréin, and he is responsible for ending the battle today."

"You know that I do not wish this," Riordan said. "I have never wished this."

Daigh nodded slowly. "That is why it must be you. Aye, I would support Brother Riordan's leadership."

Eoghan looked to the others. "What say you?"

"Not all the men will agree with you, sir—Brother Eoghan,"

Gradaigh said. "They know you as Liam's successor. They will see this breach of tradition as an end to their oaths."

"As they should," Riordan said. "The brotherhood is to end. The kingdoms are in disarray. Some of the men may feel their skills are better used in protecting their families at home."

"And the families who choose to send their boys here for protection?" Fechin asked.

"Those boys will be welcomed and trained as before." Riordan shifted and then paled again. "Anyone who wishes to leave should be allowed to leave."

"Without binding their oath?" Daigh asked.

Riordan laughed harshly. "What choice do we have? That is my decision, or it will be should you appoint me in Eoghan's place. Think hard on it now, knowing the direction I plan for our brotherhood. We may rebuild the city, provide for our brothers, continue our training, but make no mistake: this marks the end of the Fíréin. We await our High King now."

Glances rippled around the table.

"I will support you," Gradaigh said.

Six other voices added their agreement.

"I will be leaving within the week," Eoghan said. "We will need to announce this decision to the brothers tomorrow. Good night."

The men filed from the hall, heading back to their céads as if the structure of their lives were not crumbling around them, until only Riordan remained.

"Are you angry with me?" Eoghan asked him.

Riordan didn't say anything for a long while. "No. I am proud of you. This could not have been an easy decision."

Easier than you think. I never wanted to lead the brotherhood. Out loud, he said, "This is the way it is meant to be, even if Liam did not see it coming."

"Perhaps, perhaps not. You seek the harp, don't you?"

Eoghan nodded.

"You need Conor."

He nodded again.

"Then write your messages. There are ships sailing still between Seare and Aron, some of which have crewmen with connections to the Fíréin." Riordan smiled. "As you well know." He pushed himself up from the table, nearly collapsing from the pain of his hands against the furniture. "It's going to take a while to get used to this."

Eoghan supported Riordan while the man caught his breath. "I will pray for your swift healing."

"No more than I will," Riordan said. He made his way slowly to the door of the hall and then turned back before he exited. "Eoghan, do you have a sense of who we wait for?"

Eoghan just stared at him, unwilling to give away more than he already had.

Riordan nodded as if he had spoken aloud.

"Call upon Comdiu. Conor must return."

CHAPTER
THIRTY-FIVE

After Conor's ride with Briallu, he stayed as far from her as he could manage. They still ate at the same table and exchanged pleasantries in the hall, but he was careful not to put himself in a situation where he could fall prey to his inexplicable draw toward her.

Briallu possessed nothing he wanted, nothing he was missing in his own wife, besides her presence beside him. When she was out of his sight, he did not think of her. Yet the minute she neared him, his heart beat faster and every bit of sense he possessed flew out the window. It was beyond mere attraction, but whatever it was, he didn't like it.

The effort of ordering his day around Briallu's movements, coupled with days that turned into weeks without any word of Aine's whereabouts, made Conor anxious and irritable. He growled at the staff and ate his meals in sullen silence.

Whether it was because of his sudden ill humor, because his presence stretched much longer than anyone had expected, or because Briallu's mournful looks in his direction were obvious to anyone with a pair of working eyes, the guardsmen in the fortress began to scowl at him with suspicion. Conversations stopped when he entered the practice yard or the stables. Conor had originally planned to join drills to keep his skills sharp, but the resentment that radiated from the men changed his mind. In this mood, he was liable to do damage to someone, and that would not endear him to Talfryn, who alone seemed immune to the tension in the fortress.

As the weather turned colder, the guardsmen turned up in the hall in greater numbers to eat their supper by the warmth of the huge fire, and another table had to be brought into the massive space to accommodate them. One night, when Conor came to the hall for the evening meal, he found his regular place occupied by Ial, the captain of the guard.

Annoyance spiked through Conor, but it wasn't worth an argument, so he moved to the other side of the table. Another man slid onto the bench before he could take his seat.

Juvenile posturing, unworthy of a prince's guard. Conor resisted the urge to roll his eyes. He moved toward the second table. He wasn't willing to start a fight over seating.

A third man stepped in his way. "Do you not understand? You're not welcome here."

Conor held the warrior's gaze. "I think that's your lord's decision, not yours."

"Our lord is not here tonight." Ial rose. His stance communicated a clear threat. "You wear that sword of yours. Can you actually use it? Or are you just trying to fool Lady Briallu into thinking you are a man?"

Ial smirked, expecting a reaction, but for once, Conor's common sense seemed to be intact. He moved around the man blocking his way and sat down at the other table. "I don't wish to fight you."

"Because you know you can't win. Tell me, why would our prince risk his life for a worthless piece of Seareann filth?"

A servant set a goblet before Conor and scurried away before she could be caught in the dispute. Conor ignored the men and reached for his wine.

"That's enough." Briallu inserted herself between them. "There's no need to make a scene. Let us just forget it and enjoy our supper."

"This does not concern you, my lady." Ial nudged her out of the way.

Briallu grabbed his arm as if to pull him back, but he shook her off as if she were a rag doll. She stumbled into the other guardsman.

Conor's earlier irritation threatened to ignite into full-fledged anger. There was no call to treat their lady roughly. He stood. "Briallu, perhaps you should leave."

"I'm not leaving! Conor, he's not going to let you alone until you do what he wants. You might as well agree."

"The lady is right. What say you?"

"I don't want to fight," Conor said simply.

"Because you're a fraud."

"Because killing you is a poor way to repay Lord Talfryn's kindness."

Ial broke into laughter. "Kill me? As if you could manage it, boy."

Conor looked past the captain to Briallu, who looked at him pleadingly. Would fighting this man end the animosity, or would it simply escalate it?

"Very well. But we fight with wood, not steel. I will not risk Prince Talfryn's ire."

Ial smirked. "Fine. When?"

"How about now? There's still some light left."

"Good. Meet us in the practice yard."

Conor nodded and watched the men file out. This was all just some juvenile brawl, boys trying to assert their dominance.

"Did I just do something terrible?" Briallu asked at his shoulder.

He looked down at her. "If you didn't think I could fight, why did you tell me I should?"

"I thought he was bluffing. You've seen Ial practice. He's one of the best swordsmen I've ever seen. He has nothing to prove."

"That's why I asked for practice swords. He can only maim me. It's near impossible to kill with one of those."

Conor smiled to himself as he walked away. Briallu was not fooling him with her wide-eyed innocence. She was determined to make him face down Ial. Whether it was punishment for rejecting her or because she truly thought he could win, he didn't know.

She was right about one thing: Ial was very skilled.

But Conor was better.

+ + +

The number of guards in the fortress seemed to quadruple as word got out that Talfryn's guest had agreed to a "practice match" with Ial. By the time Conor got there, it felt more like villagers gathering to witness an execution than an exhibition of skill. Ial was already making experimental sweeps with the heavy wooden sword. Practice weapons or not, these would hurt if they met flesh.

"You don't have to do this," Briallu whispered behind him.

"You should have thought about that before you got me into this, my lady." He shrugged out of his silk tunic and handed it to Briallu. "Hold this. Don't want to get blood on your father's clothes."

Her eyes widened, but he just chuckled and retrieved the

practice sword. In truth, he really didn't want anything to happen to the borrowed garments. Talfryn had provided him with two changes of clothing, both finer than anything he'd worn since he was at Lisdara. Even if the prince didn't care, the frugality Conor had adopted from the brotherhood would not let him risk anything so fine.

He ignored the expectant gazes of the other men and worked through a few sword forms as warm-up, gauging his recently unused muscles. The rest seemed to have done him some good, even considering his fractured bones. When he moved to the center of the ring formed by the guards, Ial looked slightly less confident than he had before.

It didn't stop him from launching a furious attack. Conor sidestepped, parrying the blows with the flat of the wooden blade, judging the man's skill. Ial was more than good; he was excellent. Quick, strong, well-trained—except he had spent too much time fighting men with the same sort of training. He relied on a small repertoire of attacks and counters, expecting a particular response to each. When Conor did something the other man didn't expect, Ial's reaction was a split-second slower, less confident.

The men called encouragement to Ial and jeers to Conor. Best make this quick and decisive, then. Humiliating. Anything too close they would write off to bad luck and Conor would be facing challenges for the rest of his time at Cwmmaen.

He waited for his opportunity, a straight thrust. Instead of meeting the blade as Ial expected, Conor blocked and sidestepped, moving into the other man's body to deliver a sharp jab to the midsection. Ial doubled over, exposing his neck to the edge of Conor's wooden blade.

Ial straightened, fury and humiliation in his eyes.

"Again?" Conor asked.

Ial dodged away and, in answer, launched another attack. Conor avoided every blow, not bothering to counter, which only goaded Ial into a furious offense. The captain was determined to do some damage, practice sword or not. Conor ducked a wild swing meant to take his head off, stepped inside Ial's guard, and swept the man's legs out from under him. He rested the tip of the wooden blade against Ial's throat.

"Are we done?" Conor asked quietly.

Ial stared at him defiantly for a moment. Then he deflated and nodded. Conor withdrew the weapon and hauled his opponent to his feet. He winced at the twinge in his ribs and probed the bruised flesh, gauging the pain.

Ial glanced at the sickly yellow markings. "The Sofarende did that to you?"

"Took them a while to realize I wasn't a spy and didn't have any information of interest to them. It's still not completely healed."

Ial held out a hand, his bravado gone. "I stand corrected."

"Thank you." Conor gripped the captain's forearm, and then accepted his tunic from Briallu. "I've seen you at the archery range. You think you could spare some time in the morning? I'm good with a sword but rubbish with a bow."

"I'm not on duty tomorrow, unless the prince returns and requests my presence."

"It would be appreciated. Sometimes a man doesn't want to look his enemy in the eye, you know?"

Ial chuckled. "I do. After breakfast, then."

"After breakfast."

The men melted back to their regular posts, though if the jokes he already heard flying about were any indication, it would be a while before Ial lived down his loss. Good enough. Once they saw Conor's terrible showing on the archery range, the scales would be balanced.

He smiled to himself and turned to Briallu, expecting to see relief. "Satisfied?"

But she was staring at him with a disgruntled expression. Without a word, she walked away.

CHAPTER
THIRTY-SIX

The next morning, Briallu did not appear at the breakfast table. Talfryn had returned sometime in the night, though, and he took a seat across from Conor.

"I heard you fought Ial."

"Word travels fast."

"When a stranger beats the captain of the guard that soundly, it tends to." Talfryn frowned and reached for the teapot. "What brought that about? You challenge him?"

"He challenged me. Trying to make an example of me, it seems."

"Doesn't sound like Ial. He's the most even-tempered man I've ever met. I wouldn't have him in charge of this bunch of rabble otherwise. They're always devising ways of making one another black and blue."

"I think he might have designs on Briallu. He didn't seem pleased with our friendship."

Talfryn just looked at him blankly. Conor gave him a questioning smile. "Surely you've noticed how the men look at your daughter?"

"No, I suppose I haven't. When I look at her, I see a little girl. But when they look at her—"

"They see a woman." A woman so used to manipulating everyone around her, she couldn't endure the unexpected. That was the only explanation for her strange reaction to his victory. Clearly she'd wanted to cause conflict, even if Conor couldn't fathom why.

He changed the subject. "Any response to the messages?"

"My brothers have heard nothing, but they'll continue to spread the word. The only Aronans who would have received it are the Lowland clans, and it's doubtful they'll respond. We should hear something from the Highlanders soon."

"Thank you, my lord." Conor rose from the table, clutching the board for support as he swayed.

"Is something wrong?"

He didn't answer. The room swirled around him, and something tickled at the back of his mind. A whisper of a memory?

Then the sensation left as quickly as it had come. "I'm fine." He forced a smile. "Perhaps I'm not recovered from my injuries as completely as I thought."

But his heart still beat too fast as he walked down to the archery range to meet Ial, urgency squirming in his gut. The sensation was like a phantom itch that couldn't be relieved no matter how hard he scratched.

By now, he knew the touch of magic too well to dismiss it as mere imagination. Something had grabbed hold of him, seized his attention, demanded action. The question was, what was he supposed to do about it?

He shook off the musings as he entered the archery range, where Ial waited for him with several bows and two quivers of arrows.

"I feel required to warn you that I'm far better with a sword than a bow," Conor said.

Ial chuckled. "Let's see what you can do."

What he could do barely qualified as hitting the target. His arrows struck all over, even though he was drawing the bow the same way every time. In fact, he hadn't made this poor a showing since his first days at Ard Dhaimhin. He lowered the weapon and turned to Ial.

"Tell me, then. What am I doing so wrong?"

"I have no idea." Ial raised a shoulder in a helpless gesture. "Your technique is fine. Not exceptional, but not bad. You could be smoother on the draw. But, frankly, none of that explains just how . . ."

"Terrible I am?"

Ial nodded. "Maybe you're just not suited to the bow. Or maybe you've just convinced yourself that you're not."

Somehow Conor had assumed Ial would have an answer to the problem. Not that it was much of a problem. He had enough facility with his other weapons to protect himself and leave long-range attacks to those more skilled than he. Still, the fact that this challenge eluded him rankled.

He raised the bow and nocked another arrow, aware of Ial doing the same beside him. The other man's arrows flew true and struck the target squarely in the center, while Conor's still barely caught the lower edge.

It didn't make sense. Maybe it was all in his mind. After all, didn't his ability with the sword verge on the preternatural? There was clearly more at work there, not to mention the gift with the harp. Maybe he really was sabotaging his own abilities.

Conor nocked another arrow. What would happen if he truly believed he could hit the target? He imagined the arrow embedded in the center as he released the string.

It struck the bottom-left edge of the straw mat.

He frowned, thinking. Maybe just believing he could do it wasn't enough. Maybe it was about will. After all, when he'd fought Liam for his release from Ard Dhaimhin, he'd been determined to return to Aine at all costs.

This time, when he drew the bow, he thought not of the end result but of the flight of the arrow, straight to the center of the target. When he released the string, time seemed to expand as if everything moved in slow motion. He poured his will into the arrow, insisting that it strike the target true.

Then time sped up again and he was staring at the projectile embedded down to its fletching in the center ring.

"What did you do?" Ial asked, his eyes wide.

"I'm not entirely sure." Had he discovered a new gift, or merely an extension of his old one?

And, more important, if he could call on it at will for fighting, what else could he do with it?

CHAPTER
THIRTY-SEVEN

Aine waited for a sign that word of Uallas's healing had gotten out, but both the lord and the guards were true to their promises—not even a murmur hinted about what had happened in the woods that day.

Lord Uallas no longer attempted to conceal his intentions toward her. Even if she delayed her entrance to the hall, he was there to escort her to her seat. Gifts appeared in her work room without explanation—costly items like prepared myrrh and fine steel needles, of which Guaire insisted he had no knowledge. And when she began to see a trickle of patients from among the keep's staff, Uallas always seemed to find a reason to check on her. Soon the rumors of their impending betrothal whispered through Forrais's cold stone hallways. He might have insisted he would not speak words of love, but he was doing his utmost to convince her of his devotion.

"You must stop, my lord," she whispered when he slipped up behind her to take her hand just before she entered the hall for supper.

"Not until you tell me what I wish to hear." He closed his

hand around hers briefly before releasing it into the more proper formal clasp. "I want you for my wife."

"And you know why I cannot." She swallowed down her unease and pasted a vague smile onto her face as they entered the half-filled hall. She had to stop getting cornered by Lord Uallas. Not because she worried he would take liberties with her but because it was getting more difficult to put him off politely. At least in front of others, he wasn't inclined to make a scene. Uallas escorted her to the table, but instead of releasing her to her seat, he lifted her hand to his lips and brushed a lingering kiss across the backs of her fingers. Then he swept a deep bow, much deeper than was proper, before he backed away.

Aine's heart plummeted into her stomach as voices hummed through the hall. She barely restrained the impulse to glare at his back before she sat in the chair a servant held for her.

"My, my, niece," Lady Macha murmured. "Made short work of him, have you? I'll admit he's one of your better options. I just didn't think you'd come around to the reality of your situation so quickly."

"And what situation is that?"

"Legitimizing your bastard child, of course." Macha paused while a servant placed several slices of roast boar on her plate.

"I think we may be getting ahead of ourselves, Aunt. Conor—"

"Trust me," Macha continued as if Aine hadn't spoken. "You may not think this betrothal is assured, but I know the look of a man smitten when I see one. And Lord Uallas will not rest until you are his wife."

Clearly Macha just wanted Aine out of the way of her family's control of the clan's assets. A trickle of apprehension crawled over her. She'd already wondered if Macha had been behind the attack by the river. If it had not been for Uallas, Aine would be dead.

And if not for her healing gift, Uallas would be dead as well. If her aunt was really behind the attack, she knew about Aine's ability to heal.

Her heart beat so hard in her chest she was sure Macha could see it from the outside. But she tried to keep her face pleasant while she choked down slices of wild boar and honeyed parsnips. As soon as she could make a graceful exit, she excused herself and made her way from the hall.

Taran had warned her that Macha was dangerous, but somehow Aine had not thought her this subtle—pushing her into Uallas's arms as if marrying her off was the endgame, all the while trying to have her murdered. Or had she merely changed tactics when she realized Uallas's protectiveness of her?

She was so intent on the possibilities that she didn't hear the footsteps until they were right behind her. She sighed and turned, determined to lecture the island lord on the impropriety of following her to her chamber.

It was not Uallas.

She fixed on the dark eyes beneath the hooded cloak when she should have focused on the dagger in his hand. A spark of recognition lit in the back of her mind, only to be obliterated by terror when he lunged for her. She darted aside, but the edge of the blade caught her arm. Pain seared through her.

She drew the dagger from her belt, but the man grabbed her hand and slammed it against the wall once, then again, until the weapon fell from her numb fingers to clatter on the stones at her feet.

Hard hands grabbed her shoulders while his knee rammed into her midsection. She doubled over, the wind knocked out of her, and collapsed onto the ground with a pathetic wheeze.

Comdiu, help me! she cried silently as her vision faded. Her attacker raised the blade to finish the job.

And then the dagger stopped halfway through its downward arc. The assassin jerked backward as if pulled by an invisible rope. Had Comdiu answered her prayers?

Aye, but not in the way she thought. She caught a glimpse of red hair and a familiar russet tunic as Uallas downed the man with a well-aimed punch. Then, before she could catch her breath, he drew his own dagger and slit the attacker's throat.

Aine stared, stunned, for the space of two breaths. Only then did she realize she was breathing again and the ache in her mid-section was subsiding.

In an instant, Uallas was kneeling on the ground beside her. "Are you all right?" He finally registered her bloodstained sleeve. "Guards! Help! We need a physician!"

Aine pushed herself to a sitting position. "I'm fine. It's only a flesh wound." One that burned like fire, but she could tell without looking that the bleeding was not serious.

"A flesh wound?" Uallas barked an amazed laugh. "'Only a flesh wound,' she says. Truly a woman who has seen the battlefield."

Aine focused on the man lying in a slowly spreading pool of blood. "You killed him?"

"Aye, I killed him. He was trying to murder you!"

"But now we don't know who hired him. We could have questioned him." She struggled to her feet with Uallas's assistance and walked to the assassin's side. "Push back the hood."

Uallas obeyed, though reluctantly. She gasped.

"What is it? Do you know him?"

She closed her eyes. "Aye. I thought he was a friend." She opened them again, hoping for a different picture, but no—it was him. The eyes that had once looked on her with warmth now stared, glassy and distant.

Pepin.

✦ ✦ ✦

Despite the fact the wound was as shallow as she had guessed, Aine found herself under the care of one of Macha's physicians while Diocail, Guaire, and half a dozen of the keep's guards crowded around her. Uallas leaned against the wall, seemingly no more affected by slitting a man's throat than he would have been by slaughtering an animal.

"So you knew this man." Diocail's expression was dark, even if his tone was gentle. "What reason would he have to want you dead?"

"He's a mercenary," Aine said. "I assume someone paid him a large sum of money."

"I meant—"

"I know what you meant. I don't know who would want me dead. I'm just a girl. I have few enemies. Who would benefit from my death?"

Over the heads of the others, Uallas arched an eyebrow at her, clearly recognizing the question for what it was. The island lord might have been many things, but he was no fool.

The door opened, and every head turned toward the new arrival.

"You're alive," Macha said. "When I heard there had been an assassin, no one had any information."

"I'm sorry to disappoint you, my lady." Had Macha actually been concerned, it wouldn't have taken a full hour to traverse the handful of steps from the hall.

"Don't be daft, girl. What I want to know is how did an assassin get into my keep?"

Diocail stepped forward. "We are still investigating that, my lady."

"He specialized in high walls," Aine said. "If he managed the

assassination of a Ciraen senator, your fortress is hardly a challenge, my lady."

"So you do know him." Macha's voice turned frosty. "Just
how intimately?"

Until now, Aine had felt numb, weary. But at the suggestion in Macha's tone, something snapped. She stood, brushing
aside the physician's attempts to bandage her arm, and met
Macha's stare with one equally hard. "As in, did I invite him
into the keep to share my bed, after which he decided to disguise himself and kill me in full view of anyone wandering the
corridor? Come, now. Ignoring the insult to my honor—which
I only do because it's been a trying day—that makes very
little sense."

The room went silent, waiting for Macha's response. She
returned the stare for an uncomfortably long stretch and then
turned to Diocail. "Find out why and how. Anyone found shirk-
ing their duty will be severely punished." She gave Aine a cool
smile. "If something had happened to my dear niece, I'd never
have forgiven myself."

Aine had pushed as far as she dared in one night. She bowed
her head. "Thank you, Aunt."

Macha's departure seemed to be the opportunity for which
the others were waiting, and slowly the room drained of all but
Uallas, Guaire, Diocail, and Lia. Uallas stepped to her side and
whispered urgently, "May I speak with you, my lady?"

Aine glanced at the others. "Would you mind waiting outside
for a moment?" They murmured their assent, but as Guaire was
about to slip out, she called, "Leave the door ajar, please."

A trace of amusement passed over the steward's face, and he
left a full foot's gap in the entry.

Uallas grimaced. "I thought you'd learned by now you could
trust me."

"I only fear for my reputation, after your gallant behavior both in the hall and outside of it."

He grabbed her uninjured arm. "This is no jest, Aine. Assassins in the open are one thing, but in Forrais's own halls! You must leave here. We've been fortunate so far, but I'd rather rely on distance and my own men to keep you safe."

His expression softened and he took both her hands. "Marry me. I promise you, I will care for you. I will protect you. I will give you a home, children . . ."

"Love?"

Uallas appeared startled. "Love. Of course. You would be my wife—"

"And now I am not the one you are trying to convince." Aine took her hands from his. "You are a good man—an honorable man—but I cannot marry you. Just as you still love your wife, I love Conor. But unlike your wife, my husband may still be alive. If there were a chance she could return to you, would you be asking me this?"

"She's not coming back."

"But Conor might."

He held her gaze. Then he nodded. "I leave in five days. I still hope you will come with me. But I will not ask again."

"I understand. I owe you a rather great debt, Lord Uallas."

"After you pulled an arrow out of me, I'd say we're even." Uallas gave her a crooked smile. "Sleep well, my lady. Try to stay out of harm's way."

"I shall do my best. Good night, my lord."

As soon as Uallas left the room, the others slipped in. Diocail shut the door.

"You refused him," Guaire said. "Why?"

"My husband may still be alive." Then she added more quietly, "And I don't trust him."

"What makes you say that?" The steward's eyes narrowed.

Aine sighed and plopped into the chair. "I may be no great beauty, but I've had my share of admirers. I've known love, seen infatuation. Whatever he wants, it has nothing to do with me."

"If you don't trust him, what makes you trust us?" Diocail asked.

Aine spread her hands and shrugged. "I have no choice. I can only go by my intuition, and you are as close to allies as I have in this place."

"Now you sound like a daughter of your clan." Guaire's eyes sparkled. "What do you need, my lady?"

"From you? Information. Find what you can about Lord Uallas." She looked to Diocail next. "From you, I need a guard. Someone I can trust with my life, who can't be bought. Even better if he should despise my aunt."

Diocail made a sound that might have been a laugh. "Aye. I can do that, my lady. I'll post a guard on your chamber in case this man was not alone."

"Thank you, both of you." Aine smiled at them in turn, even though weariness threatened to overwhelm her.

Diocail bowed and exited the room, Guaire following close behind.

The steward paused just inside the door, his expression thoughtful. "Mark my words, my lady. Someday bards will write songs about you."

Aine stared as he shut the door behind him, her hand going to her mouth. Then the trembling began. She made it to the bed before her knees gave way.

"My lady?" Lia approached her hesitantly.

"I'm all right." Aine repeated her earlier words, but this time, she didn't feel so certain. She'd nearly been killed tonight by a man whom she'd naively trusted, and once more saved by a man who wanted to marry her. Uallas had put his life at stake for her more than once, yet all she could see were her suspicions: who might be using her, who was working against her. What was Forrais doing to her?

"Would you just unlace me, Lia? I'd like some time alone to think."

"Aye, my lady." The girl unlaced the back of the dress and retrieved a clean shift while Aine removed the bloodstained one. "At least let me comb your hair."

Lia's pleading tone spoke to her feeling of helplessness. Aine nodded and moved to the chair by the brazier, chilled despite the warmth of the room. She winced as she sat, only then remembering the blow that had taken her to the ground. He could have killed her then, but instead he'd tried to cripple her.

Or kill the child she could be carrying.

Her hands went to her stomach. She didn't know if she were actually pregnant, but if the attack had somehow caused her to lose the baby . . .

Tears pricked her eyes, opening an ache in her heart she'd done her best to ignore.

Conor, I miss you so much. Where are you? We may have a child. Or we might have before tonight. Did you ever consider that possibility? Have you hoped for it? Do you dream of me?

Somehow, pouring out her fears to her husband in the silence of her mind eased her burdened heart. Was that a sin? Wasn't that a bit like praying to an idol, someone other than Comdiu?

She hugged her arms to herself, closing her eyes while Lia combed her hair in long, slow strokes. Then the maid's hands slowed, and Aine could feel the hesitation in her movements. "What is it, Lia?"

"I shouldn't gossip, my lady. It's just that . . ."

Aine twisted in the chair. "Is there something I need to know?"

The maid chewed her lip, obviously conflicted. "You said you thought Lord Uallas wanted something from you. I overheard two of Macha's lords speaking about him in the corridor. But men don't always speak truth—"

"I understand that, Lia. But if it may help, I must know."

"They said Lord Uallas is nearly penniless and hard-pressed to defend Eilean Buidhe against the Sofarende. They said of all the women he could court, you are the wealthiest."

Aine swallowed and nodded. It only confirmed what she had suspected.

Then why did it sting so much?

"My lady, I'm sure he cares for you."

Aine waved a hand in dismissal. "Just my pride wounded, not my heart. You did well to tell me."

At least now she knew what Uallas wanted from her. The bigger question was, what would he do to get it?

CHAPTER
THIRTY-EIGHT

After Conor's victory over Ial, he enjoyed a certain level of respect from the other men. They still weren't entirely pleased with his presence, but they accepted him with only minor grumbling. He began joining the morning drills with sword and bow, rebuilding the strength he had lost through inactivity, though he still had to take care with his injuries.

Briallu kept her distance, which might also have had something to do with the men's acceptance. Perhaps she had realized there was no hope for them, or perhaps she was annoyed that Conor was on friendly terms with the guards. Either way, it was a relief. Even her presence at one of their morning practices had been enough to make him distracted and uneasy.

Word began to filter back in response to Talfryn's missives regarding Aine's whereabouts, all negative. Those who recognized her name informed him that she had been killed in Seare, while the others claimed to have no knowledge of her or anyone by her description.

Talfryn didn't seem concerned when he delivered the most

recent news at supper. "We still haven't heard from Forrais. And that is the most likely place she would have gone, is it not?"

"I'm sure it is." Conor absently rubbed his thumbnail in the crack of the wooden tabletop. "It's just . . . what if I don't find her? What if she's gone? What do I do then?"

Talfryn looked back down the table at his own wife, who was laughing with Briallu. "You don't forget; you endure. You continue on with the path Comdiu has set you."

"Aye." Hadn't he always? It was no different than the time he had spent at Ard Dhaimhin, moving forward though he had missed Aine desperately. But then he had known she was safe. She had been his reason for continuing. Always working harder, always striving to get back to her. Without her . . .

No, he couldn't follow that thought. He didn't know for sure she was gone. And even if she was, he could not turn his back on Seare. Other families—fathers, sons, wives, daughters—suffered under the reign of an evil man, and Conor might be the only one who could intervene.

Except that back in Seare, he would face another fruitless search for Meallachán's harp through enemy territory. How long would that take him? How many years until he even got a hint of its location?

The overwhelming nature of his task erased his enthusiasm for the evening. He stood. "If you'll excuse me, I think I'll retire early tonight."

"Oh, but you mustn't!" Briallu rushed to his side. "We've a bard with us tonight, just arrived. You must stay for the music."

The last thing he wanted to do was hear a merry tune or tales of valor. "I don't think so."

"Please do," Hyledd said. "If you're really to be leaving us soon, do not deprive us of your company now."

Pretty words from a woman who still seemed to dislike him.

It must be for her daughter's sake. Had Briallu changed her mind about pursuing him, or had he just misinterpreted the whole situation? He looked down at Briallu's pleading expression and sighed. He gave a single nod.

"Oh, I'm so pleased. Master Glyn is known all over Amanta for his skill with the harp."

A harpist. Wonderful. Conor steeled himself for the emotions that music normally stirred and settled in for a difficult night.

The bard, like Meallachán, was an unassuming-looking man, with nothing to hint he was a master of his craft. Conor hadn't even noticed him at the end of the table during dinner. The bard rose as one of the servants brought his harp case from the corner and found a seat at the head of the prince's table, cradling the plain but beautiful instrument in his lap.

Instead of asking Talfryn what he wished to hear, he started immediately into a haunting piece. Conor stiffened when he recognized the tune, previously one of his favorites: a ballad about a man pining over his lost love. He stared at the far wall, commanding his eyes not to well with tears, demanding his body not to show any of his turmoil. Was it just a coincidence— some cruel twist of fate—that led the man to choose that very song?

Briallu reached over and covered his hand with her own. "I'm sorry. If I had known . . ."

He shook his head sharply and withdrew his hand from hers.

When the song was over, Conor applauded with the others, then stood and strode out of the room. His feet carried him through the familiar hallway to his chamber. The servants had not yet stoked his fire, and the cold night air crept through the stones. He sank down onto the edge of the mattress, where he could just see the cold white light of the moon through one of the windows. Waxing three-quarters. That meant he had been here almost a month. Nearly two months total since he had lost Aine at sea.

Where are you, love? Are you alive? Or are you with Comdiu, waiting for me?

A light knock sounded at the door before it creaked open. "Conor?"

He twisted. Briallu stood in the doorway. "You shouldn't be here."

"I was worried about you." She glided nearer and peered into his face, the candlelight casting her features in a relief of shadow and light.

Conor turned his eyes back to the window. "Now is not the time, Briallu. I haven't the energy to spar with you."

"I know. Do you think she's still out there somewhere?"

"I have to believe she is."

"And if she's not? What are you going to do?"

"Go back to Seare. Finish my task."

"Which is?"

"Something I do not wish to discuss tonight." Conor stood and edged past her, intending to show her to the door before anyone realized she was in his chamber, but Briallu stepped in his way.

"Conor, come here." He stared at her suspiciously, and she heaved a sigh. "Men." She walked past him to the pitcher of water on his nightstand and poured it into the basin. Frowning, he moved to look over her shoulder.

She braced her hands on either side of the bowl and peered intently into the surface of the water. Conor's heart rose into his throat when he realized what she intended. "I told you—"

"Conor." She turned and put her hands on either side of his face, her green-gold eyes intent. A tingle shot down his spine. "You want to know where she is. You need to know. Why do you insist on sending messages all over Amanta when I could show you in an instant?"

"It's forbidden," he managed to choke out.

She dropped her hands. "I won't do it if you're not willing. But if she's in danger, wouldn't you rather know while something can still be done?"

He stood there, locked in her gaze, every fiber of his being screaming for him to resist. There was a reason this magic was forbidden. It was dark, unreliable . . .

"Two months, Conor. By now she must think you're dead. A highborn lady has a responsibility to her clan to marry, you know."

It was clear manipulation, but it still struck to the heart. He nodded.

She smiled and turned back to the bowl. Conor watched the glassy surface of the water, now reflecting the candlelight and the timber roof. It wasn't working. Perhaps that was a sign they really shouldn't be dabbling in this magic.

And then the image in the water changed. Conor drew in his breath, and Briallu thrust out a hand in warning. The image shimmered and then revealed a stone room not unlike the one in which they stood now. In the middle of it was Aine.

His heart squeezed in his chest. It was really her. She was alive. He swallowed down the lump in his throat and forced air into his lungs.

Then he noticed the other person in the room, a red-haired man dressed in court attire. The man took both of Aine's hands, his expression intent. "Marry me. I promise you, I will care for you. I will protect you. I will give you a home, children . . ."

"Love?"

"Love. Of course. You would be my wife."

Briallu jerked upright and the image vanished in an instant.

Conor stared at the surface of the bowl, even though it once again reflected his chamber. Surely he hadn't understood. Two months and his wife was already considering marrying another man? She had waited three years for him, and in the course of two months . . .

Briallu touched his arm. "Conor, I'm sorry. I never thought . . . I just assumed . . ."

He shook his head, not trusting his voice. He'd thought he'd understood what the bards meant when they sang about heartbreak. When he had believed Aine was dead, that had been loss, grief. This was betrayal—and a physical pain so deep he thought he might never take an easy breath again.

"The images are real, but they're open to interpretation."

"That seemed pretty clear to me." He pulled out of her reach. If Aine hadn't been receptive to this man, whoever he was, she wouldn't have allowed him into what was obviously her bedchamber.

"Conor, look at me." Briallu circled around so he had no choice but to face her. "You don't know what that's about. I'd wager that's Forrais. If you left now—"

"I could be a guest at my wife's wedding?" His vision blurred and he swiped at his eyes. He would not cry in front of Briallu. He would not let her see his whole world crumbling around him.

"Ah, love," she whispered, her arms going around him. He tensed, but she just rested against his chest while her hands stroked his back. "I'm so sorry. I want to say you were lucky to have loved so deeply, but that makes the pain that much sharper, doesn't it?"

"I didn't ask for this. I didn't want a great destiny, some great responsibility. I just wanted her."

"I know. It's too much to expect of one man. Why can you not simply live a normal life? Marry, have children . . ." She pulled back from him enough to look him in the face, her hands sliding to his waist.

He caught his breath, his heart suddenly pounding. "Briallu, you should go. This isn't proper."

She nodded, but she didn't move away. "Conor, I know that nothing I say or do will erase this betrayal, but you shouldn't have to endure it alone. I just want to be a friend to you, a comfort to you. Won't you accept that from me?" Her tone was soft, silky, and it crept into him with the same soft warmth of a melody. She said friend, comfort, but she offered so much more than that.

"I am still married, no matter what she might do." His voice felt thick and clumsy.

"Most men lack your faithfulness. I admire that about you. But she does not deserve your devotion." She sighed and stretched up on tiptoe to kiss his cheek. "I'll leave you now."

The warmth of Briallu's lips seared his skin and spread through his body, weakening his resolve. She was right. Aine had thrown their love away. She couldn't even wait two months before finding a new husband. Had she set her sights on this stranger while he was languishing in a Sofarende prison?

His hand shot out and grabbed Briallu's arm as if it were controlled by someone else. "Don't go."

She turned those remarkable green-gold eyes on him. Her voice came out breathless. "I won't. I won't ever leave you unless you ask me to."

Without any conscious decision, his lips were on hers, hard and demanding. She responded with the same urgency until he couldn't think, couldn't breathe. He was drowning, and he couldn't find it in himself to care. She pushed him back until his knees hit the bed and he was forced to sit. The part of his mind that screamed this was wrong—that part of him that still cared about things like right and wrong—got stifled when her gown slipped farther off her shoulders. He pulled her close enough to kiss her again.

Cold washed over him as if he had been plunged into the sea, bringing with it rapid flashes of images.

Shadows moved through the remnants of a ruined fortress. Mist blanketed the ground as thickly as snow, fingers of white reaching out and crawling around their legs. The beautiful woman whose arms wrapped around him dissolved into sinuous, inky smoke, carrying the smell of decay.

Conor broke the kiss and pushed Briallu away, staring in horror. Her lovely face was a mask of dismay, and her bare shoulders displayed angry red marks he didn't remember leaving. No shadows. No death. Just a young woman who had been rejected by a man she fancied.

He shivered with cold that could not be explained merely by the fall night. He remembered the touch of that unnatural cold. When she reached out to him, he jerked away.

"Conor, what's wrong?"

He opened his mouth, but nothing came out.

In a flash, the pout melted into a glare, and then the tears began to fall. She ran from the room, sobbing.

Understanding filled the once-murky corners of his mind, bringing with it a wash of dread. He'd been manipulated, so deftly he'd not seen the bigger game, the snare in which they'd all been caught—him, Talfryn, Ial, all of them. The harp music in the hall broke off, followed by a man's angry voice.

"Comdiu, help me." He knew what he had to do, and he had to do it before Briallu convinced Talfryn to kill him on sight.

He raced to the hall and skidded to a stop just before he ran into Ial's bared sword. The guard's expression was murderous.

Or so he thought until he laid eyes on Talfryn. The Gwynn

prince strode toward him, his face crimson. "You dare to take advantage of my daughter in my own palace?" He pulled his dagger and jabbed it beneath Conor's chin, hard enough to draw blood. "Haven't you anything to say for yourself?"

Conor remained as still as stone as he sized up the situation. Briallu sobbed in her mother's arms, her gown now torn and exposing far more skin than he'd seen in his chamber. Ial looked one short step from running him through, and Talfryn trembled with rage. Delicate did not even begin to describe the situation. Once more Briallu controlled the scene with the deftness of a master puppeteer.

"I can explain, my lord, but I need the harp to do it."

"You are accused of violating my daughter, and you want to *play the harp?*"

"Clearly I have nowhere to go. You're going to kill me regardless of what I say. So what have you to lose?"

Talfryn's expression didn't change, but he nodded to Ial, who withdrew his sword. Conor sighed in relief. "Master Glyn?"

"Father, you can't be serious!" Briallu cried. "He forced himself on me!"

Talfryn's jaw pulsed, but he only gestured for Conor to proceed.

Conor sat in the chair and put his hands to the strings. No power hummed through this instrument, as with Meallachán's harp. But he didn't need it. He began to play, heedless of the tune, instead pouring every bit of his will into the music, shaping its intention, its meaning with his thoughts.

Illuminate. Reveal. Strip the illusion of light and show the shadows for what they are.

The magic unleashed by the music shimmered in slow motion, hanging in the air. Conor closed his eyes and saw with his mind's eye instead, the light cloaking the room, pouring down around it like a waterfall. Washing away the illusion, revealing their surroundings.

Conor, stop! Briallu's voice came from far away, dampened by the music. Then she screamed, a piercing, otherworldly sound that couldn't have come from a human throat—so unsettling he almost stopped playing.

Only instinct and the knowledge that what he had seen in his mind was real made him continue. The tune didn't matter, only the intention, the will to call forth the light to battle the darkness. At last, the cold hand on his heart eased its grip, and the chill subsided. He let the notes fade into a deathly silence.

And then he opened his eyes.

✦ ✦ ✦

Even his brief vision did not prepare him for the sight that awaited him. The great hall, only moments ago illuminated with light and gaiety, stood dim and silent around him. The shredded tapestries hung in shards upon the ruined walls, fluttering in the breeze from the gaps in the stone. The ornate carvings that had so impressed him were ruined, hacked to pieces, timbers split.

"What have you done?" Talfryn stared like a man waking from years of slumber, unable to remember how he had gotten there.

"Revealed what Cwmmaen has truly become." Conor looked around the devastated hall and then across to Hyledd.

Gone was the beautiful woman to whom he'd been introduced. Her hair hung lank and unkempt around her sallow face, dark smudges beneath her eyes. Her dirty garments sagged from her rail-thin frame. The sumptuous feast before them had been reduced to slop not even fit for the pigs, old meat and bread covered in mold. Conor's gorge rose at the realization they had been eating the rotten food.

"My daughter," Hyledd whispered. "Briallu."

Talfryn reached for his wife. "Hyledd, darling, we have no daughter. Only sons, remember?"

She shook her head. "That's impossible. She was just here."

Talfryn looked to Conor for help.

"She was a spirit. In Seare, we call them the sidhe. We have been enwrapped in her glamour, unable to distinguish the illusion from reality."

"I—I can't remember," Lady Hyledd said. "Everything feels so distant."

"I remember everything up to the point I arrived here," the bard offered. "How could that be?"

"You have been under the influence of the illusion for far less time. The longer you spend believing the lie, the harder it is to see the truth. You have been here only a day. Me, less than a month. I can only guess it happened sometime after Talfryn left, so he wasn't as deeply ensnared. Lady Hyledd, what is the last thing you remember?"

"I don't know." She moved closer to her husband, and Talfryn put a comforting arm around her. "I remember leaving for Penafon as planned and the few days we spent there, but when we returned, all was as it should be. How?"

"Perhaps Briallu put the glamour in place so you wouldn't notice anything amiss when you returned, my lady. I take it Ial was with you?"

"Aye. And six other warriors."

"But that was nearly two months ago!" Talfryn said. "We've been under this illusion—this glamour, you called it—for this entire time?"

"It seems so," Conor said. "We should take a look at the grounds."

Hyledd rose from her chair and swayed for a moment. "I won't be left behind. Not here."

"Wife, remain here until we know all is safe. Ial, Aeron, stay with her, please." Talfryn scanned the room. "Where are my other men?"

Conor watched them process the revelation. If he'd not already witnessed the sidhe's power, he wouldn't believe it either. At last, he understood all the strange feelings he had experienced since he arrived: the wildly varying moods of the household, which seemed to echo Briallu's; the fact Conor had had so little direct interaction with the guardsmen; how easily he'd been swayed from his most deeply held principles.

Shame washed over him. Even knowing the sidhe thrived on the baser instincts of men and exploited them, he'd betrayed Aine. Was that why Briallu had been determined to sway Conor and stir up dissent with the guardsmen—to make herself strong enough that they'd never break free?

One look at the courtyard explained the disappearance of the other guardsmen. Their rotting corpses lay where they had fallen, crawling with insect life. Conor covered his mouth and nose with his hand in a futile barrier against the stench. The only signs of life outside the hall were the two stunned grooms with a handful of horses.

Conor pushed down his distaste and bent to pluck an arrow from the nearest body. He ran his fingers over the fletching, noting its construction. "Do you recognize this? It's not Gwynn, nor Aronan. Certainly not Seareann."

Talfryn took the arrow from him with surprisingly steady hands. The prince was taking the revelation better than Conor would have expected. "I saw similar ones in the Sofarende camp. It must be Norin." Then he looked at Conor with shocked, empty eyes. "How did this happen? *What* happened?"

Conor turned away from the horror before them. "If I had to guess, I would say the Sofarende attacked while you and Lady

Hyledd were away, and the sidhe placed a glamour over the place so no one would notice anything amiss when your lady wife returned."

"And now I understand why Comdiu insisted I await you in the Norin encampment. Without you, we might have wasted away beneath the glamour."

"Comdiu had far more than that in mind. I know what I must do when I return to Seare."

"You'll be leaving, then?"

"I'll help you see to the cleanup first, but aye, I must go."

"What about Aine?"

Conor closed his eyes and pushed down his anguish over the memory of what Briallu had scried. He had no way of knowing whether that had been real or just part of Briallu's attempt to keep him here. But if she felt the need to show him such a small shred of the scene before cutting it off, he could only trust that Aine still loved him.

"I can't wait. Something is calling me back. She is in Comdiu's hands, and I must trust Him to watch over her. If you find her, or you have word, please tell her where I have gone and help her get to her clan in Aron. Let her know that I will come back for her when I can."

"I will do all that is within my power. You have my word."

"Let's go back inside, then. We should try to get some sleep before we have to deal with this in the light of day."

But neither of them made any effort to return to their chambers, except to retrieve blankets to stave off the chill seeping through the broken-down walls. Instead, they sat huddled around a single table, drinking strong mulled wine until the first glimmer of light chased away the night's shadows.

CHAPTER
THIRTY-NINE

"So it's true."

"As far as I can tell, my lady." Guaire shot Aine a sympathetic glance as he wandered around her work room, looking at the collection of tonics and salves she'd amassed on the shelving. "Several men have said Lord Uallas has referred to financial difficulties at Eilean Buidhe."

Then that was the reason Uallas was so keen on marrying her. It was hard to be angry. After all, hadn't her mother done the same thing in marrying Lord Alsandair to secure Calhoun's throne? It was how the highborn remained in power. Marrying for love was not usually an option.

"Macha has said nothing about the fact I refused Uallas."

"She probably doesn't know. It's not a detail a man would put about freely."

Still, the silence made her nervous. Macha had been distant and cordial the few times Aine had supped in the hall, which in itself was disturbing. The chieftain had to be biding her time, waiting for something damning so she could . . . do what? Banish her? Seize her holdings? Worse?

"I need to leave the keep," Aine said. "I'm going mad."

"And Lachaidh or Oisean would haul you back over their shoulders before they let you be exposed again."

It shouldn't surprise her that the men Diocail assigned to keep watch over her were two who already knew—and had kept—her secret.

As if he knew her thoughts, a rap sounded on the door and Oisean poked his head in. "My lady, Rós is here to see you."

"Send her in."

Even though Rós was a young milkmaid who worked at the keep, the guard trailed her in, his hand on his sword.

"Thank you, Oisean, but I'm safe enough."

"My lady—"

She fixed him with a stern look. "Some things should not be discussed before men."

"In that case, I'll excuse myself as well." Guaire gave her an encouraging smile and slipped out the door, taking Oisean with him.

Aine reached for her gloves and slid them on with a heavy heart. How had everything gotten so complicated so fast? Enemies within, unwanted suitors. She couldn't even heal properly for fear her gifts would be found out and put her in danger, hence the gloves. Every time she touched someone, she was taking her life into her own hands.

And now she had to fear the likes of a milkmaid?

Oisean's scowl confirmed her thoughts when she emerged from her work room. "My lady, I can't protect you if you don't take my advice."

"I hardly think Rós is a threat."

"Don't be so certain. Trained assassins have already failed. If I wanted you dead, I would find someone both naive and desperate enough to slip a knife between your ribs while you treated her or to put poison in your food."

Aine stopped. Why hadn't she considered that the next move against her would be subtle? She was so used to dealing with overt threats that she had forgotten to consider the stealthy ones.

"I need a taster now?"

"That or eat only from the chief's platter," Oisean murmured as he delivered her to her chamber. "Perhaps I should test food brought directly to you."

Tightness coiled in her chest. His devotion was sincere. But she couldn't ask him to take such risks when she knew full well he was only acting under the influence of whatever ability she possessed.

"Oisean, your devotion is admirable. And appreciated. But I'm afraid you're being swayed by something outside your own will."

"This gift of yours? The one about which you spoke to Lord Uallas?"

Aine stared. "How did you know? Did he tell you?"

"No, my lady. Voices carry on the wind. I overheard."

"Then why did you agree to this duty?"

He lowered his voice. "Your father was an honorable man. We served him with devotion. You, my lady, would be a chieftain worth serving. And I am not the only one who feels this way."

Oisean gave her a precise bow and gestured for her to enter her chamber. She stepped inside and bolted the door behind her with shaky hands.

If Lady Macha hadn't had a legitimate reason to want her dead before, she most certainly did now.

✦ ✦ ✦

As Aine went about her daily duties, she was unable to shake the feeling of unease that had dogged her since Oisean's words. She avoided meals in the hall, afraid to look her aunt in the eye, lest Macha see what Aine knew.

Aine had never intended to try to supplant her aunt, but it seemed that the idea had occurred to more than one member of Macha's household.

The following night, Aine walked the perimeter of her room, worrying the button at her cuff. Lia watched her from where she mended a pair of leggings in the corner.

"My lady, you'll wear yourself out. Please lie down and rest."

"I can't." Aine couldn't explain the restlessness that had grown steadily more intense all day. She should return to her work room, but she wouldn't be able to concentrate any more there than in her own chamber.

When the heavy knock at the door came, she realized she had been waiting for it.

"Lady Aine, open the door. It's urgent."

Lord Uallas. Aine nodded, and the maid rose to unbolt the door.

Uallas rushed in, followed closely by Oisean, and bolted the door behind him. "We haven't much time, my lady. We must go."

"Go where?"

"Lady Macha has summoned the brithem. Diocail is gathering information, but she is going to call for your arrest. We have only minutes before she sends her men for you."

"I don't understand. Arrest for what?"

The bleak look on Uallas's face chilled her. "For witchcraft, my lady."

Witchcraft. She didn't even need to ask what the penalty was. She already knew.

Death.

Oisean hurried to her side and escorted her to the chair

before she could collapse, muttering under his breath. Uallas knelt before her and took both her hands.

"I can protect you, my lady, if you'll allow me. Once we escape Forrais, my men will throw them off our trail. We'll be safe on Eilean Buidhe. No one can touch us there. Even Macha will find herself powerless."

"Explain yourself, Uallas," Oisean demanded.

"We don't have time—"

"Lady Aine is not going anywhere with you until you do."

Uallas shot Oisean a hard look. When his eyes returned to Aine's face, they glittered with something cold and calculating she'd never seen before. It put a hitch in her breath. How could he have seemed so kind and sad to her before and now look so dangerous?

"This is all you need know. I'm neither as naive nor as destitute as everyone believes. I pay tribute to Lady Macha, as I do to every other clan chief between here and the island. Primarily Lord Riagain."

Aine stared. "Why?"

A smile appeared on Uallas's lips, but it was not a pleasant expression. "If one of them decided to attack my island, what do you think the other chiefs who believe they have claim would do?"

A cold admiration hung in Oisean's voice. "Very clever, my lord. They would be too busy fighting over their claim to get far in their attack. Especially when it concerns a Highlander with an island demesne."

"Indeed. A man who is beholden to all is in reality beholden to none. As long as I fill their coffers, they care little about how many men or ships I have at my disposal or where my wealth comes from."

Aine felt sick. On one hand, Uallas was certainly clever. On the other, this calculating side frightened her. No wonder he had presented marriage as a business proposal. In the absence of love, she was just a means to his own end.

"If anyone could keep you safe, it's Uallas," Oisean said.

Aine looked between the two of them, ready to say aye, ready to flee to Eilean Buidhe. But the words wouldn't come. In that moment, she knew she couldn't betray Conor. How could she break her vows before Comdiu? How could she ask her God to bless a marriage that, while legal, was a betrayal of a sacrament?

She lifted her eyes to Uallas's. "I cannot marry you. I'm sorry."

Oisean let out something that could have been a sigh or a curse. He paced away from them, his knuckles going white on the hilt of his sword.

The door shuddered under another round of pounding. Uallas gripped Aine's hand. "They're coming, my lady. This is your last chance. My offer still stands. But you must decide now."

He was confident in his ability to do what he promised. If she went with him, she would live. But the calculated edge in his voice still chilled her. "I cannot. I'm sorry."

"So am I." Uallas yanked her up, whipped her around so her back was against his chest, and laid the edge of his dagger against her throat.

Oisean took a lurching step forward, but the lord fixed him with a chilly look. "Stay right there. I don't intend to harm her unless I must. Don't make that necessary."

Her guard stopped.

"Lay down your sword."

Slowly Oisean obeyed.

"Now open the door."

"No."

"Now." Uallas pressed the edge of the blade harder to Aine's neck, and she gasped. Oisean turned pained eyes to Aine, his sense of failure written on his face.

"Do it," Aine said.

While Oisean reluctantly moved to the door, Aine whispered, "Why?"

Regret colored Uallas's voice. "If you won't go with me, I must have a plausible excuse for being here. The people of my island depend on me. For generations, Eilean Buidhe has changed hands, plundered by one chief or the next. When I took leadership, I vowed to end it. Can you understand that?"

There it was, the sadness beneath the steel. In that respect, he reminded her of Keondric, convinced to do wrong things for love of his clan. Somehow, though, she knew he would not be as easily persuaded as Keondric had been.

"I can understand that," she whispered.

The pressure relented on her throat just as the door opened and men spilled into the room, weapons bared.

"Easy, lads. I've got her," Uallas said.

Two men immediately surrounded Oisean, relieving him of his knife and holding him aside. Diocail made his way to the front and gave Uallas a slight nod. The dagger was withdrawn and Uallas released her completely.

"I'm sorry, my lady," the captain said. "It gives me no pleasure to serve this warrant from Lady Macha. You are under arrest, charged with witchcraft."

Even though she was prepared for the pronouncement, her knees still went weak. Uallas and Diocail reached out simultaneously to steady her.

What about your ability? her sense of self-preservation screamed. *You could bend them to your will.*

That would be wrong, came another voice—perhaps her conscience, her fear.

But she would live.

"Help me," she whispered to Diocail, pouring every ounce of

conviction she possessed into the plea. She willed him to feel her terror, the injustice of the situation. She could see the moment when her gift took him, a hardening of his expression, a hand straying toward his sword. "But do not kill Uallas. Wait for my word."

She met Oisean's eyes across the room, saw he already understood what she meant to do. She moved willingly toward the door, her arm in Diocail's grip as if he were carrying out his orders. As soon as they passed the doorway, she turned back to the men who had accompanied them, met each of their eyes in turn. "Please, I beg you. Do not let them take me."

"Seize Lord Uallas," Diocail ordered. "But do not kill him."

Uallas's expression changed as he realized what she had done, that he was in danger. The men descended on him, disarming him in seconds, forcing him down to the stone floor. She didn't wait to see what happened after that. Diocail grabbed her arm and dragged her down the hall at a run.

"Quickly. We must reach the stables before Lady Macha learns what has happened."

They fled down the lower hallway into the rear courtyard. It was pitch-black, and Aine stumbled on an uneven section of the ground before she could process that it was too dark. Where were the torches? "Something's wr—"

The unmistakable swish of an arrow cut off her words, followed by a muffled cry as Diocail hit the ground beside her.

"Stop right there." Macha's cold voice rang out in the dark.

Aine stumbled to a halt, instantly surrounded by a dozen guards with swords and spears. Someone jerked her hands behind her back roughly. "Please, don't let her—"

Something hard thudded into her head before she could finish the plea.

When she came to again, she was lying on her side on a

stone floor, her hands bound in front of her and a rag stuffed in her mouth. The orange glare of torchlight burned on the other side of her eyelids. Someone slapped her face, and her eyes popped open.

"She's awake, my lady," came a deep voice beside her. Uallas.

Hands hauled her upright and into a chair. She struggled to resolve her surroundings for a moment and then realized she was in Forrais's great hall. Macha stood on the dais like a queen presiding over her vassals. The keep's residents and guests crowded the room, the nobles seated at the tables, the servants packed around the edges.

Aine's heart did a little flip at the sight of the man standing beside her aunt. He was dressed like every other noble but for the sash draped over his shoulders, a symbol of office and authority. She knew the brithem who had presided over cases at Forrais for the last two decades, a fair-minded man who could be swayed by neither threats nor bribes.

This man was a stranger.

If Macha had gone to the trouble of summoning a different traveling judge, one who would presumably be more amenable to her wishes—and untainted by Aine's abilities—she had been planning this all along. No wonder she had been cordial. She hadn't wanted to take the chance Aine would flee and rob her of the pleasure of seeing her executed.

"Aine Nic Tamhais," the judge intoned, "you have been accused of the crime of witchcraft, which is punishable by death in Aron. What say you?"

Uallas removed the gag from her mouth, but before she could say anything, his knife went back to her throat.

"Nothing but the answer to his question," he murmured. "I've been instructed to kill you if you try to sway the men to your side again."

Aine swallowed, mortal fear coursing through her.

"Answer the question," the brithem said sternly.

Aine clenched her hands together. "I am no witch."

"We have witnesses who swear you have used magic to heal on more than one occasion." He raised a hand, and several people filed in front of the dais: Uallas's manservant, Oisean, Roidh, Lia. She swallowed down the sudden lump at the maid's miserable expression. Tears rolled down the girl's cheek and fell to the stone floor. What kind of threats had Macha made to ensure her compliance?

"Do you deny this?" the brithem asked.

Help, Lord. I have made a mess of this. What do I do? What do I say?

Immediately a presence filled her, like air in a bellows, wind in a sail. She lifted her head and looked the brithem straight in the eye. "No, I do not deny it."

Shocked murmurs broke out around the room.

"You admit you used magic to heal, yet you still deny a charge of witchcraft?"

"I did heal, aye. These gifts were given to me by Comdiu for the good of His people. If I did not use them, it would be an affront to my Lord."

"Heresy!" Macha jumped to her feet. "What you speak of has been long denounced by the church. And you dare speak of affronting Comdiu?"

"Who are they to pass judgment on what Comdiu has provided?" Aine returned levelly. "The gifts were given to the followers of Lord Balus, yet they have been abandoned by the church in pursuit of its own power."

"Clearly you have been ruined by your exposure to the Seareann heretics!" Macha shouted.

The brithem stopped her with an uplifted hand and addressed Aine. "You will not renounce your pagan ways?"

"I will not admit to any wrongdoing for exercising the gifts granted to me according to Comdiu's great wisdom."

"Then we will move on to the next charge. Murder."

Aine choked on the word. "Murder?"

"Do you deny you used your power on Master Diocail and his guards? That your actions directly led to his death?"

The blood drained from her head in a rush. She might be able to refute the charges of witchcraft, but she could not deny she was responsible for Diocail's actions. "He's dead?"

"It might as well have been by your own hand," Uallas said. Even if he were playing a part for Macha's benefit, his tone reminded her she was well and truly alone. Tears spilled from her eyes.

The brithem stared at her. "If you will not defend yourself, then I have no choice. I declare you guilty of witchcraft and murder and sentence you to death. Guards, escort her to the courtyard."

Gasps sounded through the room at the summary judgment. Their brithem took hours, days even, to consider the case, but Aine's guilt had already been long since determined.

Uallas stared at Macha. "My lady, the tradition is to give the condemned three days to consider their immortal soul."

"She has admitted to witchcraft! She has already sold her soul to the darkness. Three days or three years, she will not renounce the evil of her ways." Macha spoke with such pious conviction Aine could almost believe she spoke from her beliefs and not her greed. Uallas stepped back, his hands spread wide as if to concede to her judgment.

Two guards she didn't recognize replaced the gag in her mouth and unknotted the ropes that held her fast to the chair.

Their hands bruised her arms as they dragged her toward the entrance. The crowd parted and then closed around them, carrying them out the hall's doors and into the courtyard like the current of a river. Why so many? Why such an interest in where she was to be taken?

Nausea roiled through her, and her heartbeat pulsed in her ears, making her light-headed. She numbly took in the guards on the edge of the courtyard, the armed lords around her.

The guards stopped her before a wooden pole, and someone handed one of them a length of rope. Her knees went weak. She was to be burned? The guard wouldn't meet her eyes as he pushed her against the pole and began to lash her to the splintered wood. At that moment, she was actually grateful for the support. The ropes were the only thing holding her upright.

Macha stepped up before her, firelight and malice in her eyes. "Niece, this is your last chance. The brithem is willing to commute your murder sentence. Admit and repent of your witchcraft so you may be spared."

Aine's head dropped forward as tears slid down her face. Macha offered to commute the sentence she deserved if she would admit to a crime she hadn't committed. A sob built in her chest, begging to escape. What was the point? Her actions had caused the death of a good man, a loyal man, and his sacrifice had availed nothing. She deserved this death. She deserved to pay the price for the life she had stolen through selfishness and fear.

I'm sorry, Lord Balus. I failed You. I didn't trust You, so I made all the wrong decisions. Is this my punishment for my disobedience?

In her despair, she barely noticed when Macha took a torch from one of the men and touched it to the kindling at the base of the stake. It caught immediately, the flames crackling to life and slowly catching the larger pieces above them.

The crowd backed away several steps, pressed back by the ring of warriors, as the fire caught the pitch with a whoosh and engulfed the platform.

Aine moaned at the first touch of heat, terror crowding out her resignation. *Comdiu, please! Why have You abandoned me? I don't want to die!*

As if in answer, the flames licked her skin. She screamed.

Oisean lunged for the pyre, but two men restrained him. The scene grew fuzzy around the edges then, the pain distant even when the fire caught the hem of her dress. The smell of burning wool and hair surrounded her.

Then the flames morphed, the sickly orange glow changing to a pure golden light in the vague shape of a man. The heat still lapped at her skin, but pleasantly, like the sun's warmth on a winter day. Peace settled over her spirit, warming the cold places inside.

"Am I dead?" She was not in that other place, the one she'd visited when she'd died beneath the waters of Loch Eirich. Beyond the Companion, she could still see the watchers, still hear Lia's plaintive sobs.

"No. You are not finished here. You have not obeyed."

Aine bowed her head, awash in shame. "I must go back, mustn't I?"

"The forsaken city is to be rebuilt. In it lies the heart of the land, the heart of the people."

"The forsaken city?" she whispered. "Ard Dhaimhin?"

She got the impression of a smile, even though the Companion had no distinguishable features. "Go now. You have all you need to carry out our Lord's work. Have faith and you will prevail."

The ropes binding her wrists together and holding her to the pole fell away. She stepped forward through the flames, but the fire did not touch her, nor did the coals singe her feet. Cool air washed over her.

And then it began.

She's alive! She cannot be alive!

She's a spirit, come to take revenge on us all.

It cannot be.

I have failed; I have broken my oath.

The clamor of voices in her head sounded like a hall full of nobles, amplified. She pressed her hands to her head, wanting to shout for them to stop, but no one's mouth was moving. The observers stared in open-mouthed wonder.

Please stop!

Instantly, the voices subsided. A few people jerked back a step.

"Witchcraft!" one man shouted, pointing a finger at her. The murmurs began aloud this time.

"Quiet!" she screamed. Or perhaps she just thought it. Either way, the noise ceased. She looked among the crowd, focusing on individuals. Her gaze landed on Lord Uallas, who wore an expression of shock, relief—and shame.

Aine turned to the man who had decried her as a witch. "The blind will never see. This is not witchcraft but the favor of our great Maker, Comdiu, and His son, Lord Balus. The work of man will never overcome the will of the one God."

As she spoke, she felt the truth of the words flow into her. Unworthy, unfaithful as she was, Comdiu's blessing was indeed upon her. "It seems that my Lord is not finished with me yet."

Macha pushed forward through the crowd, her expression as hard as ever. But there was fear in her eyes, and her voice came out just a touch unsteadily. "I have wronged you. What claim do you make upon me?"

The formality of the words triggered a half-forgotten memory of clan law: Aine could make a formal demand of restitution, even demand trial. She opened her heart to Comdiu. His answer was quick and direct.

Aine met Macha's gaze steadily. "Only that which is mine by blood and right, so that you may understand Comdiu's great mercy toward you as He has shown toward me. It must be overseen in my absence as Father did in his lifetime. All except that which must be paid to Master Diocail's family as restitution."

"You are not staying?"

"No, my work is elsewhere." Aine looked at the people crowding Forrais's courtyard. "Comdiu is calling me home."

CHAPTER
FORTY

The carnage in Cwmmaen's courtyard was even more horrifying in the light of day. No one had slept much the night before, but all the men appeared as soon as the first strains of sunlight poured over the horizon. From the looks on their faces, they immediately wished they hadn't. Conor tied a strip of cloth over his mouth and nose, but it was little defense against the stench. And nothing could shield his eyes from the sight of decay, rotting corpses that should have been interred months ago.

"You don't have to stay," Talfryn said as they surveyed the scene. "This is not your responsibility. You have already done more than we could have asked."

"Unless I plan on walking to Aberffynnon, I suppose I should help." Conor shot Talfryn a crooked grin. "I still need a way to get there."

"In that case, we should get to work. Ial went to the village to find more workers, and Master Glyn is taking a message to my brother, but it will be days before the men from Gwingardd arrive."

Conor nodded and steeled himself for the task. Talfryn retrieved a handcart and several lengths of cloth, which they used to lift the bodies and transport them outside the fortress walls, where they would be buried. They'd already made half a dozen trips when Ial returned with an adolescent boy in tow. "My lord, look who I found in the village."

"Emrys!" Talfryn exclaimed. "Where have you been?"

"I'm sorry, my lord. I know I shouldn't have run, but they didn't notice me."

Talfryn took the boy by the arms. "No one is blaming you, Emrys. We just need to know what happened."

The boy raised tear-filled eyes. "The Northmen attacked, my lord, after you and Lady Hyledd left Cwmmaen. We thought it was a cart from Lord Neryn, but they were hiding inside . . . and then they opened the gates . . ." His voice choked on tears.

Talfryn straightened and met Ial's and Conor's eyes in turn. "The cart with which I was captured. They used it to gain entry to the fortress."

Conor's chest seized. So this was his fault. Talfryn's ploy to get himself captured in order to rescue him had directly led to the deaths of almost the entire household. He stepped away, struggling against the agony of guilt. Had he just obeyed Comdiu in the first place, none of this would have happened. Aine wouldn't be lost, Talfryn's guardsmen and servants would still be alive, and he wouldn't have broken his vows to his wife.

"Conor, you can't take responsibility for this," Talfryn said. "I obeyed Comdiu. He spared me, my wife, Ial. If it weren't for you, we would still be languishing beneath the sidhe's glamour."

It was a mark of Talfryn's nobility that he voiced the sentiment—even more that he actually seemed to believe it. But it didn't mitigate Conor's responsibility in the situation. Once more, he had blood on his hands.

Even so, if the sidhe had gone to that much trouble to ensure that Conor remain in Gwydden under the influence of her glamour, he had no doubt about where he was meant to be.

That strange sensation in the back of his mind returned, this time less of a battering ram and more of a gentle tug.

Aye. I understand. I'm coming.

Conor worked quietly until the villagers arrived. Once the slain men were carried out and given a quiet burial, the villagers set to scrubbing the stones with water and lye, washing away the putrid evidence of a battle no one could remember. Conor retreated to the bathhouse and scrubbed himself raw.

One of Talfryn's remaining servants brought Conor a change of clothes, just as fine as—if more practical than—the court attire he'd initially been given. He made his way back to the hall where Lady Hyledd was supervising the cleanup.

"My lord Conor." She dipped her head in a gesture uncomfortably close to a bow. "Or should I call you Brother Conor?"

So Talfryn had told her. It hardly mattered now anyway. "Neither, my lady. I'm just Conor."

"Somehow I doubt that." The searching look she gave him pierced him through. "What will you do now?"

"Return to Seare. It's clear to me that's where I belong."

"And what of Lady Aine?"

"I must entrust her to Comdiu."

Hyledd settled onto the bench and patted the spot beside her. "Talfryn told me about everything you've been through in Seare. You've done everything in your power to ensure her safety. How can you give up now?"

Her words struck deep. She was trying to be helpful, but she couldn't know how conflicted Conor already felt on the subject. "Please, my lady, know this is not an easy decision."

"I'm sure it is not. You must do what you feel is right. You can take a horse and go to Aberffynnon or you can ride north to Forrais. Either way, my husband has promised you an escort."

"Thank you, my lady. I will give that careful consideration."

He rose and moved quickly back to his chamber, his heart heavy. Aine had been in danger more times than he could count, more often than not because of him. He should be relieved that he would be allowed to return to Seare and finish the task he'd been given, but he felt nothing but grief at the prospect of giving up on her.

Yet Seare still tugged at him, like the moon on the tides of the ocean.

Is this what You ask of me? To give up the one person I truly love? To sacrifice her for the good of my people? Are You so cruel?

He half-expected a lightning bolt to strike him for his impertinence, perhaps even wished for it, but his accusations were met with silence.

Conor avoided supper in the hall that night, instead staring up at the moon from the newly cleaned courtyard. Two months. Two months since he had married Aine, two months of not knowing if she lived or died. Now he thought she probably lived, but she might no longer be his. Even if the scene Briallu showed him was false, how long would she wait for him? How long would she resist the pressure of her clan to marry?

This choice might mean losing her forever.

But she would be alive. And there are others who need your help. Other wives, husbands, children, whose pain is as great as your own. Would you leave them to suffer when it is in your power to change things? You must do your duty.

The thought was far too rational and unselfish to have come from him, even if it sounded like his own conscience. Comdiu had a funny way of making Himself known.

I will not.

He didn't sleep that night, tossing and turning in the drafty chamber. Had he not accused Comdiu of cruelty before, the first time he thought Aine was dead? Had Comdiu not had a greater purpose for him then?

I will not, he thought stubbornly, turning to face the stone wall.

But that tug grew steadily stronger the harder he resisted. What if this was the reason Comdiu had separated them? What if this was another test? He knew he was meant to reinstate the wards, help combat the evil that spread across Seare. Had Comdiu allowed all this—the shipwreck, the sidhe, the separation from Aine—just to get his attention?

His resistance fell from him. He should have learned long ago it was impossible to defy Comdiu's plans. With a heavy sigh, he turned his heart toward heaven.

You have my attention, Comdiu. Command me.

Prince Neryn's men arrived four days later, a full company of men with extra horses. Talfryn found Conor in his chambers, packing a change of clothing in a small knapsack and donning his weapons.

"I take it you're leaving?"

"Aye. I'm going back to Seare."

"What may I do for you, friend?"

"Transport to Aberffynnon and passage on a ship bound for Seare, if you're willing."

"Of course. We'd best leave now. You may need to spend the night in Aberffynnon anyway."

Conor thrust out his hand. "Thank you. Your assistance is much appreciated."

Talfryn grasped Conor's arm and shook his head. "No. I owe you a debt greater than passage on a ship could ever repay. Know that you have a friend in Gwydden, my lord. If there is anything I can ever do for you, you need only ask."

Conor bowed his head, overwhelmed by Talfryn's words. He could have simply thanked Conor for his service as a man. Instead, he had thanked him as a prince. It would be touching if his guilt over leaving Aine were not so sharp.

And if Conor didn't think he might someday have to call in the favor.

CHAPTER
FORTY-ONE

From the concealment of her cloak, Aine scanned the dozens of ships in port. The proprietor of the inn had said there were only two ships that traveled from Dún Caomaugh to Seare these days, and it had taken the better part of the morning to find the first. As soon as she had laid eyes on the *Verity*, however, she had felt the nudge that meant she should move on. Now she had made it to the end of the slips without any luck on the second.

The activity in the dock quarter flowed around her, no one paying any attention to the waif in their midst. A man jostled her from behind, and she reached for the dagger at her waist, but the traveler didn't give her a second look before cursing her and moving on. She was so accustomed to the deference given to a lady that she forgot that to them, she was just another bedraggled urchin. At least it proved it was an effective disguise.

Lord, protect me, she prayed, and immediately the answering reassurance filled her. It was the lesson she'd had to learn alone on the long journey south. Whereas she'd had the help of strangers on the way to Forrais, Comdiu had made it clear that this time she was to rely on only Him.

Aine was about to give up her search, when she saw a two-masted ship, a larger version of the cog that had taken her and Conor from Seare. Deckhands loaded wooden crates via a ramp on the port side. She circled to where the name had once been painted on the hull. The letters had been rubbed away, but the faint outline of a four-looped shield knot remained.

A laugh slipped out. Her Creator had a sense of humor—or perhaps just an ironic sense of provision. She waited for the men to deliver their load and go back for another before she approached the ramp.

At the bottom, however, she stopped, her heart pounding. She'd avoided thinking about the fact she'd have to board another ship to get home, but now even the lap of the water against the boat's hull sent a spike of panic through her. Three times she'd nearly drowned. Three times she had narrowly missed meeting her end in the water: first when she'd been forced into Loch Eirich by the sidhe, then in Glenmallaig's moat after Conor rescued her, and finally in the storm on the Amantine Sea.

I can't do this. I thought I could, but I can't. I'm not strong enough.

But what was the alternative? She'd already learned what happened when she didn't obey. Did she really think Comdiu would send her back to Seare and then allow her to perish on the open sea?

Her first step onto the plank was shaky, as was her second. But she forced herself up it, faster and faster, until she was standing on the deck of the ship. She snagged the first sailor she found. "Is this the *Honor*?"

He glanced at her, not unkindly, and laughed. "Aye. Best be off the ship, girl, before you get hurt. We have no need of your services." Before she could process what kind of services he thought she was offering, he turned away.

"I'm a paying passenger," she called after him, jingling her coin pouch for emphasis.

He stopped and looked at her, really looked this time. Evidently he realized she was not some street urchin and nodded toward a short, dark-haired man at the stern. "Captain Ó Meara there. You'll want to speak with him."

"Thank you." Aine strode toward the captain, dropping back her hood and throwing off one shoulder of her cloak to display her mother's marriage dagger, clear evidence of her nobility. It had been a risk, this deviation in her waif's disguise, but now she was glad she'd brought it.

"Captain Ó Meara?"

The man turned and sized her up before he spoke. "My lady? How may I assist you?"

He was sharp. He was also Seareann. Considering the Fíréin symbol, she should have expected as much, but his Aronan crew had thrown her off.

"I need passage to Seare. I understand you're making for Ballaghbán."

"Aye." The captain hesitated. "Forgive me, my lady, but you do realize that Seare is at war. The blockades have been lifted, but the cities . . . they wouldn't be safe for a lady with a full guard, let alone one traveling on her own."

A flutter of nervousness crept into her stomach, but she met his gaze. "I'm fully aware of what awaits me in Seare, sir."

He bowed his head. "Very well, then. You can take the aft cabin if you don't mind a few crates."

"That will be fine, Captain. Thank you."

He sighed heavily, the sound of a man who already regretted his decision, and then pointed her toward the small door beneath the upper deck.

The cabin was cramped and, as he had warned, stacked with

crates. Clearly he hadn't expected to take on any passengers. Not until she noticed a man's coat hanging on a peg did she realize that the captain had given her his own cabin.

Thank you, Comdiu. You are always faithful.

She took off her cloak and laid it over the top of the pack that contained her court gown and a small bag of medicines she thought might be useful on the trip. In a few weeks, she would be at Ard Dhaimhin. A giddy feeling welled up inside her, not all due to her return to Seare.

Conor was alive.

Aine closed her eyes and reached out with her mind. She had felt him immediately after the fire, when her new ability first began to manifest itself, but she'd been so overwhelmed by the press of pain and anger from those around her that it had gotten lost in the cacophony. But as the days had passed—nearly three weeks now—she had become more adept at identifying individuals. She knew for certain that one of them was Conor.

A light rap on the cabin door brought her to her feet. Captain Ó Meara poked his head into the space. "My lady, we're about to cast off. If you get seasick, you might want to come out on deck."

"Thank you, Captain. I'll be fine until we reach open water, I think."

He gave her a knowing look. Undoubtedly the captain knew the reasons a lady would need to disguise herself as a commoner. "I'll let you know when we're out of sight of land."

Her pleased frame of mind lasted only through the first part of the night, when a storm stirred up on the Amantine Sea, throwing the vessel around like a toy ship in a whirlpool. Aine stayed in her cabin, clutching a bucket and forcing herself to chew mouthfuls of the fresh mint she had brought along for this purpose. Unfortunately it was largely unsuccessful.

Closing her eyes so she couldn't see the movement of the cabin around her helped a little, but every time she tried, images from the last storm on the Amantine crowded in: the cold, the water, the terrifying slide across the decking into the sea.

Comdiu, preserve me, she prayed over and over as the ship did its acrobatic maneuvers through the waves.

"You all right?" the captain asked when he poked his head into the cabin. Aine just nodded. If she opened her mouth, bad things were liable to happen.

"The rain has abated. You might feel better out on deck in fresh air."

She shook her head. The memories were too fresh. It had been hard enough to stand on deck in the harbor.

Aine reached for Conor's mind, which grew more distant as the miles stretched between them. But she could still feel him, driven by some irresistible compulsion to return to Ard Dhaimhin. She allowed herself one brief smile at the thought of their reunion before the next wave hit and sent her scrambling for the bucket.

On the third day, Aine awoke to find that the pitching of the ship had been replaced by the steady pull of oars. Only the thud of wood in the locks broke the silence. She pushed herself up on the bunk, fighting a wave of dizziness.

She poked her head out the cabin door and blinked at the wall of white that met her, searching for the dark shapes that would indicate crew members.

"It's always like this now."

The deep voice of the captain came from the mist behind her, startling her.

"How near are we to the coast?" she asked.

"Several leagues still."

The closer they got, the more obvious it became that this was no natural phenomenon. Aine gripped the railing, assailed by the sick sense of wrongness that always accompanied the presence of the sidhe. She shivered violently and barely caught herself on the railing when her knees gave way.

"They are loosed," she whispered. "I thought—"

"Aye. It happened right after Faolán fell. Few understand why."

"But you do. You can feel the evil."

The sharp look the captain gave her made her snap her mouth shut. Instead, she reached out with her mind, trying to feel those thin, bright threads of magic she had always sensed on the isle. They were gone. The only power she sensed was dark, like oily scum floating on the surface of a pond. She shuddered.

"Perhaps you should go inside," Ó Meara murmured. "My crew are staring."

Aine straightened with his assistance and moved back to the tiny cabin, where she sank down onto the edge of the bunk.

"I don't know if I can do this." It was bad enough being able to sense the evil, which was strong, repellant. But the undercurrent of fear was so pervasive she could taste it. Seare had truly fallen.

But what other options did she have? She couldn't go back. Macha probably had agents in every port city, with instructions to kill her and dispose of her quietly. She had read almost as much in the chieftain's mind. Her aunt wouldn't attack her directly, considering people were already speaking of Aine as a saint, but Macha wouldn't take the chance that Aine would come back and seize leadership on the strength of that following.

Another reason why she'd left Aron as quickly as possible. She didn't want followers at all.

Aine closed her eyes and pretended to rest, even though her heart was heavy. The oppressive sense of evil grew as they neared shore. She curled up into a ball, forcing down the nausea that intensified with the pitch and roll of the craft as they came into port.

The captain slipped halfway into the cabin, his expression somber. "My lady, we have arrived."

"Thank you, Captain. For everything." She reached for her pouch, intending to pay the passage he had refused in Aron, but he again shook his head.

"No, my lady. It's my honor. And the least I can do for the sister of Liam Mac Cuillinn."

Aine's mouth dropped open. "You knew me? How?"

The captain just smiled and handed her a shred of paper, torn from the edge of a larger sheet. "Go to this alehouse and ask for Cuinn. Tell him I sent you. He will lodge you with his family overnight until you can move on. Don't linger in the city, though. The streets are safe for no one."

"I'm indebted to you, sir."

"No, you're not. Just be careful, Lady Aine." The captain turned and disappeared before she could say another word.

Aine rose to her feet, smoothed her dress, and said a silent prayer for strength. Then she stepped out the door, preparing to set foot in the waking nightmare Seare had become.

CHAPTER
FORTY-TWO

Eoghan shoved down his feeling of despair as he entered the port city, not entirely sure if it was the cloying mist or his disappointment in the results of his quest. When he'd left Ard Dhaimhin, his greatest worry had been whether or not he could locate Meallachán's harp. As it turned out, it had been easy to find.

Smashed into pieces and burned in the rubble of Cill Rhí. No amount of skill could reassemble the instrument into what it had once been.

At least Eoghan assumed it was the instrument in question. He had never seen it, but Liam had given him a thorough description, down to the carvings on the ivory tuning pins. Eight of those pins rested in his coin pouch now, practically the only objects that had survived the destruction of the Siomaigh monastery.

One of them was carved into the shape of a three-spoked wheel, symbol of their faith. Eoghan wanted to believe it was a sign, encouragement from the Creator, but he couldn't help feeling as though it were a warning about the future of Seare:

a symbol of Lord Balus, cast off among the ashes of a once-great edifice.

Do you trust your feelings, or do you trust Me?

Comdiu's chastisement was sharp and instantaneous, and it cut through Eoghan's dark thoughts. Even after preparing himself for it, he had succumbed to the sidhe's influence. If he could not trust his own judgment, what could he trust?

"Don't say it," he muttered aloud. "I already know."

Stay on course. Find her.

Eoghan shouldered his pack and adjusted his cloak so it concealed both his belongings and his sword. A port city of this size was infested by cutpurses and worse, all driven by fear and their baser desires, manipulated by the spirits of the mist into performing acts of which even they would not have thought themselves capable. The mist made it hard to see more than a few feet in front of him, and as he navigated his way into the rougher part of the city, he found himself dodging men with barely enough time to avoid a collision.

"Watch yourself," one man growled, hand moving to the knife at his waist. Eoghan just dipped his head and moved on before the accidental brush could escalate into bloodshed.

So this is what occurs when You remove Your influence from a land, he thought grimly, evading the reach of a young prostitute. The hollow, despairing look in the girl's eye struck him to the core, and he moved on before he could succumb to that same despair himself.

This is what happens when My people turn their backs on Me. If I removed My influence from the land, people would be wishing for this as a paradise.

Eoghan shuddered. That was a world he had no wish to see.

The mist cleared enough to show the intersection with a main thoroughfare ahead. That would be the road that led from the dock quarter. North of that, the nicer inns and drinking establishments lined the streets, or at least they once had. Eoghan had already been through this city once, and even though the mist had already begun to encroach, there hadn't been drunks propped up against the sides of buildings.

Stop.

Eoghan obeyed and looked around. He found an unoccupied corner beside the least raucous alehouse on the block and backed up against it, leaning casually as if he were waiting for someone inside. He loosened the dagger at his belt.

I'm here. What now, Lord?

Wait.

Very well, he would wait. It was hard to judge the time of day through the fog, but the vague glow from the west suggested full dark would fall in a few hours. Most of the ships would make port well before nightfall or anchor far offshore so they wouldn't be boarded by thieves or troublemakers. The few armed guards most merchants employed would not be enough to stop desperate men.

Eoghan lost track of time, suppressing a yawn with the back of his hand as the day lengthened. It wasn't until someone nearly walked into him that he realized he'd faded into the shadows. No wonder he had managed to avoid notice for so long. He straightened, vowing greater vigilance, when a tickle in his consciousness caught his attention just as surely as a tap on the shoulder.

A girl made her way down the street, struggling under the weight of a heavy pack. Men shot her curious looks, but no one addressed her—yet. The sight put his nerves on edge.

Her.

"Thank You, I hadn't guessed," Eoghan muttered under his breath. He instantly felt the sting of chastisement. Sometimes having the voice of Comdiu in his head made him forget he was talking to the Most Holy. A sense of humor his God most certainly possessed, but He didn't seem to appreciate sarcasm. Eoghan pushed away from the wall and fell into the stream of travelers, following a few paces behind so the girl wouldn't notice him.

She glanced down at a scrap of paper in her hands and then made a sharp turn at the next intersection. As she came to an alehouse from which loud music and even more raucous laughter spilled, she hesitated. He didn't blame her. No girl belonged in a place like that.

He approached her slowly, not wanting to spook her, and touched her arm. "Miss?"

She spun and, before he could react, pressed a blade to the inside of his thigh. "Move along," she said, her voice hard.

Eoghan froze, both because of her dagger's proximity to a major artery and because her identity took a second to sink in. "Lady Aine?"

She stepped back and sheathed the blade, her threatening expression melting into one of recognition. "Eoghan."

Her smile hit him straight in the gut, and she walked without hesitation into his embrace. He caught his breath before he could control his reaction.

"Comdiu is good. I was not looking forward to walking in there by myself." She stepped back and a frown creased her forehead. "What are you doing here?"

"Comdiu sent me. Of course He didn't tell me you were the one I was looking for." His relief at Aine's presence faded in favor of a sick realization. "Where's Conor?"

"Gwydden, I think. We were separated in that storm that followed us from Tigh. I feared he was lost at sea, but I sense him now. He's returning to Seare as well."

She spoke with such authority he could not doubt her. "You can tell me when we're safely away."

"Indeed. I was supposed to lodge here tonight."

"No. We can't stay in here. Even with me standing guard, I can't guarantee your safety."

"Where, then?"

"The sidhe's influence is much less outside of the city. Not as many people to draw them. I know someone who will give us shelter until we can head for Ard Dhaimhin."

"Thank you, Eoghan. You are the answer to my prayers."

Eoghan smiled and took her pack, but the warmth that crept into him at her gratitude felt like a betrayal. Aine was his best friend's wife, practically a sister to him, given his relationship with Conor. He'd best remember that. If Conor thought his friend was harboring thoughts that were anything but brotherly about Aine, he would not hesitate to stick a blade into the most convenient part of Eoghan he could reach.

CHAPTER
FORTY-THREE

Aine followed Eoghan south through town, where he turned off the noisy and crowded thoroughfare onto a quieter residential street. She had insisted on trailing behind him like a meek serving girl, even though Eoghan hadn't seemed pleased with the suggestion.

She had an ulterior motive, though. She had managed to conceal just how badly the dark magic in the city affected her, but the longer they stayed, the sicker and weaker she became. Eoghan was coddling her more than Ruarc ever had, and she didn't want to give him more reason for concern. Until they were free of the reach of the worst concentration of magic, she would not draw an easy breath.

She thought she was managing well until she stepped into a particularly cold pocket, a sign that a sidhe was nearby. She stumbled on shaking legs and barely caught herself before she went down in the dirt. Instantly, Eoghan was at her side.

"I'm fine," she insisted, but Eoghan shook his head.

"You can't go on like this. The sidhe affect you too strongly. We're going to need horses."

"I have plenty of coin—"

"Don't say that aloud." But Eoghan seemed to be thinking. "Our best choice is to send my friend back to purchase them. It'll draw less attention, and he'll know where we're least likely to be cheated."

"Can he be trusted?"

"With my life. And yours."

"I can make it. Just let me rest a few moments."

Eoghan looked unconvinced. She didn't need to read his thoughts to know he saw through her charade.

He kept up the pretenses to the edge of the city, his pace slow and steady for her benefit. Then, without a word, he swept her up in his arms.

"Please, put me down." It was an uncomfortably intimate position, pressed against his chest, his arms under her back and legs. She'd never thought she would be this close to any man but her husband.

"It's miles," Eoghan said. "You would never make it. And you weigh not much more than this bag."

Aine shifted in his arms, but that only made him flush. She stiffened. "I don't suppose I'm going to convince you otherwise."

"No." He grinned at her.

She relaxed a little and returned the smile, purposely blocking out his thoughts. She didn't want to know what he was thinking about this arrangement. She had to admit she was grateful for the rest, though. She curled her arm around Eoghan's neck and tried not to think about how it must look.

The shaky, ill feeling that had dominated since they came in sight of land began to fade the farther away they got from the center of the city. She closed her eyes and pretended to be asleep. At least then she wouldn't have to make awkward conversation with her husband's best friend, who was holding her far too close for comfort.

✦ ✦ ✦

Eoghan sensed the moment when Aine went from pretending to be asleep to actually being asleep, her muscles relaxing and her head falling forward against his shoulder. He managed to relax as well. It was more than awkward to be carrying Conor's bride in such a way, and they both knew it. But she was exhausted and would not have made it more than a few steps outside the city's borders.

Aine was clearly uncomfortable with the situation, but she couldn't possibly understand his own uneasiness. Until he ventured out of Ard Dhaimhin, he had never met a woman. Not that he had been ignorant of the full range of male-female interaction, but for a man raised among men, it was an odd experience. No one could blame him if he looked on a capable, beautiful woman such as Aine with a spark of interest, his friend's wife or not.

You'd do best to remember that, he reminded himself and shifted her in his arms.

After several stops to rest—Aine was light, but not *that* light—they came to a croft on the outskirts of the city. The glow of candlelight seeped from one of the windows. Eoghan gave Aine a little shake. "Time to wake up, my lady."

She murmured something unintelligible against his shoulder, but her eyes remained closed.

Eoghan shook her a little harder this time. "My lady, we are here."

Aine's eyelids fluttered and she looked straight into Eoghan's eyes. A flush immediately tinged her entire face and neck. "You may put me down. I'm awake."

He set her gently on her feet and stepped back while she

straightened her dress and regained her composure. "We'll be safe here. Criofan was a member of the brotherhood. He chose to leave Ard Dhaimhin to protect his family after the city was attacked."

Aine's eyes widened. "When did that happen?"

"I'll explain on the way, my lady. It's over two weeks to the forest's edge by horseback."

"And you expected us to walk?" She arched an eyebrow, reminding Eoghan she was a lady, unaccustomed to traveling by foot. She would have endured, no doubt, but she did not have the benefit of his Fíréin training.

The door of the cottage opened to illuminate the silhouette of a tall, muscular man. Criofan stepped outside and closed the door behind him, dropping them back into near-darkness. "You found her."

"Did you think Comdiu was surprised by her arrival?" Eoghan hadn't given Criofan the full story of how he'd known she would be arriving that afternoon, only that they would need a safe place to stay, away from the city.

The brother chuckled. "Come inside. My mother has supper on. You look as if you could use it."

Inside, the Fíréin brother gave Aine a little bow. "I am Criofan."

Eoghan realized he probably should have made formal introductions. "This is Lady Aine."

Aine swept back her hood and smiled. "Thank you for your hospitality, Brother Criofan. You cannot know how much I appreciate having a safe place to stay outside the city."

Criofan just stared for a moment, as if mesmerized. Then he shook himself. "It is our honor, my lady. Let me introduce my mother, Nola."

A surprisingly young woman set a pot of stew at the center of the table and strode toward them, wiping her hands on her apron.

"You are most welcome, my lady. We know what you did for our fighting men in the last days of the war. We are most grateful."

Aine took her hand. "Did you have a husband or sons fighting with Faolán, Mistress Nola?"

The woman seemed to crumple. "My husband. He never returned home to me. Did you know him, perchance? Lugaid Ó Murchadha?"

"I don't think so. What company did he fight with?"

"He was part of Lord Gainor's company, my lady."

Aine clasped the woman's hand in both of hers. "I did not know him personally, but the men with Gainor fought valiantly. It was only because of them that my brother survived the retreat."

Tears streamed down Nola's face. Aine put her arms around her. After several moments, the woman pulled away and wiped her eyes. "Forgive me. You will be hungry from the road. Please sit. Eat. It's not much, but you're welcome to it."

They huddled around the small table, where Nola had set out stew in her few scarred wooden bowls.

Eoghan ate in silence for a few moments, then set down his spoon and turned his attention to their hosts. "Tomorrow we'll need to buy horses in town. Do you know of a merchant who's trustworthy?"

Criofan chuckled. "In Ballaghbán? You'll find that a difficult task. There's a brother in town who might know. We can see him in the morning."

"Only one? There were half a dozen brothers when I passed through before."

"And all those who have identified themselves with the shield knot have been arrested and executed. The new lord at Lisdara takes great pleasure in making examples of the Fíréin they manage to capture."

Eoghan took in the information silently, though it sickened him. "I'm surprised they've managed to capture any."

"Word is they lost so many guards in the first attempts, thinking a half dozen would suffice to subdue a single warrior, they had to start sending a full company of men. Twenty years away from Ard Dhaimhin they might have been, but they were still Fíréin at heart."

"Is it only Fíréin they target?" Aine inquired.

They started at her soft voice. She had been so quiet that Eoghan had almost forgotten about her.

"No, my lady. All Balians are at risk. You need only travel to Lisdara to see. Lord Keondric has decorated the road to the fortress with their heads on pikes."

"Lord Keondric? How is that possible?"

"He seized the army from Fergus," Eoghan said. "He's the one who controls the men now."

Understanding surfaced on her face. She clearly understood the subtext of the statement even though few people knew the truth outside of the Conclave. Her throat worked. "Then we must find a way to reinstate the wards around Ard Dhaimhin. Balians need a safe haven. What better place to bring them than the city of our first Balian king?"

"My lady," Eoghan said, "Seanrós and part of Róscomain is burned. Our barrier is gone."

"If the wards are rebuilt, the Fíréin cannot hold the city?"

Eoghan and Criofan exchanged a glance, and Eoghan saw the same spark of hope rising in the other brother's eyes. "Perhaps, but the harp is gone. Destroyed."

"Where did the harp come from?" Aine asked.

"No one knows. Like all objects of power, it dates back to the Great Kingdom."

"Then it can't be the only way to reinstate the wards." Aine stood. "Mistress Nola, may I assist you in washing up?"

Eoghan watched Aine clear the table with the widow. She spoke with such conviction, it was impossible to believe that things could be other than she said. The only other person who seemed to believe so strongly in the impossible was Conor.

Could it be, Lord? Can it be done?

Comdiu did not answer directly. Still, a deep conviction crept into Eoghan's heart, a feeling that could be described only as affirmation.

CHAPTER
FORTY-FOUR

It took two weeks to reach the burned edge of Róscomain, not because of the distance, which was great enough, but because their path was constantly being diverted by patrols of Keondric's men.

"I don't understand how you manage it," Eoghan said, but Aine couldn't explain. Her powers were growing with each passing day until she could sense the presence of others who meant to do them harm or those under the influence of the sorcerer's power. Eoghan had related the Conclave's theory that the druid had inhabited Keondric's body, taking not only Diarmuid's powers but the Faolanaigh lord's as well. She could not shake the thought that the druid was aware of her presence and throwing men in their way in hopes of capturing her.

"I do not understand either," Aine said. "But I'm grateful for it."

Her gratitude was waning, though. The same awareness that allowed them to avoid the patrols made it difficult to ride with Eoghan. In town, surrounded by the constant hum of the inhabitants' thoughts and desires, it had been easy to block him out.

But here in the quiet, his thoughts intruded on every waking moment. She assumed he was talking to Comdiu, given the topics, but it was like listening to only one side of a conversation. Worse yet was when she got a glimpse of his thoughts about her. He was painfully aware of her as a woman and equally determined not to show it. Knowing she was his friend's wife only layered shame over his embarrassment.

Aine tried to turn her thoughts to other things, most often to Conor. The closer they got to their destination, the more she yearned for him. They had spent most of the last several years apart, intersecting for only months or days at a time, and knowing he was making his way back to her was nearly unbearable. She could not read his thoughts from so far away, but she could feel his presence, his intentions, in the back of her mind.

I love you, she thought just in case he could hear her. *I miss you. Hurry back to me.*

As they neared Róscomain, Eoghan detailed the assault on Ard Dhaimhin. She didn't expect the pang of anguish when he told her Liam had killed himself rather than give up vital information to the enemy. Her brother had gone to Ard Dhaimhin long before she ever came to Seare, but somewhere in the back of her mind, she had hoped they might finally establish a relationship. She'd even thought he might shed some light on this gift they shared.

Neither did she expect the extent of the damage when they reached the old forest. She had ridden through sections of these woods, visited trappers who lived on the edges. Now the trees' thick canopies were gone, leaving only charred black skeletons stretching grotesquely into the sky. The smell of smoke hung as heavily as the thick layer of ash on the forest floor. Nothing had been spared, no green in sight for hundreds of miles.

This was not just a military strategy to burn out the sentries and trackers. Aine felt that in her bones. This was a strike against the power of the Fíréin. The brotherhood had mastered the secrets of the forest so thoroughly they had kept away intruders for half a millennium. Now, with one stroke, the druid had turned them into common watchmen.

Yet he had also opened the way for the next step in Comdiu's plan. If the High King were to return and reign once more, Ard Dhaimhin would have to welcome all. The age of the brotherhood was over, but a new age would begin.

Aine smiled to herself, the wrong reaction to such destruction. It wasn't a vision exactly, not in the sense she was used to, but she felt the nudging of Comdiu anyway. She spurred her horse forward into the wasteland.

✦　✦　✦

Even prepared by Conor's and Eoghan's stories, Aine's first sight of Ard Dhaimhin took her completely off guard. It wasn't just the destruction, which was widespread—cottages burned, fields ruined, forests scarred—but also those things fire could not touch, such as Carraigmór's natural grandeur on the edge of the massive lake, and the sheer size of the Fíréin's domain.

They descended into the city by the winding switchback. Sentries watched openly, raising a hand in greeting to Eoghan as they passed and looking her over curiously.

Deeper in the city, rebuilding had already begun. Several men were busy rethatching the burned roofs of stone clochans. Others shoveled out the detritus of the battle, transferring it to large oxcarts or smaller handcarts to be taken away. Then there were the normal activities of a city: blacksmithing, candlemaking, weaving. The smell of cooking food drew her attention to the large, open-sided cookhouses.

Eoghan sent Aine a smile. "Impressive, isn't it? Even now."

"It is. It just needs a woman's touch."

"Then I know just the woman."

It will take far more than me. How would the leadership of Ard Dhaimhin receive the shocking proposal she intended to present? "Who's in charge here?"

"Brother Riordan."

"Conor's father?"

"He'll be pleased to meet his new daughter. He's already enchanted by you from the few details I gave him."

She ignored the implication, instead focusing on the sacrifice Eoghan had made. "Were you punished severely?"

"No, my lady, nothing beyond endurance." But the stroke of the lash was still fresh in his mind, as was the pain he had endured on their behalf. She winced and looked away. He had made the sacrifice willingly. She would not humiliate him by revealing she knew how harsh that punishment had been.

"We don't have stables for the horses," Eoghan said when they came to the bottom of the fortress. "We'll have to pasture them with the sheep." He caught the attention of a young, dark-haired boy and dismounted. "Breann, come!"

The boy jogged over to him, his expression brightening when he saw Eoghan. "You're back, sir!"

"I am. Have you been keeping busy?"

"Aye, sir. We've gone back to training, but we're spending our afternoons helping with the rebuilding."

"As it should be. Can you see our horses to the pasture, where they can graze? Find one of your céad mates to help you, and tell Brother Cian you need help brushing them down and removing tack."

"Aye, sir. May I tell them it's an order from you?"

"You can tell them, much good it will do you. I'm no longer in command here."

"Aye, sir, so the Conclave says. But you might need to tell the rest of the brotherhood that." He gave them a little bow and took the reins as placidly as any young groom. He gestured to another boy, and the two of them led the horses away.

"That one is far too smart for his own good," Eoghan said.

"You have no idea." Aine had gotten a glimpse of the boy's thoughts. Breann missed nothing, not the politics of the Conclave nor the dynamics of the brotherhood. And he looked up to Eoghan almost like a father.

Eoghan lifted their packs, which he'd off-loaded from their horses while Aine was focused on Breann, and gestured with his head toward the steps. "After you."

Aine stared at the hundreds of slick steps and sighed. No way to reach the top but up. She had to stop and rest several times on the way, winded by the exertion and still affected by the faint feel of the sidhe's presence in the distance. Only then did she realize that the overpowering sense of dark magic was absent.

"Are there still wards intact?" she asked.

"Not that I'm aware of, but I've never been able to feel them. Why?"

"Because the sidhe are not present."

Eoghan smiled. "That's because so many of our brothers are devout believers in Balus. We still have devotions twice a day in the amphitheater, and there are always brothers in prayer. It must be uncomfortable for them to be near so many with faith."

"I suppose so," Aine said with a hint of wonder before she continued climbing.

A brother met them at the top, and another opened the door to admit them to Carraigmór's massive hall. Aine allowed herself a moment of awe at the sheer immensity of the space and the weighty feeling of rock around them before Eoghan gestured for her to follow him down a corridor.

"You'll want to meet Brother Riordan right away, I assume. We'll try the Ceannaire's study first."

They wound up the sloping tunnel, the torches flickering in the breeze from their passage. Eoghan climbed the short flight of stairs and rapped sharply on the door before pushing it open.

"Brother Riordan, do you have a moment?"

A response came from inside, and Eoghan nodded to Aine. Suddenly timid, she brushed by Eoghan. Several men crowded around a table, but her eyes went to one man as soon as she entered. Tall and lean, with a braid in a familiar shade of brown-blond, this could only be Riordan, Conor's father. He resembled her husband so strongly that it was almost difficult to look at him.

"Brother Riordan, I'd like you to meet someone. This is Aine Nic Tamhais."

"Aine?" The color drained from his face, and he looked to Eoghan. "Where's Conor?"

"He's coming," Aine answered quickly. "Soon, I hope."

Riordan's expression melted into a smile. "Forgive me. Aine, you cannot know how long I have waited to meet you. You are every bit as beautiful as I expected you to be."

Aine's eyes went to his hands, red and raw, while she gave him a curtsy. He shook his head and circled the table. "I am perfectly entitled to give my daughter a hug."

His daughter, not his son's wife. As Riordan approached her, she didn't need to focus on his thoughts to pick up on a wave of love directed toward her. He did not know her. He only knew that his son loved her, and by extension, he loved her as well. He folded his arms around her and embraced her gently.

Without understanding why, she started to cry.

"Brothers," Riordan said quietly, "will you give us a moment alone?"

Aine was vaguely aware of the scrape of benches and the shuffle of footsteps as the room drained of its occupants. She pulled away and wiped her eyes, embarrassed by her reaction. "I'm sorry. I don't know why . . . I didn't mean . . ."

"You've clearly been through some trials, young lady." Riordan smiled and pulled out a chair for her. She sank onto it and tried to control her erratic emotions. He reached for her hand, but pulled it back before he could touch her.

"What happened?"

"Burned. Better than the alternative. I was only a few seconds away from being taken by the druid's sorcery."

Aine took his hands in her own, handling the raw skin as little as possible, but he still winced. It was bad, worse than anything she'd seen before. "This must be excruciating. How are you enduring the pain?"

"Our healers are skilled. Ointment and painkillers. It's bearable now."

Just barely, though. "Did Conor or Eoghan tell you that I'm a healer as well?"

"Aye. Your skills are well known. But I'm afraid I'm beyond help. At least I'll maintain use of my hands, even if I'll never grip a sword again."

She released his hand and folded her own in her lap. "I wouldn't be so sure of that. Sometimes things that are destroyed can be rebuilt stronger than ever."

"You speak of Ard Dhaimhin."

She nodded.

"The age of the brotherhood is over."

"But the High King is still to come. You know that. And you suspect Conor is that king."

Riordan's eyebrows lifted. "How do you know such things? Very few know our suspicions, only myself and Eoghan."

Aine blushed. "I'm afraid I have a confession to make." She told him about her ability and how it had only become stronger as time passed, though she left out the event that had precipitated it.

Riordan stared. "You and Liam share the same gifts, then. But it took him years to develop his. You must be stronger than he was at twice your age."

"That is not all," she said softly. "Look."

He followed her gaze downward and leapt out of his seat. His burned hands, raw and ruined, were covered with new pink skin. He flexed his hands as if he'd never seen them before.

"You did this?"

She nodded.

He seated himself again and grabbed her hand, determination glowing in his blue eyes.

"My lady, we have much to discuss."

CHAPTER
FORTY-FIVE

"She's amazing, isn't she?"

At Riordan's voice, Eoghan turned away from where he was watching Aine help several women plant seeds in one of the many small vegetable plots that were springing up around the city. Riordan smiled at him sympathetically.

"She's my friend's wife and your daughter," Eoghan said, a little too sharply. He couldn't deny that Aine had caught his attention by the way she'd handled herself after Conor had rescued her from Glenmallaig. But he'd written that off as his inexperience with women and how little she was like those in the stories the men liked to tell. The time he'd spent in her presence the past few weeks had only strengthened his under-standing of why Conor had fallen in love with her. She was truly a remarkable woman—a remarkable woman who was completely off-limits.

At least he wasn't the only one who thought so. Half the men in the city seemed to feel the same way. She had healed most of the wounded in her first days, and everyone knew she was responsible for the life that had been infused into the shell of the High City.

Two little girls ran by in a game of chase, squealing with laughter. That was one of the hardest things to get used to: the families. After Eoghan and Aine spent days cloistered in Riordan's office with the Conclave, it had been decided that if the brotherhood no longer functioned as it had for the last several centuries, it was pointless to allow only men. The first families to arrive were related to brothers who had decided to stay. As word got out that Ard Dhaimhin was a safe refuge, the trickle of newcomers widened to a flood.

There were still barracks for the unattached men, but the far side of the city saw an explosion of tiny cottages for families, several often sharing one space. Aine and the other women had established a garden behind each structure to help ease the burden of the burnt crops, though they would harvest little but winter greens until warmer weather in spring.

"I almost can't believe it." Eoghan shook his head.

"I can," Riordan said. "Ard Dhaimhin was once the High King's city. I imagine it looked like this when he was building the palace."

"Aye. But he had the wards to protect it."

Riordan sobered then. Until they found a way to reinstate the wards, they would always be at risk for Niall's wrath. The druid had not attacked them again because it did not serve him to lose more men without gaining the artifacts he desired. But they could expect another strike someday. And now they had women and children to protect as well.

"Come." Riordan nudged him with his elbow. "Let's find something useful to do."

"They look like they could use a hand with that garden plot."

Riordan winked at him. "I thought more like a quick bout. Don't want you to become more comfortable with a shovel than a sword."

"That sounds like a challenge." Eoghan grinned. "I accept."

Just as they turned away, an alarm rippled back to them, a trill of birdsong. The forest might be gone, but the signals were still familiar.

Someone was arriving.

✦ ✦ ✦

"Don't bury it so deep, sweeting. It only needs dirt up to your fingertip." Aine showed the little girl how much soil was necessary to cover the lettuce seed. The child smiled and brushed away the little mound she'd made. Aine patted her on the shoulder as she pushed herself to her feet and moved on to the next child working in the plot.

She was exhausted. But she was also the happiest she could remember being. The influx of families from the surrounding countryside had infused new life into Ard Dhaimhin, even though some of the warriors were taking to the idea of women and children better than others. If she judged correctly, they would see a rash of weddings come winter and spring. She smiled, taking pleasure in the idea even though it came with her own pain.

Conor was coming, she was sure of it. She had just been sure of it for the last month without any sign of him. Instead, she toiled away at Ard Dhaimhin, healing, planting, and counseling. Had she misunderstood her gift? Was it not as reliable as she thought?

A ripple of birdsong reached her ears, all the more striking because most of the animals had abandoned the forest. She had become accustomed to the signals of the sentries, even if she couldn't always distinguish their meaning. This one, though, announced that someone was arriving.

She stood, a wave of anticipation assailing her. Her heart

leapt into her throat. Could it be? Could she have missed his approach?

Aine brushed her dirty hands on her apron and rushed out onto the main thoroughfare, heart beating so hard in her chest that she swayed in time with every thud. *Please. Let it be him. Let it not be a mistake.*

A lone figure on foot descended the switchback into the city, too distant to let her distinguish features. She could barely keep herself from running toward him, but he was still at least a mile away. So she forced herself to wait, her hands twisting her apron into knots. Riordan appeared beside her, followed by Eoghan.

"Is it him?" Eoghan asked. "I can't tell from this distance."

Aine couldn't answer, afraid that speaking aloud might reveal the sight to be a hallucination. Her eyes never wavered from the man, but when he at last came within shouting distance, her knees nearly buckled. It was Conor, looking weary and haggard, his long hair shorn short, his foreign clothing streaked with dirt. She had never seen anyone more beautiful in her life.

"Go to him," Riordan murmured, steadying her with a hand on her elbow.

Aine staggered forward, drawing her husband's gaze. His eyes widened, and in a flash he was striding toward her with an intensity that almost took her knees out from beneath her again. In an instant, she was in his arms, pressed to him so tightly she could barely breathe. He shuddered and buried his face in her hair.

"You're alive," he whispered. "Comdiu be praised, you're alive."

He pulled back far enough to take her face in his hands and lean his forehead against hers, an expression close to pain on his face. "Please tell me I'm not imagining you. Let this not be another illusion." His words had the sound of a prayer.

"It's me," she whispered, seeking his eyes again. "Don't ever leave me again, promise me."

"They will have to drag me away." Then he was kissing her, pouring every last ounce of passion and grief and fear into the embrace. She didn't realize she was weeping until he pulled back enough to wipe away her tears with his thumb. "Why are you crying, my love?"

She shook her head. How could she put into words the depth of her fear and concern the last several months, the relief that she felt at finding him alive and whole before her?

She reached up and laced her fingers with his. "We've got an audience."

He kissed her again. "I don't care."

Neither do I, she thought, getting lost in the sensation of being in his arms again. She loved this man. Needed him like breath. But self-consciousness got the better of her and she backed away. "Plenty of time to . . . catch up. Your friends and your father will want to see you."

She could almost see the relief rush into him. "They're all right? Eoghan? My father? Master Liam?" Apparently he read the spark of grief in her eyes because he gripped her hand tighter. "Who?"

"Liam. Your father is in charge of the warriors now. But things have changed."

He took in his surroundings. "I can see that." Then he looked back at her and smiled. "Time enough for explanations. For now, we celebrate."

Impulsively, Aine pulled down his head and kissed him again, not wanting to let him go. She laced her fingers with his and turned to face the watchers. Riordan strode toward them, beaming, but when she sought Eoghan in the crowd, he was gone.

CHAPTER
FORTY-SIX

Only seconds after his reunion with Aine, Conor found himself surrounded, and dozens more people rushed toward him. Apparently word traveled as quickly as ever in Ard Dhaimhin. Riordan crushed him into a strong embrace. "Welcome home, son."

"Thank you," Conor said, overwhelmed by the welcome. He barely recognized the faces around him, conscious of Aine getting farther and farther away.

"The Conclave will want to speak with you. Eoghan was here a moment ago . . ."

Conor didn't hear the rest of the words as he pushed back through the crowd to Aine and seized her hand. "You didn't think you'd be rid of me that easily, did you?"

Mischief glinted in her eyes. "Don't think you'll use me as an excuse to escape from the Conclave. If I had to sit through their meetings, so do you."

Things had changed even more than he had thought. Obviously the city had been opened. He'd thought it a result of the burned forest, but as they fell in alongside Riordan and headed for Carraigmór, he realized it probably had something to do with his wife. Everyone knew her, and even more surprising, they didn't come across anyone whose name she didn't know in return.

"You have a lot to tell me," he said.

"As do you. For example, what have you been doing in Gwydden these past months?"

He looked at her in shock, but she just wore a satisfied little smile. "How do you know that?"

"Same way I know you're contemplating slipping out of the hall before the Conclave can pin you down."

It was indeed what he'd been thinking, though he doubted she knew—

"Oh, aye. I know that, too." She squeezed his hand, and a tinge of pink reached her cheeks.

"Then you know I'm not likely to be dissuaded."

It was Aine's turn to laugh. "Husband, do your duty and tell your story to the Conclave. There are things you must know." Her amusement faded. "Much has changed."

He nodded. There was plenty he needed to tell them, but he didn't want to waste this joyful reunion with Aine. Just releasing her hand to start the upward climb to Carraigmór filled him with loss.

Once they reached the hall, Riordan paused. "I'll assemble the Conclave. They'll want to speak with you right away."

"I'd like to wash and change first. And something to eat would be appreciated. I've been traveling on foot and sleeping rough for weeks."

Riordan looked startled, but he bent his head in acknowledgment. "I'll have supper brought to the hall. Aine can show you to her—your—chamber. Someone will come fetch you when the Conclave is assembled."

Conor gave a short bow and then turned to Aine. He could sense his father's disappointment. But what had he expected? Conor was no longer Fíréin, if that designation still meant anything. Did Riordan think his return to Ard Dhaimhin could overshadow seeing his wife again?

Aine led him upward to one of Carraigmór's guest chambers, sending him a sympathetic glance. "It will take time. You're his son, and his former student. He's not used to seeing you as a man, and one with other responsibilities, at that."

"How exactly are you doing that?" At first Conor had thought perhaps she'd had a vision of him in Gwydden, but this was more specific, more precise.

"A new gift," she murmured.

"You can read minds?" Conor grinned at her. "That could be fun."

Aine made a face and smacked him on the arm. "Stop that. You're supposed to be washing for supper, not contemplating other things." But her reproof was halfhearted at best.

She stopped before a door and pushed it open to reveal a sparse chamber. Apparently the opening of the city hadn't changed the brotherhood's ideas about living requirements. As Conor wandered the room, though, he saw evidence of his wife's presence: an ivory comb and a hair ribbon on a low table, a gown hanging on a hook. Aine went to a basin and poured water from a pitcher and then set a folded cloth by it, her movements precise and measured.

"If you'd waited, you could have had warm water," she said.

"And I'd have to smell like the road for the rest of the night." Conor dumped his pack out on the bed and began to remove his weapons. Aine was there before he could get very far, unbuckling his baldric with nimble fingers.

"Gwynn?" she guessed, assessing the sword before she put it aside on the bed.

"Aye." He pulled his stained tunic over his head and paused as Aine removed an embroidered garment from his pack.

"What happened, Conor? Where have you been? This is thread of gold."

How could he sum up all that had happened since leaving Seare? "I just came from Cwmmaen, Prince Talfryn's household. The rest . . . can you forgive me if I only want to tell it once?"

She looked at him then—really looked, her eyes lingering on the new scars he'd acquired—and her jaw tightened. Before she could say anything, he tugged her to him and kissed her.

"What was that for?" she asked breathlessly.

"You have to ask?" He lifted his eyebrows, trying for a teasing tone, but it fell flat. He sighed. "Can you blame me if I want to pretend for a few moments that we live an ordinary life?"

"No. I can't blame you. I want nothing more myself. But, Conor, we're at war."

He released her. "I know. The sidhe have overtaken the kingdoms, and in some way, my clan is responsible. Which means I have the obligation to make it right."

"That's too much responsibility for anyone to take on, even you."

He turned away and plunged the rag into the water, then ran it over his face and neck. "Someone has to redeem the Mac Nir name, Aine. Else what do I have to offer you?"

"You." She positioned herself between him and the basin. "That's all I've ever needed. Now wash up before they send someone for us. I want to hear your story. It's taking all my restraint not to pull it from your mind piece by piece."

He reached for her hand and brought it to his lips. "I love you, Aine. You have no idea what it was like for me, not knowing."

"I do." She stole a kiss and then slipped away before he could make good on his thoughts of a true distraction. The half smile she wore said she knew exactly what she was doing.

✦ ✦ ✦

When Conor and Aine arrived in Carraigmór's hall, the Conclave members were just sitting down to the table set with bowls of stew, fruit, and several loaves of bread with honey. Two large pitchers of mead sat in the center with a stack of cups. Conor suspected that however much the city had changed, this spread was just as unusual now as it had been under Liam's command.

Those things would shift, though. Conor didn't need Aine's mind-reading gift to know that the city would someday be the seat of a monarchy—that eventually the kingdom's customs, those the Fíréin had so carefully kept away, would start creeping in. He wasn't yet sure if that were good or bad.

Eoghan entered the hall at the last possible moment. Conor stilled, his hand on the chair back, sensing the tension in his friend's posture. Then Eoghan pressed him into a hug, thumping his back hard enough to knock the wind from him, just as he had done when Conor was a novice.

"Brother," Eoghan said, as if all he needed to express was contained in that one word.

"I told you we'd see each other again," Conor said. "I just didn't expect it to be so soon."

Riordan stood and gestured to them. "Conor, Eoghan, sit."

Eoghan circled to an empty seat next to Riordan, leaving the two chairs opposite them for Conor and Aine. Conor reached for the mead and poured a cup for himself and his wife before he spoke.

"Tell me what happened here."

Riordan launched into a lengthy explanation of the attack on Ard Dhaimhin, his account punctuated by other members of the Conclave. Conor merely nodded, even though his stomach sank with each new detail. So many casualties. Those men commanded by the druid—Keondric now, it seemed—were just as much victims as his fallen brothers.

When Riordan got to Aine's role in the reopening of the city, the first real smile touched Conor's lips. He squeezed her hand under the table. "Somehow I knew you'd be at the center of it."

He looked around the table. "What are our numbers now?"

"Two and a half thousand Fíréin remain. The rest chose to return to the kingdoms to protect their families. A few hundred warriors have joined us as well as another thousand men, women, and children. Were it not for the burnt fields, we'd have no difficulty feeding everyone, but our resources are stretched thin. We'll need this year to be our best harvest ever in order not to starve."

Conor's hopes plummeted at the new reality of Ard Dhaimhin. So many had come to the city, looking for sanctuary. Would they avoid the war and violence outside only to die of starvation here? For that matter, how long could the Fíréin hope to keep another battle from their doorstep?

"Ard Dhaimhin is vulnerable," Conor said quietly. "We must reinstate the wards."

"The harp is gone," Eoghan said. "Smashed, burned. I saw it with my own eyes." He fished a tuning pin from his pouch and slid it across the table.

Conor handled the ivory pin thoughtfully. He felt nothing—no power, no indication that this was from Meallachán's exceptional harp but for its fine craftsmanship. He pushed it back to Eoghan. "I may not need it. But I'll have to experiment with Master Liam's harp before I know for sure. Brother Gillian might have some ideas."

The table remained quiet, and once more his stomach pitched. "When?"

"Not long after the siege," Riordan said. "As far as we can tell, he went peacefully."

Conor wiped a weary hand over his face. He had been relying on Gillian's knowledge to figure the wards out. Now that he was gone, it would make his task that much more difficult.

Eoghan pulled the conversation back on track. "Tell us why you don't need the harp."

Conor detailed his last two months to rapt attention, giving only the most abbreviated version. He didn't go into how he had nearly died in a goat pen, how he had debated giving up Ard Dhaimhin's secrets to save Aine. He certainly didn't mention Briallu. Aine's hand tightened on his beneath the table with every new detail.

"What did you learn that might be useful to us here?" Daigh asked.

"I suspect the sidhe's influence is more widespread than we thought. They're present in Gwydden. Certain things Haldor said made me wonder if they haven't been encroaching on the Lakelands as well."

"Lord Balus warned me as much," Aine said softly. "Seare is only the beginning. If they are not stopped here, now, there is no hope for the rest of the world."

Conor slumped back in his chair. She was right. She'd told him of Balus's words to her, about the evil that would sweep across mankind. This was simply the first battleground. Finally he said, "The wards will only discourage the sidhe from influencing the city, assuming I can rebuild them. We need to find a permanent solution. If they're allowed to continue their dominion, there will be no Seare left to liberate."

"I've seen that firsthand," Aine murmured, exchanging a significant glance with Eoghan.

Conor frowned. Since when did his wife and his friend share thoughts?

"Comdiu sent me to retrieve Aine from Ballaghbán," Eoghan explained. "The sidhe's influence is particularly strong there. It affected her badly."

A tinge of pink touched Aine's cheeks, and Conor's frown deepened. What on earth was that about? Riordan must have caught the shift in mood because he said, "We should let you rest. You and Aine will want to talk, and you've been traveling for a long while."

Conor should have been relieved—after all, some time alone with his wife was all he'd wanted in the first place—but he couldn't help but feel that something was being kept from him. He mumbled a polite farewell to the group and offered Aine his arm to escort her from the hall.

After several seconds, he murmured, "What aren't you telling me?"

She looked genuinely surprised. "About my arrival? About Aron? I'll tell you everything. I just don't think either of us is ready to discuss it all tonight."

"That's not what I meant. I saw the way Eoghan looked at you."

Aine stiffened. So he hadn't been wrong.

"My best friend. Did he . . . ? Has he—?"

"Heavens no, Conor! He loves you. He would never . . . I shouldn't even tell you this. I wouldn't know if it weren't for my gift."

Aine's steps sped up, and Conor increased his own to keep pace with her. "If my friend has made some sort of advance toward my wife, I'd like to know."

"He can't help it," she said, a sigh in her voice. "It irritates him. It's uncomfortable for me. But you have to understand, for the men who were raised here in the brotherhood, it's a big change to have women around. I suspect we'll be seeing a lot of weddings this winter."

She was right, of course. But the idea that his best friend might have feelings for his wife—how could Conor ever look at him the same way again, even if Eoghan never acted on those feelings?

They arrived at their chamber, and Aine pushed through the door without waiting for him. "I shouldn't have told you. It would have been better for you not to know."

A horrifying thought occurred to him. He shut the door behind them while he worked up the courage to ask. "You don't . . . return those feelings, do you?"

She spun, eyes flashing. "How could you ask that? I'm your wife. I love *you*."

"Still, things change." His voice came out choked. What if it were true? She hadn't wanted to be alone with him. She'd instead encouraged him to do his duty to Ard Dhaimhin—

"Conor."

His eyes snapped to hers mid-thought. She knew what he was thinking.

"Don't be an idiot." She stepped close to him and looked into his face. "I love you and you alone." She rose on tiptoes and brushed his lips with a kiss that held as much promise as her words.

He ran his hands down her shoulders and bent for another kiss, wishing he hadn't had the doubt planted in his mind. He should still be careful with her, woo her, win her. It wasn't as if they'd had a proper courtship. Perhaps Aine just needed to be reminded of the connection they had always shared. He could be patient.

"You don't need to win me, Conor," she murmured. "I am already yours."

Then she was pulling his head down and kissing him hungrily. Her hands roamed his back, then moved to the hem of his tunic and tugged it off over his head.

"Aine," he whispered, but she silenced him with a long, eloquent kiss.

"I know," she murmured. "Me too."

Apparently words were no longer necessary.

CHAPTER
FORTY-SEVEN

Alertness seeped into Aine like the spill of early morning light. She stretched and rolled to her side, her hand splaying out beside her and touching warm skin.

Her heart immediately accelerated, carrying off the last bits of sleep. She struggled to keep her eyes closed. After all the mornings she had woken up alone, wishing for her husband beside her, part of her was sure this was a dream, that when she opened her eyes, she would find only empty space.

"I know you're awake." Conor's voice, low and teasing, rumbled in her ear.

A smile crept over her face. "No, I'm not."

His fingertips brushed her bare waist, and she squirmed away, her smile widening until she couldn't resist it any longer. She opened her eyes and found herself looking into his beautiful gray-blue ones. He lay on his side, head propped on his hand, watching her with an expression that made her already-rapid heartbeat stutter. "Good morning, love."

"Good morning to you, husband." She loved the way the

word sounded on her tongue. "Have you just been lying here watching me sleep?"

"Of course not," he said, but his smile gave lie to the words. Aine shut the door to his mind the best she could, but images still seeped around the barrier. They made her want to blush.

"What are you thinking?"

He smiled. "You first. It's only fair. You can already read my thoughts."

"You'll think I'm ridiculous."

"Try me." He took her hand and twined their fingers together between them on the mattress.

Her smile faded. "When I was in Aron, I'd sometimes dream about waking up and having you there beside me. I'm half-afraid I'm going to wake up and find myself alone."

"I'm sorry, Aine." He brought their joined hands to his lips and kissed her fingers, one by one. "I promise you, it's not a dream. And I don't intend on going anywhere."

The love that radiated through his words and shone in his eyes turned her insides to warm honey. Then she sighed. "You might as well tell me. You're trying to focus, but little shreds of your thoughts keep slipping out. What about the wards?"

Conor laughed and rolled away from her. "This gift of yours is going to take some getting used to." He reached for his tunic and trousers on the floor, giving her a view of his muscled back. She smiled. Good thing he couldn't read her mind. They had too much to do today to get distracted this early.

"The wards?" she prompted, as much for her benefit as his.

He stopped and turned, trousers donned, tunic in hand. "I'm going to try to rebuild them."

"Now? What about the harp?"

"I don't need Meallachán's harp. I learned that while in

Gwydden." His lips dragged upward into a slow grin. "I meant to tell you; I was just . . . distracted."

She bit her lip against the impulse to smile. "You can rebuild the wards with anything?"

"I think so. It has more to do with being able to control the magic. I suspect there could be others with the power to affect the wards if they have another way to direct it. For all we know, if music isn't required, it might not have been Meallachán and the harp that broke the wards at all—just someone who has an understanding of the old magic."

"That doesn't make sense."

"Doesn't it? Since when does it make sense that I should be able to *play* a ward into existence? It's like Meallachán explained to me at Lisdara: music is one of the last pure gifts of heaven left. For me it was the first indication that there was anything different about me. Whatever my intrinsic gift is, it comes out in music."

"And mine comes out in healing?"

"No. I think your gift is empathy, and healing is only a small part of it. That's why you draw people to you, why people seem to love you at first sight, why you have the ability to read minds now."

"You have no idea," she murmured. She hadn't even had the chance to tell him all that had happened at Forrais. He looked at her questioningly, but she shook her head.

If Conor's gift wasn't music, if it simply emerged through music, what was it?

"You think you can do it?"

He nodded.

"Then I'm going with you." She slid off the side of the bed, taking the coverlet with her as she retrieved her own dress from the floor. She felt his eyes on her as she slipped on the chemise and heard the ideas rattling through his head, suddenly distracted from his thoughts of wards and magic. A giddy laugh bubbled up inside her. "I know you're looking."

"I'm not going to be able to slip anything past you, am I? Let's go find something to eat before we summon the Conclave."

"I need to comb my hair first."

He wandered to a low table, where Aine had set out her personal items: the decorative brass mirror, a coil of ribbon, a carved wooden comb. He picked up the comb and gestured for her to sit.

"You're going to fix my hair?"

"I reckon I can manage a simple braid."

Aine smiled as she climbed back onto the bed and turned her back toward him. He tugged the tangled strands, taking care not to hurt her as he combed them smooth. She shivered as his fingers brushed her neck and shoulders while he worked. She didn't need to look at his thoughts to know he was doing it on purpose. Finally he decided to stop torturing her and braided her hair into a thick plait, tying the bottom with a piece of the ribbon on the table.

"There. I'll never be mistaken for a lady's maid, but it's neat enough."

She twisted around and let her gaze travel over him, drinking him in. Her husband, equal parts warrior and musician. He bore a few more scars than she remembered, but his manner was as gentle as ever, holding the delicate comb in calloused hands. Her heart knocked with painful intensity.

He'd changed. He'd always been serious and intense, but now he possessed a new air of gravity, a somberness. Was it that he'd seen too much that couldn't be undone, or was it just a sign of maturity? After all they had been through, they couldn't help but change and grow.

"What is it?" she asked.

He toyed with the end of her braid. "I can't help feeling like this was in some way my fault."

"How? You weren't even here."

"That's my point." He took her hand, absently brushing his fingers over the back of it. "I would do anything for you, Aine. From the moment I saw you, I've known . . . there is nothing I wouldn't sacrifice for you."

A small kernel of dread grew in her chest. "And I, you. We were meant to be together. Don't tell me you're doubting that again."

"No, no." He smiled and laced his fingers with hers. "But I thought it was my duty to protect you at all costs. I should have understood that you are chosen by Comdiu. He will protect you, with or without me. He tried to teach me that lesson while I was at Ard Dhaimhin, when I thought you had drowned, but I didn't learn it."

"I don't understand what you're saying."

"I've had a lot of time to think about it. The plans of men succeed only where Comdiu allows it. That's something Master Liam used to say. I think the storm was for me. Had I just put you on the ship like I was supposed to, the storm never would have come; you would have been safe in Aron. I wouldn't have had to be in captivity to learn the lesson Comdiu wanted to teach me." His voice roughened. "I could have fixed the wards and no one would have had to die."

"Look at me." When he didn't respond, Aine repeated herself, her voice harder. "This is too much responsibility to take on yourself. If you had not rescued me at Glenmallaig, I would be dead."

"Comdiu would have rescued you."

"He did. He sent you to me. Conor, you cannot second-guess your choices. Perhaps we didn't do the things we should have. I thought some of the same things you did, that I was being punished for my lack of obedience. But Comdiu made me see the truth. He does not condemn those He has called. He corrects us, aye. In my case, it took a Companion chastising me for my disobedience. But He is not finished with me."

Conor nodded, but his gaze never moved from their joined hands. It took all her will not to delve into his mind and see what still troubled him. Her chest constricted with fear. "That's not all, is it?"

One side of his mouth lifted, more a grimace than a smile. "I fear I'm more stubborn than I should be. On my way back to Ard Dhaimhin, I was certain I would do all that was required of me, no matter the cost. I would not fail Comdiu again." He lifted his eyes to hers. "But the moment I saw you, I couldn't think how I could have done anything differently."

The tightness in her chest clamped down another degree, both painful and giddy. Had she ever dreamed she would be loved by anyone with such intensity? Who was she to inspire such devotion?

Then a chill slid over her skin. *The moment I saw you, I couldn't think of how I could have done anything differently.*

Why had it not occurred to her before now? Her gift drew people to her. Aye, it had saved her life more than once, but it had cost Diocail his. What if that connection Conor felt, that knowledge he would do anything for her, was merely a compulsion?

What if their love were a lie?

She couldn't breathe. The tightness paralyzed her, made her pulse throb in her throat. She had to tell him. Uallas had said that once he realized it, it hadn't affected him again. The fact he'd been able to hold a dagger to her throat seemed to bear that out.

She opened her mouth to make the confession, but she couldn't say the words. What would happen if Conor learned he'd been duped? Would he leave? Would he not finish what he was meant to accomplish in Ard Dhaimhin?

Then came an even greater surge of fear: what if this had been Comdiu's plan all along? After all, her ability had to be a gift from Him. The Companion had said she had all the tools she needed to accomplish Comdiu's work.

But that flew in the face of everything she understood about their God. If He did not force their obedience, would He really give her the means to command Conor's devotion, great plan or not?

She pressed her fingers to her temples, where a headache had begun to throb. She needed time alone to pray, time to let Conor clear his thoughts. If he were not near her, he was free to do what Comdiu asked, away from compulsion. So much evil lurked beyond the boundaries of Ard Dhaimhin. His first priority must be the wards, not her. She shivered.

He frowned at her gooseflesh and rubbed her arms. "Are you all right, Aine?"

"I'm fine. Just a little hungry. Let's find something to eat, and then you can find Liam's harp."

Conor nodded and kissed her lightly, even though his brow remained furrowed. He could not fail to notice the sudden change in her. She pushed away the sick feeling and put on a smile instead.

If she really did have that powerful of an influence over people—especially Conor—then she would do all she could to make sure she was not interfering with what Comdiu had told him to do.

✦ ✦ ✦

Conor felt the moment Aine withdrew from him. He'd made a mistake. He shouldn't have told her the thoughts that had plagued him throughout his trek to Ard Dhaimhin. Why had he thought it was a good idea? He'd practically said the deaths in Ard Dhaimhin were her fault. *I loved you so much I let hundreds of people die.* Why would he want her to carry that burden?

He knew no more about love and women than Eoghan.

Unfortunately, that brought up another issue he didn't want to think about. As they made their way from Carraigmór to the cookhouse, where the second wave of men was queuing for the morning meal, he realized he might have no choice. Just like yesterday, more men greeted Aine than Conor. It seemed his wife had inspired devotion in more than one brother. Once he and Aine took their bowls of porridge, he steered her away from the crowd to a more secluded spot beneath a cluster of trees.

She nudged him playfully. "Afraid to share me?"

"Something like that."

Aine reached for his hand and squeezed it. "I love you and you alone. Don't forget that."

"Am I interrupting something?"

Conor glanced up to find Eoghan standing over them, arms crossed over his chest. He couldn't keep the scowl from returning. "Aye."

"Of course not," Aine said, smiling. "Join us. We were just going to come looking for you."

"We were?"

"You were." She nudged Conor again, and he sighed.

"That gift of hers is a little disconcerting, isn't it?" Eoghan said as he lowered himself down beside them.

"I try to ignore it, but sometimes you menfolk think so loud it's like you're shouting."

Eoghan grinned. Conor tensed, but he continued to spoon porridge into his mouth. No matter what Aine claimed, it was obvious she and Eoghan had formed a rapport. And why not?

Eoghan had been sent to help her, while Conor was paying the price for his disobedience.

Aine didn't seem to notice, though. Either she wasn't paying attention to his thoughts or she couldn't read them all the time. He wished he knew for sure.

"Conor is going to try to rebuild the wards," she told Eoghan. "We'll need to summon the Conclave. Will you help?"

Eoghan looked intrigued. "Of course. I'll wait for you in the hall."

Conor said nothing as the brother left, and Aine turned back to her breakfast. When they were both finished, she took his bowl and stacked it in her own. Her hand lingered on his wrist.

"Eoghan and I are just friends," she said. "I am yours, heart, body, and soul. You have nothing to fear from him or any other man."

"I don't doubt you," he said. And he didn't.

But that short discussion had changed something between them that even two months apart had not, and he had no idea how to fix it.

CHAPTER
FORTY-EIGHT

"What if it doesn't work?" Conor paused outside the great hall, where Riordan, Eoghan, and the rest of the Conclave waited, expecting to witness the rebuilding of Ard Dhaimhin's wards. He'd said he was sure he could rebuild them without Meallachán's harp after what he had done in Cwmmaen's hall, but it was all just supposition. What if he started to play and the only thing that happened was a little music? Why hadn't he tried this in private first?

"It will work." Aine stretched up to kiss him lightly and squeezed his arms in encouragement.

He nodded, buoyed by her belief in him. Whatever had happened earlier that day, the love shining in her eyes was real, as was her conviction that Comdiu had brought him here for this purpose. He actually believed it might be possible.

In a few moments, they would find out.

The harp sat beside a chair in the center of the room, innocuous, unremarkable. If he understood his gift, the actual harp should be immaterial. When he was finished, would it hum with power like Meallachán's? Or would it go back to being just a simple instrument of polished maple, never hinting at the role it played in the protection of their city?

Conor strode into the room, making his expression confident, but he needn't have bothered. The anticipation and anxiety in the room was palpable. The moment demanded he make some sort of announcement, a grand gesture, but he didn't trust his voice. Instead, he sat in the chair and lifted the harp into his lap.

Aine took up a position across from him and offered him an encouraging smile. He took a breath, put his fingers to the strings, and began to play.

Unintentionally, the notes took on the form of an old song, the one he had composed for Aine years ago at Lisdara, before he left her for the first time. And then the music began to change. He lost sight of the individual notes, the melody. In his mind's eye, he saw the music as a golden light, emanating from the harp and spreading out over the fortress.

He stretched himself further and it curved into a shining dome, encompassing the city, the forests, all the land the Fírein had laid claim to, all the land they depended on for their sustenance. When it had expanded as far as he could see in his mind's eye, he let it fall in a shimmering curtain to the ground. It was not the web of interconnecting wards that had originally protected the city and given warning to the sentries but a shield— a shield of song and magic and will, a barrier to those who meant to harm the new city that had emerged from the druid's attack.

Satisfaction swelled in him as the last notes faded. He had done it. Conor opened his eyes and scanned the room.

"Is it done?" Riordan asked.

Conor looked to Aine. Her expression cracked his confidence and sent his heart plummeting. "Tell me."

"It worked for a moment. The shield went up. But it dissipated the minute you stopped playing."

Silence fell around the room, their hope dying with her words.

"So we do need the harp," Eoghan said. "To make it permanent."

Riordan looked to Conor. "And the harp is destroyed. What do we do now?"

"I don't know." Failure washed over him, heavier than before. "If Gillian still lived, he might know a way. I thought it would work."

Where had he gone wrong? Had he not concentrated hard enough? Why had he not been able to will the outcome? He had been so sure—confident, cocky even—that he'd be able to rebuild the wards with nothing more than his gifts. Wasn't that the purpose of his experience at Cwmmaen? To show him how he was meant to save Seare? To convince him he was needed back home?

Since when does Comdiu need you to save anyone or anything?

The chastisement cut through the jumble of his thoughts, illuminating the sheer arrogance of his assumptions. He'd assumed that his rescue from captivity had been for his benefit, the storm punishment for his disobedience, but maybe all of it had been to free Talfryn and his family from the grip of the sidhe. But if that were true, why show Conor the extent of his gifts?

Unless it wasn't the extent of his gifts he was supposed to learn but rather the nature of them, their limitations.

His face burned as he realized the depth of his egotism. He'd actually believed Comdiu had given him the power to will the outcome of events, that He would hand over that sort of power to someone who hadn't even been faithful with what he'd been gifted—someone who had failed his vows to his wife, had been deceived by evil . . .

Conor jerked his head up. The nature of his gifts. Hadn't he just said to Aine that his gift was related to the control of magic?

It made sense. Everything he'd done had been beneath the influence of Briallu's glamour, including his archery session with Ial. He'd never actually been manipulating reality; he'd been manipulating the sidhe's magic.

I'm sorry, Comdiu. I've been foolish. Prideful. Disobedient. Even when I thought I was doing Your work, I only had an eye to my own glory. Please don't let Seare suffer because I was unfaithful. Show me. Tell me what to do.

He silently poured out his contrition, only vaguely aware of the conversation flowing around him, until that familiar tug cut through his thoughts. He gripped the chair as dizziness swept through him.

"Conor? What's wrong?" Aine was by his side in an instant, a hand on his arm, a concerned look on her face.

"I don't know. Just an . . . odd feeling."

"What kind of feeling?"

"Ever since I was in Gwydden, I've felt a pull to Carraigmór. At first I thought it was just Comdiu nudging me back to Seare, but it got stronger the closer I got to Ard Dhaimhin. I assumed that when I rebuilt the wards, it would go away." He winced and rubbed the back of his neck. "It's rather uncomfortable."

He noticed that the hall had fallen silent again and all the Conclave members were looking at him. "What?"

Riordan and Eoghan exchanged a glance.

"What is it?" Conor asked.

Eoghan shook his head. "Couldn't be."

"Give him a chance," Riordan said. "It would explain a great deal about what's happened here."

Conor glanced at Aine. "Do you know what this is about?"

"I do now. But I shouldn't tell you. I don't want to interfere with how this is unfolding."

Frustration welled up within him again at being the only one in the room who didn't know what was going on. "Lead the way, then, since you all have this figured out."

Aine took his hand, undoubtedly meaning to calm him, but he barely managed not to shake it off. He'd been back a day, and already he felt as if everyone around him knew his business better than he did. He turned down the corridor that led to the Ceannaire's study, making a quick turn into an intersecting corridor before they reached the stairs.

He moved forward, drawn by feel more than sight. It was here, the place, the object, whatever it was that called him so strongly. Riordan and Eoghan slowed, looking around them, talking in low tones, but he couldn't make out the words. He trailed a finger over the stone as he walked and then stopped abruptly.

"Here. Don't you see the door?" It was set seamlessly into the stone wall, almost unnoticeable even though it was wood instead of stone. He traced his finger along the joint of where the two materials met, unable to keep his eye on both at the same time. How was that possible?

"An enchantment," Aine murmured. "Old magic."

He shot her a curious glance, and when he looked back to the door, he blinked. The stone wall shimmered in front of him. "Remarkable. How do we get in?"

"There's a password," Eoghan said. "I've heard it, but I can't remember it. It should have passed to me as Liam's successor, but . . ."

A password. That tickle in the back of his mind grew. He opened his mouth and unfamiliar syllables floated out.

The door opened with a soft whoosh. Conor exchanged startled looks with the others, then pushed it open.

Beyond the doorway was a cramped passage, lit by an otherworldly glow. He hesitated before plunging into the narrow space.

He was dimly aware of the others following. This place had

a hush, as if it were cut off from the rest of Ard Dhaimhin. Perhaps it was. A sense of magic, not the light touch of the wards but something deeper and more rooted, passed over him. He stumbled.

"I feel it too," Aine whispered behind him.

At least it wasn't just his imagination. He continued downward until the corridor ended in the stone wall and then doubled back on itself at an angle. Ancient defenses, like the passageways into Ciraen cities, ambush spots. Something about this room was important enough to defend with both cunning and magic.

Feeling as if he were breaching some sort of inner sanctum, Conor stepped through the entrance.

A surge of power nearly brought him to his knees. Aine rushed forward and grabbed his arm. "Are you all right?"

"Aye."

He turned in a circle, taking in the cubbyholes, all the parchments and scrolls that filled them. "What are all these?"

"Prophecies," Eoghan said. "Writings that have been collected from all over the world since Daimhin's time. Even Liam knew only a fraction of what is contained here."

"Was this room what called you?" Riordan asked.

"No." Conor walked slowly around the chamber, letting his senses guide him, even though he saw nothing to distinguish any spot from another. Then he paused. A drawer, barely perceptible among the shelves. He grasped the ring and pulled.

A familiar case lay inside it.

"The sword." The sword that had called to him so strongly during the oath binding ceremonies, the blade upon which the clan chiefs of Seare had sworn their allegiance to King Daimhin. He removed the case and carried it to the table in the middle of the room.

There could have been discussion in the background, but

Conor heard nothing. The thrum of power, so much like the magic in Meallachán's harp, vibrated through him, aligning itself with the beat of his heart. He flipped the latch, bracing himself for a blast of power.

But it did not come. Instead, the magic faded to a mere whisper, the ripple of water over rocks in a stream. The etchings on the blade glowed in the dim light.

He closed his hand around the grip and lifted it before him, not on his palms as he would handle a ceremonial blade but as a weapon. A surge of electricity traveled up his arm and nearly took his breath away.

Then the whispers began. Echoes at first, then stronger, the sounds of men's voices vowing their allegiance to the brotherhood, to the High King. An idea began to take shape in his mind. He looked to Aine and saw the same wonder reflected in her eyes.

A smile stretched her lips. "Aye."

He replaced the sword in the case, and the voices faded, the hum of power dwindling to nothing. He closed the box and flipped the latch shut.

"This is what the druid wanted. And now I know why."

CHAPTER
FORTY-NINE

"You're getting ahead of yourself, Conor."

He stopped pacing the Hall of Prophecies and dropped his hands from where they'd been locked behind his head. "You saw it as clearly as I did. This is why I was called back. This is why the succession of Fíréin leadership passed to me and not to Eoghan."

The sword could solve so much. They needed men. Warriors, soldiers, whatever he wanted to call them. Men who would be willing to fight to retake their country, now scattered across Seare. Thanks to the sword, he knew who they were, knew he could call them back. But how?

"Aye, we need men," Aine said softly. It took him a moment to realize he hadn't voiced his thoughts aloud. "But we can't call them back until we reinstate the wards. Right now they're safe because they're scattered. The druid doesn't know who they are. But what's to keep him from just destroying the city, with all our men inside?"

"His plan must be bigger than that." But Conor couldn't discount her words. Without the wards, they were at the druid's mercy. He scrubbed his hands over his face and sighed. "So we're back to where we were before."

"Maybe there's something in these records that could tell us about the wards or the harp," Aine mused, wandering along the shelves.

"There are thousands of pieces of writing here. The right one would practically have to jump into your hands."

They met each other's eye as a thought occurred to them simultaneously. Aine put voice to it. "The timing of it . . . you felt the sword call to you right after you failed to rebuild the wards."

He winced at her word choice, but she was right. So what were they missing?

He went to the case on the table and opened it. Once more the thrum of magic vibrated through him, so different from the magic of the wards and yet similar to Meallachán's harp.

"That's it," Conor murmured. He lifted the sword from the case, this time holding it flat across his palms. Its etchings glistened in the soft light.

No, not etchings—runes.

Excitement gripped him. He peered closer at the blade. Most of the symbols he didn't recognize. He'd interpreted them originally as Odlum, but they were different somehow. Then his eyes focused on a familiar symbol: a three-spoked wheel, like the charm Aine wore around her neck—and the symbol carved into the tuning pin of Meallachán's harp.

Conor's pulse suddenly throbbed through his entire body. He could barely choke words from his tight throat. "We need Eoghan."

Ten minutes later, Conor, Eoghan, and Aine gathered in the Ceannaire's office above with the sword, the harp, and the pouch of tuning pins. Conor flipped open the sword's case as Eoghan laid out the eight pins he had salvaged from the ruins of Cill Rhí. Aine placed her charm on the table between them, its carved symbols facing up.

"They're runes," Eoghan said in surprise.

"Aye." Not all of the runes on the pins were present on the sword or vice versa, but several—the wheel, something that looked like an arrow, and a strange crosshatch—were. Conor reached for the nearest pin and held it in his hand, expecting to feel some indication of magic, but he felt nothing.

"I don't understand," Conor murmured. "I was sure this was the source of the sword's power."

"Maybe it is," Aine said. "The runes are a language, right? You can't just put random words together and expect them to mean something."

"So they only work together," Eoghan said. "Which means you need to put them in the harp. We already know these mean something or they wouldn't have been on Meallachán's instrument."

"But we have less than a third of the pins. How do we know we have the ones we need?"

They frowned as they looked over the items, all objects of power, all mysterious.

"The three have this one in common." Aine pointed to the rune that looked like a wheel charm.

Eoghan lifted it and considered. "The name of Comdiu, the three parts of our God."

Conor glanced at Eoghan, startled, and nodded. It made sense. He unscrewed the first tuning pin and replaced it with the rune pin, then tuned the string until it sounded true.

He plucked it one last time, and a deep vibration hummed inside him. His eyes widened. "What's next?"

Aine scanned the runes. "This one is common among all three as well."

Eoghan picked it up. "Protection. Actually, it's the rune for *sword*, but it means the same thing."

Conor stared at Eoghan. His friend had always insisted that he had no knowledge of languages or magic, yet now he spoke with absolute certainty. Conor didn't argue, though. He just put the pin on the end of the harp opposite the wheel.

Language or not, this was more like constructing a building than a sentence: bracket a span of notes with Comdiu's protection, fill it in with magic. It made sense in a symbolic sort of way.

"What about the rest?"

Eoghan touched each in turn. "I don't know. Your guess is as good as mine."

Conor spread each of the other six pins at even intervals along the harp. Once he had tuned each of the notes, he ran his fingers along the strings. Magic hummed on his skin.

He glanced at Eoghan and Aine. "Shall we give it another try?"

"Shouldn't we get the others first?" Aine asked.

Eoghan shook his head slightly. Conor agreed with him. As confident as he felt, this still might not work. It was like trying to speak a language of which you had only the most rudimentary knowledge. The message had the potential to get garbled in the delivery. And with only eight of the twenty-eight pins . . .

"All right, let's give it a try, then." He forced a confidence he didn't feel into his tone.

The first note sent a shiver through his body as he began to play. This time he didn't control the music. It almost wasn't even a song. It was a breath, a prayer, a plea to Comdiu—an acknowledgement that while his skills were too meager to accomplish something this vast, he served a God who was greater and more powerful than that which they battled against.

Perhaps that was the reason for the magic embedded in the

runes: a reminder that there was something bigger and more mysterious at work than what they could accomplish by their own abilities.

And then the music changed again to that golden light, spilling out like liquid metal and seeping into the city's foundation like rain. It was not a shield as he had first conceived but rather the touch of hallowed ground. A benediction. A blessing. It sped along the earth like a flood, burning away invisible shreds of mist it met along the way. And somewhere in his heart, Conor understood.

Ard Dhaimhin was not meant to be protected and shielded from the kingdom; it was to be its heart, its shield, its sword. What they built here would endure not because of any attempt to make it safe but because they were courageous enough to stand against the evil that threatened it.

When the last note died, Conor didn't need Aine to tell him it was successful. The wards tickled his skin like the crackle of an impending lightning strike. It was as if the music had become part of the city, the foundation upon which it stood.

"You did it," Aine whispered. "It's different . . . strong. It's not what it once was, but it's what we need now."

"Comdiu did it." It was no coincidence that of the twenty-eight pins Eoghan could have found, these eight accomplished something so vast. And once more, Comdiu chose to humble him by showing him the limitations of his own knowledge, the graciousness of their Lord's protection.

"It's done, then," Eoghan said quietly. "Let's tell the others."

+ + +

Word of what Conor had done spread through Ard Dhaimhin almost as quickly as the magic itself, helped in part by the fact that more than a few people could feel it.

"So we're protected," Riordan said when Conor, Eoghan, and Aine met with the Conclave in the hall. "Against what?"

Aine answered. "I'm fairly certain that anyone possessing sorcery cannot set foot within Ard Dhaimhin's borders. It's become part of the foundation of the city."

"And the sidhe?" Daigh said. "Can they pass?"

"They will be able to pass as they did with the other wards," Conor said, "but their power will be limited to affecting individuals. I don't think one could weave a full-scale illusion, not with the magic as the foundation of the city." His experiences at Cwmmaen had taught him that much.

"So you couldn't do the same thing to drive the sidhe from Seare," Gradaigh said, disappointment in his tone.

"Not on such a large scale," Conor said. "At least not yet. We have some other ideas that could be explored."

Aine jumped in. "Conor and I would like to spend some time with the texts in Master Liam's study and the Hall of Prophecies and see if there's anything of use there."

"Seems wise." Riordan paused. "There's something else we must discuss, though."

Conor's stomach sank. He could guess what was coming. "I don't think—"

"No, hear me out. Eoghan was Liam's choice for Ceannaire, but he had other duties, and now I think we know why. I fell into leadership in their absence. But it seems Carraigmór's own magic has chosen you. I think we make a grave mistake if we don't listen."

"I never wanted to lead the brotherhood," Conor said.

"Neither did Liam. But he was chosen, as I believe you are." Riordan glanced around at the members of the Conclave. "Perhaps for more. Only time will tell."

The implication of Riordan's words made him ill. "You can't possibly mean . . ."

"There's a prophecy." The hard set of Eoghan's jaw and the intense look in his eyes were at odds with his quiet tone. "It speaks of the one who will stand against the Kinslayer with 'the sword and the song.' Master Liam showed me."

Conor looked at Aine. She gave him a little nod, though he couldn't tell if it was meant to be encouragement or verification of the truth of Eoghan's words.

"Prophecy or no prophecy, the brotherhood is over," Conor said finally. "There is no Ceannaire because there is no Fíréin anymore."

Riordan looked around the table and voiced the question on all their minds: "What are we, then?"

+ + +

"You did well." Aine's soft voice snapped Conor out of his thoughts as he stared out the window in Liam's study. She slid her arms around his waist from behind and leaned her head against his back. Just that small show of support warmed him and eased a little of the tension in his body.

"Can you tell me what they're thinking?" he asked.

"You know I shouldn't have—"

"But you did. I need to know." He turned and pulled her closer, but for once he wasn't tempted off topic. "Please."

"They all believe you are meant to take leadership of the city in Liam's stead."

"And . . ."

She sighed. "A few of them—Riordan, Daigh, Eoghan— believe you are the one prophesied in the writings."

"The High King."

"Aye."

He heaved another sigh. He couldn't explain it, but what he felt was more than just fear. It was like the nudge on his spirit in the Sofarende camp, the one that prompted him to stay even though common sense—and Talfryn—told him to flee. He felt tied to Ard Dhaimhin, true, and the sword called to him. But kingship? That felt completely wrong.

"You would make a wonderful king."

"Would I?" So far he'd made a mess of things by acting on his own desires and out of his own fears. A king must make decisions for the good of his people, no matter the personal consequence. And somehow he knew if given the hard choice, he'd always choose Aine. He could sooner sacrifice himself than allow harm to come to her when it was in his power to save her.

"We just don't have all the information yet. They don't have all the information." He gestured to the piles of books spread across Liam's desk. "I still feel as if the answer is here somewhere."

"Then we read. We pray." Aine stretched to kiss him and then grinned. "And probably read some more."

Conor chuckled. "You don't need to sound so enthusiastic about that."

"And you don't need to sound so morose. I'll just send you anything in an obscure language and you can awe me with your linguistic prowess."

Conor grinned and stole one more kiss, which elicited another smile from Aine. Then he grew serious and linked his arms around her waist. "I love you, Aine. You amaze me. You make me feel like I can do anything."

"I think that's what marriage is for." She pointed to the folios and books piled high. "We should get started. If you believe there are answers here, there are probably answers."

Conor hoped so, because lately it seemed as though every answer came with another set of questions.

CHAPTER
FIFTY

It had actually been easy, Eoghan thought.

The failed first attempt aside, it seemed that Conor possessed the skills and knowledge necessary to protect the city. Carraigmór's magic had somehow chosen him to be their leader.

The only thing left to do was convince Conor that he was meant to be High King. Riordan and Daigh certainly thought so or they wouldn't have ceded him power so easily. The rest of the Conclave could be convinced. Conor might refuse the title of Ceannaire, but he was already making decisions on their behalf. Eoghan's role in the High City was over, just as he'd always intended.

So why did he feel so bereft?

Pride, he decided, as he made his way toward the training yards. He'd always known that Conor possessed abilities and education that were vast even by Fíréin standards. It was time to stop moping and make the most of what he was meant to do. Just because the brotherhood had effectively been dissolved didn't mean there weren't still men to be trained, captains to be developed. He was good with a sword, and he was good at teaching others to be good with a sword.

He paused at the edge of one yard to watch two young men, perhaps six-and-ten, bouting with wooden weapons. Eoghan recognized one as Fíréin by his fluid style. The other was kingdom trained but no less talented—a recent refugee, probably, escaping the druid's conscripted army.

"Halt," Eoghan called, and the two boys backed off in surprise. The Fíréin apprentice bowed immediately, but the other one just stared at him.

"What are your names?" Eoghan asked.

"Colm, sir," the first boy said.

Apparently the opponent figured Eoghan was someone of note because he sketched a hasty bow. "Anraí, sir."

"You've got good form, Anraí. But I want you to watch me and tell me what I'm doing that you're not." He took the sword and faced Colm. "Your attack."

Colm came at him with a series of flawless offensive strikes. The boy was going to be good someday. Eoghan easily deflected the blows without countering, trusting Anraí to pick up the nuances of his technique.

Then he stepped back and addressed the new student. "What did you note?"

The boy stared, puzzled. Then understanding dawned on his face. "Your weight. It's centered. I'm reaching."

"You're reaching," Eoghan repeated with a nod. He handed the boy his weapon and then watched as the two resumed their match. When he was satisfied that Anraí had made the correction, Eoghan moved on.

After stopping and working with half a dozen groups, a calm settled over him. Perhaps Conor's return was an answer to his prayers. He'd always known he belonged at Ard Dhaimhin, even as he chafed at the restrictions placed on him. He loved teaching, fighting, the rhythm of life in the city. Even as he mourned

Master Liam's passing, he could admit that without the pressure of living up to expectations as the Ceannaire's successor, he could be happy here.

What did it matter if Conor received the acclaim? Even though Eoghan had given his entire life to Ard Dhaimhin . . .

I see all men equally, though I may call them to different tasks.

It was both chastisement and encouragement. Eoghan bowed his head beneath the weight of Comdiu's words. *I will serve in whatever task You set before me. Forgive me.*

I still have plans for you.

Aye. Eoghan would do what Comdiu asked him, even if that meant he would never again see the world outside Ard Dhaimhin's borders, never find a woman who looked at him with the same love Aine had for Conor. If Comdiu called him to fight, he would fight. If He told him to follow, he would follow.

And if I call you to lead?

Lord?

There was no answer. Eoghan shook his head and went back to his rounds. Maybe Comdiu was just making the point that it was not his place to dictate what he would or would not do. He needed only to offer his will to obey and stand ready to respond when he was called.

He forgot about the somewhat one-sided conversation as the days passed, pushing aside the twinge of jealousy he felt as Conor stepped into the space Liam had left vacant.

He was hardly surprised, then, when one of the younger boys serving in the fortress told him he'd been summoned to the Ceannaire's office. His friend hadn't wasted any time in assuming the prerogatives of the station. And why should he? Conor was the son of a king, born to leadership. He'd already shown that he had his own path to follow, the rules and goals of the brotherhood aside.

Eoghan shoved down those thoughts and raised a silent prayer of apology to Comdiu for their bitter tone. He'd never thought of himself as being uncharitable, but then again, he'd always enjoyed a certain status within the brotherhood. How uncomfortable to realize that his humility had been just a sham.

He climbed the stairs to Carraigmór slowly, wondering what Conor could have to say to him. But when he arrived at the Ceannaire's office, it was not simply his friend waiting. Riordan and Aine were with him.

"There's something you should see," Conor said. "Sit down."

Eoghan lifted an eyebrow at the command, but he sat. A stack of scrolls on the desk drew his attention.

Aine spoke first. "I found the message from your mother, Eoghan. You said that she was a Fearghail?"

"That's right. Why?"

Aine turned a book toward him, a heavy leather-bound tome that took up half the table. "This is a genealogy of Sliebhan. Fearghail is a noble clan."

Eoghan looked between Aine and the book. "So? It's not as if they had any contact with me after I was given up."

Aine pointed to an entry near the bottom of the page. "This right here? Fionnuala Nic Fearghail? I think that's your mother. It shows she married a Beollain about five-and-twenty years ago."

When Eoghan looked at her blankly, Conor said, "Beollain is the minor royal branch in Sliebhan. Just like Laighid is to Nir, or Eirhinin is to Cuillinn."

"What are you saying? That I have claim to the throne of Sliebhan?" Eoghan laughed. "Maybe that meant something before, but Sliebhan has fallen. Royal blood hardly matters now."

"Eoghan," Aine said more gently, "have you ever heard the story of how the Great Kingdom split?"

He frowned. Everyone knew the story. "Daimhin was

disappointed his sons hadn't held true to their faith or their gifts. He named a successor who was not of his direct line, and rather than lose what they felt was their birthright, his sons killed him."

Aine nodded. "There's more, though. We found one of Daimhin's journals in the Ceannaire's study. I can only guess Liam already suspected he may have been wrong about the prophecy."

Eoghan looked at the three others in the room. They stared at him, as if willing him to read the direction of their thoughts.

"Daimhin spoke of a boy who possessed the same gift he did," Conor said.

"Music," Eoghan guessed.

"No," Conor said. "Comdiu spoke to Daimhin. Directly. As I believe Comdiu speaks to you. He wanted the High King of Seare to be guided not by his own thoughts and prejudices but directly by Comdiu himself. That is why Daimhin's sons rebelled against him: because they did not hear Comdiu's voice."

The breath left him like flame snuffed from a candle. "You can't possibly mean . . ."

"We do," Riordan said. "If we reread the prophecy in this light, it's altogether possible."

"But the sword and the song—Conor has wielded both already to restore Ard Dhaimhin. In a sense, he's already fulfilled that prophecy."

Conor shook his head. "I believe the prophecy does refer to me. But I won't wield the sword and the song. I believe I *am* the sword and the song, a tool in the hand of the one who will deliver our island from this evil."

Something unsettlingly hard glimmered in Conor's gaze as he stepped around the desk, something Eoghan couldn't reconcile with the young man he knew. But even the books had not prepared him for Conor's next words.

"I am not destined to be High King, Eoghan. You are."

Discussion Questions

1. When the sidhe are unleashed, they take control of the kingdom's citizens through their emotions. Do you think emotions can be trusted? Contrast how Eoghan and Conor deal with misleading emotions.

2. Comdiu speaks differently to each of the characters. He communicates with Eoghan directly, He sends Companions to Aine, and He uses humans for Conor. What does that say about how God relates to us as individuals?

3. The characters attempt to rely on Comdiu, but when they use their own wisdom, they get themselves into trouble. Sometimes they escape without having to take responsibility, and other times they have to bear the harsh consequences of their actions. What application do you see for your own life?

4. Conor struggles with the question of whether he did the right thing by saving Aine and bringing her home to Aron. What do you think?

5. Liam sacrificed himself in order to (he thinks) save the future of the brotherhood and Ard Dhaimhin. Do you think he was right or wrong in that action? Why?

6. Both Conor and Liam are incredibly gifted but too confident in their own abilities. How are Liam and Conor similar to Niall? How are they different?

7. All the characters deviate from Comdiu's plan for them, thinking they are doing the right thing. Liam wants to protect his city, Eoghan wants to obey Comdiu, Conor wants to save Aine—all of which are noble goals. When does the "right thing" become the wrong thing?

8. Aine, Conor, and Eoghan all undergo challenges and trials throughout the book, but they emerge understanding more about themselves and Comdiu's will for them. How does God use trials and difficulty to teach you and prepare you for your service to Him?

9. At Cwmmaen, the sidhe traps Conor and his companions within a glamour that makes everything appear to be normal, even desirable, but really just masks the corruption beneath. How is the illusion a metaphor for sin?

10. In a number of places, Conor puts Aine before himself. He tells Haldor that he loves her, so he counts her life as more important than his. Later he says there is nothing he wouldn't sacrifice for her. Is this good or bad? How does his sacrificial love—however imperfect—reflect God's love for mankind (see Ephesians 5:25)?

11. Conor believes he would not make a good king because he must be willing to sacrifice an individual for the good of the many. Is that position morally right or wrong? Is there a different standard of morality for a head of state versus an individual? Why do you think so?

Glossary

Aberffynnon (ah-ber-FIN-nuhn)—a port city on the southern coast of Gwydden

Aenghus (AYN-gus)—Lady Macha's husband

Ailís (AY-leesh)—Aine's mother, lady of Forrais and wife of Alsandair Mac Tamhais, now deceased

Aine Nic Tamhais (ON-yuh nik TAV-ish)—the "lady healer of Lisdara," married to Conor Mac Nir

Alsandair Mac Tamhais—Aine's father, lord of Forrais and chief of Clan Tamhais, now deceased

Amanta (ah-MAN-ta)—the island upon which Aron and Gwydden are located

Amantine Sea (ah-MAN-teen)—narrow sea separating Seare and Amanta

Ard Dhaimhin (ard DAV-in)—former high city of Seare, home of the Fíréin brotherhood

Arkiel (ar-KEEL)—Companion who instigated the rebellion against Comdiu

Aron (ah-RUN)—Aine's birthplace, across the Amantine Sea from Seare

Askr (as-KER)—Norin warrior god

Bain (bwen)—Forrais guard

Balian (BAH-lee-an)—the faith of those who follow Balus; a follower of Balus

Ballaghbán (bal-luh-BAHN)—port city in northern Faolán

Balus (BAH-lus)—son of Comdiu, savior of mankind

Beagan (BOG-awn)—Fíréin tracker

Bearrach (BEAR-uhk)—healer at Lisdara; Aine's instructor

Breann (BREE-ahn)—novice of the Fíréin brotherhood

Bress (bress)—King of Aron

Briallu (bree-AHL-lu)—Talfryn's daughter

Brightwater—nickname for Ionbhar Dealrach

brithem (BRITH-ev)—traveling judge in Aron who presides over serious crimes

Caerfaddyn (care-FAD-duhn)—a Gwynn castle, seat of Prince Dewyn

Calhoun Mac Cuillinn (cal-HOON mok CUL-in)—former King of Faolán, assumed deceased; Aine's half brother

carnyx (car-nix)—war horn

Carraigmór (CAIR-ig-mor)—fortress of the High King and the Fíréin brotherhood

Cass Mac Onaghan (kass mok ON-ah-han)—captain of the *Beacon*

Cé (keh)—Forrais guard

céad (ked)—a company of men; literally, one hundred

Ceannaire (KAN-na-ahr)—leader of the Fíréin brotherhood

Cill Rhí (kill ree)—Balian monastery

Cira/Ciraen (seer-AH) (seer-AY-ahn)—largest empire in history, now reduced to a small portion of the continent

Clogheen (cloh-EEN)—a market town in central Faolán

Comdiu (COM-dyoo)—God

Companions—the spirit warriors of Comdiu; angels

Conclave—the ruling body of the Fíréin brotherhood

Conor Mac Nir (CON-ner mok NEER)—Timhaigh warrior and musician, former Fíréin apprentice

Criofan (CRIH-fahn)– former Fíréin brother

Cwmmaen (coom-MINE)—a former Ciraen fortress in Gwydden, seat of Prince Talfryn

Daigh (dy)—senior member of the Fíréin brotherhood

Daimhin (DAV-in)– the first High King of Seare

Dal (DAHL)—senior member of the Fíréin brotherhood

Dewyn (DEW-ayn)—prince of Gwydden, Talfryn's brother

Diarmuid (DEER-muhd)—druid; formerly Ceannaire Niall

Diocail (dyuh-KEL)—master of Forrais's house guard

Dún Caomaugh (doon KOW-mah)—southern Aronan port city

Dyllan (DIL-lahn)—Gwynn prisoner in the Sofarende settlement

Eilean Buidhe (AY-luhn BOO-yah)—a southern island located between Aron and Seare

Eluf (ell-LOOF)—Norin warrior

Eoghan (OH-in)—Fíréin apprentice; Conor's best friend

Faolán/Faolanaigh (FEY-lahn) (FEY-lahn-aye)—northeastern kingdom in Seare, formerly ruled by Clan Cuillinn/their language and people

Fechin (feh-KEEN)—senior member of the Fíréin brotherhood

Fergus Mac Nir (FAYR-gus mok NEER)—former king of Tigh; Conor's uncle

Fermaigh (fuhr-MY)—southern Aronan port city

Fionnuala (fin-NOO-la)—Eoghan's mother; clan Fearghail (husband's clan unknown)

Fíréin (FEER-een) brotherhood—ancient brotherhood dedicated to the reinstatement of the High King

Forrais (FOR-rahs)—Aine's birthplace in the Aronan Highlands

Gabhran (GAH-ruhn)—Lord Riagain's enforcer

Gainor Mac Cuillinn (GAY-nor mok CUL-in)—tanist to King Calhoun; Calhoun's brother, assumed deceased

Galbraith Mac Nir (GOL-breth mok NEER)—king of Tigh; Conor's stepfather, now deceased

Gillian (JILL-yuhn)—elderly Fíréin brother

Glenmallaig (glen-MAL-ag)—seat of the king of Tigh; Conor's birthplace

Glyn (glin)—bard

Gradaigh (GRAH-duh)—senior member of the Fíréin brotherhood

Guaire (GUHR-yeh)—Forrais's steward

Gwingardd (GWIN-gard)—a Gwynn castle, seat of Prince Neryn

Gwydden/Gwynn (GWIH-duhn) (gwin)—a country across the Amantine Sea/ their people

Haldor (HAL-dohr)—captain of the Sofarende settlement near Cwmmaen; also known as Haldor the Brave

Hall of Prophecies—magically concealed chamber in Carraigmór that contains the Fíréin brotherhood's ancient writings

Hyledd (HY-led)—Talfryn's wife

Ial (yahl)—captain of Cwmmaen's guard

Iomhar (EE-ver)—young Fíréin brother

Ionbhar Dealrach (ee-ON-var DAL-rok)—one of the largest clan holdings in Aron; controlled by Lord Riagain

Keondric Mac Eirhinin (KEN-drick mok AYR-nin)—Lord of Rathmor; battle captain

Klasjvic (KLAH-yah-vik)—Norin capitol

Lachaidh (LAH-chee)—Forrais guardsman

Lelle (LEL-leh)—Norin god known as the "dying god"

Lia (LEE-uh)—Aine's lady's maid

Liam Mac Cuillinn (LEE-um mok CUL-in)—Ceannaire, leader of the Fíréin brotherhood; Aine's half brother

Lisdara (lis-DAR-ah)—seat of the king of Faolán

Llantawe (hlan-TAW)—a Gwynn castle, seat of King Llewellyn

Llewellyn (HLEW-ell-en)—King of Gwydden

Loch Ceo (lok kyo)—lake within Ard Dhaimhin

Lorcan (LUR-cawn)—leader of Aine's guard, presumed deceased

Macha (mah-HUH)—chieftain of Clan Tamhais, lady of Forrais

Manog (mah-NOGH)—senior member of the Fíréin brotherhood

Meallachán (MOL-luck-on)—bard

Merov/Merovian (mehr-AHV) (mehr-OHV-ee-an)—country within the Ciraen empire/their language and people

Miach (ME-ahk)—first mate of the *Beacon*

Neryn (NEHR-ehn)—prince of Gwydden, Talfryn's brother

Niall (NEE-ahl)—former Ceannaire of the Fíréin brotherhood, now Keondric

Niamh Nic Cuillinn (NEE-uv nik CUL-in)—King Calhoun's sister, assumed deceased; Aine's half sister

Norin (NOR-in)—the common name of the Northern Isles; origin of the Sofarende

Odran (OH-rawn)—Fíréin tracker

Oisean (oh-SHEEN)—Forrais guard

Pepin (pep-EEN)—Merovian mercenary

Rathmór (RATH-mohr)—seat of Clan Eirhinin, a minor royal line of Faolán

Riagain Mac Comain (REE-gan mok KO-myn)—lord of Ionbhar Dealrach (Brightwater), Aine's distant cousin

Riordan Mac Nir (REER-uh-dawn mok NEER)—Conor's father, senior member of the Fíréin brotherhood

Roidh (roy)—Forrais guard

Róscomain (ros-COM-muhn)—old forest bordering Tigh and Sliebhan

Ruarc (ROO-ark)—Aine's bodyguard, now deceased

Seanrós (SHAWN-ross)—old forest bordering Faolán

Seare/Seareann (SHAR-uh)(SHAR-uhn)—island housing the four kingdoms/its language and people

Semias (SHAY-mus)—former King of Siomar

sidhe (shee)—the evil spirits of the underworld; demons

Sigurd (SEE-gyurd)– Norin mercenary

Siomar/Siomaigh (SHO-mar) (SHO-my)—Southeastern kingdom in Seare/their language and people

Sliebhan/Sliebhanaigh (SLEEV-ahn) (SLEEV-ahn-eye)—Southwestern kingdom in Seare/their language and people

Sofarende (soeh-FUR-end-uh)—seafarers from the Northern Isles (Norin)

Talfryn (TAL-frin)—prince of Gwydden, lord of Cwmmaen

tanist—chosen successor of a Seareann king, elected by the kingdom's council of lords

Taran Mac Maolain (TAH-ruhn mok MAL-lin)—mercenary, once a Midland lord

Tigh/Timhaigh (ty) (TIH-vy)—northwestern kingdom in Seare, ruled by Clan Nir/ their language and people

Uallas (WAL-luhs)—lord of Eilean Buidhe

Ulaf (OO-lahf)—Sofarende warrior

Acknowledgments

It's a humbling thought that for so many people, "going to work" has involved sending this book into the world. My heartfelt gratitude goes to:

Meg Wallin, Rebekah Guzman, Brian Thomasson, Caitlyn Carlson, Don Pape, Reagen Reed, Jeff Rustemeyer, Debbie Johnson, Kirk DouPounce, and the rest of the combined NavPress/Tyndale teams. Even if we've never corresponded or met face-to-face, your fingerprints are seen in all the details involved in getting this book to print. Your hard work means more than you know.

And to everyone else who makes it possible to do this crazy thing called writing, both personally and professionally—I couldn't do it without you:

Rey, N and P, Mom and Dad, Steve Laube, Jeane Wynn, Serena Chase, Brandy Vallance, Evangeline Denmark, Amy Matayo, Nicole Deese, Ronie Kendig, Laurie Tomlinson, Beth Vogt, and my friendly Aurora/Parker Starbucks baristas. You keep me sane, focused, inspired, entertained, and/or caffeine-fueled. You're the best.

About the Author

C. E. Laureano's love of fantasy began with a trip through a magical wardrobe, and she has never looked back. She's happiest when her day involves martial arts, swords, and a well-choreographed fight scene, though when pressed, she'll admit to a love of theater and travel as well. Appropriately, she's the wife to a martial arts master and mom to two boys who spend most of their time jumping off things and finding objects to turn into lightsabers. They live in Denver, Colorado, with a menagerie of small pets. Visit her on the web at www.CELaureano.com, or e-mail her at connect@CELaureano.com.